TO RIDE A
WHITE HORSE

TO RIDE A

WHITE HORSE

PAMELA FORD

To Ireland.

And to Bob.

The old woman lifted the child into her arms as they reached the edge of the bluff. Below them, the sea crashed upon a shallow beach; its waves white with foam, splattered on the rocky face. Holding her granddaughter close to her chest, she pointed to the great white swells galloping across the sea, and in hushed tones told the young girl of the white horses of the Tuatha dé Danann, the Irish gods, traveling between the faerie and the mortal worlds. Of the white mare that carried the faerie princess, Niamh, and her beloved, the mortal Oisin, across the waves to the island of Tír Na nÓg, the Country of the Young, where they lived in happiness for 300 years. Of the white steed that took a homesick Oisin to see Ireland once again, then charged away when the mortal turned into a withered old man the moment his feet touched the earth. And of the white horse that appears in the waves along Ireland's shores when the moon is full, a milk-white mare carrying a heartbroken Niamh as she searches for her lost love, Oisin.

PROLOGUE

County Cork, Ireland, August 1846

KATHLEEN DUG HER fingers into the loose soil beneath the dying plants and pulled out the unripe potatoes, recoiling as they turned to mush beneath the light pressure of her grip. Rot oozed over her palm, the smell so foul she gagged and fought the urge to retch. Dear Lord, she prayed, please don't let the whole crop be blighted again. We'll not survive another year.

All morning there had been shouting and wailing as neighbors awakened in the darkness to the sulfurous stench of rot and rushed from their cottages to find the potato crop dying. On every hillside as far as she could see, families were working frantically, tearing off cankerous stalks, hoping to prevent the spread of disease even as the green leaves blackened and withered around them. 'Twas as if the fields had been ravaged in the night by some unholy creature of darkness.

The gray stone fences bounding each tiny patch of land suddenly felt like prison walls locking the families inside to await the death sentence laid upon them this morn. Kathleen shoved her hands deep into the earth beneath another stalk. She pulled a fistful of potatoes from the ground and watched in horror as they decayed in her hands. Her breath came quick and shallow. Crawling in the dirt beside her brother, Rory, she dug beneath one plant and another and another in a frantic search for healthy potatoes. There must be some. Faith, they could not have lost them all. Not again. Ireland could not starve a second year.

A vision of Danny filled her mind, her betrothed, dark curls and a jaunty grin, waving goodbye as the ship set sail five months ago for the cod fisheries in Newfoundland. Thank God he and her brother, Sean, had gone across, for the pay they brought home would help the family through the winter to come.

She glanced at her father where he dug nearby, one foot pushing a rusted spade deep into the black soil, shoulders hunched with the effort. "Da, have you found any without the blight?"

He straightened and drew a callused hand across his forehead. The dirt from his palm left a smudged trail as it blended with the sweat on his brow. She could see fear in his eyes. "A few lass, but a precious few."

Beside him, Kathleen's mother unearthed potatoes with a smaller spade, each thrust bringing forth another putrid mass of vegetation.

"A long winter again it will be," Rory murmured. "And mark me words, this time the English will watch us starve before lifting a hand to help."

Their mother shook her head slowly. "*Ní thuigeann an sách an seang.* The well-fed does not understand the lean."

Despair coursed through Kathleen and she curled her fingers into fists in the dirt. "The English." She pushed herself to standing. "Six hundred years we've lived with their heel pressed to our throat. May they be damned for what they have done to Ireland. Our land is stolen and given to their gentry, our wheat and cattle sent to feed England. And what do they leave us but rotten potatoes. 'Tis Irish land—not English. And we've grain aplenty to feed all of Ireland. So tell me now why we must starve as the English grow fat on our crops?"

Her only answer was the keening that echoed across the fields, growing in intensity as one family after another joined in to mourn the destruction. The eerie sound, carried on the breeze along with the putrid odor, sent a shiver through Kathleen and she crossed herself. Hell had returned to Ireland and there was only the hunger to come.

CHAPTER ONE

County Cork, Ireland – October 1846

SHE HEARD THE shouting long before she could make
out the words. 'Twas a woman's voice, at once urgent and
excited, floating over the fields from the road to Cobh.
Drawing a breath, Kathleen froze on hands and knees in the dirt of
the garden and tilted her head to listen, straining to make sense of
the syllables rising and falling and scattering on the breeze.

She dug her fingers into the freshly tilled earth, warm and soft
in the autumn sun, and concentrated on the sounds: "Kath—
leen...... har...bor..."

Har? Bor?

She squinted at a black bug making its way across the leaf of
a turnip plant. They'd found old Paddy O'Donoghue yesterday,
starved to death by the side of the road, his mouth stained green
from eating grass. Fear twisted her empty stomach. Some said
he was one of the Good People, trapped forever in human form.
Would it be that even the faeries were to perish?

Har-bor? Her eyes widened in comprehension. "Danny!" she
breathed aloud. Sean! With a strangled cry, she shoved herself to
her feet, throwing aside a fistful of weeds and wiping her hands on

her apron as she lifted her skirt and raced across the small patch of land to where her father was working.

"Da—do you hear?! A ship—the ship—is in harbor! Our lads have returned!"

Her father leaned on the handle of his hoe and smiled. He pulled off his cap to push his red hair off his forehead and wipe his brow. "Aye, lass, I hear. We'll go down just as soon as I finish—"

"Da! I cannot wait for you!" she exclaimed. She turned toward the stone cottage where her mother had appeared in the doorway with Kathleen's younger sister, Nora.

"Ma, me heart is near to bursting already!"

"Go on with you, lass," her mother answered with a wave. "Your father is just having fun. Tell your brother and Danny that we'll be along, just a wee bit more slowly."

Kathleen nodded and tore off her apron, throwing it to the ground as she raced down the hard dirt road toward the woman who had brought the news.

"Moira, you saw it?" she shouted, one hand waving high above her head in greeting.

"Me brother did. The ship's in harbor, but not yet at the wharf."

Laughing, Kathleen threw herself into her friend's arms, then pushed back and spun a circle. "Danny has come back," she whispered to the blue sky, her throat tight with joy, arms outstretched as if to embrace all she could see. All would be right now. Her Danny was home.

Moira touched her on the arm. "Kathleen, it's soon they'll be docking. Best I not be standing in the road but at the dock so that your brother will not think I've forgotten me marriage vows."

"Pah! How could ye forget with that big belly out in front of you?" Kathleen set out at full stride, then slacked off to keep pace with Moira's gait. "I canna wait to see Sean's face when he sees how you've changed."

Moira laughed and drew a protective hand over her swollen belly. "It's a blessing the boys went to the fisheries this year."

Kathleen nodded and glanced at the empty patches in the fields, the ground brown and bare where once had grown lush green potato plants, their small purple flowers promising a bountiful harvest. Even now, a month past the blight, she could still smell the rot.

She shook her head to force the thought away. "We've turnips missing from the ground near every morning now," she said. "And beggars at the door."

"'Tis begun," Moira answered. "The real hunger. I fear it won't be long before the landlord's crowbar brigade is at work, tearing cottages to the ground and turning families out on the road for not paying the rent."

Kathleen looked over the fields at the tiny cottages that stood as they always had, their thick stone walls and thatched roofs solid and dependable, giving no hint of the fear and misery that now lay inside. "What else would ye expect from the English?" she said quietly. "Our land, our country, is what they want—not our people. They've never wanted us."

They followed the road as it took a steep slant into Cobh, built a century ago along the waterfront by fishermen with eyes upon the cod and herring that thrived in the deep harbor. But that quaint fishing village was long gone now, replaced during the Napoleonic wars by a British naval base and fine homes for the British officers.

Kathleen refused to look at the houses as they passed. 'Twas her own small act of disrespect, for she knew that behind the elegant and formal entrances, the wealthy English entertained their friends, while paying no mind to the hunger creeping like a deathly specter across the countryside.

The two women dodged horse-drawn wagons and passersby as they hurried down the narrow street, following the twists and turns that brought them ever closer to the water. Never before had the road to the bay seemed so long.

With each downhill step, the air grew more damp and the odor of the sea became more pungent, until, suddenly, they broke out onto the wharf and Cork Harbor lay before them, hazy beneath a light mist, and obscured in part by the crowd that had gathered to welcome its sons home.

"They've docked already, Kathleen," Moira cried. She searched the faces of the young men lined along the rail of the ship waiting to disembark. The two pressed into the back of the crowd, stretching up on tiptoes to peer over the shoulders and heads blocking their view.

"I can't see," Kathleen muttered. "Moira, do you see either of them?" Lifting the front of her skirt, she jumped up. Then she jumped again.

"Stop that Kathleen! Do you want Danny to think ye an idiot?"

She sprang up once more and spotted the lean build and dark black hair of her older brother. "Sean! There's Sean coming off now! This way!" Pushing through the crowd with Moira in tow, she launched herself into her brother's arms. "Welcome home, Sean! I've brought your wife to you...and your babe!"

She pulled away to let Moira take her place, then let out a delighted laugh as Sean's expression shifted from surprise to joy.

Up on her toes again, she bobbed her head from side to side in an attempt to see around nearby people. "Sean, where's me Danny?"

Hearing no reply, she looked over to find him and Moira locked in an embrace, kissing away the months of separation. She exhaled sharply then searched the throng again. A fine sweat broke out across her shoulders. Where was Danny? Surely he was all right.

She grasped her brother by the arm and shook it in fearful desperation. "Sean!"

He tore his mouth from Moira's. "Aye?"

"Where's Danny?"

He stared at her as though struck dumb. Then he moved Moira gently aside. Never before had she seen him look like this.

"Sean?" Panic edged into her voice and her heart began to pound so hard she could hear it in her ears. "Where's Danny?" Her voice rose a notch. "Tell me."

He glanced away, then fixed his eyes on her. "I don't know where he is. He didn't come back."

Her gaze jerked from Sean to the boat and back again. "Didn't come back?"

Sean took hold of her by the arms. "Our last night on the island, Danny didna return to the boat. We sailed for Ireland the next day without him."

Her throat constricted so that she could not speak. She swallowed hard and forced the lump away. "You'll not be fooling with me, will ye Sean? For if ye are, I'll never forgive you. Not this time. I swear it. Do you hear me? I swear it."

He shook his head. "'Tis not a trick, Kathleen. If I could change the truth of it, I would. Danny didn't come back with us."

"But did you not search for him then? Knowing he was me own betrothed? Knowing we were to wed this very season?" She pressed her hand against her chest to stop the ache inside.

Sean exhaled. "'Twas not till morning I learnt he was missing—"

"So ye just left him behind? Perhaps he was hurt—"

"What do ye take me for Kathleen?" Sean snapped. "Sure, I didn't just leave him there. I asked after him. He went out for a pint with some of the lads, but none remember seeing him past midnight." His voice softened. "I couldn't go back to town, Kathleen, 'twas too late. The ship was ready to set sail. Had I gone searching, I, too, would be there still." He glanced at Moira, her belly swollen with the child she carried, and reached out to take her hand.

The silence pressed like a weight against Kathleen's lungs. "Did he know of the hunger? That the potatoes rotted again little more than a month ago?"

"Nay, none of us knew." Sean drew a slow breath as though weighing his next words. "Some of the lads thought he might have met a lass…"

She swung at him then, landing a stinging slap across his cheek. "Shame on ye, Sean. How dare you speak of Danny so," she said fiercely. "He's loved me since we were wee."

"I would never try to hurt you, Kathleen. I'm only saying what I heard." Sean tried to pull her close but she jerked away.

Moira touched her on the shoulder.

Kathleen looked at the woman who was her dearest friend in all the world and could feel nothing but jealousy that the man Moira loved had come home. And then she was filled with self-loathing for even thinking such a thing.

She turned to stare at the ship rocking softly in the light mist of the harbor, its deck now devoid of life. The air stank of fish and sweat.

He hadn't come back.

All around her was the chaos of reunion—the cries of joy, the laughter, the voices choked with emotion, the tears, the hearty slaps on the back, the fierce hugging…the kissing.

He hadn't come back.

She couldn't remember a time when she hadn't loved Danny, couldn't remember ever wanting anything except to become his wife. An emptiness settled over her; she could feel nothing but the dull ache in her chest.

"Kathleen, I'll take you home." Her brother came up behind her and tried to turn her by the shoulders.

"Leave me be." She pushed through the thinning crowd, shoving her way past the happiness, welcoming the slight jostling as if the contact could ease her pain. Reaching the edge of the dock, she looked across the harbor to the spot between two high bluffs where the water traveled to the sea, where the white horses galloped to the Country of the Young out past the western ocean.

Where was he now? Was he standing, as she, looking out over the water? Was he longing for home? Was he hurt? *Was he dead?*

Her breath caught. Nay, he lived. She was as sure of that as she was of her own heart. Tears welled in her eyes and began to slip down her cheeks.

An arm circled her waist and she turned. Ma.

"There's a reason, lass," her mother whispered. "There's always a reason." She pulled Kathleen close and cradled her head like she had when Kathleen was young and in need of comfort over the emotional bruises of childhood.

She clung to her mother, shoulders shaking as her tears rolled down to wet her mother's dress. "He's so far away, Ma, and I can't know if he is all right."

"Don't ye be thinking the worst, now. In the end all will be as it was meant to be," her mother murmured. *"Is fada an bóthar nach mbíonn casadh ann.* It's a long road that has no turning."

They stood there at the edge of the sea, not speaking, as a fine rain began to descend with the falling night. Kathleen sniffed loudly and wiped her eyes on the edge of her sleeve. The cool air sent a shiver through her and she lifted her head from her mother's shoulder, noticing for the first time that the crowd had dispersed and they were alone on the quay.

"Are you ready to go home, lass?"

"I keep thinking if I wait long enough he'll be here." She pulled out of her mother's arms.

"Aye, easy it is to feel that way. But it's growing dark and the road will seem twice as long when the sky is black." She put her hand in Kathleen's and drew her away from the water and onto the road. "There'll be other ships coming across…perhaps Danny will be on one of those."

In the graying night, the buildings rose up around them, their murky shadows gaping like dark entrances to the otherworld. Uphill they walked, the mist following them from the sea to the fields above. Kathleen looked back once, hoping, searching, but the empty road behind delivered only an aching reminder of her loss. She wrapped her arms protectively around her waist and prayed that no harm had befallen the man she loved.

CHAPTER TWO

THE SOUND OF raised voices broke into her sleep. Kathleen covered her ears with her hands and tried to block out the commotion. No doubt they caught someone stealing turnips again. She longed for the peaceful escape of slumber, that place where she could forget the potatoes had rotted, that Ireland was in famine again, *that Danny hadn't come back.* She let her hands drop to the straw pallet on which she lay and prayed the same thing she had said for three days now: *Please, let him be all right.* Tears pricked at the back of her eyes and she shoved herself to sitting. There would be no more sleep for her this morn.

Alone in the cottage she slipped into her clothes and pushed through the door, blinking as the morning sun hit her full face. Her parents and Sean stood out in the dusty road, deep in discussion, their voices rising and falling as they exchanged heated words.

"Of what are you speaking so early this morn?" she asked.

The three pivoted to face her, their expressions a mixture of guilt and dismay.

"Nothing to concern you, lass," her father said. "Go on about your business."

She pursed her lips and considered him for a moment. "Da, I wonder now what ye might be hiding from me? I've no patience anymore for games—not with the hunger, not with me Danny left in Newfoundland." She gave Sean a pointed look.

Sean stepped toward her. "I'll tell you, Kathleen. You need to know. Da has but a little money left, what with the crops failing this year—and last year too."

"Aye," she said cautiously. A kernel of fear lodged in her chest.

"And I haven't much. Hardly enough to keep Moira and me alive, but not near enough money to feed us all this winter. With the potatoes rotting again—" He shook his head. "If I'd known, I would have stayed in Newfoundland to work. And sent money home."

"'Tis a bit late to be fretting over what might have been," she muttered, not yet willing to forgive him for leaving Danny behind.

"Nay. We'll not survive another winter. Two years of famine in a row—and already I hear word has come from the English—"

"What word?"

"They'll offer no help to the Irish. It's the divine hand of providence that has delivered the famine, they say. And since it comes from the Lord, it would not be right for them to intervene."

Horror trickled into Kathleen's stomach. "But the crop has failed two years—"

"What don't you understand? They say we're lazy, that to help Ireland would make us dependent on Britain, that we must learn to feed ourselves." He spat on the ground. "They'll see us die—and be glad for it."

She drew in a sharp breath.

Sean reached out his hands in supplication. "There's money to be made in America."

"What are you saying Sean?"

"He's saying nothing, lass," her father said.

She could not drag her eyes from her brother's. "Sean?"

"Moira is with child. And once the babe is born, 'twill be deep in winter—no time to be crossing the ocean... Da and Ma, they're too old... I haven't money enough to feed us all, Kathleen."

"What are you saying Sean?"

"You have to go to America."

"Nay," she whispered.

"You must."

"Nay!" she shouted. "I'll not! How dare you ask that of me?"

"I would not ask if—"

She spun to face her parents. "What say you on this?"

Her mother stepped forward and drew Kathleen into her arms. "'Tis just your brother's idea. Your Da has been trying to talk some sense into him all morning."

"Sense?" The word burst out of Sean like a bullet. "We'll not all survive on what I've made at the fisheries! It's fact, Ma. The people are starving already and the potatoes rotted just over a month ago. There are food riots in the cities. This winter shall be far worse than the last." His voice dropped low. "If not for the babe, I would go meself. And by God, in the spring, Moira and I will take the child to America."

"You can't leave Ireland," Their mother's voice was just a whisper.

"I'll not stay here and starve to death. I've seen a better life, Ma, and my child is going to have it."

"But to leave... This is your home, your country."

"Pah! The English, will never let Ireland be ours again. We're nothing more than servants here in our own country, tilling the soil for them. Living on potatoes—and now nothing— while still they send our cattle, our grain to England—"

Tears filled Kathleen's eyes. "I canna go, Sean. What about Danny? What if Danny comes home and I am gone?"

"You'll not be going," her father roared.

Sean took her by the arms and pulled her away from their mother. "You must go. Soon. Before the winter sets in. Else we'll all be dead by the spring. Mac tells me that Irish girls are in great demand for domestic help. You'll live in a grand house and make a good wage—enough to send some home each month to help Ma and Da—"

She shook her head. She couldn't leave. Danny would be coming back and she had to be here when he arrived. She looked up at the rolling hills dotted with tiny sod and stone cottages, the dirt road beneath her feet winding across the hillside like a ribbon connecting the one home to the next, all their lives intertwined. Nay, she couldn't go. This was her home. These were her family. What if she never came back?

"…When Moira and I come in the spring, we'll be able to help you save enough for Da and Ma to come next. We'll be together in America."

She shook her head again, this time more vehemently.

"Yes, Kathleen. You must. For the family. You must go."

"Nay!" She pulled out of his grasp, swinging her hands wildly at him as if to fend off his words. "Let me be. Why do ye ask such a thing? Damn the English to hell! Damn the rotten potatoes and the hunger." A sob tore lose from her throat as the truth in his words forced itself into her brain. "Damn you, Sean Deacey and all your ideas. I don't want to go to America. I don't want to leave me home. Don't ye understand me now, Sean? I just want Danny." She turned and strode away, her steps coming more and more quickly until she was running, racing through the fields away from them in an attempt to escape her future.

*

In the late hours of night, Kathleen woke to the sound of Sean whispering in the darkness. "It must be soon," she heard him say. "Few ships will depart in the winter months."

Though Moira's reply was muffled, the anguish in her tone was clear.

"Don't weep," Sean said softly. "We'll be together in the spring, I promise. I'd rather be apart and know I'm helping ye live, then be with you here and not able to keep you and our child from dying."

Kathleen's heart stilled. Sean was leaving again. And by the spring Moira would, too. The potatoes had rotted, Danny hadn't come back, and no matter how much she wished it otherwise, nothing would ever be the same again. She pressed her hands to her ears as if blocking the conversation could prevent change from coming. The silence and darkness pressed down on her with suffocating clarity, and she spent the rest of the night drifting between her thoughts and a restless sleep.

She awakened just as dawn turned the black night to gray. Slipping out from under the covers, she stepped outside into a somber morning wet with faint rain dripping from low, leaden clouds. She pulled her scarf tight to her ears and let her gaze slip over the hillsides. 'Twas hardly sunrise and that was as she wanted it to be; she needed the dawn's quietude to still her thoughts so she might think.

She rested her hands upon the flat stones of the wall surrounding her family's small plot of land and remembered as a young child helping Da and Sean clear them from the field so crops could be planted. Stone fences crisscrossed the fields, divided the land into little plots, one per family, each so small it was hard to grow crops enough to keep a family fed even in good years. Yet, whether the crop was abundant or failed, rent was demanded by the English landlords.

She pressed her hands into the stones, felt the rough surface beneath her hands. So many stones in Ireland... So many stones and so much rain, sometimes she couldn't understand why the English were so bent on keeping this isle for themselves.

"Kathleen."

She started at the sound of Sean's voice and turned to see him coming toward her from the road to Cobh. "Where have you been off to already this morning? Is there news?" she asked.

"None you'll be wanting to hear."

She fisted her hands, pressed her fingers hard into her palms. "Stop protecting me now, Sean. I'm no longer that wee child who used to tag after you."

He nodded. "There's fever. Like last year when the crop failed. Fever is following the hunger."

"And death follows the fever," she said wearily.

"We should be all right for a while with the money I made in Newfoundland."

But only for a while. There were so many of them in the house, and three other children younger than she. If Danny had come back, they would have wed and moved into his parents' cottage. There would have been one less mouth for her parents to feed.

And one more for his.

She drew a ragged breath to calm her rising desperation. What would happen when the turnips were gone? When Sean's earnings from the fisheries were spent? No matter which way she turned, she could find no hope; the end was always the same. One of them had to go to America, and with Moira heavy with child it couldn't be Sean.

"Walk with me a bit," she said.

The rain had slowed to mist, and as the sun rose behind the dull clouds, a subdued shimmer draped itself over the landscape. A soft breeze kissed her cheek as if to convince her all would be right if she would but wait a bit longer to make a decision. 'Twas a faerie morn, sure, and she couldn't let it sway her mind. All would not be right for a long time to come.

When they were far enough from the cottage that they couldn't be overheard, she looked out over the soft hills and tried to imprint the image in her mind so she could call it up whenever she was missing home. "I'm sorry for refusing to go to America," she said.

Sean shook his head. "You're a woman grown now, Kathleen. It's your own choice to make, not mine. I should not have tried to force ye."

Her throat tightened. God, but she would miss him. And if God had any hand in this, the money she sent from across the ocean would ensure both his and Moira's survival so they might come out of Ireland next.

"I've changed me mind."

He grasped her by the arms and searched her face. "I had decided to go—"

She shook her head. "I thought as much. But you can't be leaving Moira. She carries your child and you've been gone half a year already. 'Tis my turn to help the family."

"Kathleen. Are ye sure?

"Aye." She smiled to hide the grief squeezing her chest. "But I have rules, Seanie, and you must hear me out on them. We'll not be telling Ma and Da until but a few days before I go. Else I will not be able to stand it. They will try to change my mind and I will want to change my mind and ye know sure as I there is no other choice."

"They'll not forgive you—"

"They'll forgive me soon enough when they are able to buy food for the family with the money I send." She put her hand on Sean's arm. "Do ye know how soon a ship will be leaving?"

"That's where I was this morning. Went to ask Mac about it. He said they're putting berths in the holds of cargo ships so they can carry the Irish across. Won't be more than a month and you can get passage."

A door slammed somewhere behind them and they both jerked round guiltily to see Ma shaking out her apron and two of their siblings follow her outside. Rain began to fall again.

"Sean, leave your sister be," their mother called. Though it was impossible for her to know what they were speaking of, somehow it seemed she did, just as she always had when they were children. "She'll not be doing your bidding."

Kathleen shook her head as the rain pattered cold upon her cheeks. "Don't you be fretting now, Ma. Seanie's not pushing me at all." She looked at her brother. "Did Mac know of any ships going to Newfoundland?"

"They say the work is in America—"

"That's my other rule. I'll be going to Newfoundland—not America. For I have to find Danny."

"And what if you can't?"

"At least I'll have tried." She smiled bravely though her stomach was knotted with fear. "So do ye know when a ship will be leaving?"

He nodded slowly. "To Canada, aye. But I've not heard of any bound for Newfoundland. I'll be thinking you'll be landing in New Brunswick and have to travel to Newfoundland."

A tremor of nervous anticipation rippled through her. "When? How soon does this ship leave for New Brunswick."

"Next week. There's room on a timber ship that leaves next week."

CHAPTER THREE

KATHLEEN STOOD AT the rail of the tired ship that was to be her home for the next month and watched Ireland grow smaller as the ship sliced through the blue cobalt water on its path across the ocean. Around her floated the murmurings of other emigrants, hushed voices, sorrowful and bitter at their leave-taking. Hunger had forced them from their homes; the English, by refusing to provide aid, had forced them from their country. 'Twould be a rare Irishman among them who would ever see these green hills again.

She had awoken this October morning to a soft rain pattering upon the roof. "Tears," Ma had said. "Ireland is weeping for its children, the ones it will never see again."

"Pah." Sean had waved an irritated hand at her. "Be keeping such thoughts to yourself, Ma. A day hardly passes without rain on this island. In Newfoundland, Kathleen, why, the sun shines near every day. I wouldn't doubt you'll soon be writing me to complain that it's too bright." He'd wrapped his arms around her then and pulled her close and she'd felt his pain in the trembling of his shoulders.

The rain had stopped before she boarded the ship and now the clouds were breaking apart, separated by great swaths of blue like

God had spilled a bucket of paint and it was pouring down to Earth. There could be no sky more beautiful than that over Ireland on a clear day. Above her, the sails stretched out full and white like the wings of some great bird...stealing her away from all she had ever known. Fear and nervousness tumbled over one another in her stomach.

Ireland was now just a speck on the horizon, but still she could not pull herself away from the ship's rail. As long as she could see her homeland, she would be all right.

From this distance she could almost pretend that all was still green there, that everything was as it once had been. 'Twas too far away now to see the potato fields laid bare by the blight. Too far away to see the houses torn to the ground by English landlords who cared not that the people were starving. *Too far away to see the hillside where Danny first told her he loved her.*

Danny. Her breath caught. He would not know she was coming across. God help them both if he was already on a ship bringing him home to Ireland. To famine.

Her eyes prickled and she clenched her teeth together as if to crush her grief. Nearly all the parish had come last night to see her off. They had smoked their pipes and talked in somber tones and passed along their blessings—and cursed the English. There had been no whiskey to share, yet all had stayed anyway.

In the wee hours of the morning, Ma had cried, wept like a child before all their guests, and begged her not to go—and then told her she must. And Da. She swallowed hard. Da had danced with her last night, one last jig. "Step with me, lass," he'd said. "For 'tis likely, we'll never dance together again." Facing one another, arms akimbo, they had kicked up their heels in abandon, the tears streaming down their cheeks the only sign of the pain within. He had clasped her to him then and held her tight and wished her well. And she knew his heart was breaking along with hers.

She reached out a finger as if to touch the island before it disappeared from sight. As long as she could still see Ireland—

And then it was gone.

Her eyes filled with tears and her head sagged toward her chest. A low sob escaped her throat. *May the English rot in hell for turning their backs on Ireland.*

She dragged the back of her fist across her eyes and wiped the tears away. There would be no more weeping. She lifted her head and set her jaw. Newfoundland was to be her home now. She would start a new life there and earn a good wage, enough to send money home so her family might survive another year of famine.

The breeze freshened and the ship seemed to leap forward, as if determined to leave Ireland behind as quickly as possible. Her homeland now lay beyond her sight, hidden like some faerie isle beneath the white-peaked waves rolling over and over into the brilliant blue horizon. Her mother's words came back to her then, spoken through tears like a final promise just before Kathleen boarded the small boat that carried her out to the ship anchored in Cork Harbor: "*An áit a bhfuil do chroí is ann a thabharfas do chosa thú.* Your feet will bring you to where your heart is."

Aye, she would make sure of that. She was her family's only hope; she could not fail. By all that was holy, she would survive this voyage and keep her family alive. And as God was her witness, she would find Danny.

Turning from the rail, she picked up her traveling bag and slowly made her way across the nearly-deserted deck toward the hatchway leading to the passenger section in steerage below deck. As she started down the ladder, the ship lurched on a wave and she nearly fell, dropping her bag as she scrambled to get a better grip on the rungs. Someone below shouted angrily at her and she called down a weak, "Sorry."

She stopped at the bottom to let her eyes adjust to the dim light, and her ears to the unintelligible sound of so many people talking and weeping at once. Everywhere she looked were Irish, sitting on the berths and the floor, small bags beside them crammed with the few belongings they had brought from home. *A lifetime in Ireland squashed into one small satchel—just as she had done.*

Grasping her bag in a tight fist, feet wide for balance, she picked her way through the throng of thin, haggard people camped on the floor, past the children in threadbare clothing laughing and scrabbling about, past row upon row of double berths, each wide enough it seemed that it could hold four or five adults—and already did. Faith, but had she lost her chance for a place to sleep by staying topsides so long?

She turned and began to retrace her steps, glancing left and right, searching even the floor for a spot she might call her own. Women shook their heads sympathetically, saying, "We've no room—six already in this one," or "Five children, we have, besides us."

She thought she heard someone call her name above the din and turned uncertainly. Was her mind simply creating what she longed to hear? She squinted into darkness and spotted a woman a few berths down motioning to her.

"It's Lucy," the woman called.

Lucy McKenna. In the chaos of coming aboard and the pain of leaving Ireland, she'd forgotten the McKenna family was on this ship. Kathleen waved a hand and made her way to where Lucy stood.

"I was wondering where you might be," Lucy said. "Here, your ma asked me to watch over—"

"She didn't," Kathleen said, embarrassed. "You've enough of your own to worry over—"

"Och, 'tis every mother's blessing to watch out for other mother's children." She glanced around steerage and shook her head. "They've sold more tickets than they have space. I hope they've food enough for so many."

Kathleen nodded, grateful for the oatmeal and bread her mother had tucked into her bag even though the family could ill afford to give it up.

"You can share with us. Do you remember Maegan and Molly?" Lucy motioned at a lower berth where her two daughters sat swinging their skinny legs back and forth in the space underneath. The girls looked at her but did not smile, though they'd met Kathleen several times before.

"Aye." She knew the family had two sons as well—with Kathleen that would make seven in the berth. "But have you room?"

"The children are small. Won't be much different from what we left behind."

"I'll be thanking you. I feared the only place left was the floor. But even with that, I didn't know where I would fit." She pushed her bag under the bottom berth and held onto the bunk as the ship rolled a little. She smiled at the two girls. "I'm a bit nervous about this voyage," she said. "Are you?"

Maegan shook her head. "Molly is."

"I'm not," Molly protested.

"Well then, I shall take courage from the two of you, all right? I'm not so sure me own little sister would be so brave."

"That's because she's ten," Maegan said. "I'm eleven."

"You're probably right." A pang of homesickness swept through her. "Do ye know about Canada? My brother has told me stories."

Maegan leaned forward. "Has he been there?"

"He was in Newfoundland, which is part of Canada. And I shall tell you everything he's said so ye'll know just what to expect."

Both girls grinned and Kathleen felt her spirits lift. With the McKennas near, perhaps she wouldn't miss her own family quite so much. She straightened and touched Lucy's arm. "I'll be thanking you."

Lucy nodded, then tilted her head toward a man lying in a nearby berth. "There's some down here that are looking none too well already," she said under her breath. "The fever, I wager. Best that we all stay topside whenever we can."

*

Lucy's words were a prescient warning. Three weeks later, the first Irishman died. Kathleen hung back among the crowd on deck, watching, as he was wrapped in a piece of sailcloth, prayers were murmured over his body, and he was slipped into the ocean.

Her heart chilled at the feeling that others would likely follow. The air in steerage had become a breeding ground for death—each day it seemed another person had taken ill with the fever. The stench of disease and excrement mingled with the odors of rotten food and too many unwashed people. And the lice, everywhere were the lice.

"No doubt the crew will be celebrating the first Irish death," Lucy murmured. She pulled Maegan close and kissed the top of her head.

Kathleen glanced sharply at her friend. "It cannot happen

to us, Lucy. We've not left our homes to die on the ocean, to be thrown into a watery grave."

Her temper flared at the shipboard conditions. The biscuits were wormy, the rations shorted, the water shared grudgingly. When the weather was stormy, the Irish were locked in the fetid darkness below deck, denied access to the cooking stoves and privies for days at a time. Water leaked through from the deck above soaking everything and hastening illness, and still the hatches stayed locked tight.

"God help us," Lucy said, "if we could but get across this endless ocean. Just two weeks more they say." She pressed her palm to her daughter's cheek, flushed pink with fever.

Kathleen tamped down the fear that hovered at the edge of her mind. So many onboard were unwell. And now, sweet Maegan was sick. "The conditions in steerage are what breeds the illness. If the crew would but let some of us sleep on deck—"

"Too dangerous they say."

"And 'tis less dangerous to sleep where the air hangs heavy with disease? Pah! This English crew cares not how the Irish fare, so long as their own bunks are clean and their rations plenty."

Lucy smiled in weary acquiescence.

All Kathleen had ever wanted was a simple life, to wed Danny, to bear his children, to grow old with her family close about her. But the famine had changed all that. And now the lives of her entire family rested on her shoulders. "If we're to survive this voyage, we can't stay in steerage any longer." She took a step back and looked around.

The deck was so crowded with provisions, gear, and people there was little space for the Irish to walk about. Many passengers simply stood and sucked in great breaths of fresh air to cleanse their lungs. The smell of disease and decay rose up from their ragged clothing and filthy skin. Even in the freshening breeze, the odor did not dissipate. Kathleen grimaced. No doubt she smelled as bad.

She gritted her teeth and began to make her way along the outer edges of the throng. Sure, there must be somewhere they could hide after dark, somewhere they wouldn't be seen. Nearby, a man put a hand to his mouth and coughed, a hacking, painful sound, thick with mucous. Kathleen jerked away, unsettled.

Near the lifeboats, the extra sails had been tossed on the deck, jammed into a corner amid casks and extra spars and piles of coiled lines. Several sailors sat amongst the clutter, legs outstretched for balance as they mended sails and tarred ropes.

She watched them a moment, an idea forming in her mind. The crew did not do stitching work at night; that jumbled mess of sails and supplies would be deserted after dusk. If they could but slip beneath the sails in the darkness, the water casks would hide them from view. No one would know she and the McKennas were still on deck. She allowed herself a small smile. The sails that opened aloft like angel's wings, would be their salvation down here on the deck.

She worked her way back to where Lucy stood with Maegan and described her plan, glancing around to make sure she wasn't overhead. "I truly think it's worth a try," she said.

"There are so many of us. Never would we be able to keep the children quiet. 'Twould be over before it began."

"We can try—"

Lucy shook her head.

"I'll do it first. If all goes well—"

"I promised your mother to keep you safe. What will I say to her if something happens to ye up here?"

"Tell her I had as much chance of dying below deck as I did topsides."

Lucy sighed. "Aye. There is that." She stroked her daughter's hair, then pressed a hand to her forehead. "*There is that*. All right then, you try. I hope it works. But even if it does, we'll not be joining you, not with so many children."

"Perhaps Maegan…"

Lucy shook her head, but Kathleen pushed forward. "'Tis getting worse and worse below deck. We've only two weeks left, perhaps the fresh air will cleanse the fever from her."

After a long moment, Lucy yielded with a sad smile. "I fear ye may be right. Keep her up here, then. And keep my darling girl safe."

Several hours later, long after the sun had slid into the ocean, its light extinguished like a torch dropped into a puddle, Kathleen waited with Maegan in the shadows near the water casks and gathered her courage. The bell had just rung for the change of the watch and the crew was intent on trading places. If luck was with her, none would notice them.

She glanced up at the sky. Not a star penetrated the coal black universe, the clouds so thick and low, evening had fallen early. It was a perfect first night.

A shiver rippled through her, as much from fear as from the evening's chill. Feigning nonchalance, she glanced around the deck, waiting until all the crew members were occupied and the few passengers still topsides had their attention on other things. She motioned for Maegan to follow, then dropped to her knees and crawled onto the pile of dingy sails. Her eyes were locked on their destination—the furthest corner.

In her haste, her knees trapped her skirt beneath her, nearly flopping her onto her stomach. "Jesus, Mary, and Joseph," she muttered under her breath. She tugged at her skirt and silently cursed again.

Male voices sounded nearby and she froze, straining to hear better, to gauge how close the two speakers might be. Faith, but they couldn't be found out already. She yanked her skirt free and slid her legs under the sails. As Maegan scrambled in next to her, Kathleen pulled the white canvas over their heads and grasped Maegan's hand in her own. She could feel the child's fear in her grip.

Flat on her back, Kathleen held her breath, terrified that the sails might rise and fall with her breathing and give them away. Try as she might, she could hear nothing but the blood pounding in her ears. Her lungs ached with the need for air and still she did not inhale, counting seconds in her head to distract herself, fighting against the will to breathe until she could stand the pressure no longer. When finally she exhaled, the air burst out of her like she had taken a blow to the stomach.

Holding the worn canvas inches off her face, she quietly gulped in breaths, the air musty and tasting of salt. If they were to be caught, now would be the moment. She tensed in anticipation, awaiting the angry voice, the kick in the ribs, the rough hand that would haul them from beneath the sails and throw them below deck into that squalid hold with its lice and fever.

A minute passed and then another, and still she waited several more before accepting that no one had spotted them. She gave Maegan's hand a squeeze. Then she smiled and the canvas of their white haven kissed her cheek. They had made it.

She slept fitfully, her dreams nonsensical and frightening, of angels with great wings carrying her to America as she tried to tell them she was bound for Canada, of being discovered by the crew and forced back below deck. As dawn began to lighten the day, she slid the sail from her face and saw the first rays of morning sun unfurling across the sky like shimmering white horses racing across the ocean waves. Grinning triumphantly, she shook Maegan awake, then made for the privy with the young girl in tow. 'Twas a brilliant ploy—to any of the crew who might see them, they would look to have just come up from below deck for their morning relief.

The next few nights passed as smoothly as the first. Though Maegan seemed no better, she was also no worse, which they all took as a good sign. Tucked safely beneath the sails once again, Maegan's hand clasped in her own, Kathleen let her fear and apprehension ease with the gently rocking motion of the ship. She fell asleep picturing how Sean would laugh when she described exactly how she'd bested the English.

Hours later, she came awake groggily to the sound of a low moan, vibrating and rising until it became a shriek that splintered the night. She slid the sails off her head and pushed up slowly on her elbows. A blast of icy air slapped her in the face and she flinched at the sudden temperature change. The darkness was endless, a mass of solid black. *Like the inside of a casket.*

Maegan clutched Kathleen's arm and curled against her side. "What is it," she whispered.

The screech sounded again and Kathleen gasped in terror, expecting at any moment to see a wailing woman shrouded in a dark, misty cloak—the harbinger of death. It couldn't be the banshee. Not now. They couldn't die with Canada so close.

The eerie wail wove through the rigging, breaking off abruptly as the ship heeled beneath the stiff breeze and the leeward rail skimmed the water's surface. Cold spray drenched the deck and spattered the sails covering them. In the darkness, the ocean looked like ink, ready to swallow forever that which dared to cross its surface.

"Batten the hatches! Reef the sails! It's a Nor'easter and she's coming on fast!" The words shouted by the captain were echoed from sailor to sailor scaling the rigging above her. Lightning convulsed across the sky, snapping and cracking as if enraged at the ship in the water below. Kathleen jerked back in panic. "We need get below deck. Now, before they lock the hatches."

Making no effort to hide, she took Maegan's hand and stumbled toward the hatchway. The ship pitched beneath them, lurching under powerful blasts of wind. Icy spray burst over the bulwark and pierced Kathleen's skin like the sharp fingernails of the banshee. Maegan lost her balance and dragged them both to their knees on the wet deck. Kathleen landed hard; pain shot up one leg. Somewhere in the survival side of her brain, she knew they had but a few minutes more before the storm hit full force and their chance of getting below deck was gone.

"Crawl, Maegan!" she screamed. The young girl looked at her, dazed and feverish. On hands and knees, Kathleen began to push her toward the hatch opening. Sailors shouted from high in the rigging, but she didn't look up. Her eyes were locked on the hatchway that led to safety. Still on her knees, she half dragged Maegan across the wet deck and got her onto the ladder down to steerage. The moment Maegan disappeared below deck, Kathleen reached for the rungs so she could follow.

The ship slammed into a great swell and heeled over sharply, tearing Kathleen's fingers from her hold on the ladder and sending her sliding toward the low side. She clutched at the deck in a frantic effort to halt her descent. The wood tore at her palms and she cried out, screaming for help, but her voice was swallowed by the roaring wind.

Another pitch of the ship flung her against the leeward rail gasping for breath. Furious lightning rent the sky, illuminating the ship beneath its stark light. The mizzenmast was bent nearly to breaking. Sailors dangled from the rigging, struggling to keep from being swept into the ocean. And then rain exploded from the clouds, plummeting with such force she felt like her face was being pierced by a thousand needles.

Grunting in fear, she began to claw her way across the deck, eyes fixed on the hatchway leading below. The ship slammed into another wave and the water casks broke loose from their lashings, tumbling across the deck like cannonballs. Three casks roped together rammed into her, shoving her back and down against the bulwark. "Danny!" she screamed through the icy water rushing over her face.

The masts groaned beneath the onslaught of the shrieking wind, the shrouds and stays creaked as they strained to hold the spars in place. All around her was shouting and panic as sailors struggled to cut loose the sails before any of the spars broke.

Frantic, she shoved at the barrels that pinned her against the half-submerged bulwark. Water surged over her face and she gagged it out, gasping for air. Oh, mother of God—

The sea pulled at her as it receded and she clung to the loose lashing on the casks to keep from washing overboard. Her fingers slipped on the wet hemp and she thrust both hands beneath the lashings, twisting the rope around her wrists until it bit into her skin. Then she closed her fingers over the rough hemp and gripped it with all her strength. She'd not go into the sea without a fight.

The bow crashed down on a monstrous swell and water flooded over her again. She threw back her head, coughing and gagging and praying to live. As the ship heeled precariously beneath her, the three casks rose on the foaming waves and rolled over the bulwark, dragging her with it into the raging sea.

'Twas the banshee after all. Today she was to die.

CHAPTER FOUR

"CAPTAIN, UP OFF the starboard bow—due east. What do you make of it?" Will Matson, the ship's first mate, pointed into the distance.

Jack Montgomery leaned on the rail of his whaling ship and squinted at the small dark shape bobbing on the ocean swells in the distance. Choppy seas and a low ceiling of dark clouds were all that remained of last night's ferocious storm. He shook his head. For a few minutes during the worst of it, he'd actually worried they might lose their main mast, but the ship had ridden out the storm intact and all three spars were standing tall when the wind finally subsided.

"Flotsam is my guess," he finally answered. "Washed off some ship." In the dim light, it was impossible to tell what the thing was. And frankly, who the hell cared?

He turned his attention midships, to where half of the crew was cutting in the whale they'd caught that morning. Nearly twenty men were on this six-hour watch, each focused on performing a specific task, knowing that the faster they finished with this whale, the sooner they could search for the next—and the sooner they could go home.

Great chunks of whale meat were piled across the deck, blood and oil oozing in thick shiny streams across the planking. Forward, fires roared in brick furnaces that held the trypots, two huge iron cauldrons where they were boiling the blubber to remove the oil, and boiling the oil to remove contaminants.

Thick black smoke from the tryworks' chimneys wove up the ship's foremast, and the fire belched up great gusts of flame as though the temperature was too much for even the tryworks itself to bear. The oil was now hot enough to melt lead, and the air was just as scorching.

"Hard to believe this is nearly your last voyage," Matson said. "I still say you're going to miss it."

"I may never get the chance to miss it. We've been out six months already and the hold is only half full. I never thought the Davis Straits would be as fished out as the rest of the Atlantic."

Matson rested his elbows on the rail and grinned. "Well... we've always done well in the South Pacific."

Jack snorted. "That's for you to chase. My whaling days are almost done—and none too soon, either." Twice already he'd taken the long, treacherous route around Cape Horn, the southern tip of South America, to whale hunt for two years in the Pacific. But after losing three men during the last rounding, his ship nearly driven onto the rocks, he had no desire to visit that sailor's graveyard again. The lives of his crew members were as important to him as his own.

He wiped the sweat off his face with his sleeve and watched his men work, their skin and clothing covered with a black sheen of mingled grease and smoke. The choppy sea tossed the ship, splashing oil from the trypots into the fire and sending the flames flaring high. The men at the trypots glowed crimson in the reflected light.

Twelve years he'd been at this. Twelve years of blood, oil and grime. Twelve years of the reeking, sweet rotten stench of whale processing, a smell so repulsive that other ships avoided being near them when the tryworks were burning.

He'd hated whaling since his first voyage. But he'd signed aboard time and again because it offered opportunities he knew he would never see on land—advancement at a young age, a faster path to financial security. He'd worked his way up and built a decent nest egg. If this trip was successful, he would need just one more voyage before he had enough money put aside to become one of the ship's principal owners, perhaps even managing partner, instead of a minor partner like he was now. If these last two voyages did well enough, he might even have enough to invest in shares of other whaling ships. He would move to the other side of the balance sheet, live a businessman's life, marry well, and put the ghosts of his past to rest.

Overhead the sagging sails gave a listless snap that jerked him from his thoughts. The white shapes glowed an eerie lurid yellow in the smoke-filled dusk. There was a savageness to this process, a wildness not of this earth. And now, with the blubber boiling over fierce fires, thick, black smoke filling the sky above and trailing behind them for miles, it was like stepping into hell itself.

"Captain, you might want to take another look," Matson said.

"If it's not a whale, I don't care."

"Jack, take a look."

He glanced at Matson, then put the offered spyglass to his eye and held his breath to steady his arm. Three wooden barrels lashed together came into view; a dark shape lay across the top of them. He watched as the casks bobbed in and out of sight with the waves.

"What the hell…" He pulled the spyglass away. "What is that?"

"Don't know. Almost looks like an animal."

Jack shoved the glass to his eye again. "Hard to see, it's getting so dark." He concentrated on the casks. "Hell, Will, I think it's a person."

He handed the spyglass to Matson who took another look then let out a low whistle.

That was all the confirmation Jack needed. He spun and shouted at the nearest crew members, "Man overboard! Due east. You four—drop the starboard boat!"

The men leapt to the task. The rest of the crew watched from their posts as an oarboat was dropped so quickly it slapped the water. The men sprang aboard and each took hold of an oar and leaned into it, determination evident in their every stroke. They were driven by the unwritten rule of the sea—help those in trouble on the water.

As the oarboat bounced over the waves, a few officers moved to stand at the rail beside Jack. He held his breath in uneasy anticipation, only vaguely aware of the crew's murmurings and the nearly empty sails flapping overhead. Putting the glass to his eye once more, he focused on the body, and silently cursed the rapidly falling night.

The person wasn't moving. *Probably dead.* Damn, but this was the last thing he needed with a crew of superstitious sailors—a body, like a bad omen, portending an ill future for this voyage. People died all the time on the ocean, but they usually disappeared beneath its surface never to be seen again.

The oarboat surged up one side of each dying wave and down the other until it drew even with the casks. As the men pulled the body into the boat, Jack could see a long black skirt tangled about its legs.

"Jesus, it's a woman," he muttered. His words echoed from man to man behind him.

Matson exhaled. "A ship full of men, six months to sea, and we haul aboard a woman." He took the glass from Jack and put it to his eye. "She's probably dead."

An unnatural hush fell over the ship as the crew watched the boat slowly return, up one wave and down the next with the woman lying across the seats and the casks in tow. Once it was within shouting distance, one of the men on the oarboat stood and waved his hands above his head. "Alive!" he yelled and a whoop went up from the crew.

Jack blew out a breath. *Thank God.* And just as quickly, that thought was replaced by another—they were bringing a woman aboard a whaling ship filled with men, and they wouldn't be going into a port for months.

The oarboat bumped up against the whaler and the crew quickly winched it up to deck level. Eager hands lifted the woman from the boat and laid her on her back on the deck. The crew pressed forward.

The woman's face was gray and crusted with salt, her lips cracked, her red hair a thick matted mass, and both wrists were bleeding. Jack could see no sign that she was breathing.

"She was tied to the casks, sir," one of the men offered. "Lines wrapped so tight about her wrists, they bit her skin raw. We had to cut her free."

Shock reverberated through Jack. "If she went overboard during last night's gale, she spent at least ten hours in the ocean."

"Lucky to be alive," Matson said.

Jack knelt to take her pulse at her throat. As the ship's captain, he also served by tradition as the ship's doctor. It was up to him to save her. Feeling no heartbeat against his fingertips, he pressed a little harder. If she died, the crew would be talking about bad luck and ill-fated voyages for the rest of this trip.

He waved a hand at the gathered men. "Let's give her some air. Back to work, boys. It's nearly dark and we have a whale to finish cutting in."

He waited until only a few officers remained, then checked her pulse again. Behind him, the fires in the furnace roared back to life. One man shouted something, another answered, and then came the crackling sizzle of whale blubber as it landed in a scorching trywork pot.

He pressed his fingers harder against the artery in her neck and finally felt the whisper of a heartbeat in response. He allowed himself a bit of grim satisfaction. Still alive; that's all that mattered.

"Let's put her—" His brow furrowed. Where? She couldn't stay in the forecastle—no telling what some in this bunch would do while she lay unconscious. Jack tensed his jaw. What the devil was he supposed to do with her? "Put her in my berth for now. If she doesn't warm soon, the chill will kill her."

Her eyelids fluttered.

"I'll be damned," he said. "She's coming to."

*

Kathleen forced her eyelids open. Crusty pieces of salt dropped into her eyes, stinging, as her lashes separated. Her vision swam in and out of focus as she fought to make sense of the sight before her. Man-like beings, soot-blackened and naked to the waist, labored near blazing fires, their skin glistening red as they sliced chunks of flesh with great knives. Beside them, other beings stirred huge cauldrons. Shadows rose and fell with the contortions of the flames, casting some and then others in and out of her sight.

She drew a shaky breath and fought the horror and confusion that flooded her exhausted mind. One incoherent thought rambled over the next as she tried to pull them into order. She had gone overboard, but then what—

The banshee. *She had heard the banshee.*

A worker forked chunks of flesh into the seething liquid. The oil hissed and sent up a stream of smoke as it enveloped each new piece, bubbling the sickening odor of death into the air. Other pieces, fried until they were but twisted chunks, were scooped from the pot and tossed into a nearby tub. Bile rose in the back of her throat.

She had died. *And this was hell.*

Her breath came in short gasps as she tried to still her terror and tear her gaze away, and failed. Jesus, Mary and Joseph, they were burning people up. That's what happened in hell—hadn't Thomas Kinney told her as much when they were wee? To be sure, Ma had said he'd made it up, but now, dear Lord, 'twas clear that Tommy had been right all along.

Within the billows of black smoke, the devil's helpers feverishly worked, slicing and boiling those they had already killed. The demon with the big fork grabbed one of the fried scraps and jammed it in his mouth, a greedy grin splitting his face.

Heart pounding, Kathleen turned away. She had to escape from here. She tried to push herself up, but her hands slipped on the thick, slimy liquid oozing over the planks. A low croaking moan escaped the back of her throat as she drew her hand to her nose in horror—*blood*. Faith, but the floor was awash in blood.

Into her vision came the oily, blackened face of a dark-haired demon with eyes the color of an underworld midnight. *Sure, this was the devil himself.* She cringed back, drawing one ragged breath upon another in an effort to control the panic pressing outward from within her chest, the hysteria exploding in her mind.

How could this have happened when she had always gone to mass except just a few times she missed and hadn't she always said her prayers and how could this have happened when Father McCarthy had blessed her before she left home and said the Lord would keep her safe—

In a broken rush, she began to croak out what she could remember of her prayers. "Hail Mary, full of grace the Lord is with thee, blessed—blessed are— Our Father, who art in heaven, hallowed be—Our Father who art—Our Father—Oh my God I am heartily sorry for—"

She couldn't think, her prayers were gone. She could hardly breathe. "Oh my God, I am heartily sorry for having offended thee…"

A deathly silence greeted her from the circle of demons gazing down at her. Crumbling beneath her own terror, she passed into unconsciousness again.

*

"Delirious or mad," Jack muttered. What the hell kind of disaster had he just brought on board his ship? "Dammit. Donnelly, get some hot tea and bring it to my cabin. The rest of you—get back to work." He gave command of the ship over to Matson, then scooped the woman up and carried her below deck to his quarters. As captain, he had a spacious living space—a sitting room with a built-in upholstered sofa and large light-filled skylight; a separate stateroom containing his bed, dresser and washbasin; and a private head. Without a doubt, his quarters would be the best place for her to recover.

She was lighter than he'd expected, skinny, the bones in her shoulders and legs easily felt through her worn clothing. He lay her in his stateroom berth, then shook his head. Until she recovered? More like, if she recovered. Her pulse was weak, her breathing shallow and irregular. Who knew how much salt water she had ingested—or how long she had been in the ocean exposed to the elements?

He pushed the sodden mass of hair off her face, then dipped a cloth into the pitcher of water on his commode and wiped the dried salt from her face. Laying a palm against her cheek, he winced at the coldness of her skin. The wet clothing had to go. He tried to pull off her blouse and the threadbare fabric stuck to her arm and tore. Irritated, he stripped it off and tossed it to the floor. Her skirt, shift, and stockings followed.

She had so little fat it was hard to believe she been able to survive at all in the ocean. Shifting her gently, he slid the blankets over her nakedness and tucked them tight to keep the warmth close to her body. The fire from the tryworks on deck was already heating up his quarters, and for the first time he was actually glad for the extra warmth.

A tap at the sitting room door broke his concentration. Donnelly stepped into the room and set a small tray on the chart table. "Captain, here's the tea." He peered into the stateroom at the woman in the bed. "Will she live, do you think?"

"I don't know. She's barely breathing and has the pulse of a bird."

Donnelly murmured something in Irish.

"What did you say?"

"Just a blessing sir, for one of me own."

"You think she's Irish?"

Donnelly nodded. "Could you not hear it in her voice?"

"I could hardly hear her at all."

"She was born on the Isle, sure. You've not seen the banshee, have you?"

"Banshee?"

"Aye, the spirit of death. Shows herself only before someone passes on. Wrapped in a gray cloak, wailing, her eyes red from the weeping—"

"Nonsense."

Donnelly nodded. "I meself saw the banshee before me own grandmother passed on. Pray you don't see her, Captain. It's a frightening thing to know of coming death." He paused. "Will you be needing anything else, sir?"

Jack shook his head. He barely heard the dull thud of the door closing as Donnelly took his leave. *Irish.* There had been news a year or more ago, of the Irish potato crop failing. If Donnelly was right about her being Irish, that might explain why she was so thin. For a moment he wondered where she had been headed and how she ended up in the ocean. Had she been seeking a new life or was something else at play, something underhanded?

He poured some tea into a cup and blew on the steam curling above the amber liquid, waiting a few moments for it to cool. "You made it this far," he murmured as he turned toward the bed. "Don't give up now."

Sliding a hand beneath her neck, he raised her head and held the cup to her lips, hoping she might wake enough to swallow. The liquid dribbled down the sides of her cheeks and onto the blankets.

He set the cup back on the table, drew another blanket from a locker in the sitting room, and lay it over her. Heat was what she needed; she likely wouldn't awaken until her body had warmed. Until then, all he could do was wait. He glanced at the door and back at the woman. He didn't feel right about leaving her alone, but the cutting-in process had to be completed quickly or the blubber would rot.

Conflicting thoughts argued in his mind. She was unconscious; she might awake and need help. One of the men could sit with her; every man was needed topside.

"Damnation!" They had a whale to process...and playing nursemaid did nothing to help him run his ship, nor make a living for every man on this ship. He picked up her ragged clothing to throw into the fire, then let himself out of his cabin. Surely she could spend a few hours unattended.

CHAPTER FIVE

LONG AFTER MIDNIGHT, Jack dragged himself into his quarters, aching and exhausted. They hadn't even gotten a quarter of the way through the job but he needed some sleep. Last night's storm had kept him and the crew on deck until nearly dawn—and then they had spotted the whale and taken up the chase. It had been a long thirty-six hours with little rest for anyone.

He turned up the wick on the oil lamp hanging from the bulkhead, then took a towel from a locker and wiped the greasy soot from his face and arms as he stepped into his stateroom to check on the woman. Even though she was unconscious and below deck, her presence was already having an effect on the crew.

Donnelly had gone topsides after delivering the tea and told the men about the banshee, this spirit that foretold death. After that he'd spent hours regaling them with stories about Irish spirits and fairies. How the Sheerie used sorcery to lead people astray after dark, and the Grey Man wore a cloak of swirling fog to hide rocks along the coast so ships would run aground. He'd spun tales until the combination of the stories, the darkness, the smoke and the fires and the dead whale and the exhaustion had most of the men glancing nervously over their shoulders. And throughout it all, there had been more gossiping, more bravado, more bawdy talk, more posturing than he'd ever seen among the crew…as though each of them thought he might win the woman's favor once she came to.

Despite his cautionary words, the men seemed convinced that she would soon be up and about. God only knew what the ship would be like if that happened—one woman and all these men currying her favor.

Setting a hand on her forehead, he frowned at the icy cold that met his palm. She was no warmer than before. How could that be? It was so hot down here from the tryworks fires it was almost unbearable. He leaned forward to watch her. Was her chest moving or not? Dammit, wasn't she breathing? He pressed his fingers against a vein beneath the soft skin of her throat. Nothing. He pressed harder, this time gently slapping her cheeks with his other hand. Damn, where was her pulse? *Don't die.* He held his breath. *Come on, come on.* How could she have died? It had only been a few hours since he'd last checked on her.

A tiny beat pulsed against his fingertip. There it was. He exhaled and let his head drop to his chest. With shaking hands, he smoothed her damp hair back from her brow.

"You can't die. It would not bode well for this voyage." He collapsed into the chair at his chart table, disconcerted by his concern for her and knowing that his reason for wanting her to live went far deeper than simply the success of this voyage. He'd not have another death on his conscience, not again, not ever.

Returning to the bed, he reached beneath the blankets and vigorously rubbed her arms and legs. A sense of foreboding rolled over him. She was so cold.

Death. The word slammed into his brain and he jerked upright. His father's death. Skin rigid and cold, limbs stiff. *I couldn't save him.*

Jack looked around the room, his thoughts almost frantic as he tried to shove the memory away before the wound was torn open. *I couldn't save him—there was nothing I could do.*

Damn, she couldn't die. Not on his ship, not with him on watch. He had to get her warm—now. Striding across the cabin, he slammed the lock into place on the door, then pulled off his shoes and flipped them into the corner. He knew what to do; his grandfather had taught him years ago from his own experience on the sea. The fastest way to warm a person was with your own body.

He turned down the lamp, then peeled off his shirt and pants and dropped them in the chair, all the while keeping his eyes focused on the woman's face, as though shifting his gaze away might mean the difference between her living and dying. Wearing only his drawers, he stepped toward the bed then stopped. Though her life was clearly in his hands, he still owed it to her to preserve her decency.

He slid under the blankets, making sure to keep the sheet between the two of them. Then he wrapped his arms around her bony shoulders and pulled her close. As her chill crossed the thin cotton barrier, he sucked in a quick breath and shifted her head into the hollow between his chin and shoulder. The smell of the sea lingered on her damp hair, the odor so strong he could almost taste the salt.

He tried to will his warmth over her. Fatigue played with his thoughts, slid his eyelids shut. Finally his tense muscles slackened and he slept.

Hours later he woke with a start. He'd dreamed of his father again—the same dream he'd had since he was a child.

A trickle of sweat ran between his shoulder blades and he slid a numb arm from beneath the woman. The lantern had gone out, and the darkness of his cabin was broken only by a reed of moonlight filtering through a porthole. He ran a hand down the woman's arm, noting with satisfaction that her skin was warmer. Deep in slumber, she exhaled softly. At last she was breathing normally.

He rolled onto his back and stared into the darkness. The dream was always the same. He was running home, carrying a canvas bag to give his father. With every step, the bag became heavier and his legs grew harder to lift. He struggled to keep going, his steps growing shorter until finally he couldn't move his feet and the bag slipped from his hands, tearing open on the ground, the coins inside rolling out in every direction. He tried frantically to scoop them up, crawling as he tried to push them back into the bag, all the while calling to his father, shouting as if his words could change what happened, as if his words could save his father's life.

Jack drew a long, slow breath. He knew he couldn't have saved his father, had reasoned it out time and again. Yet, even now, twenty years later, some part of his mind still clung to that possibility, was still plagued by the guilt.

The woman whimpered. Jack shoved himself up on one elbow and focused on her eyes, searching for a sign of consciousness but finding none. In the pale mist of moonlight, Donnelly's words returned to him and Jack felt a prickle of anticipation. Suppressing a shudder, he looked across his empty stateroom.

For an instant, the moonlight wavered as though something crossed its path. Jack froze, caught in a moment that seemed to hover between life and afterlife. The hair on his arms rose, and suddenly he was sure she was there, the spirit in the gray cloak, the banshee.

"Be gone, woman." The fierceness in his voice surprised him. "This one lives. She belongs to me."

He pulled the woman closer as though daring the spirit to defy him. Several long moments passed before he gave his head a shake. What was he doing? One day with this woman on board and now *he* believed in Irish spirits? Donnelly would be so pleased.

He relaxed into the bed and forced his mind to still. The layers of blankets warmed him and sleep beckoned again. Exhausted, he slid into the nebulous world between unconscious and awake. His thoughts floated, blending with his dreams. There was a woman beside him but he knew not why, nor did he care. Drifting ever closer to slumber, he snuggled his head in next to hers. She was here, she was his…and that was enough.

*

Lord it was hot. So hot. Like the sun had gotten beneath her skin and was trying to burn its way out. Sweat dribbled down her chest along the curves of her breasts. Damp fabric stuck to her, warm and wrinkled.

Kathleen tried to ask for help, but the words stuck in her parched throat and the effort brought tears to her closed eyes. Thirsty. She gulped at the air, heavy and stale and rancid. Water. She needed water. She couldn't breathe—God help her she was wrapped in something, buried—suffocating she was.

Panicked, she shoved at the weight that pressed down on her and struggled to free herself. Her muscles burned from the effort, her breath came in short, shallow bursts.

And then the weight shifted and spoke in a low voice, heavy with sleep. "Easy," a man murmured.

She forced her eyelids open. A black haired man slept beside her—nay, held her in his arms so close his every breath touched her cheek. She struggled to comprehend. Delirious thoughts and images tumbled over one another in her mind so she couldn't tell what was real and what was dream. The room seemed to rock as though she were still on the boat, but that couldn't be, she had gone overboard. She drew a shaky breath. Had she been rescued? Then why was this man in her bed?

Suddenly a memory loomed before her—flames, thick smoke from a blazing fire, and oily, blackened demons boiling the dead. Nay, it couldn't be real. She had to get out of this heat, had to find water, talk to Lucy McKenna. Aye, surely Lucy would know what had happened. Maegan had been on deck with her—where was wee Maegan?

The banshee. Panic rippled through her. Was this a dream or— She tried to move again but found herself restrained, wrapped in a cloth, white and smooth…a burial shroud.

Mother of God, could she really have died? But then who—

She considered the black-haired man once again. The devil? Sure, she was not sleeping with the devil? She'd made no pact with the faeries, no bargains that would have sent her here. Surely this was not hell. Surely—

But it was so hot.

She tried to focus on the man beside her, but her vision wavered and she fought to keep from sinking into unconsciousness again. Gathering her strength, she slid one arm up her side and poked him hard in the chest. His lids opened just a crack, but it was enough for her to see the orbs within, black as only the devil's eyes could be. Her heart fell as her fears were confirmed. A sob lodged in her parched throat and she whispered the only word that mattered right now: "Thirsty."

He did not respond. So. Even water was to be denied her in this fiery place. Drained, she let her eyes close. "You devil be damned," she muttered.

Without warning, he shoved her away and scrambled from the bed. The sudden movement sent her heart pounding and she cringed back, eyes widening at his underdrawers. Beneath the blankets she brought a hand to her chest and gasped. She was even more naked than he.

Where were her clothes? And what had she done with him in this bed? A flash of heat raced through her and she gripped the covers tight to her neck. Had she lost her virginity to the devil? Her stomach lurched. Would such a thing be a sin if she was already in hell? Panic lodged like a rock on her chest, pressing downward, squeezing her ability to draw a full breath.

He leaned over her, black eyes so close she could have poked them out if she had the strength. She tried to remember what she might have done with him but could draw no memory forward.

"You *are* awake." His voice held a decidedly familiar accent. "Water? Is it water you want?"

She nodded. Och, the devil was English. It didn't surprise her a bit.

He retrieved a mug from the other room and held it to her mouth. As she gulped at the water, some trickled over her cracked lips, soothing as it dribbled down her chin. The devil gently wiped the wayward liquid away with his thumb. And then he smiled.

Faith, but the devil was a handsome man.

Sure and she must already be embracing his evil ways for such a thought to have come into her head.

"Are you hungry?"

She shook her head, then nodded in confusion. Tired, hungry, she wasn't sure. It took all her effort just to keep from passing out again.

He drew a hand over the dark stubble on his jaw. "I'll get you something to eat."

He shrugged into a black shirt and pulled on some pants, impatiently jamming the shirttails in at the waist. Kathleen watched him through slitted eyes, imagining what Moira might say if she were here: *A handsome man is easily dressed.* Och, and now here she was thinking impure thoughts.

For all those years of going to mass, she was adjusting quickly enough to hell.

"I'll not be long." The devil stepped out the door.

Her eyes slid shut and her thoughts drifted as fatigue played with her mind. *The devil wore drawers.* Had she any strength she would have laughed. Who would have ever guessed the devil wore underdrawers?

*

Jack knew he was grinning like a fool—and he didn't care. She was awake. *She was alive.* He sprinted up the companionway two steps at a time and kicked the door shut behind him once he was on deck. The tryworks were spitting fire toward the sky, black smoke rolling heavenward as daybreak washed the horizon with gold. It was a beautiful morning already.

"Captain," a voice called from the rigging. "How's the lady?"

He tilted his head back and shaded his eyes as he looked up. "Awake," he shouted. "And thirsty."

Laughter tittered around him.

"I'm a might thirsty, too," the man answered. "For a lady who—"

"Let's have some respect." Jack waved a hand to catch the steward's attention. "She would like something to eat."

"Aye, sir! That's a good sign."

A wide grin broke across the blackened, oily face of a nearby sailor. He slapped his hands together and broke into song.

Had a girl back home, awaiting,
Waiting by the sea,
But out upon the ocean, boys,
What good does that do me?

Jack turned toward the singer, as the man rolled into the chorus, now accompanied by almost every crewman on deck, many of whom were taking a break from their work to clap their hands. After Donnelly had fed their superstitions last night, it was good to see they were back to their usual selves.

So be cheery, my lads, be cheery. Let your hearts never fail.
We may not have the girl we want, but we surely got the whale!

Might be years before I see her,
That gentle girl again,
So in the balmy Southern Seas,
I get it when I kin!"

So be cheery, my lads, be cheery...

"Jack, you've turned a miracle. The way she looked yesterday, I would have bet against her." Matson fell into step beside him.

He nodded. "I, too."

A whoop went up among the men, dissolving into laughter and

shouts about girlfriends, and wives, and regrets that this voyage wasn't headed to the South Pacific where the native women were known to be open-minded about relations outside of marriage. Someone began another song and soon the men were singing at the top of their lungs and stomping the deck in accompaniment.

"How'd you do it?" Matson asked.

Jack remembered the warmth of her in his arms, the feel of her body close to his. "I—ah—blankets. Wool blankets…during the night. And hot tea. That helped. I checked on her all night. She wants more tea. I'd better tell the steward." He smiled woodenly at his friend and walked away.

Jesus, he had to be careful. One wrong word and the woman's reputation would be ruined. If the crew learned he had spent the night in bed with her, she be considered fair game. The last thing he needed on this voyage was the added job of protecting her from this crew starved for female companionship.

A thought assailed him, a memory of holding her, caressing her. He jerked to a halt. Good God, had he done anything improper while he'd slept beside her? He inhaled sharply as the memory came clearer. No, he had only dreamed of loving her.

The words caught him by surprise. Never, in all the times he'd lain with a woman had he considered it anything but a release, a fulfillment of his needs, a man's right. He frowned. If this was where his thoughts were headed, he'd been at sea too long already. Damnation, if he was thinking this way about her, he could only imagine what some of his crew had on their minds—and she had yet to even take a step on deck.

CHAPTER SIX

THE SOUND OF a door closing tugged her towards consciousness. Kathleen eased one eye open a crack and peered through her lashes. Lord, the devil had returned. And he'd brought nothing to eat like he'd promised. Her stomach knotted. Had her time come now to be cut into pieces and boiled in seething oil?

He took a quiet step toward her.

Or was he expecting to climb into her bed again? In a desperate attempt to forestall his intentions, she opened her eyes and blurted out the first thing that came into her rambling mind.

"You're not what I expected to find on the other side." She couldn't bring herself to utter the word *hell* aloud, as if not saying it might change the truth of where she was.

He raised an eyebrow. "The other side?"

Slowly she pushed herself to sitting, blankets clutched to her chin. Dizziness washed through her and she closed her eyes until the feeling passed.

"Are you all right?" He leaned toward her.

She opened her eyes and nodded. How could the devil be so comely? He was supposed to be hideous, with horns. Perhaps he made himself handsome so he could seduce each new soul as they arrived. Before he boiled them for supper.

She fixed her gaze on the dawn light streaming through the portholes and watched the dust motes dance in the yellow rays. Was it to be that this netherworld sunrise would be the last she—

Sunrise? Realization hit her fatigued mind so hard it was as if she had been slapped. There could never be a sunrise in hell. Exhilaration shot through her and brought all her thoughts into focus. She hadn't died.

And this man was not the devil.

"The other side?" he asked again.

She sat up a little straighter, a slow burn sliding up her cheeks. For the first time she noticed the commode at the end of the room, the pitcher of water, the towel—all things no devil would need. How could she be so...addled? And how could she explain her words without sounding daft? She shook her head. "I—I've been a wee bit...confused."

He nodded and waited for her to continue.

"I washed overboard in a storm. Thought I was to die. So when I—opened me eyes—and saw... The fires and the smoke and those men cooking..." She grimaced. "What are ye doing up there?"

"Cutting in a whale. It's how we get the oil. What did you *think* we were doing?" After a moment, his mouth curved in a knowing grin. "*On the other side.*"

She glanced away and shrugged.

He let out a small laugh before smothering his amusement. A moment later, a guffaw broke loose and then he threw back his head and roared. When finally he looked at her again, tears were coursing down his cheeks.

She tamped down her irritation and lifted her chin. "Are ye quite finished yet?"

He wiped his eyes on his sleeve and swallowed his smile. "Forgive me. I understand, truly. What with the flames, the smell." The corners of his mouth twitched.

"Where am I?" she asked before laughter could overtake him again.

"You're on the Cyrena, a whaling ship. We fished you out of the ocean yesterday afternoon. I'm the captain—Jack Montgomery."

English accent, English name. Her spirits plummeted. Jesus, Mary, and holy Joseph, please don't let him be taking this ship to England. She couldn't end up on the same side of the ocean as she had begun.

"I'm Kathleen Deacey. And, I'll be thanking you, sir, for saving me life." She reached for the mug of water and took a long swallow to put off asking where he was headed.

"From Ireland?"

"Aye. And is your home port England, Captain?" She held her breath, praying that she was wrong.

He shook his head. "We're out of Boston—"

"Boston," she breathed. "We're going to America?" She remembered the map Sean had showed her, how he'd pointed out New York and Boston in case she would need to travel there for work if she didn't find Danny.

"Eventually. We won't return to Boston until the hold is filled with whale oil."

"How long will that take?"

"We had hoped to be home by Christmas, but things haven't gone as planned, so..." He shrugged. "It's hard to say, but that's our goal."

Christmas was almost two months away. By the time she found work and then sent money to Ireland, it would nearly be spring before any funds would reach her family. They needed help soon, not months from now.

"I was going to Canada. To work and send money home to me family...so that they, too, might come across." She hesitated, not certain how much to tell this English captain, uncertain whether he would be understanding of her family's plight or willing to be party to it. Certainly there was no need to tell him of Danny and her plans to go to Newfoundland to find him.

The captain shook his head apologetically. "There are hundreds of ships in this ocean. We often cross paths with others headed for home. You may be able to catch on with one of them."

"And if not?" Surely she wouldn't be stuck out here for months.

His brow wrinkled as though the thought pained him. Clearly he was no more excited to have her on board than she was to be here.

She leaned forward. "Just how often do you catch these whales, sir?"

"Depends... We could have a run of luck, but..." The corners of his mouth turned down. "Sometimes we go months without a sighting." His voice held a note of resignation.

"So ye bob about on the ocean, hoping a whale will just pass you by?"

"Not exactly—there are whaling grounds—"

"I wonder now, with all this wasted time between sightings, why you couldn't just take me into port and then go out again. You'd probably not see the same whales ye wouldn't see if you were out here the whole time."

She leaned back into the pillow pleased with her solution.

The Captain laughed. "Are you suggesting, Miss Deacey, that I put into Boston *now*, so that you can get off the ship?"

"Imagine the joy of your wife, seeing you after—how long have you been away?"

"Ahhh. No wife."

"Well, surely a special woman waiting for ye."

He shook his head.

She wasn't surprised to learn it. "Well, then, your crew, how pleased they would be with a wee break to see their families."

He let out a snort. "First, we're weeks away from Boston. Second, the moment I dock, I'll lose my crew. Do you think they like sitting out here, bored most of the time? Half have never been on a whaling ship before, and once it's over a great many will never sign aboard one again."

She nodded. "Perhaps if it was just a quick stop—"

"You still think I should take you in?"

"Well, if you could see how important this is to me family..."

He shook his head and an edge crept into his voice. "This is not a transport line, Miss Deacey. It's a business. We go home when the hold is full—and not before. I stand to make a great deal of money on this voyage and I'll *not* give up that profit. You are on board for the duration—whether it be one week, one month, or one—"

"It best not be one year, Captain Montgomery!"

"He leveled a critical gaze on her, then strode out of the cabin.

"She's all yours," he snapped at someone outside the door. "Don't bother me about her today unless there's a problem." After a long pause, he added, "And if she's too much trouble—as I expect she'll be—you have my permission to throw her back overboard."

Kathleen squeezed back tears of frustration. She was trapped, floating about on the ocean while in Ireland her family starved. The captain may well live in America, but 'twas clear his heart pumped only English blood.

A man poked his head through the doorway and nervously cleared his throat. "I'll leave the food here on the chart table, Miss," he said. "Pork and biscuits, hot coffee and gingerbread." He escaped without awaiting an answer.

Kathleen swiped a hand across her eyes. She couldn't give up so easily. First, she needed her strength back, and for that she needed to eat. "The devil take you, Captain Montgomery." She swung her legs off the bed and stood unsteadily. "'Twas God's hand that kept me alive on that ocean so I might help me family. Now I've only you to persuade."

*

Late that evening, Jack stepped off the bottom stair of the companionway. Heat assailed him and he wiped the sweat from his brow. Though they'd finished cutting in the whale and the tryworks were no longer burning, the air below deck was ungodly hot.

He entered his after cabin, his private sitting room, and ran a hand irritably through his hair. After the full day topsides, he had yet to forget Miss Deacey's entreaty that he take her to America. He understood why she didn't want to stay on the ship—he didn't want her on board for the next two months either.

Moonlight streamed through the large skylight above the room, providing enough light for him to move about without turning up the lamp. Larger quarters and natural light helped him manage this job.

Much as he admired her determination, much as he wondered what it would be like to have a family worthy of such loyalty, he would lose more than just money if he took her in. He had six other partners in this vessel. The others could easily decide the decision had been so poor he wouldn't ever be trusted with a larger share of ownership, let alone be considered for managing partner.

He opened the door to his stateroom and frowned at Kathleen Deacey asleep in his bed. Stepping quietly to the washstand, he poured some water from the pitcher into the sink and quickly washed his face and hands. Then he grabbed clean pants and a shirt from his chest and went back to his sitting room.

He couldn't take her to an American port; the risks were too great. But somewhere else… Perhaps she could get off at Fayal, one of the Western Islands off the coast of Portugal, when they stopped to re-provision. She could probably catch on with another ship from there. As long as the consul agreed to let her stay, they could drop her in Fayal.

Still, the Western Islands were two weeks away even if the winds held. Two weeks too long. He pulled the fresh shirt over his head and willed himself to be patient. She was but a temporary inconvenience that would soon be gone. As long as he limited her contact with the crew and kept the men focused on their work, he'd be able to prevent her from disrupting the operation of his ship.

Hell, who was he fooling? She was already disrupting the operation of his ship and the men hadn't even met her yet.

He tugged on the clean pants, spread open a light blanket, and stretched out beneath it on the sofa, all the while trying not to think about what lay ahead for him—a night fighting to keep from rolling onto the floor whenever the ship lurched on a wave. Meanwhile, Kathleen Deacey would be sleeping comfortably, the gimbaled design of his bed ensuring that it always hung level regardless of the ship's angle in the water.

Hours later, a ragged, high-pitched shriek ripped open the night and he jerked upright. He fumbled to turn up the lantern and clear his mind. Understanding flared with the light; the Irish woman must be dreaming. He muttered an oath.

Another hysterical scream shattered the silence and Jack crossed the room and hauled open the door. Pale light filtered in from behind him, and he could just make out the woman standing beside the bed, bent at the waist, hands in her long hair, head swinging from side to side. A cacophony of grunts and feral sounds spewed from her mouth. By God, perhaps she was mad after all.

The woman jumped backward and lifted her head, staring at him through tangled hair for one stunned moment before letting loose with another screech.

She was wearing one of his shirts.

"They're all over me!" She swatted at her arms and legs and shook her head, whipping her hair across her face. Raising one hand, she threw something at him. A cockroach hit the floor at his feet and scurried away. She shrieked again and he strode forward to grab her by the shoulders.

"Quiet! They're just cockroaches! Driven aft by the heat of the trypots." He squeezed her bony shoulders tighter to still her shaking. "Surely you've seen roaches before?"

"Not crawling over me face while I slept!"

His irritation dissipated. He well remembered how unnerving it had been the first time the little buggers swarmed over him in his sleep. Hell, even after all these years of whaling he still didn't like it. "I know. It's okay. You'll get used to it…a little anyway." He dropped his hands from her shoulders and motioned gently toward the bed.

She didn't move. "Once me eyes are closed, they'll be crawling over me again."

"It helps to pull the blankets over your head." He returned to his sitting room and shut the door.

Outside his cabin he heard the door to an officer's room latch shut. Damn. What must his men be thinking was going on in here?

He yanked his door open knowing full well that he owed no explanation—and the crew didn't expect one. "Cockroaches!" he shouted to anyone who might be listening.

He slammed the door, flicked open a cabinet and pulled out a decanter of whiskey. At this point, he needed a good stiff drink to help him get back to sleep. Hell, if he was honest about it, he needed that drink just to forget he'd rescued a woman on the ocean and she was wreaking havoc on his well-ordered life.

The muffled sound of crying reached him from behind the closed stateroom door. He exhaled sharply. If he was to get any sleep tonight, he would have to get Kathleen Deacey settled first. Holding his temper in check, he gently opened the door. She had already climbed back into bed.

"The roaches won't be running much longer," he said evenly. "Only until the temperature drops. The fires are out, so by tomorrow it should be over."

She whipped one hand across her eyes, while the other clutched the untied drawstrings at the neck of the shirt. Sympathy stirred in him and he let out a sigh, then stepped to the side of the bed and eased the fabric from her grasp to smooth it into place. His fingers brushed the soft nape of her neck and the contact slowed him, making him suddenly aware of what he was doing. Unsettled, he fumbled to tie her collar closed, suddenly anxious to be out of the room. "Don't forget to cover your head," he said as he shut the door firmly between them.

He slid under the blanket on the sofa again. God help him, he had a ship to run, money to make. He couldn't afford distractions right now and he couldn't afford to care—especially not about a poor Irish woman on her way to America.

He had hardly fallen asleep before her muffled cries jerked him to consciousness again. This would be far too long a voyage if he had to put up with this every time they were trying out a whale.

He jammed the pillow over his head to block out the sound. If they arrived in Fayal tomorrow it wouldn't be soon enough. He didn't care whether the consul objected or not—he was leaving Kathleen Deacey behind. Let the consul look after the woman until some other ship came along. He'd saved her life; he owed her no more. Now she owed it to his sanity to get off his ship.

CHAPTER SEVEN

KATHLEEN STOOD AT the ship's rail and raised her face to the late afternoon sun. Already a week had passed since she'd asked the captain to take her to America, a week during which she had grown stronger and healthier with plenty to eat. Guilt and worry gnawed at her; it was as if she were on holiday while her family struggled to survive. She gripped the rail in frustration, filled with the same helplessness she felt the day the potatoes rotted.

Across the boat, crewmen lounged—playing backgammon, carving scrimshaw from whalebone, napping in the sun. Chickens clucked in their crates, contentedly laying eggs. And the ocean stretched outward like an endless empty plateau, teasing them with the hope that at any moment one of the great gray beasts they sought would burst through its surface.

She crossed the ship to stand beside Matson at the windward rail. "How do you not go mad from the boredom?"

He laughed. "Ah, but you haven't yet experienced the thrill of catching a whale."

"I don't know if I wish to experience it, now that the ship no longer stinks to the heavens." Once the oil had been sealed in casks, the crew had scrubbed everything down with saltwater and sand and thoroughly washed all the soiled clothing and bedding. Everything had been restored to order.

Matson swept a hand across the view. "Still it's a beautiful sight is it not?"

"Aye, though not as lovely as America I'd wager."

"Touché."

"Can you tell me, sir, is there any hope Captain Montgomery might change his mind about taking me there?" She would have pressed the captain herself on the issue if she ever saw him for more than a minute. He spent most of his time on deck or at the officers' dining table, and the few curt sentences he spoke to her each day left no room for conversation.

She spotted him aft, strolling leisurely along the bulwark, dark hair mussed by the steady breeze. Lord, but was he strutting? Aye, as only an Englishman would.

Matson raised his eyebrows as though surprised by her question. "No. There's no chance. We're not very close to Boston. But more important, if he takes the ship in now, he and his partners will lose a great deal of money."

"But here's what I'll not be understanding. Could you not be catching whales all the way back? Then not a bit of the time is wasted."

"I know it sounds reasonable. But the Atlantic is so fished out along the American shore, we won't find any whales there."

He drew a pipe from his pocket and tamped down the tobacco in the bowl. "A lot of money was put out at the front end of this voyage for food and outfitting the ship. Contracts were drawn between the investing partners guaranteeing them a percentage of the profits. We've not taken enough oil... The investors would be furious if this ship suddenly appeared back in Boston."

He lit his pipe and puffed thoughtfully. "Frankly, I can't think of anything that would make him—"

The captain came up beside them and rested his hands on the rail. "Don't stop talking on my behalf," he said.

Kathleen cleared her throat and gathered her courage. "I was just asking Mr. Matson whether he thought you might reconsider taking me to Boston."

Matson coughed out a mouthful of smoke.

The captain cast a sideways glance at him. "And what was his reply?"

"I said it was something she'd have to take up with you." Matson rolled his eyes. "If you'll excuse me, I need to get some more tobacco."

"Captain, I know you have good reasons for not returning to Boston, but could you not take me to some other port in America instead? One far enough from Boston so your investors wouldna ever learn you'd come ashore?"

A muscle tightened in his jaw. She raced forward so he wouldn't be able to answer too quickly and destroy her hopes without considering the idea. "Doesn't that seem like it would take care of all your concerns?"

"There'd be no hiding this ship from anyone, Miss Deacey. Word travels with every other ship and it would soon get back to Boston."

"So, again you say *no*?"

"What makes you think my answer would change?"

"If you were wearing my shoes, would your family expect any less of you than I am trying to do for me own?"

"My family?" He let out a sharp laugh. "My family would expect nothing from me...nor I from them."

She glanced away from his irritated gaze.

"I can't help you, Miss Deacey. Don't ask me again." His voice was even and low, but pain hovered along its edges. "Now if you don't mind, I'd like to be able to continue this voyage without any more disruptions from you."

She bit back the retort that leapt to the tip of her tongue. If the man thought he'd just put an end to this topic, he was mistaken. She'd not give up until she was finally in America, until she knew she had done all she could to ensure her family's safety.

"By all means, Captain. Have your peace." *For the moment.* Lifting her chin, she retreated to the other side of the deck.

*

Jack watched her go and tried to ignore the tightening beneath his breastbone. He wasn't a cold-hearted man. God knew he wished he could help her. But he had duties, responsibilities, obligations. He silently cursed as she sashayed toward the bow, slim hips perfectly filling out the men's pants she wore. A prickle of awareness slid over him.

Dammit to hell, she was skinny and red-haired. What was the matter with him? Since almost the moment she'd awakened, he'd felt this pull toward her—and he'd fought it back. No doubt it had to do with the length of time he'd been at sea already. Besides, he liked his women blond, buxom, experienced, and undemanding.

And Kathleen Deacey was anything but blond, buxom, and experienced. To say nothing of undemanding.

He glanced aft to see Matson watching him, then walked slowly across the stern to stand beside him. "We're dropping her in Fayal," he said, almost cringing at the snarl in his voice.

"Getting to you, is she?"

"Yes." He followed Matson's gaze to where Kathleen stood near the bow talking to one of the crew. She laughed and dropped her head back, and his every nerve heightened. Christ, he'd gone from protector to rutting buck.

No good could come of this inexplicable attraction. He had to avoid her until they reached Fayal. If she was at the bow, he'd stay at the stern. If she was at the dining table, he'd eat later. And if she was in his quarters, *in his bed…* His determination faltered at the picture his mind conjured. Hell, if she was in his bed, like she'd been every night since he'd rescued her, he'd just keep sleeping on the sofa.

*

Sounds filtered through the quiet to Kathleen—an occasional laugh, the murmur of conversation, the slap of the ship's hull upon the waves. The boat heeled slightly as it cut through the foam. Like a shadow, a sense of foreboding passed over her, a sudden fear that her family was suffering, waiting for her to send funds to them, *dying in Ireland,* while she drifted across the ocean searching for whales.

She cast a glance at the captain. There must be something she could say or do to make him change his mind. An image slid into her thoughts, a memory of lying naked with him the night he'd saved her life. Warmth raced upward across her cheeks and she turned away. Nay, she couldn't offer *that*; she was no woman of loose virtue willing to give herself to any man who came along. And how would she admit such a thing in the confessional? What if the priest refused to give her absolution?

And there was Danny to think of. What would her betrothed think when she told him? Would he turn away from her?

She twisted her fingers together and squeezed her eyes shut for a long moment. But what else, pray, had she to bargain with?

She gave her head a shake and steeled her thoughts against her conscience. Her virginity would be a sorry companion if all her family were dead.

Slowly, she raised her eyes to look at Captain Montgomery again. He'd not had a woman since he'd set sail some six months ago—perhaps even longer. If what she'd heard of men was true, surely he'd be having needs by now. *Surely he would be open to some sort of agreement.*

Watching him across the deck, she contemplated what it might be like to sleep with him. The thought of his unclothed body pressed to hers made her stomach tremble and her legs weaken. Her cheeks flamed. She took a slow breath and tried to still the racing of her heart.

Could she do such a thing? *Aye.* For her family, she could. But it had to be soon, for if she had too much time to think on it, she wouldn't be able to follow through. Perhaps tomorrow would be best. Or even the day after that.

She let out a slow exhale. Her family had not the luxury of time. Sure, and what would be wrong with tonight?

She swallowed hard and confronted her fears head on. It must be tonight. This evening, when finally the captain came to his cabin, she would offer him the only thing of value she had, her virginity, a night of love, in return for his taking her to America.

The decision made, she turned quickly away, suddenly terrified of nightfall.

"Thar she blows!" The lookout at the top of the mast thrust a hand in the air. Like a row of rolling gray hills, a pod of whales appeared not far off the leeward rail.

"Call all hands! Back the main topsail! Get your tubs in your boats." The captain paced the deck, dark eyes intent on the whales as he shouted orders. What followed was nothing short of a stampede as the crew took their places in preparation for lowering the six oarboats hanging at the ready—three on each side of the ship.

The captain turned, catching her accidentally in his gaze, and he grinned wide and happy, and she pictured his mouth on hers. Shaken by her mind's involuntary response, she jerked her eyes away.

"Stand by to lower!" the captain shouted. "All ready?"

"Ready, sir!"

"Away the boats!"

Six oarboats smacked the water in unison. Shoes kicked to the side, the men leapt over the rail and took up their positions in the boats. A large gray hump rose from the water not more than fifteen yards off the ship's bow. Kathleen let out a gasp at the size of the beast and took several steps backward.

The captain spotted the animal and cursed as he leaned over the rail and shouted, "Take the calf first!"

The calf? Sure if there wasn't a wee one swimming alongside the beast. A baby. She glanced at the captain. *Take the calf first?* Fear snaked into her belly.

Two of the whaleboats rowed to close the distance to the mother and calf. The boatsteerer and mates cheered the men on with every stroke. "Pull lads, pull ahead! It'll be a bottle of the best for you on shore!"

Within minutes they had reached the two whales. Maneuvering to windward, they stole up quietly while the boatsteerer lifted a harpoon over his shoulder and took his position in the bow, waiting. Kathleen held her breath, suddenly afraid of what she was about to see.

The man arched back, then sprang forward to drive his harpoon deep into the calf's flank.

The animal let loose a cry that wrapped itself around Kathleen's chest. One hand over her mouth, she watched as the mother swam nearby, agitated by the cries and convulsions of her offspring. The cow dove and then shot up through the water, slapping her flukes upon the surface and spraying the men in the whaleboat. Her baby was caught, was dying, and the mother could do nothing to help. Yet she would not abandon it.

For a brief instant, Kathleen thought of Moira, Sean and their baby yet to be born. And Ireland dying all around them.

She strode to where the captain watched.

"Captain Montgomery, is this necessary? How much oil can you get from a wee one like that?"

"The mother won't leave the calf. We catch the baby first—and the cow is ours for the taking." He began to walk toward the bow.

"You kill the babe for its mother?"

"Yes." He walked away from her and she stared at his back. How could she have thought to offer herself to this man? She took a step toward him, wanting to call him every vile name she could think of, to make him somehow see that the easy way was not always the right way.

The men on the second whaleboat were switching places now, the boatsteerer moving to the bow, harpoon in hand. 'Twas only a few minutes more before the cow herself was caught.

"Go!" She screamed at the beast as she raced to the rail. "Go! Swim away ye stupid thing!" She knew the captain was staring at her, that he thought her absurd. And she didn't care. Just once she wanted the hunted to win, to prevail over those who held its life in their hands and did not care. But the beast, bound by some deep maternal instinct stayed near, nuzzling her calf as it cried out for her.

"Flee…" Kathleen pleaded.

"Take it now," the captain muttered.

The boatsteerer arched back and released his iron into the cow's flank. The animal let loose with a roar, blood gushing from her wound. She flung her flukes into the air spraying a fine drizzle over the men in the whaleboat. And then she sounded, plummeting straight down into the ocean, the line attached to her running out of the tub so fast Kathleen could not tell it was moving at all.

The cow rose in a frenzy of anger and slapped the water again with her flukes, the motion sending bloody spray over the ship's deck. Kathleen wiped her face and looked into the sea, crimson with blood, gruesome red foam lapping up against the ship. The calf cried out for its mother, and the mother answered, the sounds of agony from both animals mingling into a deep lamenting cry of despair. Kathleen fought the sobs gathering in her chest.

Hours passed as the great beast fought, dragging the oarboat miles across the ocean by the rope that held her fast, while the mother ship followed.

Kathleen refused to leave the rail, forced herself to watch this battle for life. And when finally the cow tired, the men hauled the line in, hand over hand, until they were beside her again. The mate stepped into the oarboat's bow and with nary an ounce of resistance from the whale, drove a lance into her lungs. She slapped her flukes again and swam in a frenzy, the mist spouting from her air hole suddenly thick with red, as it poured out her life into the sea. And then, without warning, the cow rolled belly up, dead.

A cheer went up among the men. And Kathleen vomited into the crimson sea.

She stumbled down to the cabin and threw herself onto the sofa, sobbing. She wept for the death of a whale that wouldn't abandon its calf. She wept for her family, for Danny, for Ireland, for the injustice foisted upon the weak. And she wept for herself, knowing that even as she despised the captain, she must still strike a bargain with him, must use him for her own ends just as he used the calf to catch its mother.

CHAPTER EIGHT

WHERE COULD HE be? Kathleen paced across the small after-cabin. 'Twas nearly midnight and the captain had not come below deck since taking the whales. Perhaps he was up there dancing in the blood, she thought spitefully. Her stomach knotted in revulsion. To be sure, she was now on such an edge she didn't know if she could even go through with her plan. Perhaps he wouldn't be coming below for hours. And if that were so, she should find out so she could go to bed... alone.

An eerie sight greeted her as she stepped on deck. Flames leapt from the tryworks and lamps had been lit atop all three masts. In the light, the sails glowed an otherworldly yellow. And though the whales were tied off the stern of the ship, no one worked, nor talked.

Several crew members were perched high in the crosstrees, while others lined the rail. The captain stood at the bow, staring out over the ocean. He called up to the look-outs, "Do you see any lights?"

"None yet, sir."

Neither moon nor star penetrated the night's solid black, so the ship in the darkness looked to be afire—even to those who were on it. The flames danced in the rising wind and shuddered each time the ship struck a larger wave.

Kathleen moved to stand beside the helmsman. She gestured at the men in the rigging. "What are they doing?"

"Searching. Two boats are lost—they went after other whales in the pod. They'll have lit their lanterns so we can find them."

She let her gaze move across the ocean and saw nothing that looked like lights. "But you always find them?"

When the helmsman didn't answer, Kathleen realized that the silence on deck was that of fear.

"Twelve men?"

He nodded. Her heart dropped. Twelve lives. "Is the wind coming up?" she asked, almost afraid of the answer.

"Could be a storm blowing in. If it hits before we find them…" He shook his head. "We've lit our fires hoping the boats will be able to spot us."

The captain left his position at the bow and made his way toward them. The garish light accentuated the circles under his eyes, the troubled expression on his face.

"The wind is shifting." He rubbed a hand across his eyes. "God forgive me if the whales smashed their boats," he murmured.

Kathleen touched his arm, but could think of nothing to say that would ease his mind.

"Let's come about," he said to the helmsman, then shouted the order to the crew. They complied in silence, the only sounds the creaking of the ship and the rattle of rigging as the sails changed position and popped full with air on the other side.

"Anything?" Captain Montgomery called aloft.

"No, sir. No lights," a man answered.

The fear that had settled over the ship began to deepen into despondency. The captain walked to the bow again.

A half hour turned into an hour, and then another. The temperature dropped and the rising wind began to clatter the rigging. The crew changed places in the crosstrees, as though fresh eyes might see something others had missed. No one went off watch.

Kathleen followed the captain to the bow hoping to have her own fears calmed.

"It's my responsibility to keep my crew safe," he said without glancing her way. "There are those who say death is an unavoidable partner with whaling. I can't accept that."

She nodded, beginning to see that bringing all his men home alive was much more than simply responsibility for him.

"I lost three men on our last voyage as we rounded the tip of South America. Nearly lost the ship… Some said we were lucky to just lose three." He shook his head. "It was three too many."

She nodded again, well aware that his fears needed calming much more than hers. "They may not yet be lost, sir," she whispered. "Me ma would say, '*Ar scáth a chéile a mhaireann na daoine.* Under the shelter of each other, people survive.' They are not alone, for they have you, determined to find them."

He looked at her then, really looked at her, as though she was someone other than just a troublesome woman he'd pulled from the ocean. "Few men spend their childhoods dreaming of being whale hunters. But adulthood comes and a living must be had… and for some whaling is all they have to choose." His jaw tightened. "They put their lives in my hands."

He searched the murky ocean again, and Kathleen had a sense

that he was talking as much about himself as he was his men. Suddenly a cry from the masthead startled them both.

"Lights! Two lights!"

Joyous shouts rained down from the rigging.

"Lights." The captain bowed his head.

"We found them." Kathleen wanted to throw her arms around him.

"We found them." He grinned at her, then grabbed her by the shoulders and lifted her to her toes and planted a kiss hard on her mouth before striding back to the stern.

Kathleen blushed in the darkness and touched a hand to her lips. Warmth spread through her. "I didna give you leave to be kissing me," she whispered. But though she tried, she could muster no anger.

They chased the lights that flickered far in the distance, raced the squall that threatened to break overhead. As they drew near, greetings and mock insults were tossed back and forth between the mother ship and the oarboats, words that masked the men's fear and relief. At the sight of the large whale trailing off the boats, the greetings turned to cheers.

"She's a hundred barrels or more, Captain! We couldn't let her get away from us!" someone shouted.

The captain welcomed each man aboard with a hearty handshake and a clap on the back. He let the crew celebrate for a few minutes before stepping into their midst to remind them of the job ahead—stripping off the whales' blubber and boiling it to remove the oil. With two large beasts taken, the cutting-in could take several days.

"A fine job, boys. Get yourself something to eat and drink and then get back topsides. We'll start cutting in without you. The rest of you know your duties. Stoke the fires and fasten the blubber hook. Then I'll take the beast's head off." He motioned to the steward who handed him a razor-sharp cutting spade. "Look lively, men. Let's get some of this done before the sharks come calling."

As the cutting-in process began again, Kathleen retreated to the captain's quarters and climbed into bed. She would have to try her plan some other night.

Outside, the wind rattled the rigging and light rain pattered the deck. The storm had turned out to be more bluster than bite... much like the captain, she was beginning to think.

Without question, Da would have hunted whales if it had put money in his pocket and food on their table. She could almost hear Ma admonishing her, "*Is crua a cheannaíonn an droim an bolg.* The back must slave to feed the belly." Aye, men did what they must to earn a living.

A small smile slipped unbidden across her face. The captain had kissed her; perhaps she should try her plan tonight after all. She let herself relive the way he had grasped her by the arms and pressed his mouth to hers. Her heart quickened. To be sure, it seemed tonight would be best. All she had to do was stay awake until he came below deck.

*

Nothing could dampen his mood this night. All his men were safe and they'd taken several whales besides. Before too many more days, they would anchor in Fayal and Kathleen would be off his ship. Things were definitely on the upswing.

Jack hesitated outside his cabin door. His mind had given him little peace during the two weeks Kathleen had been on board. It seemed the more he purposely avoided her, the more she was all he could think of. Yet, he would not act on this attraction; there was nothing good that could come of it.

He went into his quarters and turned up the lamp, then pulled his wet shirt over his head and tossed it to the floor. Kathleen Deacey could only complicate matters. He had responsibilities back in Boston...plans and commitments. She could bring none of what he'd worked for—not the wealth, not the status, and especially not the security such things would give him. Better that he stay focused on what he wanted, what he needed, and leave his base desires to be fulfilled by other women.

As he wiped the whale oil off his hands, the stateroom door opened. Kathleen stood in the doorway wearing only his shirt. Desire shot through him. He mentally cursed and tried not to look at her bare legs.

"Did you need something?" He gestured at the privy, but she shook her head.

"I...have to ask you..." Her voice, silky with sleep, wrapped around him like a woman's embrace.

He mentally shook it off. "Yes?"

She glanced away as though uncertain what to say next. She'd probably been dreaming, was likely not even fully awake now. He took a step toward her to hurry her back to bed—and away from him. "You can ask me tomorrow."

"But, I—"

"Tomorrow would really be better."

As she stepped back into the stateroom, he grasped the door handle, anxious to close it behind her as if the physical barrier would still his desires.

"Captain." Her voice floated back to him.

"Yes?"

"Will you be wanting…me?"

His stomach tightened and he froze with his hand on the door, certain he was misunderstanding her meaning. "Wanting—you?" he asked as evenly as he could muster.

"Aye." She turned to face him. "In your bed."

He needed to get this woman off his ship. "Are you offering?"

She hesitated a split second before nodding. And he hesitated a split second before closing the gap between them, his own misgivings quashed by her apparent lack of inhibition. He ran a finger down her cheek and along her jaw, then tipped her chin up. Every inch of his body burned with anticipation.

Kathleen took a step back. "Captain," she said in a quiet voice. "There's to be more to this than just one night of love."

He couldn't believe his good fortune. Perhaps he wouldn't drop her in Fayal after all; perhaps he'd keep her with him the entire voyage. "Certainly…there can be more…I have no objection to many, many nights of—"

He took a step toward her and she took another back, stopping only because she bumped up against the wall.

"Nay," she said. "You misunderstand. It's a bargain I seek. I spend a night in your bed and…" She looked down.

He stepped so close to her he could feel the heat of her body. "And?"

"And in return, you take me to America…right away." She raised defiant eyes to meet his.

*

Anger flashed across his expression, and then it was gone, replaced by something darker, almost frightening. His black eyes locked with hers as though he could read her mind and know the truth—the very nearness of him set her stomach trembling.

She tore her gaze away. Faith, but it could only mean he was about to agree and, may the good Lord and Danny forgive her, she was no longer afraid but willing for this night to occur. Her heart began to beat a rhythm in anticipation. She wanted to run her hands up the muscles of his arms and down the dark hair on his chest, across his belly... Only then did she notice how his pants, wet with rain, clung to him, exposing every muscle in his thighs, and nearly everything between them. Cheeks flaming, she tore her gaze away and looked up into his face.

He smirked at her. Slowly, deliberately, he braced his hands on the wall on either side of her shoulders and dipped his head toward hers.

"S-So, Captain. Have we a bargain?"

"It would take more nights than just one to bring me to such an agreement," he said in a low voice.

She stared into his devil black eyes and, God help her, nodded.

He crushed her lips beneath his as his body pressed her back against the wall, one hand cupping her buttocks and molding her hard to him. She could feel the evidence of his desire and knew she had won; there would be no turning back now. A shiver of excitement rippled through her and she yielded to the insistent pressure of his mouth, responding as he deepened the kiss, his tongue thrusting between her lips to explore her mouth. He tasted of tobacco and whiskey warmed beneath the afternoon sun.

His roughened hands skimmed beneath her shirt, teasing the soft skin of her back, one hand slipping round to caress her breasts, plying the tips beneath his thumb. Her knees weakened and she leaned into him, fingers splayed across the black hair on his chest. He pressed a thigh between her legs and murmured something low into her ear but she couldn't make out his words and before she could even think he had undone the ties at the neck of her shirt and pulled it down off her shoulders. He kissed the line of her throat spreading a trail of fire to the tips of her breasts. He took one and then the other in his mouth, hard and hot, and she clutched at him, pulling him closer as she gasped out his name.

He froze. "Damn it to hell," he muttered. He jerked the shirt back up onto to her shoulders.

She dragged her eyes open as though drugged. "Captain?"

He took a step back and drew a ragged breath. "We have no bargain, Miss Deacey." He stepped toward the sitting room, turning back just as he reached the door.

"Once we finish trying-out these whales we'll be stopping in the Western Islands—on Fayal—for provisions."

She clutched the neck of her shirt together and nodded in confusion as she tried to still the pounding of her heart.

"Their actual name is the Azores Islands—there are nine of them in the middle of the Atlantic," he said as if he were giving a geography lesson, as if she cared. "If the American consul there agrees, you'll get off at Fayal. He'll help you catch on with a ship bound for America."

She struggled to pull all this new information together. "How soon will we reach these islands?

"A week or less."

"Thank you…for telling me instead of…" She felt a profound sense of relief.

"Yes… Well, it's best for us all this way." He closed the door between them, casting the stateroom into almost complete darkness.

America! She would soon be on her way to America.

She felt her way to the bed and slipped beneath the covers.

A vague sense of disappointment nagged at the silvery edges of her joy. Wrapped in a cocoon of blankets and darkness, she felt again the touch of Jack Montgomery's lips on hers and the roughness of his calloused fingers on her skin. Her body tightened at the memory. God help her, but at this moment she would go willingly to his bed if he were to ask, bargain or no. Faith, what was happening to her? She was betrothed to Danny O'Sheehan.

Aye, and she had never wanted Danny like this.

*

The first scream pierced Jack's sleep shortly before dawn. He grabbed his pillow and smashed it over his head to block out the sound. The cockroaches must be running from the heat again—all over Kathleen Deacey. Just a few more days and he'd be free of her. Just a few more days.

The thought of her gone from his ship sent a vague loneliness through him, a muted ache deep in his gut. For the price of a bargain, he could have had her willingly this night, could have pressed her body deep into the mattress with his, could have roused her to passions she didn't yet know even existed. For the price of a bargain—

Hell, what was the matter with him? He had seduced enough women to know he could have had Kathleen Deacey whether he agreed to her bargain or not. But he couldn't do it. He would have felt bound to honor the agreement. And the cost would have been too great. Better that he stay focused on his goals and set her ashore in Fayal where the American consul could help her get passage on another ship.

Guilt pricked at him. The Western Islands were a favorite stop for whalers on the beginning leg of a South Pacific voyage, he just wasn't sure how many came through on their way home. The usual return route along the coast of South America, didn't venture close to Fayal. Still, merchant ships put into port there...and whaling vessels returning home from the Indian Ocean. Hopefully, she wouldn't have to wait too long before a ship heading for America came into port.

Maybe he shouldn't do this to her.

Another scream sounded, along with the sound of her jumping up and down as she tried to dislodge the little buggers from her hair. Then again, this was perhaps the best decision he'd ever made in his life.

CHAPTER NINE

SEAN RESTED HIS hands on the stone fence and leaned forward into the bitter wind. Heavy, wet snow whipped against his face, sticking for a moment before slipping down onto his jacket. The blood was high in his cheeks, his skin stinging.

"So much cold and snow," he muttered to his father beside him. "And November not even past." What manner of God was this, to send such a winter on top of the famine?

A scream pierced the air, louder and longer now than the ones before it. He flinched and gripped the cold stone before glancing toward the cottage. How much longer could this go on? Eighteen hours already to Moira's labor, and no end it seemed in sight.

As if reading his thoughts, his father placed a hand on Sean's shoulder. "The first child is always the hardest. Your ma took even longer when she was birthing you."

Sean nodded, unwilling to speak aloud the thoughts that darkened his mind. The baby was too soon, nearly two months early if Moira had figured right. He prayed that she had been wrong even as he prayed for her strength. She had weakened in the last month; though they had tried to make sure she had more to eat, the shortage of food had taken a greater toll on her what with the babe growing within.

He tensed, anticipating the next sounds from his wife, but minutes passed with only silence. He looked at his father in question.

The older man pulled his collar closer and turned his back to the bitter wind. "Your Ma will tell us when the child has arrived," he finally said with a shrug. "Nature is in charge here and our job is but to wait. Still the pay you get at the end is the best you'll ever have—a child of your own blood, of your ancestors before ye, passed down—"

An anguished wail sounded from within the house, a sound haunting and filled with pain. The door banged open and his mother stepped out into the driving snow, motioning them toward her. Sean was at her side in seconds. "Ma? Is everything all right?"

She motioned him to silence as she took her husband's arm. "Micheal, you must go for the doctor." She brushed the falling snow off her face. "Hurry now. Tell him I canna stop the bleeding."

"The babe is here?" he asked.

"Aye, now go. Hurry." In her eyes and the curtness of her reply, Sean could tell she was warning his father away from asking anything else.

The older man pulled his collar up and quickly set off down the snow-covered road, shoulders hunched against the gusting wind.

"Ma, I heard no baby's cry."

She took his hands in her own. "Twins. Two wee lads." There was no joy in her voice and he could not make himself ask about her sorrow for fear of what she might say. His mind slammed shut and for just this moment he pretended that nothing was wrong, that his wife waited within the house with a newborn babe in each arm.

Tears filled his mother's eyes. "Two perfect little boys—" Her voice broke.

"Nay!" He tugged a hand free from hers and waved it between them as though he could create a barrier her words could not penetrate. "Don't be telling me, not yet—"

"We've no time for this. They've gone back to heaven already. Gone before they were born."

The force of her words nearly brought him to his knees. He tried to draw a breath, but the wind stole the air and he had the sudden sense that he was suffocating. The whole world seemed to draw to a halt around him. His wife's grief would be boundless. "Moira."

"She needs you now. Ye heard me say I cannot stop the bleeding," his mother said. "She'll need your strength to get through this, Sean. And with the loss of her babes, she'll need a will to live, too." She took his arm and pulled him into the cottage.

He knelt on the dirt floor next to where his wife lay on a bed of straw. Taking a hand between his own, he rubbed her cold fingers, then raised her hand to his mouth and laid a kiss upon her palm. All the words he longed to say were trapped in his throat, lodged behind a lump that he could not dislodge. He wanted to tell her that it was all right, that there would be other babies...

"I'm sorry," she whispered.

Sorry? "Ye've nothing to be sorry for. I love you, Moira," he said. "And nothing, not a child nor the lack of one will ever be changing that."

She smiled weakly and tears slipped down the side of her face. "Aye. But I wanted to give you a child, so much I wanted to, Sean—"

"And ye will, love. There will be other babes for us. So many that someday you'll be asking me what we were thinking bringing so many children into one family."

"Aye." She closed her eyes.

Ma lifted the blood-soaked blankets around Moira's hips and shook her head. "Don't let her sleep."

Panicked, he pushed against her shoulder. "Moira." She opened her eyes and stared at him. Nay, stared past him, off into a corner of the room.

"Ma?" she asked. "Sean, me Ma is come to visit."

He swiveled round to stare in horror at the empty room behind him, at the shadows flickering on the wall from a lit candle. Moira's mother had been dead some five years already.

"Nay, love. 'Tisn't your ma, she isn't here. Look at me."

"She's holding our boys. Look how beautiful they are, Seanie," she whispered.

"Tell her to go away," Sean said.

"They have your eyes. Ma? Where did she go?"

"Let her go, Moira." Fear edged his words. "There'll be other children for us."

His mother gently pressed her palms against Moira's cheeks. "The doctor is coming, Moira. Stay here with us, lass."

"Two fine lads we have, Sean. They'll be needing me, they will." Her voice began to drift off so that Sean had to strain to hear her. "They'll be needing me…"

Her eyes closed and she took in one last soft breath. Sean knew the moment her spirit left her body, could feel it brush past him on its way beyond. It was not cold as he had always heard, but enveloping, as though Moira had wrapped her arms around him one last time.

He stayed at her side until his father returned with the doctor.

Then he pressed a kiss into her forehead. "Give our wee boys me love," he whispered. Then he shoved himself to his feet and quietly let himself out the door into the storm. The wind spared him no quarter and he welcomed its bite, the pain on his flesh far more the tolerable than that in his heart.

CHAPTER TEN

"**M**ISS DEACEY!" CAPTAIN Montgomery pointed into the distance at a row of dark shapes rising out of the frothy blue waves. "The Western Islands."

Fayal. Her future lay ahead. She glanced at the captain and felt a flush of warmth. They'd not spoken again of her offer to him, indeed had hardly spoken at all since that night. Yet she couldn't seem to forget how it had felt in his arms, how she would have given herself willingly to him. 'Twas good she would be getting off his ship, for then her thoughts would be only of Danny.

Fayal grew larger as they drew near, its summit the crater of a volcano, its rich green hills crisscrossed with stone fences like those on the island she had left behind—her Ireland. Seagulls swooped in the air around them, crying out in their sad voices. She grasped the rail and drew a shaky breath. Oh, to be sailing into Cork Harbor instead of here.

Waves battered the island's rocky coast, spray and foam engulfing the stones in a shimmer of silver-blue and green. How would they anchor along this dangerous shore? And then she spotted a crescent-shaped bay with clusters of small white buildings stretched along its border. In the middle stood a fort with at least ten mounted guns, and at each end of the town yet another fort.

"That's Horta, the principal city," the captain said.

"It's lovely. I can almost feel the magic from here," she said.

He rolled his eyes.

Across the bay, an anchored three-masted schooner was flying the American ensign from its mast. A grin burst across her face. "Look, an American ship! Just waiting to take me across." She danced a few steps and when the captain raised an eyebrow at her, she let out a joyful laugh. "Come now, Captain. You're to be free of me. I'll be thinking 'tis worth a bit of celebration."

They set an anchor and lowered an oarboat to take several of them to the island. A government officer met them at the pier and allowed them to land only after receiving assurances from the captain that they had no sick crew members aboard.

As soon as they stepped ashore, the peasantry swarmed them, men and women of all ages carrying baskets laden with melons, potatoes and other foods to sell to the crew. All were chattering in a tongue she couldn't understand—Portuguese, the captain had told her on the ship.

Most of the women were dressed in short frocks of blue or green, their jet black hair tied back beneath white handkerchiefs, while the men wore coarsely woven frock coats and small cloth caps.

The captain waved them away and set off down the pier. He motioned for Kathleen to follow. "The American Consulate is this way."

She lengthened her stride to keep up. "I'm rocking as though I were on the ship still."

"It'll pass."

She glanced at him sharply. Let him have his unpleasant mood this day, she'd not let it dim her happiness. As they made their way through the narrow streets, a band of shabbily-dressed, sun-browned urchins followed them, jockeying with one another as though whomever was closest would receive some sort of reward.

They reached the Consulate's office and the captain held open the door to let her enter first. The consul bounced up from behind his desk to welcome them, a wide smile on his round face, his robust middle jiggling. Kathleen felt a burst of excitement at his enthusiasm; this was the person who would help her get to America.

The two men greeted one another as friends, then Captain Montgomery quickly explained Kathleen's situation. The consul nodded steadily, his eyes shifting back and forth between her and the captain as the story unfolded.

"She's welcome to stay," he interrupted. "The fee's the same, whether you drop sick or well. Thirty-six dollars."

She gasped and glanced at the captain. An enormous sum. He'd not let her stay—not for that cost. Her passage from Ireland had not been even a quarter as much.

Without looking at her, the captain drew out his purse and counted thirty-six dollars into the consul's hand. For a moment, Kathleen could hardly breathe. She touched his arm. "Captain Montgomery, I owe you, my family owes you a great debt. Thank you."

He shook his head, refusing her gratitude. "Best of luck to you. I hope...you get to America in time." He pulled open the door. "Take care of yourself."

As the door latched shut behind him, she brought a hand to her chest. They hadn't always gotten on so well, but more than once, she'd glimpsed something in the captain that she'd never expected to see in an Englishman—kindness.

"Miss Deacey?"

She turned an expectant face to the consul.

"I'll arrange a place for you to stay—"

"Oh, but I'll not need somewhere to stay. If you would just talk to the captain of that ship in harbor, I'll be happy to take passage with them to America."

"That whaling vessel?" He frowned. "They're headed for the Indian Ocean. Not America."

"They're not?" Her shoulders sagged. "How soon, I'll be wondering, would you think a ship bound for America might be coming into harbor?"

"Hard to tell. Merchant ships come through, but where they're headed, it could be anywhere. I suspect it will simply be a waiting game for you." He brought his hands together and gave her sailor's pants a disapproving glance. "Let's get you settled. I'll have my wife find something more appropriate for you to wear."

She smoothed the tangled hair back from her forehead and forced out a disappointed, "Thank you."

"You know..." He smiled sympathetically. "We had a ship going to the States just last week, and a couple of others heading through to ports in Spain and Portugal." He shuffled through the papers on his desk. "Yes, here there are. I expect we'll see them on their homeward voyages, but of course, there's no telling when."

She nodded. "I thought—the captain said—" She reached out a hand and let it drop. "Captain Montgomery had hoped to be in America by Christmas. Do you think it will be possible for me to get there sooner?"

He rolled the papers in his hands. "I don't know. We could see a ship bound for America next week or we might not see one for a month. Or more. I don't mean to be discouraging, but it all depends on—"

"Whether a ship comes through. I understand," she said. It seemed she had gained nothing by getting off Captain Montgomery's ship. Irritation pricked beneath her skin. And sure as the sun rose in the east, Jack Montgomery knew it as well. The man had dropped her here to help himself…not her. It seemed she'd been right about him in the beginning.

*

Hours later, settled into a room on the second floor of a small inn, Kathleen tugged a brush through her snarled ginger curls and glared at her reflection in the long mirror over the bureau. Even in the floral day dress the consul's wife had lent her from the woman's own closet, more lovely than anything she had ever worn, she couldn't see herself as anything but stupid. "How could you trust him? How could you think one Englishman would be different than any other?"

But he'd been so concerned about his missing crew members. "You silly fool!" she snapped at her reflection. "It was the kisses." That meaningless, impulsive kiss he'd given her on the deck, and the others they'd shared that night in his stateroom when she'd nearly given herself to him. 'Twas then she'd begun to let down her guard, to trust him. And now her foolish trust meant she would likely not get to America until after Captain Montgomery's own ship had arrived.

The brush snagged in her hair and she let loose a cry that was equal parts pain and frustration. "Damn ye, Captain Montgomery." She flung the brush across the room, taking satisfaction in the loud clatter it made as it skittered across the planked wood floor.

She went to the window and rested her hands upon the ledge.

Out in the harbor, the Cyrena was still anchored, while small boats rowed back and forth between the quay and the ship ferrying supplies for the next leg of the journey. Under other circumstances she might have found the sight breathtaking—a solitary three-masted brig, the bay glistening turquoise between lush green peaks, the pink-streaked sky gently fading to violet as the sun sank below the horizon.

But there was no beauty in this scene today. Not now when she knew Captain Montgomery would depart in the morning and his ship may well have been her fastest way to America. She considered asking someone to row her out there so she could ask him to let her come aboard again, but immediately discarded the idea. The man had paid nearly a king's ransom to get her off his ship; he'd not be welcoming her back under any circumstances.

It had never occurred to her that the other whaler might not be going to America. Nor had it occurred to her that she might have to stay on this island for any length of time. And Captain Montgomery had not seen fit to mention either point.

Her spirit felt bruised with the pain of betrayal.

She leaned forward through the open window. The streets below were now deserted, and the number of rowboats ferrying supplies out to the ship had dwindled to just a few. An idea took root. She didn't need to ask the captain, nor change his mind; she just needed to get on board. If he was not to learn she was there until they were well out to sea, he'd have no choice but to keep her with them until they reached Boston.

All she had to do was get on the ship without getting caught.

She strode from the window and stripped off the dress, feeling only a moment's regret as it slid to the floor and she pulled on the dirty, ill-fitting pants and shirt the captain had given her. Once her hair was tugged firmly back into a knot, she snatched up the dress and marched out the door. She would need money to put her plan into action—and the consul had thirty-six dollars he had no right to keep if she was leaving.

Ten minutes later she was standing in the foyer of the consul's spacious home trying to appear rational as she made her case. "And so, after thinking it all over, I've realized that me best choice is to stay on with Captain Montgomery," she said.

Doubt flicked across the man's face and she sped up. "I've spoken with the captain and he's come round to your way of thinking—that is, that I'll likely arrive in Boston with him long before I will on some other ship. If you please, sir, he's asked me to get his thirty-six dollars back."

She shoved the blue dress into the man's arms and waited for his answer. The blood roared in her ears. The silence seemed to drag on for minutes. Then he smiled.

"Of course. By all means. If you aren't staying on, the fee should be refunded."

He went down the corridor and returned a few minutes later to hand her a small drawstring bag. "Tell Captain Montgomery to have a safe voyage."

Kathleen pulled out the bills and counted them. "He'll be none too pleased if I bring back less than he paid," she said with an apologetic smile. "I see it's all here, so I'll be thanking you for your help and be on me way."

She didn't start running until she heard the door latch solidly behind her. Jesus, Mary, and Joseph, but she'd done it so far. *She had the money.* More money than ever she had seen in her life. Now she need only get on board the ship.

Reaching the waterfront, she hung back in the shadows

between two buildings and watched the native men secure their rowboats for the night. Though the moon was barely more than a sliver and darkness was on her side, 'twas far too early to try to board the ship. No doubt some crew members would still be topsides, stowing and securing the food that had been brought aboard. Still if she didn't arrange something now, all the native men would be gone—and so would her chance to sneak onto the ship.

The breeze tugged some of her hair loose and it danced across her eyes. She smiled and brushed it away. The rising wind was just what she needed, for once the ship weighed anchor, a strong wind would quickly carry them far away from Fayal.

She pulled two dollar bills from the small bag, shoved one deep into her pocket and crumpled the other within a tight fist. Then she pushed the bag deep into her other pocket. Steeling her courage, she walked slowly toward the few men who still labored near their boats.

"I need to get out to that whaling ship," she said in a quiet voice. "Can you help me?" She patted her chest, then pointed at the ship.

A short, thick man straightened and replied in Portuguese. Kathleen shook her head and raised her hands palm up to show him she didn't understand.

"Got tobac?" he asked.

"I'm sorry, I don't under—"

"Tobac smoke?" he said impatiently.

Oh. "Nay."

"No got tobac smoke? Tobac chew?" He gestured at the ship. "Get tobac?"

She exhaled and shook her head.

He said something in Portuguese to the others and they all laughed.

"Please. I'll be needing your help." She opened her fist and showed them the dollar bill. The man snatched it from her palm and waved it for the others to see, then pointed from her to his boat to the whaler. She smiled and nodded, relieved at how easy it had been to communicate.

The man began to push his boat toward the water, and Kathleen waved her hands. "Nay, nay. Not yet. Later, when the men are asleep." She put her palms together, then lay her head against them, miming sleep.

His eyes widened and several of the men laughed out loud. Portuguese words flew around her like gnats. She looked from one face to the next in a vain attempt to understand what was being said.

The man with the dollar stepped closer and patted her bottom. "Chummie," he said with a wide grin.

She swatted his hand away and took two steps back. *Chummie?* His meaning dawned on her.

"Oh, nay! No chummie. No, no chummie! The boat—I'll be needing to get to that ship." She pointed frantically at the ship. A fine sweat beaded on the back of her neck and she glanced at the dark street behind them. What had she been thinking coming out here like this? Anything could happen.

The man took a step toward her, moving his hips from side to side. "Me like. Chummie. Me chummie. Good."

He reached for her and she leaped back with a screech. "Jesus, Mary and Joseph! No chummie! No, no, no."

The others laughed and bantered back and forth in Portuguese, while he and Kathleen stared each other down.

"No chummie," she said from between clenched teeth.

"No chummie?"

The watching men began to drift away.

She pointed to herself and then to the whaler. "Me. Go to ship. Do ye understand?"

He gave his rowboat another shove toward the water.

She shook her head from side to side in exasperation. "Not now. Later."

He touched two fingers to his forehead, muttered something beneath his breath, then pushed the dollar into her hand and started to walk away. Panicked, she ran to catch up with him. "Where are ye going?"

He kept walking.

Kathleen dug in her pocket for the second bill and waved both at him. "All right, ye win, ye win. I'll go now. Right now." She thrust the money into his hand. "Ye buy yourself tobac—lots of tobac." She grasped his arm and pointed at the boat. "Aye? Yes?"

He rolled his eyes and nodded.

"Faith, but ye drive a hard bargain," she muttered. "You'd get along just fine with me brother."

CHAPTER ELEVEN

T HE WATER IN the harbor was growing choppier by the minute with the wind coming from the south as it was, straight off the ocean. Not only did they have to row against the waves, but now against the wind as well. With each wave, salt water sprayed out from the dark sea and over the side of the boat. The Portuguese man muttered beneath his breath and though Kathleen could not understand a word, she was fairly certain he was cursing. She pulled her arms in close to her body for warmth.

Clouds kept blowing in with the wind, piling atop one another until the sky was hidden and the moon's dim light extinguished. Kathleen narrowed her eyes into the darkness. The ship lay directly in front of them, a dark, forbidding shape rising up like a sea monster come to the surface. Her stomach fluttered with nervousness and she started to shiver, more from anticipation than from cold. If she was caught, the captain would surely put her ashore again.

So she must not be caught.

As they drew near the ship, she strained to hear—was anyone on deck besides the night watch?

She pointed to the falls, a rope ladder hanging down the hull directly beneath the whaleboats that were secured at deck level. As the man brought his boat alongside the ship, Kathleen took hold of the wet rope and awkwardly stepped onto the lowest rung.

The man whispered something in Portuguese, then pushed off, leaving her alone in the black night, hanging to a rope ladder to keep from plunging into the sea. The wind skimmed loose the surface water and sprayed her with icy droplets. She squeezed her eyes shut and said a prayer before finally forcing herself to look up.

It wasn't so far, not really, to climb to the deck. She drew a shaking breath and willed herself to move, slowly, hand over fist, painstaking in her determination not to slip nor make the slightest noise. The coarse, wet line chafed her palms. The wind tugged at her.

"Hey! What are you doing?" a man shouted from the deck.

She jerked and almost lost her grip on the slippery rope. Mother of God, she couldn't be caught already. She pressed her body against the hull and raised her head to scan the full length of the gunwale. No one was there.

A reply floated back over the water from the Portuguese man, a steady stream of information in a language that no one on board understood. She let out a relieved breath and inched her head past the top of the bulwark to look around. Only two crewmen were topside, and both were at the bow watching the Portuguese man row away. Fear made her freeze, then propelled her forward. She quietly crawled up and over the rail, grateful that she wore men's pants. This climb would have been next to impossible in a dress.

Crouching low in the shadows, she slipped into the galley, a small room on deck, pushed back into a dark corner, and slid to the floor so she would be hard to spot if anyone opened the door. She could hide in here for hours if she had to. Once it was late enough that she could be certain the captain and his officers were asleep, she would sneak below deck into the captain's private pantry and hide there. If luck was with her, she would have at least a day or more before anyone discovered her on board.

The ship rocked on a wave and hanging pans clanked against one another. She started, cracking her head against the edge of a shelf. Gritting her teeth to keep from crying out, she cursed Jack Montgomery for the mess she was in. Nay! She'd not be thinking of him now. It would only make her angrier and she needed to be keeping her wits about her if she were to get below deck unseen.

Just a bit more time, she told herself. She couldn't make her move until later, when the men on deck had settled into the boredom that accompanied the night watch. She rested her head on the wall behind her, closed her eyes, and willed her shaking limbs to still. Her plan would work. It had to.

*

She woke with a start to the sound of the wind rising and the rigging clattering. She blinked her eyes hard. How had she fallen asleep? It was still dark, but how much closer was it to dawn already? If the crew came topsides, she'd be caught in an instant.

She pushed herself to standing, wincing as pain shot through her legs, tight and numb from being held so long in a cramped position. Cracking open the door, she peered out into the darkness. Not a man in sight.

Now. She must go now.

The chill wind wove its fingers through her clothes and she shivered. A storm was coming for certain. Bending low, she slipped across the deck and tiptoed down the companionway leading to the captain's and officers' quarters. May the Lord protect her from meeting Captain Montgomery here in the passageway.

Below deck, the blackness was nearly solid. Legs wide apart for balance, she stretched her arms out before her like a blind woman, sliding one foot in front of the other as she made her way to the pantry with only memory as her guide. When her fingers touched the pantry door handle, she grasped it like the hand of a long-lost friend and stepped inside the room.

Relief raced through her. *She had made it.* The ship bucked against its anchor and she stumbled, grabbing hold of a shelf to keep from falling. She followed the shelf as far back as it went, then slid to the floor in a corner, blessing the darkness. They'd not know she was on board until 'twas far too late to do anything about it. She leaned her head against the wall and tried to smile but her lips only quivered. Pulling up her legs, she wrapped her arms around her knees, dropped her head and quietly wept.

Something tripped across the back of her hand. She let out a strangled cry and leapt to her feet, swatting at her clothing. Roaches. Her breath came hard, her mind raced with visions of the hard-shelled creatures crawling about in the room. Shaking, breath hissing through gritted teeth, she forced down the urge to scream.

A minute passed and another with her standing, fighting to hold her balance against the roll of the ship. Finally, she leaned her arms against a shelf and reminded herself of her plan. *One day.* She needed to stay hidden for just one day. If the winds were good, the ship would surely be far enough to sea that Captain Montgomery wouldn't turn back.

She felt a tickle against her wrist and swung at it, grunting in satisfaction when she felt a crunch beneath her fist. "Wee bastard," she muttered, not at all certain whether she was talking about the roach...or the captain.

Before long, her legs ached from standing, from holding her balance against the rolling of the ship. She shivered, chilled through by the damp air. The captain had said they would cast off at first light, but she had no idea how much longer that might be. Exhaustion was making it hard for her to estimate the passage of time. A loud knocking brought her instantly alert and she crept to the door to listen.

"Captain, a squall's coming in from the south," Matson said. "The anchor won't hold in this deep harbor."

She couldn't make out the captain's reply, but heard Matson's footsteps as he returned up the companionway.

What had the captain said? Were they to weigh anchor? Would they not need some light to bring the ship out of the harbor safely with a storm brewing? A bell rang overhead to call all hands on deck. Perhaps dawn had already risen and the sun was up. It was almost more than she dared to hope.

Moments later, doors banged shut as the captain and several officers exited their quarters. She could hear them discussing their imminent departure from Fayal as they stomped up the companionway. As soon as she heard only silence, Kathleen cracked open the door and tiptoed across the officer's dining room and into the captain's quarters.

From above came shouts as the sails unfurled. She knew the moment a blast of air filled the white bellies; the ship heeled slightly and leapt forward from the force, causing her to grab hold of a locker for balance. The powerful wind was more than she could have asked for, so strong they would be far from the Western Islands by nightfall.

She took a blanket from the captain's bed, lifted an oil lamp from its holder, and grabbed two books from the shelves lining the wall of his sitting room. Though she'd not had much formal schooling, Ma had insisted all the children learn to read.

Back in the pantry, she turned the lantern wick so low the lamp gave off but a tiny sphere of light, just enough to keep the cockroaches at bay and give her the courage to make herself a spot on the floor.

The light illuminated the food on the shelves, the captain's personal stock of biscuits and various kinds of fruit. She'd not have to worry about hunger. Faith, there were even several jugs of whiskey in a crate. She grinned. Da and Sean would surely appreciate her circumstances.

She settled back against the wall, picked up one of the books, and ran a finger over the leather cover. *Ballads and Other Poems by Henry Wadsworth Longfellow.* The captain read poetry? An ivory woman's handkerchief lay pressed between the pages and she ran a finger over the soft linen, spread it open so the lace-trimmed edges fanned across the open book like an angel's wings. With her finger, she traced the initials embroidered on one corner: E.C.

The captain had a lady friend? Somehow she never would have thought it. Unsettled, she snapped the book shut and leaned her head back against the wall.

The ship creaked and moaned as the hull sliced through the storm-stirred sea. Even below deck she could feel the speed with which they were moving away from Fayal. She allowed herself a small nod of satisfaction that Captain Montgomery wouldn't be getting rid of her so easily.

A shiver coursed through her and she wrapped the blanket around her shoulders. What she would give to be climbing into a warm bed right now. She let her eyes drift shut for an instant, as though teasing herself with the prospect of slumber, then jerked them open again. She didn't dare sleep for fear the lantern might tip and start a fire.

The cold was getting heavier now, the chill breath of the storm seeping insidiously through the boat. She stretched her stiff legs, and thought of her family and Danny and how far away she was from everyone she loved. If they could but hold on, surely she would be in America by Christmas.

'Twould be a lonely holiday indeed without them, but at least she would know she was helping them survive. In the old days, her father always managed to have a jug of poitín for the holidays, to share with friends when they stopped by to bestow Christmas greetings and blessings. "Just a nip to warm the soul," he would say. Then the men would raise their glasses and he would toast, *"Sláinte chuig na fír, agus go mairfidh na mna go deo.* Health to the men and may the women live forever."

She looked at the jugs of whiskey on the shelf. Maybe a nip to warm the soul was what she needed to fend off the chill. She lifted a jug from the crate, pulled the cork from its neck, and took a sniff. It wasn't bitter as she'd expected, but not sweet either.

Raising the jug to her lips, she took a large swallow and grimaced as it burned its way down her throat. She savored the warm sensation for a moment, then took another gulp, shivering as the liquor coursed a hot path from her mouth to her stomach. A few drops had dribbled over her bottom lip and she licked them away as she recorked the jug. Da was right. She felt warmer already…invigorated even.

She eyed the jug. Perhaps a wee bit more would be best to ensure her comfort down here. She pulled the cork and put the jug to her mouth again. Aye, who was to know anyhow?

CHAPTER TWELVE

"THAT SQUALL SURE sent us flying," Jack mused aloud as he crossed the foredeck with Matson. After a full day of sailing under stormy skies, the bleak cloud cover was finally splintering and pale blue was shining through the cracks.

"Yes, we're well away from…Fayal."

Jack gave his friend a sharp look. "Are you trying to say something?"

"Not a thing."

"You think I was wrong to leave her there." He gestured in the direction from which they'd sailed.

"Her?"

"Kathleen Deacey."

Matson shrugged.

Jack stopped and slapped a hand on the rail. "What do you think I should have done with her? Don't answer that—I don't want to know." He looked out over the ocean for several long moments. "We couldn't have kept her with us for two more months."

"I know."

"This ship is a business—"

"You're absolutely right."

"A business. There is no room for a woman—"

"I *agree* with you."

"She'll catch on with a ship at Fayal."

"Eventually."

"Damn it, Matson. You think I was wrong."

"No, not wrong…" Matson shook his head.

"It isn't enough that I save her life, but now you want me to feel guilty for leaving her on Fayal so she can get passage on a merchant ship?"

"*If* she gets passage."

"Enough. I'm going to my quarters to get out of these wet clothes." He turned away, then spun back. "*My* quarters, mind you, which now happen to be peaceful due to the departure of one half-wit Irish woman who spent her nights screaming because of cockroaches."

He stalked off, but not before he saw a grin pop across Matson's face. Devil take it, what did the man expect of him?

He'd saved the woman's life and deposited her on land, safe and sound. No one could expect more. No one.

So why did he expect more of himself?

He let himself down the companionway, anxious for a change of clothes and some solitude before dinner. His first night back in his own bed had amounted to a broken night's sleep, hours of tossing and turning. It had been a relief when that storm front had come in and forced their early departure from Fayal.

A sound from the direction of his pantry caught his attention and his mood soured even further. No doubt, rats were in the food again. He shook his head. Worms in the biscuits, rats eating the fruit, and roaches in everything else. He would not miss the shipboard life when his time was done.

He whipped open the pantry door and let loose with a bellow

to scare the rodents off. The sound was drowned out by an ear-splitting scream from a woman sitting on the floor in the pantry, a blanket from his bed wrapped around her shoulders.

Kathleen Deacey?

Irrational relief shot through him. He took a step back and blinked. For a moment he thought guilt was making him see things. And then he realized guilt had nothing to do with it. "Dammit to hell! What are you doing here?"

Kathleen looked up at him, her face almost glowing in the soft lamplight. "Your language leaves something to be desired, Captain."

"How did you get back on my ship?" Then it hit him. He turned, half expecting to find his first mate behind him, grinning. "Matson. He helped you, didn't he?"

"A fine how d'ye do to you too. Do you often shout into the pantry when you're alone?"

"I'll kill him." He tried to muster anger and couldn't.

"The man knows not that I am here. I came aboard meself."

"So then how— I must be dreaming."

She pushed herself to her feet, swaying unsteadily. "Do ye see any horses? If you dream of horses, good luck you'll have—"

"I'm not dreaming," he said between gritted teeth. "How did you get back on my ship?"

"I swam."

She was grinning at him, a loose, devil-may-care smile. What was the matter with her? "The truth, Kathleen. And spare me the lies."

"Oh, aye. Let us talk of lies, Captain. Like the one that I might get quick passage to America from Fayal."

"You might have."

"And I might not have." She took an unsteady step and shook a finger at him. "I'll be reaching America as quick—or quicker—if I stay with you. The consul said as much. So I came back to you, sir."

Whiskey—he smelled whiskey. "Have you been drinking?"

A sloppy grin spread across her face. "Me Da used to say, what butter and whiskey won't cure, there's no cure for." She looked pensive for a moment. "Still, I had no butter, but I was cold and now I'm warm as—"

He spotted a jug tucked into the corner behind her and strode forward to pick it up. "*My* whiskey?" he choked out.

At her nod, he had a sudden vision of what the remainder of this voyage would be like—one disruption after another. His head began to throb. Without a word, he turned and left the pantry.

Back in his quarters, he poured himself a shot and threw it down. Not exactly the best dinner he'd ever had, but it fit the bill today. All he wanted—needed—was to fill his hold with oil. But somehow this Kathleen Deacey had... He filled his glass again.

A knock sounded and then the door opened. Kathleen smiled at him from across the threshold. "I'm wondering sir, since you know already I'm here, must I stay in that pantry any longer?"

"Yes!" he snapped. "That is now officially your quarters!"

She put one hand out against the doorframe for support. "But 'tis crawling with roaches in there."

He clenched his teeth together so tight he thought they might crack. "And rats, too, I don't doubt."

She nodded.

Damn her. From the moment he'd brought her aboard, she'd created nothing but trouble. His mind kicked back to the night she had tried to seduce him in exchange for passage home, to the measures she was willing to take to get to America...to the bond her family must share. He massaged the bridge of his nose as the whiskey's amber glow spread through him. With his eyes shut, he could almost pretend that she really was gone. That his cabin was his own, that things were as they had been before she'd been rescued.

"Captain?"

Almost.

He opened his eyes and looked into the face of the woman he'd been avoiding for weeks simply because of the effect she had on him. "I may live to regret this the rest of my life."

"The floor's moving," Kathleen slurred.

"It should be—we're on a ship. Sit down before you fall." He sighed. "You don't have to stay in the pantry."

"You've changed your mind?" She pulled a small purse from her pocket. "Your money, Captain. That you paid the consul for me." She held it toward him, then lost her balance and dropped onto the sofa.

Jack opened the bag, incredulous.

"Not the whole of it, I'm afraid," she said. "Two dollars went to the man who rowed me out here last evening."

"I thought you swam."

She grinned loopily, then nodded toward the empty glass in his hand. "If you'll be filling that again sir, would you mind sharing a spot with me?"

He raised his eyebrows. "I don't think— Oh hell, why not? Why bloody not?"

He got out another glass and poured her a finger's worth.

She raised her glass. "To a swift return to America."

"After a successful voyage," he countered.

Kathleen laughed and shook her head. "It's rather good once

you get used to the taste, don't you think?" She held her glass out for more. "Don't be tight with it now, Captain. I saw how much ye have in the pantry."

He poured her a couple more fingers of the amber liquid. "That was to last the trip, Miss Deacey, not just this night."

"My friends call me Kathleen."

He felt a tightening beneath his breastbone and had the sensation that he was slipping down the long side of a wave into water too dark to see through. "My friends…call me Jack."

Her eyes met his for a long moment and then she grinned and the tension broke. "Me Da would think he'd gone to heaven if he saw all those jugs." Her voice sobered. "And me brother, Sean, too, I'd say. Been a long time since we've had whiskey…"

"They've given up the drink?"

She leaned toward him as though imparting a secret. "They've not given it up—there's no money for whiskey."

Jack finished off his glass. "Didn't you say you'll be sending them money? Won't be that many more months they'll have to go without."

"If my family is still alive when I reach America, Captain, the money I send will be for food," she said, an edge in her voice. "Ireland is starving. The potato crop has rotted."

He'd heard of this problem last spring. "I know. I heard about it last year."

She shook her head irritably. "Aye, and this year too. We didna think it could happen again. Two years in a row. But just like that, on a fine August morning, the blight returned, our potato plants began to die. We dug the potatoes from the earth praying we got them out in time." Her voice dropped to a whisper. "Nearly all me family's food for the coming year was lost on that day. Nearly everyone's was."

"A second crop failure?" He'd been on the ship since April and had heard nothing of this.

"Far worse than last year's."

"Didn't England send food when the crop failed last year? Surely it will help again."

She snorted. "Ye've been at sea too long. The Head of the Treasury, Charles Trevelyan himself, said the Irish need to stand on our own feet. That it was up to the Irish to get themselves out of this trouble."

She gestured at him with her glass and some of the whiskey sloshed over the top. "But how are we to do that, I'll ask you? Our land is owned by the English, our livestock sent to England as payment for rent—"

"The English won't let the Irish die."

"What don't you understand...Jack. The English are saying that God has delivered the famine, and they cannot intervene against the divine," she said in a low voice. "There's no food, and no way to earn money. Ireland grows grain and oats aplenty, but the harvest is guarded by English soldiers so that none can be had by the people."

"Why don't the Irish fight for it then?"

Kathleen let out a snort. "They've tried. The struggles turned to riots...and then the starving died by the English bullet."

"They fired at the people?" This couldn't be true.

"Aye. They give the Irish a choice you see—quick death by shooting or slow death praying for help that will never come. So tell me now, if there is no work and no money and all the food we grow is sent away, just how are the Irish supposed to feed the Irish?"

The horror of her words trickled into the pit of his stomach. "Surely you exaggerate—"

"On me grandmother's grave I swear. Someday history will bear me out on this and it will not be kind to the English." Her voice grew softer still. "Only the Irish care about saving the Irish. And the only way we will do it…is from America."

He could not speak for the image of death in his mind. His father. His father. His father. *And hers.*

By the time he looked back at her, she was asleep, curled up on one end of the sofa, her red hair spread like flames across the armrest. His annoyance was gone, diffused by the whiskey and by her words—*and by her presence.*

He poured himself another finger of whiskey and downed it as he stood and watched her. She looked so untroubled, dark lashes above cheeks rosy from fresh air, her breathing deep and even in slumber. But her peacefulness was only illusion; she carried a burden many others would have not have had the strength to shoulder. And though he knew there was little he could do to help her, he found himself admiring her determination to not give up, and hoping he would soon fill the hold with oil so he could get her to America.

Her eyes opened, and she pushed herself to sitting as she stifled a yawn. "'Twas a long night I had with little sleep at all, so I'll be needing a wee nap, I will."

He watched her walk slowly into his stateroom, one hand on the wall for support, and felt not even the slightest irritation that she had just taken his bed without asking.

CHAPTER THIRTEEN

KATHLEEN PACED THE deck. Weeks had passed since they left Fayal and yet there was no sign of the island, Bermuda, where the captain had said was a bountiful whaling ground. She glared at the sky. Once again the wind had died at sunset, slowing them to a turtle's pace.

A ship appeared in the distance and she watched it inch across the horizon, wondering whether it, too, was headed for Bermuda. In all of November, they'd taken but two whales and now December was upon them. Though she abhorred the killing, she'd come to accept it, for if they didn't catch several more whales soon they'd never be in Boston before the new year.

At least the horizon was streaked with pink—*red sky at night, sailor's delight,* Matson had told her. That meant the winds would be good tomorrow. Perhaps it would be enough to deliver them to Bermuda.

An odd screak startled her and she turned, spotting Donnelly standing amidships, a fiddle under his chin and a grin on his face. He winked at her and she felt the warmth of his friendship. Only he, Mr. Matson, and the captain knew of her worries about her family...but Donnelly, being Irish, understood most what another famine meant.

His bow struck up a joyous tune and several of the crew clapped along, a respite from the boredom on the ship. The beat was infectious and Kathleen tapped her fingers against the bulwark and absently gazed out over the nearly flat ocean, now a sea of reflected pinks and golds.

The schooner she'd spotted earlier had tacked onto a course heading straight toward them. One of the men pointed the ship out to the others and most scrambled to their feet, their conversation now an excited buzz. Matson slipped down the companionway to alert the captain.

When the ship finally came within hailing distance, its helmsman took advantage of the remaining breeze to deftly maneuver closer, then haul back the main yard.

"I'll be damned," the steward said. "They want to gam." He grinned at Kathleen. "Visit back and forth across the ships. Let's hope the captain is in the mood for a party tonight."

As if in answer, Jack's voice rang out aft, "Heave to!" The crew let out a cheer as the helmsman brought the bow of the ship around until it was head-to-wind and all forward momentum had stopped.

An oarboat dropped into the water beside the other ship, and moments later four men rowed across the short distance to come on board. Kathleen hung back in the shadows, watching as hands were shaken and introductions made. The other ship's captain was one of the four, a handsome dark-haired man, perhaps five years older than Captain Montgomery.

"Are you heading back to the States?" he asked.

Jack nodded. "All we need is one more good run of whales and we'll be steering for Boston."

And some wind, Kathleen thought, enough wind to get us there.

"Outstanding. Could you post our mail? A couple of the men are newly married," the other said with a grin.

Jack let out a laugh. "We'll make certain it goes out." He held out a hand, palm up. "Can I get you a drink, Captain?"

"Lead the way."

Before heading below deck to break out his private stock, the captain gave the order for shrub to be mixed up—a concoction of lemon juice, molasses, rum and water—and gave a group of men permission to row over to the other ship.

By late evening, parties were in full swing on both ships, the drink flowing freely and the men jabbering like so many magpies set free after a long imprisonment.

Jack had gone to the other ship hours ago to partake of that captain's liquor, leaving her in the protection of Mr. Matson. She squinted through the night at the deck of the other ship, illuminated by lanterns lit in the cross trees, and wondered whether one of the dark shapes on deck was Jack.

Jesus, Mary and Joseph, but she was foolish. If she didn't know better she might think she was missing his company. Foolish, indeed. A ship with men from one end to the other and her longing for one not here.

From the foredeck came the wiry sounds of a fiddle, a lively tune soon accompanied by men stomping their feet and clapping along. The scent of tobacco wafted through the air, carrying with it snatches of boisterous conversation, tales of whaling chases and heroic deeds, and descriptions of exotic islands, hard drinking, native women, and whoring the night away.

Did Jack partake in such doings? Kathleen felt her cheeks warm.

"A fine party, don't you think?" Matson tipped up his mug and took a swallow. "They'll be dancing now that everyone's loosened up."

"A grand sight that will be," she said with a laugh.

Matson held out a hand. "May I?" he asked. "Before we get crowded out by the men?"

She hadn't danced since the night she'd left Ireland. Her throat constricted at the memory. "I'll not be thinking—"

"Have pity on me." Before she could protest again, he took hold of her hand and pulled her out into the open space.

As they twirled the makeshift dance floor, Kathleen tipped her head back to look up at the starry night. A joyous laugh escaped her. Other sailors began to join them, joking with one another as one man of each pair took the lady's part. Soon the deck was crowded with dancers, all trying to lead, laughing and shouting as they accidentally stepped on each other's toes.

The fiddler left little time between songs, and Kathleen finally begged off and scampered to the side to catch her breath. As she tapped her foot to the music, the sound of second fiddle joined the first, and the steward stepped into the illuminated area, grinning. The other fiddler rose to the challenge, his bow flying over the strings. A cheer went up when he finished, then the steward answered with a solo of his own.

"A draw!" someone shouted.

"And a toast to it!" another answered and every man agreed by taking a hearty swallow of his shrub.

The two played together then, the music so vibrant and the dancers so spirited 'twas as if the ship itself had come to life. After several more songs, the steward bent to confer with the other fiddler, then raised his bow in the air and the gathering quieted. "This one is for our lady," he said, nodding at Kathleen.

The music they played slid off the two fiddles and into her heart. A love song. An Irish melody, the words if sung, of Ireland and love lost. This one she almost couldn't bear, not with Danny missing and Ireland starving. Nay, she would weep, sure, if she stayed for every note. She gave the fiddlers a tremulous smile and a tiny salute, then slipped away from the crowd to move as far from the music as she could, into the darkness near the stern.

Yet even there the melody pursued her. She stared out across the midnight sea and prayed for her parents, for Sean and Moira's baby, for her own brothers and sister. And she longed to be home just once more.

"I'd think the only lady around for miles would be in constant demand on the dance floor," a low voice murmured in her ear.

Her stomach leaped. *Jack.* She couldn't stop a smile from breaking across her face. "I'm catching my breath."

"This one they're playing, do you know it?" he asked.

"Aye." But she had no interest in talking of it. "I thought you were on the other ship."

"It looked more fun over here."

"Ye may be right."

He leaned against the bulwark beside her, so close she could smell his shaving soap.

"Almost too much fun," he said. "I hope the men are able to function tomorrow."

"So they'll be ready to sail about with nothing to do?"

He frowned and she laughed. "I mean no offense, Captain, it's just what it is."

"We're not far off Bermuda. If the whaling grounds are generous, we could have a lot of work ahead."

"Best you be getting your dancing in now, then. Or isn't that allowed for whaling masters?"

He shrugged. "Somehow I've just never wanted to dance with…Matson."

She choked on a laugh. "Ah, then Donnelly?"

"Him either."

This time her laugh bubbled over. He slid close enough that their arms touched. "We could dance, I suppose," he said.

Shyness swept through her even as her stomach turned over in anticipation. She glanced toward the foredeck where the fiddlers were conferring about what to play next. "But there is no music."

As though in charge of a great orchestra, he lifted one hand in the air and the music began again. A cloud slipped across the moon and Kathleen shivered. Though their words were in jest, she couldn't shake the feeling that something else was at work here, something outside their control.

"Well?" Jack asked.

Nay, her mind warned even as the idea made her almost giddy. She shook her head.

"Why not?"

"Ye'll laugh."

"At your dancing? Never."

She considered him carefully. "It's a faerie night," she finally said. "And if you laugh at that I'll not tell you more."

"I'm not laughing."

"If I'd been paying attention at all, I would have known before, for I can feel it now in the air about us."

Jack glanced cautiously to either side. "Feel what?"

"If ye were Irish—ah, but you aren't. Have you not ever felt it, something amiss that you canna quite put your finger on, something not of this earth?"

He screwed up his face.

"Ah, so you have. Don't deny it, Jack, for I can see it plain on your face. There are faeries on board here tonight, with mischief in mind and maybe worse." She nodded. "I'll tell you a story so you understand. A very long time ago, a girl came upon a crowd that had gathered round a blazing fire. A handsome lad with long yellow hair asked her to dance.

"And the girl said, 'Now 'tis a foolish thing, sir, for you ask me to dance when there is no music.' And he raised up one hand, just like ye did, and instantly the sweetest music played all around them."

She gave Jack a pointed look. "Do you see now why I say the faeries are about? You and I just nearly did the same as the story. Best that we stop the mischief before the wee ones can play it."

Jack frowned. "Nothing bad happened in your story."

"But I haven't finished. The girl danced with him, she did, until the moon and stars went down. Then he asked her to supper and led her down a stairway into the ground, to a beautiful hall, shimmering with gold and silver. The table was covered with delicious food, and wine was poured into golden cups."

She took hold of Jack's forearm. "But when she went to drink from a goblet, a man whispered to her, *Eat no food nor drink any wine or you'll never see your home again.* The girl refused to drink the wine and the people grew angry. Then the man took her by the hand and led her out."

"I fail to see—"

"He gave her a branch of ground ivy and said that no one could harm her as long as she held it in her hand. She ran all the way home with them chasing her. When she reached her home, she barred the door. Outside, voices called to her, warning that when next she danced to the music on the hill, she would stay with the wee ones forever."

She stepped closer to Jack. "Don't you see? We played out the beginning of the tale." She gestured toward the companionway and shook her head. "And there is the stairway that leads below, like the one in the story. Who is to say—"

"Captain!"

They both started at Matson's call, and the mystical flow of the moment shattered. Kathleen took a step back and let out a shaky breath.

"We've run through all the shrub," Matson said. "I wasn't sure you'd want the men to make more."

Jack shook his head. "The wind is certain to pick up before morning. I don't want the entire crew a half seas over when we need to trim the sails."

"I'd thought as much." Matson headed toward the bow.

"Time we bid our guests good-night." Jack started to follow Matson, then turned back for a moment. He reached out to touch her cheek. "If you'd danced with me, I'd still have let you go home."

She watched him walk away. "Would you, now?" she murmured into the night. "'Tis the faeries at work here this evening. And I've saved us from their doings."

CHAPTER FOURTEEN

MINUTES AFTER THE captain went forward, the crew from the other ship loaded into their oarboats and rowed across the unruffled ocean to their own ship. *Like faeries following a glimmer of moonlight.*

The thought sent Kathleen fleeing down the companionway to Jack's quarters. She couldn't be topsides when he returned to the afterdeck. She had to protect him...and her. As Ma used to say, once you set off down the path of the faeries, you seldom have a say where it leads.

And sure it was faerie mischief that made her heart quicken when she was near the man. Mischief that made her insides tingle and her skin flush with heat at the thought of kissing him again.

She had been right not to dance with him. For if she had, if she ever dared to care for him, an Englishman, she would lose her family. And like the story, 'twould be the same as if she were never to go home again.

She needed to forget about Jack Montgomery, needed to keep her thoughts focused on anything but him. She closed herself into the stateroom and began to brush out her hair. *We could dance, I suppose.* Faith, but the man haunted her even when she tried not to think of him.

Something thudded to the deck directly above her, and angry shouting broke out. What could they be doing at this time of night? A minute later, the commotion that had been topsides came down the companionway and into Jack's sitting room, the sound carrying through the closed door.

"Just hand me the whiskey and I'll be fine," Jack said. "Son of a bitch."

She strained to hear Matson's reply, his voice so low she couldn't make out the words.

"Give me the damn rag then," Jack snapped. "Yes, yes. I'll hold it tight. Yes… Go away and let me drink off the pain."

Matson muttered a few other unintelligible sentences, then there was the sound of the door opening and closing. Something was wrong. Another crash in the sitting room propelled her to push open the door between their rooms. "Is everything all right— Jesus, Mary and Joseph!"

Jack sat slouched into the sofa, a blood-stained cloth pressed to his nose with one hand, a glass of whiskey in his other. A trail of blood ran down his chin. His left eye was beginning to swell shut, a bruise forming beneath it like a purple crown above the blood splattered on his cheek.

As she stepped toward him, her foot hit a pan of water on the floor and it splashed in every direction. She struggled to regain her balance. "What happened to you?" she cried. "Your nose looks to be broken."

"It not only looks to be, but it is. What do you want?"

"You must straighten that thing out right away or it will heal crooked." She bent over him. "How in God's heaven did this happen? I swear by the devil, but the faeries were at work tonight.

Angry they were, no doubt, at you for not dancing with me. Let me take a look." She reached to remove the cloth.

He swatted her hand away. "You were the one who wouldn't dance. Seems to me they should be breaking your nose, not mine. Now, what is it you want?"

"I heard all the noise and was worried about you, sir. Och, but you do need me help. I can straighten it out for you. I had to do this once for me brother, Sean."

She stretched her hands out in front of her and wiggled her fingers. "Isn't so hard to do, really, you just need an eye for getting it straight. Now lie back here on the sofa. You've no idea what a mess you look—"

"Oh, I do. I'll straighten it out myself once this whiskey sufficiently numbs me."

Kathleen frowned at him. Mighty sorry he'd be come the morn if he let that thing set the way it now looked. "Nay, Captain. I'll not go until you let me take care of it. And if you don't, I promise I'll sit in here and talk about it until you wish you'd never let me in the room, indeed that you'd never brought me on board."

"Don't think I've never yet thought *that* before," he muttered.

Her mouth nearly dropped open at the admission. And this from the same man who had just asked her to dance up on deck? She stuck out her chin. "Sure, you've a foul mood now, don't you?"

He rolled his eyes.

"Lie down." With a flat hand, she gave his shoulder a hard shove, sending him off balance so that he rolled onto his back on the sofa.

"Dammit!"

"Watch your language, sir!" She seated herself on the edge of the cushion and removed the bloody cloth he had been holding to his nose. "Och, but you've a split lip as well?" She touched a finger to his lip and shook her head. "This will hurt a wee bit," she said. One side of her was a little glad that it would. He deserved it for the mean thing he'd just said.

She held one hand alongside his nose and used the other to gently push the cartilage back into position. Finally she sat back and eyed her handiwork. 'Twas hard to tell exactly, what with the dim light and the bruising, but... "That looks close to what you had before," she said as she pressed the cloth to his nose once more. "Now, have you a large key?"

"What for?" He didn't even open his eyes.

"To stop the bleeding."

"Oh." His brow furrowed, but still he didn't open his eyes. "In the top drawer. You aren't going to stick a key up my nose are you?"

She drew a ring of keys from the drawer and removed the largest one. "I doubt it would fit up your nose. Nay, this works another way."

Before he had a moment more to contemplate her intention, she lifted his head a bit and pressed the cold key to the back of his neck.

He let out a blood-curdling yell and twisted away from her. "What are you doing! Christ almighty, I just hit my nose on the back of the sofa! Look at it," he demanded. "Is it crooked again?"

"It looks fine. Now leave the key behind your neck to stop the bleeding."

"The hell it will." Jack sat up, wet rag pressed to his nose. "I'll show you how to stop the bleeding." He took another swallow of whiskey.

Kathleen ignored him. "I suppose we could crush some pig's

dung on it—or you might eat some. Either way works on the bleeding."

"This is working just fine," he said tersely. He lifted the cloth off his nose. "Look. The bleeding's about stopped anyhow. There's no need to keep searching for remedies."

She eyed him cautiously. "You're getting quite a black eye, Captain. How did this happen?"

"A fist."

"You mean like on the end of someone's arm?"

He nodded.

"You mean to tell me, ye've been popped in the nose?"

He gave her a tight smile. "I *popped* him a couple better before he landed this one."

"You had a fist fight? Why Jack, I'd never have thought it of you. Surely not with one of your own men?"

"The captain of the other ship."

She lowered herself into the chart table chair. "You got in a fight with the other captain? This is not good. Pray tell, sir, over what?"

Jack's eyes raked over her. "He wanted a woman tonight."

"So you popped him one for it? I don't understand. Is this a man sort of thing, to inhibit the desire, so to speak?"

"So to speak."

"I'm surprised the whole crew isn't up there popping one another in the nose, since there are no women around here to be had." She nodded knowingly.

"Kathleen, he wanted *you*."

"Me?" Realization dawned and her eyes widened. "Surely you cannot be implying that the other captain thought I—I—"

"Oh, yes. He was quite drunk and quite determined to have you."

Kathleen blew out her breath slowly. "And so you popped him one…"

Jack nodded without lifting his head off the back of the sofa.

"You broke your nose protecting me honor?"

His closed mouth curved up in a smile, grotesquely stretching his bloodied and bruised face. Yet he'd never looked more appealing than he did at that moment. Indeed, it was all she could do to keep herself from throwing her arms around him.

She dipped the cloth into the pan of water and wiped the blood off his chin, then gently sponged the red trails off his throat. "Let me have another look at that nose of yours," she said softly.

*

Jack opened the lid on his unbruised eye and perused the room, bathed in the soft yellow morning sun that flowed like liquid through the skylight. His head throbbed. His eye hurt. His nose ached. He ran a finger down the bridge of his nose, feeling once again Kathleen's gentle touch as she ministered to him.

He remembered the story she'd told him last night, of the girl who danced with the faeries. Though he'd wanted to laugh at first, by the time she finished the telling he had felt like he'd been spirited off his ship to some mystical, mythical place. As much as he had wanted to call her foolish for believing such nonsense, he was hard-pressed to explain his own reaction. Maybe it was the rum he'd had on the other ship that did him in, or perhaps the whiskey on his own ship afterward.

Or maybe it was Kathleen…maybe she was enchanted.

Hell, what was he thinking now?

The boat heeled to one side and he could almost hear the hull humming as it carved through the water. They were making good speed; Bermuda couldn't be much further.

Before coming below last night, he'd instructed the men on watch to set sail immediately. Actually, what he'd said was, "Get us the hell out of here."

He'd been anxious to put some distance between them and the other ship, to ensure there wouldn't be a repeat of last night's demand from the other captain. But he'd also had other reasons to get moving as quickly as possible. He'd learned on the other ship the latest news from Ireland—that the famine was far worse than the year before. Just as Kathleen had said, the entire potato crop had perished and people were starving and dying all over the country. For her family's sake, he needed to fill the hold with oil as quickly as possible and get back to Boston.

For Kathleen's sake.

For his. Somehow their lives had become entwined, and he knew there would be no peace for his mind until he got her safely onto the next stage of her journey.

He forced himself to sitting, then paused to still the pounding in his head and the sensation of needles being jabbed into the skin under his eye. A moment passed before he realized someone was tapping at the door.

Kathleen stepped into the room, a large mug in one hand. The smell of coffee wafted toward him.

"How are ye faring this morning?" she asked as she handed him the mug and bent forward to look more closely at his face. "Your nose looks straight."

The nearness of her sent the blood rushing to his head and increased the pounding between his eyes.

"You're plenty bruised, though." She straightened and put

her hands on her hips. "I think you should rest today…put cold compresses on your eye and nose."

He opened his mouth to tell her that he would make such decisions, that he would take care of himself, that he was the captain and if he wanted to hold his men's respect he couldn't be resting whenever he had the slightest problem.

But then she brushed the hair off his forehead and touched his eye. "Ye need a little time to heal. Let someone else take care of you a bit."

He relaxed beneath the caress of her fingers. The idea of being nursed back to health by Kathleen held a definite appeal.

"I've set up a schedule with the officers. Each will be at your call for two hours at a time."

The officers? He jerked upright, wincing as pain shot through his eye. Enough. He'd didn't need nursing by his crew for a broken nose. He could almost hear them snickering. How had he even begun to consider her plan? "No."

"But—"

"No." He pressed his fingers into the skin under his cheekbone to lessen the pain. Weeks ago he'd vowed not to let her disrupt the operation of his ship. Yet here he was, a broken nose because of her, and about to take the day off for no reason other than the appealing thought that she might tend to him.

"I am going to wash my face and change my clothes," he said. "Then I'm going topsides to run my ship—black eye, broken nose, and all." To prove his point he stood, keeping his expression neutral despite the pain that had shot through his head when he moved.

"Are ye sure?"

A shout rang out topsides: "She blows! Thar she blows!"

A flurry of footsteps pounded the wooden deck above them.

Jack glanced upward, somehow relieved that there was no chance he could change his mind. "Absolutely."

She sighed. "I'll tell the men you'll not be needing them." At the door, she turned back as if assessing the truthfulness of his words.

He forced a reassuring smile past the throbbing in his eye. When finally the door latched shut behind her, he eased himself back onto the sofa. What he needed right now wasn't doctoring, what he needed was to finish this ill-fated journey so he could get Kathleen Deacey off his ship and out of his life. The sooner he got her to Boston, the better it would be for all of them.

CHAPTER FIFTEEN

KATHLEEN SAT AMIDSHIPS, alone in the darkness, and hugged her knees. It was Christmas Eve and she would spend this holiday on the ocean far from everyone she loved.

True to Jack's predictions, the Bermuda whaling grounds had been plentiful. They'd quickly taken enough whales to finish filling the hold with barrels of oil, then set a course for Boston. If the winds held, he predicted they would dock in a fortnight or less. Two weeks. Just two weeks and she could find work.

Overhead, the ebony sky glinted with sharp-edged stars, millions of pinpoints flickering like tiny fires lighting the universe. The crew had gathered forward and one man was reading aloud from the Bible, a retelling of the nativity. In the silence of the nearly calm night, his voice echoed across the deck, and his words filled Kathleen with hope…and longing.

She squeezed her eyes shut as if to quash the ache. Nearly three months had passed since she'd left Ireland. She could only pray that all her family was fine, and that the famine would not prevent Moira from birthing a healthy baby.

If her parents hadn't heard from the McKennas yet, it was only a matter of time before they did. They would think she had died—and their hopes would die along with her. "I live," she whispered to the universe. "Hold on just a while longer."

A bank of wispy clouds drifted across the milky half moon and she waited for them to clear. She needed to see the moon this night—needed a clear path from her heart to its glow. For she knew that in Ireland her own family would look upon the Christmas Eve moon and think of her, just as she was thinking of them. And later, when sleep had come to them all on this holy night, their souls would rise up to meet, to dance on the beams from the moon and for just that bit of time she would be home with them once more.

The men were singing now, softly at first, gaining strength with each word: *...oh come all ye faith-ful, joy-ful and tri-um-phant...* Their voices wafted into the night and wrapped around her homesickness like a too-small bandage.

Without a pause, the crew swung into another carol and then another until their voices were booming with joy. *Deck the halls with boughs of holly...* It quickly became obvious that only a few of the men knew the words to all the verses, so they led the singing, and were joined by the others for rousing choruses of *fa-la-la.* By the time the song was nearing its end, they were clapping their hands and thunderously stomping their feet.

Unnoticed in the darkness, she stood and stretched, then made her way to the companionway. 'Twas late, and she was eager to sleep, for it meant that by the time she awoke they would be that many more hours closer to Boston.

At the bottom of the stairs, Jack and Matson sat at the officers' dining table, a jug of whiskey and two glasses between them. The lantern flame flicked shadows across Jack's nearly healed face, darkening the faint bruising that remained and giving him a dangerous air.

"Sure, but this is where the real Christmas Eve party is," she teased.

Matson gestured with his pipe for her to join them.

"I don't mean to be interrupting."

"You're not." Matson looked at Jack. "Is she?"

Jack held up his glass in answer, the faintest of smiles on his face. "Any for you?"

For a moment she thought he was mocking her from that night she'd sneaked back onto the ship, but the warmth in his eyes convinced her otherwise. She slid onto the bench next to Matson. "Not that I'm making a habit of it, but since 'tis Christmas Eve... perhaps a wee bit will help me sleep."

Jack retrieved another glass from his quarters and poured two fingers worth. "Just a wee bit." As he handed her the glass, his eyes caught hers and held. She jerked her gaze away, her thoughts suddenly sliding off balance as if her mind had tilted.

"I-I was thinking," she stammered, "you might tell me a bit about Boston. Some friends from me parish, the Boyles, went there a few years ago, and I'll be hoping to find them."

"So many Irish in Boston, it won't be easy." Jack took a swallow of his whiskey.

"Still, the Irish all settle near one another," Matson said. "It may make your search a little easier."

He went on to describe the neighborhoods, then Jack interrupted to talk about the weather, then they argued over religion for a few minutes, and then slid into a spirited discussion about local politics, each trying to convince Kathleen of his point of view.

She sipped her whiskey, thoroughly entertained and more than a little nervous about her life ahead. Finally Jack grinned at her and said, "Don't worry. Once you're there a while, this will all be old news. You'll come to know the city like a native—"

"Ah, well, I'll not be staying too long in Boston—only until I've saved enough money for passage to Newfoundland."

"Newfoundland? What do you want up in that Godforsaken place?" Matson asked.

She just stared at him. Jesus, Mary and Joseph, but she'd let the whisky loosen her tongue. She'd gone all this time without speaking of Danny, had kept that part of her life to herself for fear that talking about him might somehow ruin her chances of finding him. She set her elbows on the table and considered how much to share.

They both looked at her, waiting.

She mentally sighed. "Oh, well, it's simple actually. I…my betrothed is there."

Matson nodded and puffed on his pipe. "Well. What a surprise. Jack, did you—"

"I had no idea."

Kathleen felt her cheeks grow warm under his gaze. The silence begin to grow.

Matson cleared his throat. "You could write him. I would think, being your betrothed, he'd pay the passage to bring you there."

"Aye, but you see, I'll not be knowing exactly where he is. He left Ireland last spring to work at the fisheries in Newfoundland. And never came home. I pray that he is all right, that I'll be able to find him."

"And if you can't?" Jack asked.

A tightness gripped her throat, radiated through her body until even her fingertips hurt. She shook her head. "For all I know, he may have already taken another ship back to Ireland."

"Will you return to Ireland then?" he pressed.

She thought of this second famine, of the relentless poverty and hopeless despair, of the English pressing the Irish ever lower, stealing away their living and with it their dignity. And then she faced the truth she had kept from herself since the day she'd told Sean she was coming across. "I doubt I shall ever see Ireland again."

She raised her glass to her lips and took a large swallow, welcoming the burn down the back of her throat like a balm on her sorrow. And then she changed the subject. "I know you are married, Mr. Matson. But not you, Captain. Have ye a lady friend in Boston?"

He hesitated before answering. *Too long,* she thought.

"When I have need of a woman, I find one."

Matson choked out a mouthful of smoke. Kathleen refused to succumb to embarrassment. "But do you not want someone to love? To bear your children? To make ye a home?" she asked.

"All good questions," Matson said with a grin. "And I think I hear the steward calling." He downed his whiskey in one gulp, then slid off the bench and hustled up the companionway.

Her questions hung in the air unanswered and Kathleen scrambled for something to say that would fill the void and ease the sudden tension. She gripped her glass to steady her hands. "I'm sorry if I've overstepped, Captain. I just thought—"

He waved a hand. "No apology necessary."

"Ah, well, perhaps you'll accept a thank you then," she said. "For saving my life and letting me to stay on board after Fayal."

"No thanks necessary either."

She laughed. "It seems you're an easy man to please.

Nonetheless, 'tis Christmas and I wish I could give you a gift so you know, so you'll never forget how grateful I am. But all I have are me words." She smiled softly. "So to you…an English captain, with I think, a bit of the soul of an Irishman, I give ye an Irish blessing. May you be poor in misfortune, rich in blessings, slow to make enemies, fast to make friends, but rich or poor, slow or fast, may ye know only happiness from this day out."

Jack took a swallow of his whiskey. After a long moment, he slid forward on the bench and raised his glass. "A toast. To your future happiness—and mine. May we each find what we are seeking."

"Aye. To that."

Their glasses met with a dull clunk, then he slowly slid his glass upward along the side of hers. His knuckles brushed the back of her hand. She could not move, a captive of his black eyes and her trembling soul. And she knew if he asked her this moment what it was she was seeking, Danny's name wouldn't cross her lips.

*

America. Two weeks past Christmas and they were nearly there. Kathleen pulled her seaman's coat closer and allowed herself a cautious smile. From this distance, the shoreline looked like any other, but there wasn't a person on board who wouldn't have agreed 'twas the finest sight they'd ever seen. She exhaled and her breath curled white in the January air, like a spirit come across from the other side to accompany her on the next leg of her journey. The crew was jubilant. Several had already announced they would never again make the mistake of signing aboard a whaling vessel.

By dusk they reached the Cape Cod lighthouse and headed into the harbor. She had not left the deck since land had been sighted, and now her stomach was wound into tight knots, excitement and fear blending into nausea.

She had made it to America. And now what?

They glided past several ships anchored in the harbor, great ships with tall masts gently rocking on the navy sea. The city pressed out in every direction, golden lamps already burning in many windows, gray ribbons of smoke rising from every chimney to mingle above the rooftops in the frosty air.

The city was much larger than she had envisioned. Fear threatened to overwhelm her and tears of panic stung her eyes, blurring the scene into a haze. In a short while she would be on her own in a city where she knew no one, herself but a tiny spec in a huge unfamiliar country.

She had no money, no friends, and no idea what to do after the ship docked. And night was near upon them already. If only she knew whether the Boyles had settled here, at least she would have them to lean on for a few days. A childhood prayer stumbled through her mind, the words tripping over one another in barely remembered confusion. How had her plans come to such an uncertain end?

Ní dhéanfaidh smaoineamh an treabhadh duit. She heard the words as if they had been spoken aloud. *You'll never plough a field by turning it over in your mind.* "Ma?" she whispered. She straightened and glanced around, but there was no one near. She could almost hear what her mother would be saying if she were here: *What is the good of all this worry? It won't change what you must do in the end.*

Aye. She brushed the dampness from her eyes and moved aft to stand beside Jack.

"Welcome to America," he said, a half smile on his face, his dark eyes friendly. "Nervous?"

"A bit. Not every day one lands in a new country." She locked her fingers together to still the trembling of her hands. "I'll be wondering, Captain, if you might lend me a wee bit of coin once we dock. So I might rent a room."

He frowned, and panic blew through her, cold and afraid. "I promise to be paying you back as soon as I find work," she said in a rush. "My word is true."

"No, no. Of course, I'll lend you money. I don't know what I've been thinking." He spun toward the crewmen gathered on the foredeck and shouted, "Donnelly!"

The man came running. "Sir?"

"Miss Deacey is going to need some help getting around Boston. You're Irish—you know where your people have settled. Once we've docked, can you help her find a room?"

Donnelly gave her a pointed look. "Can you pay?"

"She has money," Jack said curtly.

"It will be dark when we dock. No time for a lady to be seeking a room…if you'll be understanding me meaning." Donnelly pursed his lips. "You might stay at me sister's tonight—that's where I'll be though she doesn't know it yet." He grinned. "They've two rooms, a bit full with seven children, but fine people they are, they'll not turn away someone in need."

Jack grimaced. "Two rooms for ten of you? Never mind."

"I've no problem staying at his sister's," Kathleen said. Indeed it sounded better than spending her first night in this new city alone. "I'm used to so many—"

"Me sister will not be minding," Donnelly said.

"Ridiculous. I'll help her find a room once we've unloaded." Jack waved Donnelly away.

"But it's no problem for me to stay there, Captain. In the

morning, I'll be able to find me own room," Kathleen said desperately as Donnelly headed back to the foredeck. "I'm sure his sister will know of some places—"

Jack shook his head, an expression of disgust on his face, and went to give some directions to the men dropping the sails.

Despite the cold, Kathleen stayed topsides until the ship docked and the men began to unload the barrels of oil. Finally the chill drove her below to warm up in the captain's sitting room, feet tucked under her on the sofa, a blanket across her lap and another around her shoulders. As the hour grew later, she began to regret not insisting that she go with Donnelly. At least then she would be moving forward with a friend beside her. As it was, the longer she waited, the more her nerves frayed and her stomach churned. Surely they must be done soon.

Finally the door opened and Jack stepped inside, grinning. "We're done. The oil's unloaded and sold. The men have headed for their homes. Are you ready to meet Boston?"

With a quick nod, she threw the blankets aside and followed him topsides. A damp fog had settled in from the sea making the city barely visible; the once bright lantern lights were now just a hazy glow, diffuse beneath the gray mist spreading eerily over the wharf. She shivered. They disembarked in silence, the sound of their footsteps on the wooden gangplank just a muffled thud in the thickening fog.

The waterfront was nearly deserted, the warehouses locked tight against the night and the creeping fog. Kathleen glanced over her shoulder not knowing what she expected to see, then quickened her steps to keep up with Jack's longer stride.

"Is there a certain place we're going?" she asked, hoping he would tell her of a friend who owned a lovely boarding house.

They walked another half minute before he answered. "We took too long unloading. It's too late to find you a room tonight. Too dark...too cold." He rubbed a hand across his jaw. "I share a house with my grandfather. You can stay with us until tomorrow."

Relief skipped through her. "Oh, thank you. How much easier to begin a new life at the start of the day instead of the close. Is it far to go?"

He shook his head.

They walked in silence, turning at one corner, then another, leaving the harbor behind. The fog so obscured her vision, she could hardly see six feet ahead, could only catch glimpses of the buildings they passed, here or there a stately front entrance or an imposing brick facade. She stumbled once on the cobblestones and the captain caught her arm. "Careful," he murmured and she nodded though he didn't see it.

By the time they reached his home some ten minutes later, her teeth had begun to chatter. Jack mounted the steps to a red brick townhome and unlocked the front door. "It's late enough my grandfather is likely abed already."

He grasped the heavy brass handle and pushed the door open, then stepped back to let Kathleen enter first. A paneled oak staircase led to the second floor from the spacious foyer. As she followed the banister with her eyes, the heat of the room collided with the chill in her bones and sent a shudder rippling through her.

"Let's get you warmed up." Jack stepped across the parlor and stoked the fire in the hearth until it flared bright with orange and yellow flames. Kathleen followed him into the room, her feet sinking into the thick rug. She held her hands out toward the heat, then turned to warm her back. Her gaze drifted across the room, taking in the rich tapestry on the chairs and sofa, the elegant detailing on the tables, the lovely paintings on the walls. The captain was no poor man, that was sure.

"'Tis a lovely home," she said.

"It's my grandfather's mostly—"

A door slammed on the second floor. "Who's here? Margaret?" a male voice demanded from upstairs.

"My grandfather," Jack whispered in warning. "He can be… gruff."

As Jack went out to the foyer, Kathleen shifted a little to the left so she had a better view of the staircase. A stout, white-haired man limped down the stairs, one hand on the railing, the other holding a cane. "Jack!" he cried. "Welcome back! When we didn't see you by Christmas, I was afraid you'd run into bad luck."

Jack reached out to steady the old man as he came down the last stair. "We did have our share of bad luck, but Bermuda was the pay off. Feels good to be home."

Before they turned toward the parlor, Kathleen took two quick steps out of their line of sight and brushed her hands over her cheeks and hair. Good Lord, what must she look like in her men's clothing, and after months at sea? What if the old man was upset that Jack had brought her here?

The two men walked slowly into the room. Jack stopped and gestured toward Kathleen. "Grandfather, this is Miss Deacey. We rescued her on the ocean."

"You what?"

Kathleen put on her warmest smile in an effort to deflect his obvious dismay. "'Tis pleased I am to be meeting you, sir," she said. "My life I owe to your grandson."

"She's not from Boston, had nowhere to go," Jack said. "So she'll be staying the night. Tomorrow I'll take her to rent a room."

The grandfather eyed her for a moment before giving a stiff, disapproving nod, and she could tell he hadn't missed a thing—not her ill-fitting sailor's clothes, not her unruly red hair, not the Irish lilt in her voice.

Jack took a seat near the hearth and motioned Kathleen into a nearby chair. "Grandfather, join us?"

The old man limped forward and eased himself onto the sofa.

"Where's Margaret?" Jack looked around. "We'll need beds made up, something to eat."

When his grandfather didn't answer, Jack asked more loudly, "Where's Margaret." He glanced at Kathleen. "His hearing's not so good."

"She quit."

"Another one quit?"

The old man held up a placating hand. "Don't start. I've got a new woman lined up next week—"

"What's going on while I'm at sea? We've gone through more maids than the queen herself. Margaret was capable enough—"

"Irish."

"What?" The faint word slipped from Kathleen's mouth before she could stop it.

The old man didn't hear her.

"Stupid, lazy Irish."

Kathleen clamped her teeth together and gripped the armrests of her chair. She could say nothing. This was Jack's grandfather—and she needed a place to stay tonight.

Jack leaned forward as if his body could slice through the

tension in the room. "Fine, well just as long as you've got someone new—"

"She'll be here Monday."

"Looks like I'll have to get the rooms ready," Jack said with false joviality.

The old man scowled. "Wake the cook."

Jack threw a smile at Kathleen. "She'll have my hide if I wake her—she's nearly as old as my grandfather. Still..." He looked between his grandfather and Kathleen, hesitating as if afraid to leave the two of them alone. Finally he pushed himself to standing and went upstairs.

Kathleen clasped her hands together in her lap and smiled nervously at the grandfather.

He glared back. "What was your name? Daisy?"

"Deacey. Kathleen Deacey."

"Irish are you?"

She nodded.

"I'd thought as much. The North End, Fort Hill... that's where your people live. You'll find yourself a nice hovel there." His eyes narrowed. "Are you aware, Miss Deacey, that my grandson is nearly engaged?"

She opened her mouth to reply, but was so flabbergasted she couldn't speak. To be sure, the man was senile. Jack himself had said there was no woman in his life and he had no reason to lie to her.

The old man nodded. "A fine woman from an upstanding family. Jack will never give her up. Be assured, whatever transpired between the two of you on shipboard, it will not continue here."

Disconcerted by his declaration, she sat up straight and stared the old man down. "Nothing transpired between us. I meself am already engaged and have no interest in your grandson whatsoever. He can wed whom he likes!"

"Good. So long as we're in agreement."

They sat in stony silence for several minutes before Jack finally reappeared. "Everyone getting on in here?" he asked.

"Wonderfully," the old man said with a tight smile.

"Couldn't be better," Kathleen added.

CHAPTER SIXTEEN

SEAN BURST INTO the house joyfully and handed the envelope to his mother. Finally, word from Kathleen. "You open it, Ma. 'Tis addressed to you and Da after all."

Tears sprang to Anna's eyes. "Och, I've been so worried," she said as she peeled back the flap with excited fingers.

Sean nodded, relieved that her fears would finally be put to rest. More than once, his mother had voiced her regret about sending Kathleen across the ocean. More than once she dreamed that the ship had gone down, had told Sean she had seen Kathleen crying out for help—and none coming. But now all would finally be right, for here was a letter to them from Kathleen, safely landed in Canada.

His siblings crowded around Ma, their thin bodies pressing in on her from every side. "Do you suppose she'll have sent money already?" his younger sister asked.

"She'd have had to find work awfully quickly," Da answered.

"But at least she's there." Ma smiled broadly before unfolding the single sheet and reading aloud:

"*My dear friends*—" Her eyes widened and she took a step backward. "It's not from Kathleen, Micheal."

"Read, Anna. Perhaps there is word of her."

Ma swallowed and began again:

"My dear friends—

*We were safely landed in Canada yesterday, with many
fewer passengers than set off from Cobh that fine morning in
October. The voyage was far worse then you could imagine,
with filth and disease and always the hunger. Our dear
Maegan succumbed to the fever as did so many others on the
ship. Anna, I don't know any better way to tell you except
that Kathleen is not with us."*

Ma put a hand to her mouth and a low sound escaped her throat.
Her voice quivered as she read on.

*"There was a terrible storm and Kathleen was washed
overboard during it. I wish I did not have to bring you
this news and pray it will not be too hard to bear. If Sean
is still determined to come over, tell him he is welcome to
stay with us until he is able to get settled. I will write again
when we have a proper address. Our love to you and our
old neighbors. We will pray for your strength and for all of
Ireland."*

Your old friend,

Lucy McKenna

Ma carefully refolded the letter and slid it into the envelope.
Tears slid down her cheeks. "My baby girl. What a fine woman she'd
become." She collapsed into Micheal's arms, and her tears gave way
to sobs.

Sean couldn't move. He had been the one to insist Kathleen
emigrate, had said she had no choice. He had sent her to her death.

And for what? If she had stayed here, at least she would still be alive. He pulled his sister into his arms. Lord, the girl was little more than bones beneath her rags. How much longer would it be before she died, too?

His mother began to wail, her face contorted with the pain of a wound torn open. Though he knew what it was to lose a child, he could scarce imagine the torment of losing that child after raising her to adulthood.

He pushed himself back from his sister and stepped toward the door.

"Sean!" his mother said.

He turned back. Ma's face was flooded with tears.

"You can't be going to America. Not with this."

He raised his hands in a gesture of helplessness.

"I'll not lose another child of mine to the ocean," she whispered.

"We said all this, Ma. Before Kathleen left." His voice dropped. "Before Moira died. If there is no money coming in, then we'll all starve here." He shook his head. "My passage is booked to Newfoundland. I am going still."

He slammed the door behind him, the sound interrupting his pain for the briefest moment. He trudged through the snow, deep like he'd never seen before, and hoisted himself upon the stone fence outside the cottage. Snow swirled around him and he pulled his jacket closer against the chill, wishing only to be able to hold his wife in his arms once more and the tiny baby boys she had delivered.

Ah, Kathleen, how could this have happened? He thought he had it all figured. His eyes clouded with tears. He'd forced her to go, had believed it would all work out, had even held out hope that she might find Danny.

But everything was weighted against them.

He stared out into the gathering dusk, could just barely see the ruin of a nearby cottage, torn to the ground hours ago by the landlord's brigade. The Collins family shuffled down the road toward him, a brood of children behind the parents, the youngest in his father's arms and the mother keening a mournful wail. As they drew near, Sean could see the tears streaking the woman's gaunt face, the resignation in the sag of her shoulders. His throat tightened. He had known these people all his life and, now, when they needed help so badly, he could offer them nothing.

The woman reached out to gather her children close, as if her love could keep them safe and well on this journey with no destination. Sean nodded as they passed. "God be on your road," he murmured.

He watched until he could see them no more, until the night had fallen and hidden away any trace of their passing, until the moon shimmered in the snow that kept falling and hid their footprints. From far away in the darkness then the woman's wail came again, a sound of pain so deep it drew the tears from Sean's eyes and sent them rolling over his cheeks.

Ireland was dying. It was as if a shroud had been dropped over the countryside, suffocating the people until their spirit had been stilled and silence ruled the land. The music, the laughter, the afternoon gatherings, the nightly story telling—all had been abandoned since the potato crop had failed. The blight had destroyed their very Irishness in a way the English, for all their trying, had never been able to do.

Sean dropped his head and wept for his people, for his sister, for the wife he had lost and the sons he would never see to adulthood, and he knew that sleep would be a long way off for him this night.

CHAPTER SEVENTEEN

L ATE THE NEXT morning, Jack sat into the carriage seat across from Kathleen and allowed himself a small smile of satisfaction as he considered her appearance. Clothed in a new cloak, black dress, and white apron, her hair pulled back into a knot at her nape, she looked for all the world like a respectable house servant. He hadn't planned on buying her new clothing, but he couldn't very well have sent her off dressed in men's pants.

"I'll be thanking you again for posting my letter home," Kathleen said. "I only wish me family could know right now that I'm alive."

Though packet ships crossed the ocean quickly, delivering mail in as little as a month at times, the trip was still long when the news was important.

Kathleen peered out the window. "How much further to the next boarding house?"

He shrugged and shook his head. It was one thing to refer to Fort Hill as a destination—quite another to find her a place to live there, the area teeming as it was with tens of thousands of Irish immigrants jammed shoulder-to-shoulder in tenements two and three stories tall. Their driver was familiar with the area and had already taken them to several rooming houses in Fort Hill, but Jack had found none acceptable. He had no problem leaving Kathleen on her own, but he didn't want to simply deposit her into squalor…and then return to his comfortable home.

He looked out the window and watched the snow that was trying to fall, small wispy flakes dropping into the crisp gray air. It would be best if they got her settled before a real storm decided to hit.

He hadn't shown Kathleen the newspaper he'd seen this morning, the report that the British government was now admitting it could no longer save the situation in Ireland. Whole communities were completely without food and many people were dying every day of starvation. He'd not wanted to panic her when there was nothing she could yet do to ease her family's plight. But it was clear to him that she would need to get settled and find work immediately if she were to help them before it was too late.

The carriage drew to a stop just past a tavern and the driver jumped down and opened the door. "Perhaps this one will be better, sir. It's the last I know of, but I've no doubt there are others."

Jack stepped to the ground. They were now in the heart of the Irish district, both sides of the street lined with tired three-story buildings, paint peeling and shutters sagging. If the driver hadn't said this was a new place, he would have thought they'd already been here. The street, the buildings, looked no different than all the others they'd seen over the past few hours, the alleys behind criss-crossed with rope clotheslines strung from window to window, sagging beneath the weight of wet clothing even in this cold weather.

"Which is the boarding house?"

The man pointed across the street. Jack gave the building a skeptical perusal before reaching out to help Kathleen down from the carriage. "You're certain you don't know anyone in Boston with whom you might stay?" he asked.

"Donnelly—"

"Besides him."

"Only the Boyles, like I've said before. But even if they're here still, how would we find them?" She pulled her hood up against the wind.

Jack nodded. She was right; it would be next to impossible to find someone in this city, especially in one day. He looked down the nearly empty street. Only a peddler and several underdressed and unsupervised children were outside, but he knew that the apartments inside were crowded with Irish families.

They crossed the street and stopped outside an old boarding house; a sign in the window announced there were no rooms to let. He cursed under his breath and pounded on the door anyway.

"Jack, it's full," Kathleen said. "The sign says—"

A thin, weary old woman pulled open the door and eyed Jack warily. "Yes?"

"I'm sorry to bother you," Jack said. "But we're looking for a room to let and wondered if you might know of one in the neighborhood."

She eyed him up and down. "The two of you?"

"No, no. Just for her."

"I've just come across," Kathleen said.

The old woman's face softened. "Ah, well, lass, you might try the building on the corner—there on the left." She pointed down the block. "They may still have a room open. It's a grand one, I hear."

"Sounds perfect, thank you." Jack waved for the carriage to follow, then set off at a fast clip on foot, slowing a little to let

Kathleen catch up with him. *A grand one.* He certainly hoped so. Finally he could get Kathleen settled, then head home and do his damndest to forget about her.

They neared the building, its exterior as decrepit as every other they had seen. He stopped and let out a slow breath as his gaze slid up the three story tenement. *Grand?* It looked no better than any they had seen today.

"It's probably nicer inside," Kathleen said hopefully.

He nodded, knowing that any optimism was little more than wishful thinking. He pulled open the door and the knob wobbled loosely in his hand. As he stepped into the hallway, the acid odor of ammonia met his nostrils. Urine. He curled one hand into a fist of frustration and forced his mind to stay open—surely the room for let would be *grand* as the woman had said.

A sign directed them to the manager on the second floor and they started up the sagging stairs, most worn so thin in the center they didn't look strong enough to take the full weight of a man. He warned Kathleen to be careful, then stepped gingerly on the outside edges.

Stained walls lined the dim second floor hallway. Jack stopped at the first open door; a brood of children playfully tumbled and screeched in the dingy room. What little plaster remained on the walls was yellowed and greasy.

Jack stole a glance at Kathleen but she showed no reaction

He hesitated, his uncertainty growing, then made himself knock firmly on the doorframe. A woman appeared out of some other room. "Aye?" She pushed her black hair behind her ears.

"We're here about the room for let," he said. "Are you the manager?"

"Last door on the left." She looked Kathleen up and down. "Where are you from?"

Kathleen nodded. "Cobh."

"If ye have no luck, we might take you in here if you can pay. Have you work?"

Kathleen shook her head.

"The factories are hiring girls. It's a long workday, but—"

"Me brother thought I might find work as household staff."

"Aye, that too. Most likely a maid—or a housekeeper. Either way, you'll get a room free then at the house."

Half-listening, Jack went ahead down the hallway. He knocked at the manager's door and found himself almost hoping the man wasn't in. As the door opened, he gave himself a mental shake and asked about the available room. The manager grinned. "Yes, yes, still open," he said. "As nice as you'll find in all the area. Let me show you."

He led Jack and Kathleen back down the stairs to the cellar. "Cool in the summer, warm in the winter as it's half below ground, you know," he chatted.

As they stepped into the basement room, a dank odor assailed them. Mildew stained the walls in a line a few inches above the floor, and discolored the corners of the ceiling. Jack nodded at the ground-level windows. "When it rains—is there any problem with water?"

The man turned to Kathleen. "Basement apartments are first choice by most—"

"Does it get water?" Jack asked.

The landlord made a face. "Perhaps a wee bit, sure. Still, because of that I'll let ye have it for half the price—just a dollar a week instead of two. Paid in advance of course."

Kathleen smiled. "It's certainly more affordable than the others we've seen. I think it will be fine."

He didn't doubt she could live in these conditions, he just didn't know if he could leave her in them. It felt like minutes passed as he said nothing, just played everything over in his mind.

"You want it then?" the manager asked.

Jack took a step back. "No. It won't do. Not this place. But thank you for showing it to us." He grabbed Kathleen's hand and tugged her up the stairs and into the street.

The snow was falling more heavily now, wet and heavy, a sharp wind driving it against the buildings making them look to be freshly whitewashed. He pulled Kathleen round to face him. Wet flakes dropped on her cheeks and melted from her warmth. She reached up a hand to brush the dampness away.

"You can't stay there," he said.

"I know it looks horrid to you," she answered. "But the basement room, or with Donnelly's sister, or even with that family on the second floor... Jack, 'tis no worse than my home in Ireland. In some ways, it might even be better, what with me being the only one living there. And the rent, so cheap—"

He threw his hands up and cursed. "Don't tell me. I don't want to know any more. I don't want to know." He looked up at the building again. Damn her. If he left her here, he might as well condemn her to a life no better than the one she'd left behind. *If he left her here, he might never see her again.* The thought left a hollow in his chest.

He took hold of her arm and pulled her toward the carriage. "You're not staying here. You're going to be a maid and have a room of your own in a nice house."

"What? Jack, what are you doing?"

The carriage driver jumped down to open the door and Jack propelled Kathleen inside.

"Take us home. We've had enough." He followed Kathleen into the carriage and took a seat.

"Jack, what are you saying?"

"You're going to be a maid, Kathleen. For my grandfather."

*

Kathleen let out an incredulous laugh. "Are ye mad?"

"To the contrary, this is perhaps the sanest thing I've done all day."

"Nay, sir. 'Tis insanity. Your grandfather has no use for the Irish." *Faith, but the old man would think they were lovers for certain.* She crossed her arms over her chest. "I'll not work for him. And he'll not have me anyway."

"He will. It might not be a pretty discussion, but in the end, he'll come around."

"Why would you do this to me?"

"Kathleen. Believe it or not, I'm helping you. It's a job—with room and board included—"

"Working for an Englishman who believes the Irish are lazy and stupid." She shook her head. She couldn't do it, couldn't work for a man just like those who had forced her from her country. "He'll have fired me within the week."

Jack snorted. "Even Margaret lasted several months—"

"It's my life we're speaking of, Captain. Not some jest."

"You need work, Kathleen, to save your family. I'm offering you work. Yes, my grandfather can be difficult to get along with— and he may not be immediately agreeable to this plan. But, believe me, he *will* agree."

Panic pressed against her lungs. "But he's hired someone else already."

Jack shrugged.

"He'll let me go as soon as you are out to sea again."

"No. I'll make certain of that. You'll have a job as long as you want one."

"But he...has no use for the Irish." Her voice dropped to a whisper. "And he thinks..."

"Thinks what?"

She looked directly into his dark eyes and forced herself to hold his gaze. "He thinks you and I are...lovers. Said so last evening when you were out of the room."

Jack threw back his head and laughed. Then he took her hand and kissed her knuckles. "Kathleen Deacey, I'm half tempted to scandalize him by making it come true."

She jerked her hand away. "It's nothing to joke about, sir. I'll find some other job. In a factory, perhaps. I'll not work for an Englishman who hates the Irish and thinks me a woman of no virtue besides!"

She could tell by the set of Jack's jaw that he was not happy with her response. After several tense moments, he banged on the carriage ceiling.

She pushed back in her seat? Was he going to put her out right here and now?

Before the carriage had even rolled to a stop, he shoved open the door and jumped out into the falling snow. Minutes later he slid into the seat opposite her, shook the snow off a newspaper, and pointed to a story about Ireland. "Read this."

Angling the paper toward the light, she read only the first paragraph before fear slipped its fingers around her gut and squeezed. She read the rest of the story, then rubbed a hand across her brow. Her country was faring far worse than she had even imagined. What did that mean for her family?

Jack took the newspaper and flipped through several pages before turning it back on itself and handing it to her again. "Now look at this page."

She glanced at the page of Help Wanted advertisements. "There are many job openings…"

He moved across to sit beside her and pointed to a prominent ad. "Read that line."

"None need apply but Americans."

He pointed to another ad. "And that."

"No Irish need apply." She sucked in a breath.

"And that." He pointed again.

"English, Scotch, Welsh, German, or any country or color *except Irish* may apply."

He pointed again and again.

Finally, she let the newspaper drop into her lap. Things were no different here than in Ireland. The English would make sure the Irish didn't survive in any country. She closed her eyes and put a hand to the bridge of her nose.

"I'm offering you a job," Jack said quietly. "And your employer will be no worse than any other you might get. Kathleen—do you understand?"

She thought back to the day she left Ireland, how she had vowed to survive, to do whatever it took to help her family. This was what it would take. Eyes still shut, she nodded.

*

"Absolutely not!"

The captain's grandfather pushed himself off the settee and

shuffled across the sitting room, jamming his cane into the carpet with each step for effect, even though the thick rug swallowed any sound. "I'm done employing the—"

He stopped in front of the hearth and tossed a glance at Kathleen where she stood inside the doorway. "I've hired a woman—an *Englishwoman*. Hardworking, reliable, honest."

Jack settled into a wingback chair and motioned for Kathleen to take the matching chair next to him. "Then un-hire her."

"No." The old man glowered at her.

He probably thought this was her idea so she and Jack could continue with their dalliance. She bit her tongue to keep from making some comment to that effect.

Jack crossed his arms. "I've hired Miss Deacey—"

"And I've hired Miss…Englishwoman…"

If their disagreement wasn't so vehement, Kathleen might have laughed.

"Miss Deacey has some knowledge of nursing so she'll be able to help you with your rheumatism, your aches," Jack said matter-of-factly.

She blanched. Jesus, Mary, and holy Joseph, but he was lying outright now. What would happen when the old man learned the truth? "Captain you flatter me. I would not go so far as to—"

"Irish superstition, most likely," the grandfather muttered. "Faerie and leprechaun nonsense."

"Watch what you're saying, sir." Kathleen made sure her voice was loud enough for him to hear. "The Good People do not take kindly to slurs against—"

"And you expect me to live with this every day?" The old man almost lost his balance as he twisted round to confront Jack face to face.

And I to live with the likes of him? her mind shot back. With all she had endured to get to America, she could hardly stomach the idea of working for someone who despised her only because of her nationality—and had no fear of making it known.

Jack raised an eyebrow at his grandfather. "She'll make a good maid."

"I *hired* a good maid."

"I doubt it."

The two men stared at one another, neither speaking nor yielding.

"I was thinking of getting out of the whaling business," Jack said finally. "Give up my ownership share of the ship. Move away. Maybe try farming."

Kathleen caught her breath. What was he doing?

The grandfather laughed. "You never would."

"Try me. You know I've hated whaling since the beginning."

"You would quit when you're so close to reaching so many goals?"

Jack sat back in his chair and nodded.

"You son of—" the old man said through clenched teeth.

"Son of your son." Jack smiled.

The old man rammed the end of his cane into the carpet again. "That you are."

Eyes narrowed, he limped back to the settee and slowly lowered himself to the cushion. He waved a dismissive hand at her. "You know which room is the maid's—you slept in it last night. Mind you, if you give me but one reason, I'll send you on your way."

She had no doubt of that.

"She'll work out fine." Jack smiled reassuringly at her. "Now tell me where to find the woman you hired," he said to his grandfather, "and I'll let her know the job is no longer available."

The old man muttered something unintelligible.

"What?"

"I hadn't actually hired anyone yet. Margaret only just quit day before yesterday and I figured Emma could handle everything for a while."

"The cook? She's too old to handle both duties."

The old man ignored him and pointed his cane at Kathleen. "I don't recall your name…Bridget, Molly, Colleen…"

She straightened her shoulders and raised her chin. "Kathleen. Kathleen Deacey."

"Ah, yes. Daisy. Doesn't sound very Irish."

"'Tis Deacey. Not daisy."

"Yes, well. I hope you know your place—*Kathleen*. My breakfast is served at seven."

*

She closed the bedroom door behind her and sagged against the wall. How could Jack expect this to work? His grandfather had so much contempt for the Irish and here she was living in his home. Yet if the newspaper advertisements were any indication—*no Irish need apply*—most of Boston was prejudiced against the Irish.

Sean had told her so many things before she'd left Ireland, but most often what he'd said was that America was the land of opportunity, that anyone could have a better life in America. Sure, it would be a bitter pill for him to swallow when he learned that bigotry was alive and well even here.

She turned and looked around the room—*her room*. It had a real bed—not straw. And there was carpet on the floor, and a writing table and chest of drawers against the wall. After all the wretched places they had seen today… Her heart warmed at Jack's generosity, so different from his grandfather. There might be hope for the Irish in America if there were more people like Jack.

She stepped past the bed and went to the window, pressed her hands to the sill and let her forehead rest against the cold glass. She'd never been very good at holding her temper, and now to spend each day with this Englishman who hated her…

How could she do it?

How could she not?

Da would tell her to be glad for the work in these difficult times. And Ma, Kathleen could see her shaking her head and gently admonishing, "*Brígh gach cluiche gu dheireadh*. The essence of a game is at its end."

She pulled the tiebacks off the drapes and let the heavy fabric fall across the window. She had no right to be complaining about dealing with one man's prejudice, not when thousands of Irish were facing that same prejudice every day—and dying because of it.

If she must endure the tirades of an Englishman so that her family might live, so be it, she would suffer without complaint. 'Twould give her great satisfaction to know that by paying her, this man who so despised the Irish would unwittingly rescue them.

CHAPTER EIGHTEEN

EIGHT O'CLOCK IN the morning and already the old man was complaining. Kathleen brushed the feather duster across the dark wood of the fireplace mantel. In the four days since she'd been hired, she had yet to see a smile cross his face. Now she could hear him grumbling to Jack in the dining room.

"I thought I'd taken a copy of the Post," he was saying. "And instead I grabbed this Irish rag."

"Just because you have it doesn't mean you have to read it."

"I should burn this thing. They're blaming England for the famine."

"Who is?"

"The Irish."

Kathleen stiffened.

"It's an Irish paper, what do you expect?" Jack said. "Besides, it may be true."

"What?" The old man snapped out the word so hard it sounded like a slap.

"England isn't doing much to help—"

"Those people need to help themselves. The Irish need to take responsibility for their lives, get jobs. If they weren't so lazy—"

"How?" Jack's voice took on an edge. "Their potato crop failed two years in a row. The country is in famine. How does a starving man make food? How does he find work when there are no jobs? Don't tell me you've forgotten why my mother and I landed on your doorstep."

After a long pause, the old man answered, "I haven't forgotten."

Kathleen stared in the direction of the dining room, waited to hear more, but not even the scrape of a fork on a plate broke the heavy silence that followed. Finally, she set down the duster, pasted a smile on her face and went into the room to clear away the dishes. She stopped beside the grandfather's chair. "Are you done with your breakfast…sir?"

He shoved his plate toward her without looking up from the newspaper.

"And you, Captain?"

"Yes. Thank you, Miss Deacey."

The grandfather's head jerked up. "Kathleen," he bit out. "She's a domestic—not a lady."

Jack's expression froze and Kathleen could tell he was debating whether this was a battle worth fighting. She drew herself up proudly and let the insult roll past.

Finally, Jack gave the old man an almost imperceptible nod. "Thank you…Kathleen."

Her name rolled off his tongue, smooth and fine, and for a moment she was wrapped in the warmth of his voice. She cleared the table, knowing that for all of Jack's kindness, his grandfather's disdain could make her life very difficult. He had made his views clear her first morning on the job, as soon as Jack had left the house.

"I expect you to be truthful, conscientious, and obliging," he'd said. "In other words, aspire to reach the class of an *Englishwoman*. Complaints about your wages will be grounds for dismissal. As will any display of ambition toward my grandson."

He may have yielded to Jack's demand that she be hired, but he was determined to make her quit. She allowed herself a tight smile. What the old man didn't know was that she'd never been one to back down from a challenge. To be sure, it had been her undoing often enough as a child, but it wouldn't be happening here. 'Twas steady work when so many others refused to hire the Irish. Her own room, plenty to eat, and two afternoons off a week. This job was a fine gift and she would make it work if it killed her.

"What's for supper this evening?" the old man asked when she returned for the last of the dishes.

She hesitated.

"You do remember Emma has the night off. You can cook, can't you?"

By God, it might kill her after all. Of course she remembered. "I was thinking of making a fine stew for you, sir."

He looked at Jack pointedly. "I should have known."

"I never learned to make much else, for we seldom had much else to cook." The words were out of her mouth before she had a chance to stop them.

The old man's face reddened. Jack brought his hands together with a clap and rubbed his palms against one other. "Stew it is," he said. "And I can't wait."

"I'll have my tea by the fire." The grandfather pushed back his chair and eased himself up. "Jack? Can you join me before your appointment?"

"A few minutes."

Kathleen knew that over the past few days Jack had been

meeting with investors about his next whaling voyage. Last night she'd heard him tell his grandfather things were smoothly falling into place. Her stomach took a nervous jump. She understood that he had to go to sea to earn a living, but the thought of staying here alone with his grandfather sent a wave of anxiety through her. She feared the old man might have a mind to let her go as soon as Jack set sail.

"Have you given a thought to anything besides business these past days?" the grandfather asked as they left the room.

"Such as?"

"Such as Emily Cuthbert."

Kathleen slowed her steps toward the kitchen as she remembered the handkerchief in the book of poetry in Jack's quarters, a lace-edged square with E C embroidered in the corner. A muscle beneath her breastbone tightened into a knot. Was this the woman his grandfather had said Jack was to marry?

"Jack?" the grandfather asked.

"Not yet."

"For God's sake, when?"

Jack shrugged.

"At least call on her. You've been back four days and made no effort."

"I will."

Kathleen could delay no longer without appearing obvious. She hurried into the kitchen and quickly gathered the tea service, but by the time she brought the tray to the parlor, the discussion had turned to whaling and Jack seemed distracted.

On her way back to the kitchen, she spied the discarded newspaper on the dining table and scooped it up. An *Irish rag* the old man had called it, and she was eager to see what he had been so upset about. Her prize tucked under one arm, she retreated to the kitchen.

"You'll have to teach me something about cooking," she said to Emma as she spread the newspaper open on the small table in the corner meant for staff meals. She perched on the edge of a chair. "Sure and the old man won't be agreeing to stew every time you've got half a day off."

Emma wiped her flour-covered hands on the apron stretched around her ample frame. Her white hair was loosely rolled in a knot at her nape that showed the last few inches of her long hair still to be brown. "Serve him right it would," she muttered, the sagging skin on her cheeks and neck wobbling with irritation. "Crotchety old goat could try to be nice."

"Especially to the Irish." Kathleen quickly browsed the articles about Ireland—news of widespread starvation, evictions and deaths, of the worst winter in memory. She gripped the edge of the table. Da and Ma were no longer so young. And with three children still at home, plus Sean and Moira, what little food they'd had when she left Ireland must nearly be gone by now. Panic surged through her.

"Emma, but I canna hardly bear the not knowing," she said. "A month will have passed before me family receives the letter I sent…and another beyond that before I hear back. It takes so long to hear anything."

Emma pressed her plump fingers into a large ball of dough and kneaded forcefully. "They've invented a machine that sends messages over a wire, quick as you can read a letter. My grandson read it to me from the newspaper a while back."

"Over a wire? Impossible." Kathleen squinted at Emma and shook her head.

"Telegraph, it's called. They set up a wire between Washington DC and New York, and now they're sending messages back and forth. *Right on that wire.*"

Kathleen sat back in her chair and shook her head. "The world moves forward with leaps and bounds, yet the best Ireland can ever hope for is survival."

She turned the newspaper page and spotted the Help Wanted ads spewing their prejudiced hatred against the Irish. Messages were traveling over wires and yet, even in the land of opportunity, the Irish couldn't get jobs. How had it come to be like this?

She flipped another page, then stopped and slowly turned back, searching for something she had seen, a sentence, a phrase that had caught her subconscious. When she spotted it again, she gasped. "Emma, sure but ye'll not be believing what I've found. Listen to this."

She began to read aloud. "Kevin McDermott, who is supposed to be in Toronto, Canada, will please write to Ignatius Goggins, No. 26, Butolph Street, Boston, Massachusetts... Mary Hurley, who left Ireland last March, and when last heard from was at Long Island, New York. She is a native of county Roscommon, parish of Cloonfinlough. Any information respecting her will be thankfully received by her brother, Patrick Hurley, care of Valentine Edmonds, Newtown Centre, Massachusetts."

"Are these friends of yours?" Emma asked.

"Nay. Don't you see, the Irish are advertising to find one another. Look here, a whole column of notices. Someone seeks word of Patrick O'Connell, from County Westmeath, who was supposed to be in New York; and John Clark's wife is looking for him. Why it says she has not heard from him since last July and does not even know what part of the country he is in."

"A terrible thing." Emma clucked her tongue.

"Think of what this means—I might find the Boyles," Kathleen exclaimed. "And look here, half the listings are for people in other places…like New York and Canada."

Emma smiled knowingly. "Will you place a notice, then, in Newfoundland?"

Kathleen gave a jubilant laugh. She could search for Danny without giving up her job, without having to travel to Newfoundland. Faith, but the old man had again helped her without even knowing it. 'Twas a grand day after all.

"I've a wee bit of money the captain advanced me," she said. And tomorrow afternoon off. It would seem to make sense I place a notice for the Boyles, don't you think? And post a letter to the newspaper up in Newfoundland."

"Seems most sensible to me."

Kathleen pursed her lips. She would have to compose the notices later tonight once she was off duty. The writing would be easy if she could copy the wording straight from the newspaper. But if the old man threw it on the fire like he'd threatened… She glanced at the door before hurriedly removing the page, folding it in half, and pushing it into the cookie jar to retrieve later. 'Twasn't likely the old man would notice the page missing, even if he bothered to look at the paper again.

*

Twelve hours later she dragged herself up the stairs to her room. Her head ached as much as her legs. Jack had brought two friends home for supper, one of them Matson, the first mate from the ship. It had been wonderful to see Matson again, but of what could Jack have been thinking, bringing guests home on a night when the cook was off?

At least the men had liked the stew; even the grandfather hadn't said a bad word about it, which was probably the best she could ever expect from him. Still, between cooking and serving and cleaning up, she hadn't stopped moving since four o'clock. And then, just when she thought the men were about to leave, they had retired to the parlor for drinks and cards.

She threw herself face down on the bed and closed her eyes, too exhausted to undress, too weary to climb beneath the blankets. Just a few minutes she'd lie here, just a few. Thank goodness tomorrow was but a half a day of work—

The notices.

Her eyes rolled open and she wanted to weep. She had not yet written the advertisements; and the newspaper page was still in the cookie jar. She stared at the wall and willed the thought to go away even as she knew she would push herself from the bed and do this thing this night. She had no choice; if she didn't place the notices tomorrow, she would have to wait days before she had time off again.

"Done soon enough if you'll just get started," she muttered and forced herself to her feet. Holding a lamp in front of her, she crept down the stairs to the flickering light. The shadows tripped and danced, and she had the sense that she wasn't alone, though she knew the captain and his grandfather were both abed. Late enough it was for certain faeries to be about—and none she would ever want to be seeing. Though truth be told, she'd never heard mention of the Good People being in America; perhaps they were smart enough not to leave Ireland.

She pushed through the door to the kitchen and let out a startled cry at the sight of a figure in the shadows hunched over the kitchen table.

"Easy Kathleen," Jack murmured. He took a cookie off the pile he'd set on the table, dipped it into a glass of milk, then proceeded to eat it as he bent over the newspaper spread before him.

She narrowed her eyes in the dim light to better see what he was reading. 'Twas *her* newspaper page, the one with the Irish notices in it, from the cookie jar. Her stomach plunged. Lord save her, should she admit it was hers and ask forgiveness for tearing the grandfather's newspaper?

"I found this in the cookies." He patted the paper.

She mentally raced through replies, discarding each as quickly as it came to mind. She could almost see her mother shaking a finger and saying, "One lie begets another." And yet…if she thought on it, more than once Ma had said, "Necessity knows no law." Oh, but clearly her mother would be of little help this eve.

"I'm surprised that milk isn't curdling in your belly after all the whiskey ye had tonight," she said, grinning.

Jack raised an eyebrow.

She sighed. "Oh fine, it's me newspaper," she said. "I'm sorry. I shouldn't have taken it."

He shrugged. "Doesn't matter to me." He held up a cookie. "There aren't any nuts."

"What?"

"Nuts. These cookies need nuts."

Kathleen gaped at him. Clearly the man was well into his cups. "I'll tell Emma tomorrow."

"Did you see these notices?"

"Aye," she said cautiously.

"I didn't know the Irish were doing this—searching for people this way."

"Nor I, until this morning."

"Anyone you know?" he asked.

"Excuse me?"

He gestured at the page. "Listed here. Anyone you know?"

She shook her head.

"Want a cookie?" Jack shoved a chair out from the table with his foot and gestured for her to take a seat.

What she really wanted was that newspaper, so she could be getting her advertisements written and get off to bed, but it didn't appear Jack would be giving it up yet. She slid into the chair without answering and took a cookie off the pile.

"What was the name of those friends of yours—in Boston?"

"Boyle." She took a big bite of her cookie.

"Perhaps you could find them this way. Place a notice. What do you think?"

She felt a rush of warmth so great a smile burst across her face and a chunk of cookie dropped from her mouth. "What a grand idea. I'd been thinking the same," she said with her mouth full.

A piece of cookie stuck in her throat and she leaned forward, coughing. Jack shoved his glass at her and she took several swallows in quick succession, coughing again as the milk burned its way down her throat and tears sprang to her eyes.

"What have ye in that?" she asked with a gasp.

He gave her a lopsided grin. "A little whiskey, a bit of sugar. Milk punch it's called."

"Are ye certain you're not Irish after all?"

He laughed outright. "Can I get you a glass of your own?"

"No thank you."

"It'll help you sleep."

"I'll need no help sleeping this night. I've notices to write and I must keep me wits about me."

"And work on the morrow."

"Aye, that too…" She rubbed a tired hand across her eyes. "So, Jack, are you quite done with that page now?"

"We haven't written your notice."

She shook her head. "You need not help me."

"I insist."

"I think the whiskey's talking now. You might be better off getting some sleep."

"Don't go anywhere." Jack left the room and returned moments later with pen, ink and paper. "You dictate, I'll write," he said, dropping back into his chair.

"Best not be letting your grandfather catch ye working for the help. Who knows what holy hell might ensue." She slid the newspaper page around so she could check the wording in the notices, then dictated a notice for the Boyles. As she neared the end, she slowed her words. "…Any information should be sent to Kathleen Deacey at—" She hesitated. "I suppose replies should be sent to the local postmaster."

"Have them sent here. It'll be easier," Jack said as he wrote down his address.

"But your grandfather—"

He shoved the paper across the table for her approval. "If he complains, I'll handle it. You shouldn't have to run around town to get your replies."

She shoved the paper back. "One more notice, first. I'll be doing one more. For me Danny."

He looked at her hard for a split second before he raised his glass to his lips and finished off what remained of the milk punch. Then he took up the pen and fixed his attention on her. The joviality was gone from his eyes. "Speak."

"Of Daniel O'Sheehan, native of—"

"How's he going to see this if he's in Newfoundland?"

"There are plenty of others placing notices for people last heard from in cities other than Boston. It's worth trying. For all we know, he could be in Boston now anyway."

"Undoubtedly," Jack muttered.

"It would be my greatest joy if he were here." She dictated the notice, finishing it off with: "...When last heard from, he was working at the fisheries in Newfoundland. Any information respecting him will be thankfully received by...his betrothed... Kathleen Deacey, care of Captain Jack Montgomery, Boston, Massachusetts."

Jack finished writing, then slouched back into his chair. "Be careful what you wish for, Kathleen. You might just get it."

"What mean ye by that?"

He shrugged. "Maybe Danny doesn't want to be found. Maybe he stayed behind for a reason."

He had just said aloud what she wouldn't even let herself think. "You've had too much drink tonight to be making sense," she said evenly.

"Perhaps. And perhaps I've had so much to drink I see things all the clearer."

Her stomach lurched. She pressed her lips together in a tight smile and gathered together the papers. "Now that we've finished, it's time I retired. Thank you for your help, Captain."

"Do you know where the newspaper office is?"

"No, but I can ask—"

"Take the street to market, turn—" He paused, thinking. His eyes began to slide shut. "It's a little complicated."

"Perhaps even more so because you're so into your cups," she said under her breath.

"What?"

She shook her head. "Emma can tell me how to get there."

"You're off tomorrow afternoon."

"Aye."

"I'll take you."

"Oh, no," she said. "It's not necessary. Emma will tell me the way."

Jack stretched his legs out under the table, put his hands behind his head and closed his eyes. "I'll come back for you about one o'clock."

"I don't think—"

"Don't think, Kathleen. Go to bed." His voice had the soft tones of a man slipping into sleep.

"A fine idea. Perhaps you should take your own advice before ye spend the night down here."

"Sweet dreams," he murmured.

She shook her head as she stepped across the kitchen and into the hall; the man would be asleep before she reached the top stair. And surely his head would be aching tomorrow. 'Twas likely he would not be remembering anything he'd said here tonight. Just as well. This was her business, her problem, after all, not his. She'd find the newspaper office herself.

She took the stairs slowly and contemplated Jack's remarks about Danny. Drunk or not, the man had no right to say what he had. Her betrothed wasn't some scoundrel who cared not whether he broke her heart. He would never have *chosen* to stay behind—not with Kathleen and his homeland waiting for him across the ocean. He would never willingly hurt her.

Damn Jack Montgomery. How dare he say such a thing about someone he'd never even met? She pushed open her bedroom door, her mind now restless with the possibility that Jack was right.

There was but one solution to her turmoil—she must find Danny. His presence would put these troubling thoughts to rest. Fighting exhaustion, she seated herself at the small desk in the corner and penned a letter to the newspaper in St. John's, Newfoundland, asking them to run a notice to help her find Danny O'Sheehan, a missing friend from Ireland.

CHAPTER NINETEEN

JACK PICKED HIS steps carefully along the frozen walk. A chill wind spun snow down from low charcoal clouds. Head down, he squinted pained eyes against the overcast day and rued the amount of whiskey he'd had to drink the evening before. He hardly remembered saying goodbye to his friends and definitely didn't remember going to bed.

His foot skidded across an icy patch and he fought to hold his balance, wincing as his brain banged against the inside of his skull. Though the brisk winter air had eased his headache, the cold added a fresh layer of discomfort.

Thank God, he was almost home. He'd gotten little work done this morning and finally gave up, deciding what he needed more than anything was a nap. A nap and a quiet afternoon at home.

As he neared his front steps, a woman's voice cut through his mental haze. "I can't believe you remembered," she said. "I almost didn't wait."

He raised his head. Kathleen stood directly in front of him, the hood of her dark cloak sprinkled with flakes of snow.

"Remembered what?" he asked.

She grinned. "And I'll be guessing I was right."

The wind caught a nearby door and slammed it shut; the noise reverberated down his spine. He should know better than to drink so much.

She laughed and the sound smoothed some of the rough edges in his head. "It's all right, you don't have to take me," she said. "Emma told me how to get there."

"Good." He tried to force his sluggish brain to figure out what she was talking about. "So you're going now, are you?"

"One o'clock, just like we said."

We did?

"If you don't mind me saying so, you look a wee bit peaked. I'll be thinking a nap might do ye good." As she moved to step past him, she slipped in the dusting of snow and let out a squeal.

"Careful," Jack said. "It's treacherous today." He looked at her worn shoes and berated himself for not getting her a new pair that first day when he bought her clothing. "Perhaps you should put off this errand a day or two."

She shook her head. "If I hurry, I'll be done in no time."

If she hurried in those shoes, she'd end up with a broken leg. "I really think you should wait."

"It's far too important to wait. You said as much yourself last night."

He blew out an irritated breath and pushed away the vision of napping that had been fixed in his mind all morning. "Fine, then I'll walk you—"

"It truly isn't necessary—"

"I said I would last night…" He took a wild guess. "Didn't I?"

She smiled. "That ye did."

"Well then." He held out an arm and she took hold of it. "Where was our first stop again?" he asked.

"Just the one. The Boston Pilot."

"Oh, yes, the newspaper." Why the hell were they going there? He considered asking but didn't want to let her know how little he remembered of the night before.

They walked the entire distance without exchanging more than a sentence or two, and most of those words simply involved pointing out one patch of ice or another. Jack knew he wasn't being particularly mannerly but the pain in his head and the churning in his gut were enough to keep him from caring.

Inside the newspaper office, Kathleen drew a piece of paper from beneath her cloak, smoothed it on the dark polished wood counter, and described to the clerk the notices she wished to place. Jack leaned against the counter for support, the dull throb in his head growing in the warmth of the building. Absently he gazed at the words on the sheet Kathleen had laid out, then drew back in surprise when he recognized the handwriting. *It was his.*

He tried to remember penning those words and offering to accompany Kathleen today. A memory hovered around the edges of his mind, teasing and vague, like a thin puff of smoke seen only for an instant before it dissipates. As he mentally tugged the recollection toward consciousness, it slipped away.

By the time they headed back out into the cold, he couldn't contain his curiosity. "Do you think it will work? Placing a notice like that?" he asked.

"You saw the listings yourself, Captain. It must be working for some, else why would so many be doing it?"

He'd read the listings? He gave up trying to remember.

The snow was falling more heavily now, swirling in the gusty breeze and scattering like spring blossoms months ahead of schedule. The wind raced up the empty street toward them and Jack bent his head against its bite, eyes on the slick walk ahead.

"Perhaps you should take my arm," he murmured.

Kathleen leaned toward him, brow furrowed. "What did you say?"

Her foot hit a patch of ice hidden beneath the fresh dusting of snow and she slid awkwardly, shoulders jerking up. She teetered, arms flailing as she fought to keep her balance. Jack grasped her arms, she grabbed hold of his coat, and they hung suspended for a brief moment before her momentum carried them down. He landed hard, left leg twisting as the whole of Kathleen's weight slammed into his calf and shoved it back. Pain exploded through his ankle.

Kathleen scrambled up, brushing at the snow on her skirt and apologizing profusely. "Captain, are ye all right? I heard something pop when I landed. It wasn't a bone breaking now, was it?"

"I hope not." His ankle throbbed. He ran a hand down his lower leg and gently probed the painful area. "I don't think so."

With Kathleen's help, he struggled to his feet and gingerly tried to put some weight on his injured leg. A grunt of pain forced its way out of his mouth.

"Ye can't walk," she cried. "Faith, but how are we to get you home?"

"I can walk." The words came out harsh from between gritted teeth. "Just let me lean on you."

He pulled her close and rested his arm across the back of her shoulders though she was much shorter than he. All he'd wanted was a nap. And now that nap was getting further and further away.

After several minutes of slow going, he stopped to let the pain in his ankle ease.

"Are you all right?" she asked, dismayed.

"My headache is gone."

"Well I suppose that's good."

"Next time—" He pushed the words out from between clenched teeth. "Next time, go without me if I'm late."

"I wasn't waiting for ye. If you'd been any more minutes late, I'd have been gone already."

He grunted aloud and cursed silently.

"After all you had to drink the night before, I had no idea whether you even remembered one o'clock. And if I were supposed to go alone, why then, it didn't really matter whether I went at that time anyway."

Jack felt the stirrings of his headache returning. He stepped too hard on his injured leg and sucked in his breath to ease the pain. "I remembered, dammit, I remembered," he lied.

"There's no reason to curse, now, Captain."

"Oh yes there is."

They made slow progress; what should have been a fifteen minute walk took nearly half an hour. By the time they reached home, his shirt was wet with sweat despite the cold. Kathleen got him settled onto the sofa with his leg elevated, then ran to find his grandfather.

Several minutes later, the old man hobbled into the room. "How the devil did this happen?" he demanded.

"I fell." Jack shifted uncomfortably and the movement sent a stab of pain through his ankle. "Pour me some whiskey, Gramps, will you? I've got to take the edge off this."

"I've sent Kathleen to fetch the doctor." His grandfather filled a glass and watched as Jack threw the whole thing down in several gulps. "If you've broken something, it'll be many months before you set sail again."

"Nothing's broken."

"What were you doing with that Irish girl?" The old man lowered himself into a chair.

"I just showed her the way to the Pilot office."

"The newspaper?" His grandfather's face lightened. "Is she looking for a new job?"

Jack laughed despite his pain. "She's trying to find some friends she thinks are in Boston. She's worried about her family and hoping they may have heard something—"

"Ah yes, they're starving in Ireland—again. And they're starving here in Boston, too, in their slums." The old man slapped the armrest. "If they'd ever learned to put in an honest day's work… Well, the Irish need to quit crying about their lot and set about improving it."

From the foyer, came the sound of the entrance door slamming shut.

"They'd have far better luck improving their lot if some of the fine English in America would see fit to hire them." Kathleen's muttered words carried into the room. She rounded the corner followed by the doctor.

Jack glanced at his grandfather, but the old man appeared not to have heard. For once he was grateful his grandfather's hearing had begun to fail.

Kathleen waited in the doorway while the doctor pulled a hard-backed chair to the sofa and set his bag on the floor. "So you've hurt your ankle. Let's take a look," he said.

"Bring some tea, Kathleen," his grandfather said brusquely.

Jack eased his trouser leg up, pain rippling through his ankle even from that slight movement. One glance at the swollen joint and, even without the doctor's prognosis, he was quite certain he would be laid up for a while.

After a thorough examination and several questions, the doctor sat back into his chair with a sigh. "You're lucky. Nothing's broken, but you have a nasty sprain. I wouldn't doubt if you separated the muscle."

"How long?"

"Until you're healed? A simple sprain would be…" He shrugged. "Two weeks. But this will take several at least, perhaps a month. You need to stay off that foot. And keep it elevated."

His grandfather turned his head to hear better. "How long?" he asked.

"Could be a month," the doctor said in a louder voice.

The old man cursed. "Mark my words, you'll live to rue the day you saved that girl."

Jack nodded, his anger putting him in sullen agreement with his grandfather for once. "I already have. Several times."

*

Tea service in hand, Kathleen froze in the hallway. Jack Montgomery—the closest thing she had to a friend in America— wished he'd never saved her. She swallowed hard, then raised her chin and went into the parlor to offer tea in the cheeriest voice she could muster. The doctor declined, but she poured a cup for both Jack and his grandfather, then left the service on the table.

Then, because it was still her afternoon off, she stepped quietly away and went up to her room, locking the door behind her as if the wood panel could block the hurt caused by Jack's words.

She stoked the fire, stabbed at it, taking bitter satisfaction in the sparks that landed on the hearth rug, glowing red for a moment before she ground them out with her foot. Had she truly been such a curse? She set another log on the fire and watched it disappear into the yellow flames that engulfed it. Like it had never existed at all.

She felt an overwhelming yearning for home, a longing to be somewhere she was accepted and loved. This country was so different, so fast and busy, like it was in a hurry to leave the past behind. While Ireland held tight to its past so its people would never forget what true freedom felt like.

She pictured Ireland before the famine, the gentle green hills and gray stone fences, the rain falling soft and steady, the gardens and neighbors and singing and laughter.

Reality burst in and quashed the memory. There would be no escaping the reason she was so far from home, no escaping that the Ireland she longed for no longer existed, and her life would never again be as she had known it.

She thought of Jack's angry words. Truth be told, she had been a bit of trouble for him these past few months…perhaps even more than a bit. Sure and today was the worst. If she hadna insisted on going to the Pilot today, he wouldn't have fallen. He wouldn't be trapped at home, unable to walk for perhaps a month, nor would he be thinking about pushing his next voyage back. Her shoulders slumped in resignation. If their positions were reversed, she supposed she would be more than a wee bit angry too.

There was only one way to be fixing it. She would help the captain get well. She may have been trouble for him up until now, but she knew just how to make it right—she would cure his injury.

Not that she would try right away; she had sense enough to know just what his grandfather would be thinking of Irish treatments. Better that she let the doctor try his methods first. And if Jack wasn't up and about before too long, why then, she would offer to try an old Irish remedy. She tapped a finger against her lip and mulled over her options. There were several that could be tried. To be sure, one of them would get the captain on his feet in no time.

Then surely he would be glad he'd saved her that day on the ocean.

CHAPTER TWENTY

JACK WAS RINGING that bell again—that damned wee silver bell on the table beside his bed.

"I'm on me way, your majesty," Kathleen muttered. "On me way." She sprinkled a bit of extra salt on his eggs, a little payback, so to speak, for all his demands this past week.

By the saints, she had done her very best to be understanding, she had. But Jack was not a very good patient. In fact, she'd not seen the likes of such a sour temperament in many a year.

The doctor had insisted he stay off his leg, so he was confined to the upstairs—confined and driving her mad all the while. And with each passing day his disposition seemed to grow worse, until now she thought she might strangle the man if she heard that bell ring once more. And to think there had been times—surely very long ago—she had actually thought him...kind. He was a shape-changer, that one, and she could hardly bear him any longer.

A touch of remorse broke into her thoughts. 'Twas *her* fault he was an invalid now, however temporary the condition might be. She must try to be more patient. From upstairs, the bell tinkled again and she gritted her teeth as she mounted the stairs, breakfast tray in hand.

Her guilt quickly gave way to irritation. Aye, she may have

gotten him here, but the fact he was no better had nothing to do with her. Jack had resisted all her efforts to heal him, had insisted the doctor knew best. Still, it had been several days since she'd last offered to treat his injury; perhaps he would be more willing now. Sure, 'twas worth a try, for if he wasn't soon cured, he might be soon dead—by her hand.

She balanced the tray on one hand, gave a quick tap on the door with the other, and let herself in without waiting for a reply. He was reading in bed, propped against the headboard and wrapped in a robe. Though he looked up when she entered, he didn't smile.

She set the tray on the table beside the bed directly next to the silver bell, and ignored the temptation to snatch the thing up and throw it out the window. It might do him a bit of good to lose his precious bell for a bit, to learn he wasn't completely helpless and that he could actually pull up his blankets by himself.

"How are you feeling this fine morning, Captain?"

He grunted.

Why did she bother to ask? She swept across the room to open the drapes and let in the dull light filtering through a low lying bank of gray clouds. Another overcast day. Would they never have a break in this weather? Even in Ireland with all its rain, they saw the sun between the showers.

She came back to the bed and set the tray on his lap. "Anything else I can get you, sir?"

"A new ankle," he snapped.

Her patience snapped too. A new disposition was what the man needed most. "Your ailment might be easier to bear, Captain, if ye try accepting your situation—"

"I have."

"Nay, ye have not, acting as a child like you do."

"Excuse me?"

"A child. A pouting child. A spoiled, demanding child with a little silver bell who—"

"I get the idea." He drew the cover off his plate and stared at his food. "What's for breakfast?"

"You're pouting now."

He gave her a fake smile. "Scrambled eggs and ham, I see."

He took a bite of food and washed it down with a big swallow of tea. "A bit heavy on the salt this morning, Kathleen."

"Oh?" She gave him an innocent look and walked around the foot of the bed to stand near the bedside table. Her hand dangled at her side just inches from the offending bell. Holy Mary, but she was so close to it now, if he would concentrate on his food for but a moment more, she would soon have the damned thing tucked safely in her pocket.

"I seem to recall that the bell was *your* idea," he said around a mouthful of food.

"Aye, but how was I to know you would ring it a hundred times a day?" She picked it up and shook it so hard the ringer clanged harshly against the sides.

"It's not a hundred times a day."

"Close." She casually slid the bell into her apron pocket, two fingers holding tight to the ringer so that it couldn't make any noise. "If that's all, then…"

"You could be right about my disposition," he conceded.

"Could be?"

He shrugged. "It's just incredibly difficult to stay in bed all day…" He took another bite. "…alone," he said so low she almost couldn't hear him.

"Aye. What?" She took a step back and peered at him,

wondering whether she had just heard—had just agreed with—what she thought she had. Nay, the man wouldna dare to say such a thing to her...would he?

He chewed his food and smiled at her and said nothing to clarify his words.

"Well, then, I'd best be getting downstairs now," she said, eager to escape with the prize in her pocket.

"Take me with you, Kathleen, please. I have to get out of this room."

She sighed. "Jack, you need to do as your doctor says or it'll take all the longer to heal."

"If you won't help, I'll go alone."

"You'll not."

"Are you saying you'll stop me?"

"Jack." She looked at him through narrowed eyes, then shook her head. "All right. I'll help you downstairs. But I have me terms."

"Terms?"

"Aye. Before I help, you must let me try curing your ankle."

"Oh no, no, no." Jack waved his fork back and forth.

"But I have nursing skills, don't ye remember? You said as much to your grandfather that night we arrived." She gave him a sweet smile. "These are me great grandmother's cures, passed down to her from her own grandmother, and hers before that. Otherwise on your own, ye are."

Jack frowned, a dubious expression on his face, as though he wanted to refuse but knew he didn't have any leverage. Finally he scowled. "I won't eat pig dung or lice...or anything like that."

"I told you on the ship you only eat pig dung to stop bleeding. And lice, well eating lice will..." She quickly searched her memory. "Lice is but a remedy for the jaundice. And you don't look yellow to me—though suddenly you do look wee bit pale. Are ye all right?"

"Fine, I'm fine. What exactly is the cure you're proposing?"

"Well, I'll be needing some time to ponder it, get my thoughts in order and gather what I'll need. I'll be back in a while and we'll get to work."

He nodded hesitantly.

She laughed and headed for the door. "Now don't you be worrying, Captain. All of Ireland can't be wrong now can it?"

"Kathleen—"

She turned back. "Aye?"

"The bell?"

"Bell?"

"In your pocket."

She sighed and pulled the bell out. It gave a merry jingle as though amused at her effort. "I didn't think you would be needing it, sir. Since you'll be coming downstairs."

A laugh burst from him. "Oh, I'll need it, Kathleen. It's you who could live without it." As soon as she set it down, he gave it a shake.

"Be forewarned," she said. "If you ring that bell soon, I'll not be coming right away. I've other chores to do—your grandfather left me quite a list before he went out this morning." She turned toward the door. "And then I'll not help you cure your ankle either."

"Promise?" He grinned and gave the bell a hard shake.

*

Partway through her duties, Kathleen dropped into a chair in the kitchen and tried to think. What was the treatment for a twist in the ankle, a sprain? Ma had always told her to pay better attention to the remedies. She would have if she'd ever expected to be away from Ireland. How was she to know that someday she'd have no one but herself to rely on for the cures? She drummed her fingers on the wooden table. Now that Jack had agreed to let her treat him, it would not do for her to admit she couldn't remember even one remedy for a sprain.

There was something about bog onions… Aye, soaking bog onions to make a poultice. But where in Boston could she get bog onions? Cook would surely know but she was gone to market already, and it would not do to wait too long, for Jack could change his mind at any minute.

There were other cures, sure… She mulled over her choices, a bit discouraged that she couldn't try the bog onions first. She would just have to save that remedy for her final treatment if nothing else worked.

She filled a tray with the few items she needed—butter, a towel, and a red cloth. It had taken a bit of time to find a piece of red cloth in the rag bin, and even then it was more orange than red, but it would just have to do. Satisfied, she mounted the stairs to the second floor, pausing for a moment outside Jack's door, suddenly unsure about her doctoring skills. Faith, but what had she to be nervous about? He'd not know the difference even if she did make a mistake. She pushed open the door and stepped into the room before she could change her mind.

"Are you ready for your treatment?" Her voice sounded over bright, her smile too broad.

"Oh, quite," he said dryly. "Does this cure work immediately?"

She set the tray on the table without answering.

Jack sat up straighter. "You mean I might not even need your help getting downstairs?"

"I'll not be appreciating your making fun, sir. I've a few cures we might try. So, we'll do the first one and if we see no results, why we'll just move on."

"Grand." He slumped back into the bed pillows.

Kathleen sat on the edge of the bed facing him and slowly peeled back the covers from his ankle. Though the swelling had gone down a bit since that first day, the skin was stained shades of black, purple, and blue. "I fear you've a ways to before you're on your feet again," she said.

"Good thing you're here to cure me then."

She tied the strip of red cloth around his ankle and began to knot it. "Nine knots we'll need," she said. "And then we'll wait—"

"*That's* the cure?"

"Aye."

"Nine knots in a cloth?"

"A *red* cloth."

"Ohh. Quite the modern medicine you have in Ireland."

"A skeptic, are ye?" She clucked her tongue and pulled back to look at her handiwork, beginning to feel a bit of skepticism herself. Maybe she was leaving something out; it did seem like there should be more to the cure than this. "Why, I do believe your ankle might look better already," she said, though she thought nothing of the sort. "I'll run your breakfast dishes downstairs and check back in a bit."

"Perhaps by then I'll be running down the stairs to meet you," he said.

"Perhaps you will." She slipped through the open door and shut it quickly behind her so she wouldn't have to hear his reply.

After stalling for nearly an hour, she forced herself upstairs more than a little concerned about the effectiveness of the treatment. Jack had his hands behind his head and was grinning like he hadn't been able to wait for her to return. She lifted the blanket and peered at his ankle. Just as she feared; it didn't look any different. If only Ma were here to tell her what she was doing wrong and what really worked.

"Am I healed?" he asked.

"Not yet, but I think it's improving," she lied. "'Tis unfortuante I couldn't get some corpse linen."

"As in, for dead bodies?"

"Aye. A wrap of corpse linen would cure your swelling in no time." She looked at his ankle again. "I just don't know anyone who has died recently."

"Pity. I did so want to walk today."

She frowned. "I'm not certain how long we must wait—"

"Might I suggest we move right on to the next cure? Perhaps the effect will be greater when several treatments are combined."

He sounded downright jovial. At least her treatments were improving the man's disposition. "I suppose we could try the next one then."

She stepped to the hearth and held her hands toward the fire to warm them, then took a seat on the foot of the bed and folded the blankets back to bare his leg to the knee. "I've only watched others do this cure," she said, suddenly self-conscious. "I've not actually done it meself."

"There's a first time for everything," Jack said gamely. "Cure away."

She nodded but didn't move. Drawing a breath for courage, she finally put her hands around his swollen ankle and murmured, "Our Lord was going over the mountain and his foal's foot he sprained. Down he got and touched the sprain and said he: 'Bone to bone, blood to blood, nerve to nerve, and every sinew in its proper place.'

Without looking up, she took the butter from the tray and spread it on her palms. Then she slid her hands over the swollen ankle and gently kneaded the muscles. Over and again she slipped her hands along the same path, massaging his ankle to reduce the swelling and draw out the pain. She ran her hands over the top of his foot and around to the back, cupped his heel in one hand while she gently worked the muscles in front with the other.

It wasn't so hard, after all. Her fingers caught once in the red cloth tied around his ankle and she glanced up at the captain, a sheepish grin on her face. He did not return the smile.

"How is the pain now? Is it any better?" She stroked a rhythm across his ankle and lower calf.

"Quite."

"Is there a spot that hurts worse?"

"My—shin—when we fell…" he said in a strangled voice.

"Jack—you never said a word. I thought 'twas only your ankle that was injured." She ran her hands up his leg to his knee. He sucked in a rough breath and she looked at him sharply. "Am I hurting ye?"

"No. My knee—" he choked out.

"Don't worry—I can treat that too." She reached for more butter and spread it liberally across his knee and calf, then began to massage once more, fingers kneading, probing, feeling the outlines of his muscles beneath her fingers, firm, strong, powerful… so different from her own…a man's leg, to be sure—

The tightening began in her chest, across her breasts, a prickling that traveled slowly down her body as it turned into a need. She could hardly breathe. *A man's leg.* She felt the rush of color to her face, and willed her fingers to stop. But 'twas almost as if she were under a spell cast by the Good People, for her hands continued to massage, and she, God save her, wanted to remember every bone, every muscle, to savor the feel of him, the warmth of his skin.

She had to stop. Now. He must not know what she was feeling. Yet her fingers continued their work, sliding, slipping, over, around—

"Kathleen," he said in a low, ragged voice.

Jesus, Mary, and Joseph, *he knew.*

CHAPTER TWENTY-ONE

HER FACE BURNED with mortification and she crisply wiped her hands on her apron without looking at him. "Sure, that should be enough now to help you—"

He grasped her arms and drew her toward him until their faces were inches apart, his eyes smoldering. She felt a shiver of anticipation—and a dose of fear. "Jack, I—" He covered her mouth with his, not a gentle kiss but one demanding, conquering, giving no quarter as he staked his claim. She tried to pull back but he gripped her arms more tightly and kissed her harder until all coherent thought fled and every inch of her was aware of him— and wanting. She leaned into him and he sank back into the pillows, drawing her down across his chest and hips, his fingers in her hair, his lips on her throat, her cheek, her eyes. One hand roamed down her back and side to caress the soft curve of her breast. She gasped and he took her mouth again, kissing her deeper, drawing her further away from reality and this place.

A door slammed.

She jerked back.

"Kathleen?" a voice shouted from downstairs.

"Your grandfather!" She scrambled to get up, pushing off Jack's chest and frantically yanking at her skirt to free her legs from its tangle. In her haste, she banged a foot against his swollen ankle.

He winced and muttered an oath.

She gasped out an apology and reached for his ankle just as he did. His hand covered hers and their eyes met—and held. And she wanted him to kiss her again more than anything in the world.

"Jack?" The grandfather's voice rolled down the hall.

"He's coming upstairs!" Heart racing, she flipped the blankets over Jack's bare leg and smoothed her skirt and bodice.

"Your hair."

She glanced into the mirror and blanched. Most of her hair had come loose from the thick knot she had wound it into this morning. She pulled out the dangling hairpins, twisted her hair quickly, and shoved a couple of pins in place.

The door opened. "Kathleen!"

She spun round, clasping the extra hairpins behind her back. "Yes, sir?" There was but the slightest quiver in her voice.

"Why didn't you answer?"

"I'm sorry sir," she said breathlessly. "Were you calling? I didn't know you were yet home." She tightened her grip on the hairpins and prayed her hair would stay put until she was able to get downstairs and properly fix it.

"How could you not hear me? I was shouting—"

"The house is solid," Jack said.

"Humphh. What the devil is this?" The old man gestured at the butter on the table.

Kathleen threw a pleading look at Jack. The grandfather could not find out she had been treating his ankle or the old man would most certainly explode.

"Kathleen's healing me," Jack said with a grin.

She gritted her teeth. For the love of Jesus, if she lost her job because of this, she would make certain to strangle Captain Montgomery before she departed.

The blood rushed into the old man's face. "Faerie cures," he said in disgust. "What are you thinking Jack? You've got a doctor—"

"My ankle's feeling better."

The grandfather barked out a laugh.

"And the swelling's going down too." Jack looked directly at Kathleen, narrowed his eyes to slits and brushed the back of his knuckles across his lips. "All because of her treatment."

Heat rolled through her.

The grandfather lifted the blankets around Jack's foot. "Pah. It looks the same to me." He sniffed. "What's that on it?"

"Butter." Jack looked a little sheepish.

"Butter? What's that orange thing?"

"It's got nine knots," Jack said gamely. "I probably would be completely healed already if we only could have found a piece of corpse linen, but we had to settle for red cloth…"

The old man slammed the tip of his cane down into the carpet and lowered himself into a nearby chair. "Don't be ridiculous."

Jack shrugged. "My ankle feels better."

"For God's sake, what's come over you? Your ankle looks no different than it did yesterday."

"I respectfully disagree."

The grandfather gave his head a disgusted shake. "Well, then, if this treatment is so effective, perhaps Kathleen should do it for you every day—so you'll be healed all the sooner."

A broad grin split Jack's face. "A splendid idea. Kathleen?"

Her cheeks burned. Nay, she'd not be touching Jack

Montgomery again, not after what had just happened between them. "I could, sir. But I think we best wait to see how successful this treatment is. You may not need any others."

"I'm not so sure," he countered. "It was a bad sprain. And I've had a week already with no improvement—until today. I vote to continue treatment."

She gave him a small glare.

"Tomorrow morning, then? You can check my ankle and we'll decide whether another treatment is warranted." He flashed an impertinent grin.

"Oh aye," she said. "And might I say, it's good to see your disposition so improved, Captain."

The grandfather cleared his throat. "You may return to your duties, Kathleen."

She slipped from the room and raced down the stairs. Jack wanted further treatments? Of what could he be thinking? She rolled her eyes. Oh, aye, she knew, she well knew. She stopped before the mirror in the hall and fixed her hair, shoving the hairpins in with vehemence.

He had kissed her and she had kissed him back. And lain across him. She could still feel his lips on hers, his hands in her hair, could still hear the way he'd murmured her name—

She gave her head a shake to dislodge the memory. What was the matter with her? Danny was who she longed to kiss, it was Danny's arms she wanted around her. Yet here she was just a few weeks in America and already she was thinking about someone else, betraying her betrothed and her family for the kiss of an Englishman.

Nay, she couldn't do another cure. Not tomorrow, not the day after that, not ever. For God only knew what would happen if she touched Jack Montgomery again.

*

Late that afternoon, Kathleen went from room to room, lighting the lamps before dusk turned to night. She hadn't seen Jack since she'd left his room that morning; had even feigned a bout of lightheadedness to force Emma to take the afternoon meal up to him. All day she had pushed away thoughts about what had transpired between them. Surely he was as mortified as she, for he had not rung that silver bell all day.

To be sure, it had been a gift not to hear the bell. And yet as the hours passed with only silence from his room, 'twas hard not to wonder how he could have kissed her like he had, and not wish to see her again... if for nothing else than to apologize, certainly.

She sighed. Night was falling and she couldn't just leave him in his room in the dark. She had no choice but to face him, for the lamps must be lit. What was she to say, how was she to behave toward the man after what had happened this morning?

She wetted her lips nervously with her tongue, then wiped them dry with the back of her hand.

He must not know that his kiss had sent her mind reeling all day, that much as she tried she had been able to think of little else. Aye, she would march into his room, she would, and light the lamp just as she did every evening. She would smile and ask, 'Will you be needing anything, sir?' just like every evening. And then she would leave. Simple. Easy. Just like every other evening.

Before she could waste another second thinking about it, she turned the knob and stepped briskly into the room. "Good evening, Captain," she said, eyes focused on an oil lamp on the wall. "I'll just be giving you a bit of light." Hands trembling slightly, she lifted the glass chimney off the lamp to light the wick, then reposition the chimney back in place. Nervously she turned the wick too high and the flame flared up into the chimney. "Jesus, Mary, and Joseph," she muttered as she turned it down and watched a curl of black smoke waft up the glass tube.

"Kathleen."

Startled, she jerked round to look at him.

"Sit with me a moment." He set a hand on the bed.

She moved to perch on the edge of a nearby chair. "Did you wish something, sir? You'll not be needing another treatment for a few days." And even if she was forced to give him one, it most certainly would not be the same as this morning.

His eyes narrowed. "It's not the treatment I want," he said in a low voice. "It's the side effects."

Her heart hammered. Her mouth went dry, her brain emptied. She belonged to Danny, to Ireland. She could not care about this Englishman—should not want him. And surely, even if she did, she could not have him. She needed to get out of this room, away from this man, away from those eyes that seemed to see into her very soul and know truths that she would not even admit to herself.

She stood stiffly. "I've other duties to complete."

As she swept past, he grasped her arm and pulled her down to sit on the bed beside him. "I could take what I want," he said, his face just inches from hers, his breath warm against her cheek.

"No." Lord help her, there was no strength in her protest.

His lips touched the lobe of her ear and his rough cheek scratched against hers as he gently forced her head around to face him. "No?"

Perhaps just once more, she thought as she looked into his

devil's eyes. Just this once. And then she wouldn't do it again. What could be the harm?

He slid one hand along the side of her neck and pulled her head toward his.

Perhaps just once more.

His lips brushed gently across hers, then trailed over to kiss the edge of her jaw. She sighed and her eyes slid shut as she waited for his mouth to cover hers again—but nothing happened. Slowly she opened her eyes. He was watching her, a roguish grin on his face.

"No?" he repeated.

"Yes," she whispered.

He kissed her then and she leaned up into him, longing for the connection they had found that morning. When finally they pulled apart, she was breathless. Never in all her life had she been kissed like that. Jack took her face between his hands and kissed her again, so soft it was, like silk slipping over her lips, a whisper of a kiss, the kind one saves for true love. *Like Danny.*

"I have to go." She pulled away and stood beside the bed.

"Why?"

Because I'm betrothed. Because I love Danny. Because you are English and you make me feel different than I've ever felt before and it scares me. "It's not right—"

"It's more right than many of the things I've done in my life."

"But I'm to wed."

His expression hardened. "And what if you never find him, Kathleen? How long will you wait?"

"He is my betrothed. I've loved him since we were children."

"But do you still?"

A lump rose in her throat and she forced it down. "Don't ask such a question of me. I can't give up on him. 'Twould be like giving up on meself."

"So you'll give up on us instead?"

"There is no *us*."

"I don't quit that easily—"

"Stop!" She sliced the air with one hand. "If you care at all about me, you will quit. Promise me, Jack."

He stared at her for a long minute before giving a curt nod; she left the room before he could see the tears welling up in her eyes. Somehow, over the past weeks and months, she had let her heart go untended and feelings for Jack had slipped in and taken hold like a weed in a garden. And now the weed had blossomed into a wildflower and she was loathe to pull it out.

She shook her head. She could not have this—would not accept it. He was an Englishman. And if not for the English she would still be in Ireland—and Danny with her.

And what if she never found Danny? Jack's heart seemed good and true, more Irish than some whose blood was such. Faith, but how could she be thinking this, her own thoughts betraying the man to whom she was to pledge her life.

She stopped at the window on the landing halfway down the stairs and gazed out at the city, at the smoke curling from the chimneys and vaporizing in the winter air. She pressed a hand against the frosted window and willed the cold into her veins and heart, hoping it might freeze her feelings for Jack—even as she held onto the foolish sliver of hope that there might somehow be a chance for them.

She looked upward. "I'll be needing a sign," she murmured. "And don't be whispering it. I need you to shout it loud enough so

I might not miss it. Which way am I to turn? Is Danny still...is my past still my future?"

She started down the stairway, then stopped, one hand on the railing. "And soon, if ye might be able to manage it," she whispered. "Dear God, but I need to know soon. For the faeries have bewitched me, and the Captain as well, and faith help us both but I don't know how to put a stop to their mischief."

CHAPTER TWENTY-TWO

CHURCH BELLS BEGAN ringing as Kathleen rounded the street corner the next morning, a block from Holy Cross Cathedral. Mass would begin in just a minute or two and here she was still finding her way to the church. 'Twas the first time she would be going since arriving in Boston, and now late she would be. To think she had thought to be there early, to pray about Danny and Jack, to beg God to put an end to the faeries' tomfoolery…and here she was, late.

She quickened her steps and looked ahead to the simple stone church halfway down the block, a short steeple jutting from its roof. It must be Holy Cross, for the steeple was just as stubby as Emma had described it.

She hurried up the stairs with the other latecomers, all racing, it seemed, to get inside before the bells finally stopped chiming. Inside the doorway she stopped to gaze about in awe. The church was near to overflowing. Every pew was full and even the side aisles were lined with people standing; Emma had said the church held near to a thousand, but she'd not thought it could be true. She could hear the brogues on so many whispered voices and, for a heartbeat, had the sense that she had somehow been transported back to Ireland.

Though people were shoulder to shoulder already, they pressed still closer to make room for the stragglers; Kathleen squeezed between two women leaning against the wall near the confessional.

The priest stepped up to the altar, and a thousand voices raised in unison to sing joyfully the opening song. Her heart soared with the notes. She had awakened in the wee hours longing for home, aching to speak with Ma about this confusion she felt over Danny. And before the sun had even cracked the horizon she knew she must come to mass today, knew it as clear as if Ma had said it herself.

She followed along with the mass, listening intently to the gospel reading as she searched for meaning relevant to her, to the question she had asked God yesterday. But there was nothing. Her shoulders drooped in disappointment. To be sure, the Lord had greater things to concern himself with than who Kathleen Deacey should love.

She waited for the priest to begin the homily, holding out a faint hope that since the gospel had not spoken to her, perhaps today's sermon would deliver the message she sought. She leaned forward so as not to miss a word.

"Our Bishop, John Fitzpatrick, has come to speak to us today," the priest said in a solemn voice before seating himself in one of the fine upholstered chairs at the back of the altar.

A murmur of surprise ran through the crowd. Kathleen made the sign of the cross in reverence to this holy man.

The Bishop ascended the pulpit looking resplendent in his deep green robes. A large crucifix hung from a chain around his neck and rested on his ample belly. He laid several sheets of paper out before him, then lifted his gaze to the congregation. The murmuring dissipated into awed silence and they waited.

Finally he spoke. *"A voice comes to us from across the ocean,"* he said slowly. *"It is the voice of Ireland. This hapless country forgets her past griefs, great as they were, because one greater than all has come upon her...she bewails her sons and her daughters and her little children suffering, starving, and dead."*

As the Bishop's words rang out in the hall, all movement ceased. Kathleen caught her breath and held it, afraid to exhale lest she miss his words, and yet terrified to hear all he might say.

"If...we were to behold..." he continued in a voice edged with pain, *"men and women, and children, dying of hunger...if we heard with our own ears their wild shrieks of famine and despair, heard them crying out for a morsel of food to save them from the grasp of death, we should justly deem ourselves not only unchristian but inhuman, if we hesitated to share with them our last loaf of bread. This is what charity would dictate and command, and unless we obey this...we should be faithless to our obligations as Christians."*

The bishop paused and not a person stirred. A knot formed in Kathleen's throat so tight she thought she could suffocate here. 'Twas worse than what they had been hearing. And what of her family? What if they were dead already?

"...It is vain and idle, at a time like this, to discuss the causes to which such calamities may be traced...to discuss the duties of Parliament and of landlords. In the meantime, men that are our brethren walk the earth like specters, crawl over the ground like worms, and die because they have no food."

His voice, filled with compassion, grew stronger in determination. *"Let us arise and we shall not be alone, for throughout this vast country all those who love the faith, and all those who love that country...will be at our side."*

He called for the people to put aside their own wants in order to help Ireland. And when he spoke no more, his powerful words echoed in the cathedral, leaving a trail of fear and despair in their wake, a horrified silence broken only by weeping and murmuring of prayers.

The woman beside Kathleen shook her head and whispered. "And on top of the famine, they say 'tis Ireland's worst winter on record. Bitter winds and snow to the rooftops. The roads are closed, no one can work outside."

Kathleen's heart stilled. The newspapers had written some of this but she had hoped it to be an exaggeration. Most winters Ireland got no snow at all. "Are you certain?"

"Aye. I've letters from me sister. None have money or food. No firewood. Nor clothing warm enough. They're dying." She made the sign of the cross. "And the fever is spreading like poison through the air."

Kathleen reached into her bag, removed her rosary and held the crucifix between her fingers as she began to silently pray. The service continued, but she heard none of it. Her thoughts were of only her family and her homeland. When the mass finally ended and the church emptied around her, she went forward to kneel in a pew near the front of the church, eyes locked on the cross high on the wall behind the altar, lips barely moving as she recited the prayer for each bead on her rosary.

When she finished, she silently thanked God for bringing her to America so that she might help her family. She thanked him for Jack Montgomery without whom she would be dead. And then she leaned her head on the pew in front of her and wept.

After several minutes she slid out of the pew and headed for home. Snow had begun to fall but she would never complain about it again. 'Twould be a gift if God would put it all here instead of in Ireland.

If only there was something more she could do. Here she was, safe in America, sending a few dollars home each week. The money would help her own family, sure, but what was to become of those without someone in America?

Ar scáth a chéile a mhaireann na daoine, her mind whispered. *Under the shelter of each other, people survive.* It was what she had said to Jack when he thought he'd lost twelve men on the ocean. Aye, alone they were nothing, but together—

She stopped. All of Ireland was part of her family. And that family was suffering. She had to offer her services to the bishop's cause.

Heavy snow pelted her as she stood there. She had two afternoons off each week that she could offer to help the Irish relief cause. She turned and began to retrace her steps. "*Ar scáth a chéile a mhaireann na daoine*," she shouted into the wind.

A gentleman nearby glanced at her in surprise. She let out a laugh. Never mind what he thought, she was going to help save Ireland.

Five minutes later she stood outside the door to the rectory and brushed the snow off her cloak. She stared at the knocker for a long moment before raising a hand to thump it upon the door.

Doubt suddenly filled her mind. She had no funds to offer— only time—and Ireland didn't need her two afternoons off, they needed money for food and clothing. Perhaps she should run now, before she embarrassed herself and the priest with her meager offering. And then it was too late, for the door was open and the housekeeper was asking her to come in from the cold.

She stepped through the open doorway and pushed back her

hood. "Is Reverend Williams about? I heard Bishop Fitzpatrick speak at mass," she said in a rush. "And I wanted to volunteer me services—to help however I can."

The room's warmth touched her face and she relaxed, somewhat abashed at the abruptness of her statement. "And a good morning to you, I might add," she said.

A broad smile opened the housekeeper's plump face. "He'll be glad you've come."

"I haven't any money. But, time, I've a bit. Two afternoons off a week and I could help out then. Whatever needs to be done…"

The woman patted her on the arm. "Give me your name, child, and where you can be reached and I'll pass it along to Father. He's meeting this evening with the Bishop himself on this very subject." She kept talking as she reached into the drawer of a nearby desk and procured paper and a pen. "Much is happening. The diocese is meeting tonight in the crypt of the cathedral to create a committee to help Ireland."

"Already?" Kathleen felt a glimmer of cautious optimism. She bent over the desk to write out the necessary information, then handed the sheet to the housekeeper.

The woman set the paper on a large stack of others tucked under a weight on the desk. "These are all names of people who have come to offer their help and make donations since mass this morning," she said. "The response has been wonderful. I'm sure you'll be needed very soon."

*

Kathleen let herself in through the kitchen and shook the snow off her cloak before hanging it on a hook inside the door. She made a quick walk through the house to see if the old man was about even though she wouldn't be on duty for a couple hours more. Now more than ever, she felt the need to keep the grandfather happy—to ensure she kept herself employed.

When she didn't find him downstairs, she stopped at the front windows to gaze out at the falling snow, pattering as it drove against the windows, sticking for a moment before sliding down to accumulate on the outside sills. Warm and safe, she gazed out at the escalating storm and felt her heart chill.

Yesterday's paper had described bodies left in streets and alleys, torn apart by starving dogs and rats. She had not wanted to believe it, but now she knew the worst was true. She drew a fisted hand to her chest.

And still the English insisted that the best path was non-interference, that all would right itself if nature was left to take its course. And so the Irish kept dying—and the English landlords kept happily claiming the vacated land for themselves.

And she had no news of her family. She could hardly bear the not knowing. There were times her imagination left her nearly frantic at what they must be enduring. She prayed that the bank draft she had recently sent across would soon reach them.

The tinkle of a bell drew her attention and she turned slightly. Now how did Jack know she was back? She didn't want to face the man right now. Though a full day had already passed, the memory of his kisses was still so fresh in her mind the thought brought a flush to her cheeks even now.

Still, what had she to fear? She had made it clear that her heart belonged to Danny.

The bell tinkled again and she headed into the foyer, stopping short at the sight of Jack sitting on the top step, silver bell at his side. He had not bothered to tie the neck of his shirt, nor tuck the tails into the loose trousers he wore. Kathleen caught her breath; even disheveled, Jack Montgomery made a handsome picture.

She shook her head and put her hands on her hips. "What are ye doing there, Captain?"

"We made a bargain. I agreed to let you do your Irish treatments if you would help me downstairs. I upheld my part."

"I'll not be thinking you're well enough yet." She put on a stern expression, and started up the steps. "Now, back to bed with you."

"Am I to assume your word has no honor?"

"Pah!"

"Well, am I?"

"It's not a matter of honor." She hesitated. "It's…"

"Yes?"

She sighed in defeat. "Oh, aye, I'll keep me word."

"Well, then, let's be quick about it shall we?"

At least Jack was acting like his old self, like nothing had happened between them. She slanted a glance at him and frowned. And he must not have cared much for her at all if he had gotten over her so quickly. She raised her chin a notch.

"How are ye expecting to do this?" She went slowly up the remaining stairs until she stood directly before him. "I certainly cannot lift ye down."

"Nor shall you have to. Just hold my leg out in front of me so it doesn't bump on the stairs and I'll come down behind it."

"On your—your—" She raised her eyebrows.

"Exactly."

She swallowed a smile at the thought of him coming down the stairs on his bottom like a child, and seated herself on the stair below him. Gingerly, she lifted his foot so that his leg was extended straight forward. "Does this pain your knee at all?"

He leaned toward her. "My knee?"

She could smell the soap on his skin, the faint odor of tobacco lingering on his clothes. His breath was warm on the nape of her neck and it was all she could do to keep herself from leaning into him.

"Aye...yesterday you said—you hurt your knee—when you fell." She could hardly force the words from her mouth, for the nearness of him.

"Oh that—no—no it's fine. Kathleen?"

"Aye?" She didn't dare turn back toward him. He was too close. And it wasn't him she was needing to be worried about—it was her. If she looked at him now, she might just throw her arms around him. God help her, what were these thoughts?

Desperate to get away from her feelings, she slid to the next stair, taking care not to jar his leg. He followed without a word. In unison, they scooted down another stair and then another, the tension notching higher with each silent moment.

She searched for something to say, finally coming out with, "Won't your grandfather be surprised to find you downstairs when he returns from church, now?" When he didn't reply she twisted round. "Don't you think?"

"I nodded," he said defensively. They slid down another step and a grimace twisted his face.

"Does this hurt?"

"No."

"As if I am to believe you now. Your grandfather won't be surprised, but angry, when he sees you thus. What can ye be thinking, Jack, coming downstairs like this with your ankle in such a way?"

"I thought you cured me yesterday."

She shook her head. "And you didn't know I hadn't till this very minute, aye?"

"Perhaps what I need is another treatment. Before my grandfather comes home."

They scooted down another step. God himself only knew what would happen if she did the treatment while the old man was gone.

"If you feel inclined," Jack said as they scooted down the next couple of steps, "I also landed on my shoulder when I fell. Perhaps the treatment might also help with that."

She caught her breath. It seemed that if Jack had his way, it wouldn't be long before she would be massaging but all of his naked body. A picture slipped into her mind and a wave of heat rolled through her. Faith, but her own brain was betraying her even when she tried to deny it.

"I'm wondering now, how you've been able to bear all these injuries since your fall." She kept her tone even, her voice light. "You complained of naught but your ankle until yesterday when you mentioned your knee. And now your shoulder is paining you as well. Pray tell, out with it now. Have you any other aches I should be knowing about?" She glanced back, laughing, then froze as his eyes met hers.

"Just one," he said in a low voice.

CHAPTER TWENTY-THREE

KATHLEEN TORE HER gaze away and slid down another step. She didn't want to know. The blood pounded in her ears so that she could hardly hear. *Danny, she was betrothed to Danny.* "The bishop spoke at mass today," she said in a choked voice.

After a pause, he asked, "Is that good?"

"It's not common in Ireland, that's certain." She took the final stair and slowly lowered his leg to the floor. Jack slid onto the step beside her.

"He spoke of the people starving in Ireland. Called for the Irish in America to send aid." Her voice caught.

"You're worried about your family."

"Aye," she whispered. She sat still. "The paper says..." She faltered. "It says..."

"I know," he said. "I've read the same stories. But at least your family has you. You are here, Kathleen. You've sent them money already. They cannot starve as long as you are in America."

She stood and leaned toward him, taking his hands to help him up. There were calluses on his palms, rough hands that just yesterday had caressed her cheeks. She pulled gently back, providing balance as he used the strength of his good leg to rise.

Their clasped hands came up between them, her small white fingers engulfed in his. She stared at his chest, too afraid to look into his face, knowing that if she did, all her words yesterday would be a lie. She had said her peace, had made clear that her loyalty lay with Danny. So why was she wanting Jack Montgomery to kiss her again?

"Kathleen..."

She took a quick panicked breath and didn't look up.

"Help me to the sofa, will you please?"

She exhaled. "Oh, aye."

He rested one arm across her shoulders and she placed her own across his lower back, holding tight to his waist as they hobbled across the foyer. His hip brushed against hers with each step—and she angrily compelled her mind to think of Danny.

She slanted a glance at him. His jaw was tight, determined, and she knew even this small movement was causing him pain. By the time he settled on the sofa, leg stretched across the cushions, she wasn't sure which of them was the more relieved.

She straightened and put her hands on her hips. "I'll be thinking you won't be getting off that sofa anytime—"

The knocker thudded against the front door and she glanced toward the foyer. "Now who could be coming here on a Sunday morning?" she muttered as she stepped from the room.

She pulled open the door and felt her jaw drop at the sight of a diminutive woman waiting on the stoop. "Mrs. Boyle?" She dashed outside and threw her arms around the other. "I can hardly believe it! I hoped ye might be in Boston, but—you saw my notice, did you now?"

"We were so surprised to read it—"

Kathleen laughed in delight and half dragged the woman into

the house as she simultaneously brushed the snow off her cloak. "Come in, come in, and tell me all you know, all the news of home. 'Tis so good to see you, a face from the old—come in, we'll go into the kitchen."

She paused in the doorway to the sitting room. "Captain! The notice worked. Mrs. Boyle has found me!" She turned to the woman and gestured. "This is Captain Montgomery, my employer. He saved me life, but, oh, I'll tell you of that later. Do you mind, sir, if Mrs. Boyle comes into the kitchen for a wee bit?"

He shook his head.

"Will you be needing anything else then?"

"Just some tea would be nice."

In the kitchen, she embraced Mrs. Boyle again, as if the nearness of her fellow countrywoman could salve the pain of her worry. Then she busied herself setting water on to boil. "Tell me now the news from Cobh," she said over her shoulder. "Have you any word of my family?"

The smile slid off Mrs. Boyle's face and she took a seat at the table. "We had a letter from my brother's wife not more than a few weeks ago." She shook her head. "Things are not good—and that news was old by the time we got it. The snow—blizzards like never before. The people are starving. Och, there is food to be had, but the English won't give it out unless the Irish pay—and few have any money left."

"I've heard some of this." Kathleen watched the other carefully, afraid to ask—and terrified not to. "And my family? Was there any word on how me family is faring? By now, Moira should have had the baby."

Mrs. Boyle swallowed. "Ah, Kathleen."

"Jesus, Mary, and Joseph. Something is wrong isn't it?" She

dropped to her knees on the floor next to Mrs. Boyle and took the older woman's hands between her own. "Tell me it's not. Please tell me."

The other shook her head slowly.

Kathleen drew a sharp breath and tightened her grip. The room seemed to gray, as if she had stepped into the opaque mist of a nightmare. Nothing seemed real anymore. This wasn't true, none of it. Mrs. Boyle wasn't here, it was but a dream.

"I don't want to know," she whispered. "Don't be telling me, I don't want to know." Her head sagged forward to touch her hands and a whimper escaped her throat. Her brain raged with frantic prayers—don't let it be Da, don't let it be Ma, nor her brothers and sister, or—dear Lord, don't let it be anybody, let everyone she knew be all right. "I don't want to know," she repeated. "And I can't bear not to."

"It's Moira," Mrs. Boyle said softly. "She bore twins, two sons, but they were too early, stillborn they were. From the hunger, I wager." Her voice caught. "The birth was too much for her. Without food, her strength was gone and 'twas not long before she followed her wee babes across."

"No..." Kathleen covered her mouth with her hands and shook her head. "Not our Moira. And twins..." A sob wrenched out of her throat. "Why Moira? Dear, sweet Moira. Why not someone else? Why not the English? Why can't it ever be the English who are dying instead of us once again?"

She pressed tight fists into her cheeks and began to rock back and forth to ease the pain. The ache in her chest squeezed the air from her lungs. "I could have saved her. I should have been working in Canada. They sent me here to help, don't you know?" Her voice broke. "They sent me here and I failed them." She dropped her head to her chest and Mrs. Boyle pulled her close.

"It's not your fault, not your fault, Kathleen."

"If I had been here sooner—" She pressed her hands to her face and sobbed.

Jack called from the other room. After a moment, she drew a slow, shuddering breath and stood. "He wants his tea, I'd wager," she said in a dull voice. She wiped her apron across her eyes, blew her nose into a cloth napkin, and lifted the teapot.

*

Jack smiled as Kathleen entered the room, hopeful that Mrs. Boyle had brought word that would put her fears to rest. "Has she heard from your family?" he asked.

Kathleen did not look directly at him while she poured his tea, but he saw the dampness on her cheeks and the tremble of her hand. "Is everything all right?" he asked. "Do you have news?"

"Aye." Her eyes were wide and rimmed with red.

"What is it? What's happened?"

"Our Moira, my brother's wife. She's died. And their babies, two little boys, just born. Just born—and now already gone back to heaven."

"I'm so sorry." His words felt miniscule in the face of her pain. He reached out a hand, wanting to gather her to him, wishing he could somehow protect her from any more heartbreak out of Ireland.

She took a step back. "I can't stop thinking of all that they'll miss. They'll never run over the hillsides, nor stand at a bluff overlooking the ocean and watch the white horses ride out to Tír Na nÓg, the land of the ever young. They'll never dance with a lass, nor fall in love, nor play the fiddle." Her voice quavered.

"They'll never laugh. Two wee lads, just two more dead in Ireland. Who will ever know they were even born? Who will even care?"

Tears slipped down her cheeks and she whipped a hand across her eyes. "Perhaps I should be grateful," she said, bitterness underlining each word. "They've been spared from ever knowing what it is to live as dirt beneath the English foot...spared from ever knowing the hunger."

Her shoulders shook and he wished he could say something that mattered, wished he could promise time would heal her wounds when he didn't believe it himself.

"I should have been in Canada," she cried. "I should have been across the ocean and sending money home."

"It's not your fault."

"I couldn't even stay on board my own ship, couldn't even cross the ocean without falling overboard. And Moira died waiting for the money I was to send."

"It's not your fault," he repeated more forcefully.

"Oh aye, at least some of it is." Her eyes narrowed. "And some of it is your fault, too. Moira and her babes died waiting for me help. And I was waiting all the while for you to take me to America."

She spun on her heel and marched back to the kitchen before he could form a reply.

His fault? Jack took a large swallow of tea, mentally cursing as the hot liquid scalded his mouth and throat. He slammed the cup down on the china saucer, shattering the fragile plate and splashing tea over the sides of the cup to burn his fingers. He cursed again and wiped his hand on his pants leg.

"Excuse me, sir."

Jack jerked his head up as Mrs. Boyle crossed the room.

He followed her gaze to the broken pieces of saucer and the tea splattered over the table. "Yes?"

She drew a handkerchief from her pocket and wiped up the spill, then collected the largest pieces of broken china. "I'll be asking for a bit of compassion for Kathleen. It's a hard thing to live through, death is."

He nodded, chest tight from remembering.

"Moira was her dearest friend, like sisters those two were. And closer yet they got once Moira wed Kathleen's brother. I'll be asking you to forgive her words. The shock is what's making her say such things—and the fear of what might lie ahead."

He nodded.

"Is there anything else you'll be needing?"

"Nothing." He waved her away but Mrs. Boyle didn't move.

"If you've any fondness for the lass, she'll be needing a friend. The news from Ireland is getting worse—and I haven't told her everything I know."

His anger evaporated. "There's more?"

"Me brother's wife writes that Kathleen's mother is giving most of her own share of food to her other children. She is starving herself to give the others a better chance at life. I'll not tell Kathleen this, for what can she change of it?" Her voice shook. "I'm telling you, Captain, for you are here with her, and perhaps you might take pity. She'll be needing support when the news comes—as it will, soon enough—of her own mother's death. Will ye help her?"

He nodded, for he could not speak.

Long after she'd left, he still stared after her. He looked across the room, out the window at the falling snow and knew now that spring would not come soon enough for Ireland. One by one, Kathleen would lose everyone she loved.

He remembered the day he had found his father's body, the pain of his death so overwhelming he had lashed out at everyone around him, wanting to find someone to blame—to pass his own guilt, his own grief, his own fear to someone else so he might not suffocate beneath the weight of it. And then his mother had left, abandoned him to his grandfather so she could chase life with a wealthier man.

His mother would never understand Kathleen's mother sacrificing herself for her children. There was a time he might not have understood either. But that was so long ago. Before Kathleen.

*

Kathleen stood in the kitchen, arms wrapped around her waist and wished more than anything she were in Ireland. Moira was killed by the English as surely as if they'd put a dagger through her heart. She could only imagine Sean's anguish at losing his wife and sons.

Mrs. Boyle put an arm around her shoulders. "Cry it out, lass. And then move on. For you've others to think of, still living, who are depending on you."

"But I cannot *stop* thinking of them! If Moira was hungry, then surely the rest of them are too." Fresh tears burned her eyes. She didn't think she could go on if she lost anyone else.

Mrs. Boyle pressed a paper into Kathleen's hand on which was scrawled a man's name and an address. "If you need reach me, I work here every day."

"Do you live there?"

"We don't. We rent a room above Murphy's Pub." She looked around the kitchen. "You've been lucky, Kathleen. And the captain seems to be a fine man. It does you no good to be blaming him for things not his fault." She folded Kathleen in a tight embrace, then slipped out the back way.

Kathleen set her hands on the wooden top of the table and let her head drop forward. Guilt pricked at her. Aye, the captain was not at fault and well she knew it. An apology she owed him straightaway for her outburst. The man may be English, but he was kind and generous, far different than any Englishman she had ever known.

She wished her parents might meet him, to see that perhaps not every Englishman was the same. She'd written as much to them in a letter describing her voyage and rescue.

But with sudden clarity she saw the events through their eyes. To be sure, they would be grateful that Jack had saved her, but they would not overlook his refusal to take her to America and his attempt to leave her behind on Fayal while Moira hungered and died. Had she herself not done just the same thing minutes ago?

Already Da did not say 'England' without adding a curse to his words. How much greater his hatred, and Sean's and Ma's, would be now with Moira's death. They would not care that Jack Montgomery was a fine man. They would care only that he was English.

She squeezed her eyes shut. A sign she had prayed for just a few hours ago. And a sign she had already received. God had shouted it to her just as loudly as she'd asked. There was no place in her life for Jack. Her future lay with an Irishman. And his name was Danny O'Sheehan.

CHAPTER TWENTY-FOUR

KATHLEEN REACHED A hand into her apron pocket and touched the letter that had arrived that morning, just days after Mrs. Boyle had come to the door. The handwriting on the envelope belonged to neither her parents, nor Danny. Try as she might, she could think of only one reason why someone else would write her…to deliver bad news.

She had shoved the envelope into her apron pocket and purposely ignored it all day, like a lingering headache one hopes will simply disappear on its own. Ignorance is bliss, Ma would have said. Aye, and with the envelope unopened she could cherish the illusion that all was right with her family.

Now finally off-duty, she could delay opening the envelope no longer. She pulled it from her pocket, turned it over in her hands several times, ran her fingers over the corners, felt the creamy smoothness of the paper—and tried to stifle her fear.

So much was suddenly happening to help the Irish, it hardly seemed right that she should now receive word of new troubles. After speaking at mass last week, the Bishop had formed the Relief Association for Ireland, and the papers reported donations pouring in from all of New England. Every day letters in the Boston Pilot called for a citywide public meeting to launch an even greater relief effort. And yesterday she'd read that the Vice President of the United States had called upon the citizens of every city to organize relief programs for Ireland. The tide was turning; she did not want to discover today that it was still too late for someone she loved.

Steeling her courage, she peeled open the flap and withdrew the single sheet.

Dear Miss Deacey,

She gripped the paper between tight fingers and glanced at the bottom of the page to find the writer's name. Mary Reilly. She didn't know anyone by that name. Quickly she returned to the top and began to scan the letter. The woman knew Danny, had met him in New York months ago. Kathleen lowered herself to the edge of the bed and read on.

Danny had been working in New York until December, then he moved to Lowell, Massachusetts to work in the mills. Kathleen let out a slow, relieved breath. This was not bad news but good, a stranger helping her find the man she loved.

The man she loved. Danny. Here he was, found, and hardly more than down the road from her. Sure, but this was another sign so soon after the first one. A sound, half laugh, half sob, escaped her throat. She stared at the paper in her hand and felt panic rise in her chest. What was wrong with her? *Danny was found.*

Surely the problem was she had no one to share her news with. Aye, what good was good news if there was no one to celebrate with you?

She hurried down the back stairway and burst into the kitchen waving the letter. "Emma, me Danny is found!" she cried. "Right here in Massachusetts! It's a grand day if I've ever seen one."

The old woman frowned. "Does he say why he never came back to Ireland?"

"'Tisn't actually from him, you see. Someone else has written—"

"Hummphh." Emma returned to her chopping. "Then you don't know that you've found him if it isn't the man himself who's come forward."

Kathleen danced toward her. "Doesn't matter. I'll be going to him. He's but in Lowell. Lowell, Massachusetts. Do you know where it is? Can't be too far, can it, if it's in the same state?"

"Far enough. More than a few hours by coach. Now how will you pay for that?"

"I have a little money saved. And, well…perhaps you might lend me the rest?" Kathleen tip-toed around the back of the older woman and leaned close to her on the other side. "You know I'll be good for paying it back."

Emma's knife came down hard on a fat carrot. "You write that man and let him come to you. No self-respecting woman should go chasing after the man who jilted her." She pushed the round slices to the side and lay another carrot on the board. "There's other fish in the sea," she muttered low.

"He didn't jilt me."

"Call it what you will. I say let him come after you."

Kathleen pressed her lips together. She had no patience for sending a letter and awaiting a reply. She folded the page and shoved it into the pocket of her apron. "Fine. I'll ask Captain Montgomery for help. He knows what this means to me."

Emma snorted. "Oh yes, ask the captain. I'm sure he'll be ever so pleased to help you find that man."

*

Jack felt resignation set in. From his chair by the hearth, he fixed his gaze on Kathleen. "You want to hire a coach?"

"If you don't mind, sir, the day after tomorrow. I've the afternoon off anyway, then I'd just need half a day more. I know it's a lot to ask, but if you'll just lend me the rest of what I need, I'll be thinking ye might deduct a bit from me pay each week for reimbursement—or I might work longer each day to make up the extra hours. Whatever you—"

"Why don't you just write and have him come here?" Jack folded his hands in his lap.

"You've been around Emma too long. That's what she said."

"Always knew she had common sense. Are you even sure it's him?"

Kathleen rolled her eyes. "I can feel it. That's why I need to go. I cannot wait for a letter to find him and then for him to find his way here. Weeks could pass with all that waiting. What if he were to decide to leave Lowell before me letter even got delivered?" Her words tumbled over themselves, and Jack envied the man who was the cause of her enthusiasm. For the first time since learning of Moira's death, her blue eyes shone, and he couldn't help wishing that he had been part of restoring her spirit.

He could refuse to help her, he supposed, force her to wait until she was able to save the money she needed. Hope that Danny was long gone by the time she was finally able to get to Lowell. "You're talking about a trip several hours long—Lowell isn't exactly around the next corner—"

"I'm not afraid of travel. I crossed the ocean—"

"What if something happens, the carriage breaks down—"

"I'll have the driver—"

"And he'll have you, no doubt. For God's sake, Kathleen, you can't just go driving around the country alone with some driver you don't even know."

Ye've an appalling lack of trust, Jack."

"Do you have any idea how many mills are in Lowell? At least twenty, maybe thirty or more. Did the letter say which one he's at?"

She blinked.

"It'll take an entire day just to go from mill to—"

"If you don't want to lend me the money, then just be telling me. I'll find some other way to get there."

"I didn't say I wouldn't lend you money," he said irritably.

"Well, then what is it that you're saying?"

I don't want you to find him. He sighed. "Nothing. I'll go with you."

*

Panic shot through her. Jack couldn't be with her when she found Danny, not after what had transpired between them. "Don't be… silly. That isn't necessary." She seized upon the first thought that came to mind. "Besides, your ankle is still healing—"

He barked out a laugh and picked up his cane. "I'm getting about well enough. I've been stuck home so long, I'm bored out of my mind. Going to Lowell will be a nice excursion."

"I thought you were going to your club tomorrow night— that's an even nicer excursion."

"I am, but—"

"But with all the snow and ice, you might fall again," she said firmly. "If ye'll just lend me the money—"

"What if Danny isn't at any of the mills?" he asked. "You certainly can't go looking for him all over town by yourself—"

Faith, but the man seemed as determined to prevail as she was to dissuade him. "And why not?"

"Into taverns and the like?"

Oh. She hesitated, frantically searching for a reason that would convince Jack not to accompany her. She wanted to be alone when first she saw Danny after nearly a year apart, wanted time enough with him to banish Jack Montgomery from her heart.

As though sensing an advantage, Jack pushed forward. "You can't go running about the country—"

"Yes I can," she insisted.

"No," he said with quiet firmness. "You can't."

She bit her lower lip and looked away. 'Twas not the way she had pictured her reunion with Danny. She'd not expected to have another man beside her when finally she found her betrothed. What would Danny think when he saw Jack? *What would the Jack think when he saw Danny?*

"But he's my betrothed," she said in desperation.

"And I'm your employer. Trust me, there isn't a problem here, Kathleen. I'll make the arrangements."

She left the room in a daze. For all the signs God had given in answer to her prayers, he was surely making things difficult. Perhaps he meant for her to see the two men side-by-side, so she could easily know the depth of her feelings for Danny.

If that was his plan, so be it. This was one test she was determined not to fail.

*

Two days later they left Boston at first light, their hired carriage a bit worn, but plenty road worthy. Kathleen shivered in the winter chill and wrapped herself tightly in the heavy blankets that had been supplied with the carriage. She moved her feet closer to the hot bricks on the floor, grateful for the warmth.

The landscape rumbled by—dead weeds punching through snow-covered fields, ice frozen in ditches, forests thick and deep, and every now and again, a small house squatting beside the road.

Four hours, the driver had said when they set off. Four hours before they would reach Lowell and she would see Danny. Now nearly halfway there, so close to having him with her again, she could hardly contain the jumping of her stomach.

Jack had fallen asleep in the opposite seat, a blanket wrapped around his shoulders, his head resting on the back cushion. Her heart stirred and she attributed the feeling to gratitude. Indeed, she was much indebted to him for all he had done to help her these past months.

As though sensing her regard, he opened his eyes a crack. A slow, sleepy smile slid across his face and she let herself wonder what it would be like to awaken beside him—and then quickly chastised herself for the thought.

"I almost forgot to tell you," he said. "News out of Washington, more aid for the Irish." He pushed himself out of his slouch. "Congress has authorized the Navy to lend a warship—the U.S.S. Jamestown—to the Boston merchants to carry food to Ireland."

She gasped. "How do you come to know this?"

"It was all the talk last night. Heard it straight from the men who proposed the idea—Captain Robert Forbes and his brother John."

"And Congress agreed just like that?"

He shrugged. "Appears so. The Forbes brothers are very influential. Both are highly respected China trade merchants. They knew the Jamestown was sitting idle in the Charleston Navy Yard, so they put together a plan and petitioned Congress." He pulled his collar closer against the chill. "Robert offered to command the ship without pay, using an all-volunteer crew. Word is the President has called a cabinet meeting to discuss it." He leaned toward her. "This is epic. They government has never before given command of a warship to a civilian."

"Do you think he'll get it?"

"I do. He's been a captain over twenty years," he said. "And he's lining up a stellar crew. Several other well-respected captains have volunteered to serve as officers on the voyage. If all goes to plan, they'll leave before the end of March."

Hope soared within her. "Do you know where they'll be docking?"

"Cork Harbor."

She leaned forward to give his arm an excited shake. "My family's outside Cobh, right on the harbor."

"Perhaps this will help them directly. The ship will bring a ballast cargo back to sell in Boston, and that money will also go into the relief effort."

"What a fine country this is." She pressed hand to her heart. "To help Ireland when England has turned her back."

"There is serendipity to this it seems, for the Irish saved America long ago. There was talk last night of the winter of 1676. Do you know of it?"

She shook her head.

"The American colonies were starving. Massachusetts, Connecticut, and Plymouth, all were ravaged by a devastating winter. Ireland sent a ship to Boston with relief supplies. Poor as it was, Ireland sent aid. If not for the Irish, those English colonists would have died…and perhaps the face of America would have turned out entirely different."

"When you've never had much, you come to know what a difference just a little can make. That what is most important is not things—but life itself."

Pain flashed across Jack's eyes before he shuttered them. "I thought I learned that lesson years ago—somehow I guess I lost it."

"Me ma would say some lessons need more than one smack against the head to sink in."

"I suppose. Though I wouldn't have expected that one to—my father died when I was eight."

Sympathy stirred within her. "I'm sorry."

"Killed himself actually. In England. During the Panic of 1825. The stock market crashed. More than seventy banks failed in the first month. Factories closed, people were out of work. There were evictions for nonpayment of rent..."

Like Ireland.

"Like Ireland," he said.

She looked at him sharply.

"By the end of the next year, almost three thousand companies had gone bankrupt, including my father's. Two weeks later, he put a gun to his head. I found him."

He steepled his fingers and dropped his head to his chest. "My mother and I went to live with my grandfather. She left us soon after, married again, to a wealthy aristocrat...who didn't want any reminders that his new wife had been married before."

"You mean...you?"

He nodded. And her heart twisted.

"My grandfather decided then to teach me what he knew— whaling. Eventually we came to America because the English whaling industry was in serious decline—and it was going strong here. I haven't seen my mother in years."

He locked eyes with Kathleen. "What I felt upon my father's death, what I have lived with since... I would never wish that sense of loss on anyone. I am truly sorry that your Moira died, that the English have not done what they should to prevent this tragedy in your country."

Kathleen looked down at her hands, clenched tightly together in her lap. She didn't want to hear him apologize for something that wasn't his fault, didn't want to know he had felt pain in his life, *didn't want to like him like this.* Not with Danny coming back into her life.

"Sorry won't bring her back," she said with more bite than she intended.

"No it won't." He reached across to run a finger along the curve of her jaw, under her chin, up across her lips. "I just wanted you to know I understand."

Unconsciously, she closed her eyes and leaned into his hand. She could hardly breathe. "Aye," she whispered finally.

They reached Lowell late in the morning, the carriage drawing to an abrupt halt at the entrance to the first cotton mill they came across. Kathleen stared out the window and self-consciously smoothed her hair. Her palms were moist, her stomach knotted. She threw a tremulous smile at Jack and willed herself to move. "I'll go in alone."

"You're sure?"

She nodded with more confidence than she felt.

Taking the driver's offered hand, she stepped down from the carriage, eyes on the entrance to the large brick building. A brisk wind swirled around her and she pulled her cloak close to block the cold. What if Danny wasn't here? *Faith, what if he was?*

She twisted round to look back at the carriage, at Jack watching her through the window. He smiled and her stomach lurched. Drawing a breath for courage, she took a step toward the building, and then another, her determination wavering. What if the Danny she found was no longer the Danny she bid goodbye to almost a year ago? She pushed herself forward.

Inside the building, she explained her mission to the clerk at the main desk. He gave her a weary smile, as though he'd been asked the same sort of question a million times before, then pulled open a drawer, rifled through a file and checked names on a long list. He shoved the drawer shut. "Doesn't work here. Sorry."

Disappointment dropped into her stomach like a stone. Disappointment...and relief. For the love of Jesus, how could she be feeling relief? Mortified at her response, she fled back to the carriage.

The next stop brought the same answer, as did the third, and the fourth. By the time she pushed through the door into the thirteenth mill, her nerves were on edge—and she wanted to find Danny more than anything in the world. He had to be in Lowell. He just had to be here. She laced her fingers together, squeezing tight to restrain her hope as the clerk checked the files.

"Daniel O'Sheehan." He looked up with a smile. "Yes, he's here."

She gasped. "Would I be able to see him?" Excitement put a tremor in her voice. "I've come all the way from Boston—and Ireland before that."

"I can't call him off the floor, but there will be a break soon, another quarter hour or so. I'll fetch him down then."

"Tell him 'tis Kathleen waiting. God bless you, sir." She dashed back to the carriage and clambered aboard without waiting for the driver to lend a hand.

"He's here! Danny is here. He'll be coming out in a bit, during a break."

"You're sure it's him?"

"Aye, it must be. *Daniel O'Sheehan*, the man said. Surely 'twas no accident that I learned of him here."

He lifted an eyebrow, but did not smile.

She smoothed her hair and straightened her collar. "Tell me now, Jack, how do I look?"

He scrutinized her carefully, his gaze lingering on her lips for a moment before their eyes met. His appreciative perusal left her with a nagging sense of irritation. She was about to be reunited with her betrothed after all. "Well?"

"When he sees you, Danny will surely regret not coming back to Ireland last fall."

She grinned. "I hope you're right." She spread a blanket over her lap, flattened it carefully, then tossed it aside. "I'll not be able to sit still for even five minutes it seems. 'Tis too warm in here anyway."

Pulling up her hood, she climbed down from the carriage and briskly walked to the end of the block, then spun round and walked far in the other direction, the crisp wind bringing tears to her eyes. Turning again, she saw the clerk step out of the building and point toward her. A dark-haired man followed him outside and put a hand up to shield his eyes against the sun as he looked her way.

Danny? She lifted the front of her skirt and began to hurry toward him, each step coming faster than the last. He looked thinner than when he left…and his hair wasn't as curly…

She stopped. *And he was shorter.* She felt as though she had been kicked in the stomach. She took another few steps like it might change something, like she might find 'twas Danny after all. Now that she wasn't to get him back, suddenly she wanted him more than ever. She blinked hard forcing back tears.

"Do I know you?" the man asked as she drew nearer.

"I was thinking you were someone else—another Danny O'Sheehan."

"I'm sorry."

She couldn't stand the pity in his eyes, yet couldn't turn away, for that would bring finality to her search. "Did you know Mary Reilly in New York?" she asked, knowing well that if his answer was yes, there would be no reason to visit the remaining mills. She'd not find her Danny in Lowell.

The man blew on his bare fingers and nodded. "She's a friend. Is there news from her?"

"Nay. She is who told me you were here. She thought you were...my Danny. I'm sorry to have bothered ye." Kathleen glanced at the waiting carriage, at the driver adjusting the harness on one of the horses, and wanted only to get out of Lowell and as far away from this foolish escapade as she could. Danny was gone, he hadn't come home to Ireland, he wasn't in Lowell, and she might never find him again. Her advertisement for him had surely run in the Newfoundland newspaper by now. Someone who knew him surely would have seen it and pointed it out to him; that was, if he hadn't already seen it himself and chosen not to respond.

Enough. Enough of Danny now.

She walked stiffly over to the driver. "We can be going back to Boston." Taking his hand, she stepped up into the carriage and sat down next to Jack.

"It wasn't him," she said quietly. The carriage started off with a jolt, the motion just enough to spill the brimming tears from her eyes.

*

Jack slid a blanket around her shoulders and tucked another gently across her lap. He was still surprised at the possessiveness that had come over him the past few minutes. His stomach had lurched when Danny came out of the mill. His breath had stalled, waiting. And when it became clear that this man was not the Danny

O'Sheehan that Kathleen had been searching for, relief had rushed through him.

He pulled a white handkerchief from his pocket and pressed it into her hand. Then he put an arm around her shoulders and pulled her close, held her as she alternately railed against Danny and wept, held her until she finally drifted into an exhausted slumber. Then he touched a finger gently to her cheek and murmured, "I could love you Kathleen Deacey."

CHAPTER TWENTY-FIVE

S EAN STEPPED DOWN from the coach and pulled the collar of his coat close to his neck. Though it was only mid-afternoon, heavy gray clouds were darkening the day and the bite that accompanied dusk was already apparent.

He picked up his small travelling bag where the driver had tossed it on the ground, and set off slowly in the direction of the fishery office. Though what he wanted most was to sleep, now that he had reached Newfoundland, nothing was more important than finding work. After a few minutes, his legs began to tire from the exertion and his breathing grew heavy. He pushed himself forward, ignoring the discomfort.

He'd nearly succumbed to the fever on the voyage over. Shifting his bag to his other hand, he thought of Kathleen dying on the ocean and wondered whether her voyage had been as horrific as his. The cold and the wild sea, the passengers locked below deck without privies, and the fever, killing the weakest first, the wee babes and the old people, then spreading to the stronger passengers and taking their lives, too.

He had lain in his filthy bunk, in straw infested with lice, too sick to care, dreaming of water and the rain in Ireland. By the time the ship reached Canada, he had been too feverish to know. The sick had been taken off the ship to be quarantined at Middle Island until they recovered or died. He had been one of the lucky ones. As soon as he was strong enough, he'd come to Newfoundland.

He stopped to take a room at a boarding house, reluctantly handing over a few of the coins he had brought across, then set off again. All around the area, new buildings were going up, and the steady pounding of hammers told him that St. John's was fast recovering from the massive fire that had nearly destroyed it last June.

A few buildings from the fishery office, he stopped to catch his breath. It would be no good if he was winded when he went in to ask for work, for if the owners thought him sick he would never get hired on.

Once his breathing calmed, he crossed the street, entered the fishery office and gamely smiled at the woman behind the desk. "Excuse me," he said. "I'll be looking for work. I was out on one of your cod ships all last summer—"

"The cod won't be running for months."

"Aye," he said evenly. "I was hoping I might get aboard a sealing ship."

The woman smiled sympathetically. "We've got more men what want the berths than we've got space," she said. "Besides, the ships are out already."

"But I've worked for you before. Do the ships ever come in to unload?"

"Not until they're done. Sorry."

For the first time since beginning this journey, Sean felt fear. "Have you any other sort of work I might do? Anything."

The woman eyed him silently, then disappeared through a door into the back part of the building. Legs weak, Sean sat in a straight-backed chair to wait. He'd not be leaving. He had no idea where the woman had gone or what she was doing, but he'd not be giving up here until he knew without a doubt they had no work for him.

He listened to the muffled pounding from the nearby buildings, then grinned. Sure, but he might find work with a construction crew. The thought sent his spirits soaring.

A few minutes later, the door punched open from the other side and the clerk returned with a tall, black-haired man in her wake. *Danny?*

Sean jumped to his feet, took a step forward, and stuck out a hand in greeting. "Danny O'Sheehan, is it you?"

The two men stared at one another, incredulous, Sean's hand still stretched out in front of him like the limb of a tree.

"Sean?" Danny let loose a sound that was both laughter and shout as he grabbed the other's hand and pumped it up and down. "Jaysus, I almost didn't recognize ye. You've lost some weight Seanie."

"Aye. On the voyage over. But I'll get it back soon. And you— you must be doing well for it appears ye've put on a bit of it yourself."

Danny laughed. "For once in me life, too much to eat. But, Seanie, tell me, what are you doing here?"

"Looking for work."

"Besides that, I mean. What are you doing back in Newfoundland? Ah, well, wait a bit. We'll be closing down the office in a few minutes and then we can run out for a pint and you tell me everything."

He motioned at the woman behind the desk. "Fix Mr. O'Sheehan up with something quick to eat and some hot coffee while he waits, Margaret." He glanced at Sean. "I'll be right back."

Every muscle in Sean's body relaxed with the confidence that he would soon have work. This turn of events was more than he ever could have hoped for. Somehow Danny had secured a good position within the company. Sure, he must have some influence with the owners.

Half an hour later, the two men were seated at a tavern down the street, a frothy pint of dark ale on the bar in front of each of them.

Danny slapped some bills on the counter. "This is on me. Well enough I'll be doing, to treat an old friend to a few pints." He took a big swallow of ale, then wiped his mouth on his sleeve. "Just like old times, eh Sean?"

"Aye." Sean lifted his glass to his mouth and followed suit, savoring the rich flavor as it rolled over his tongue and down his throat. He took another long draw of his ale and listened to the voices around him blending into a steady drone punctuated by bursts of laughter and the clink of glasses. After all the starvation and death in Ireland, after the horror of his voyage, the moment felt more like a dream conjured up by his mind out of longing. Tobacco smoke wafted like silver streaks though the air, and he looked at Danny, the picture of health and success. He set his glass on the bar.

"You're looking to be doing well," he said. "But what happened to ye last fall? Why didn't you return to the ship that night?"

Danny shrugged and dropped his gaze. "I don't know. I was out drinking and, somehow, I couldn't bring meself to go back to that wretched poverty. What hope did we have in Ireland, Sean, ever under the English fist?"

Sean took another swallow of ale. "But what of Kathleen?

You should have written her then. She worried something terrible happened."

"If I had written, would she have come here to live?"

Sean sighed, remembering how Kathleen had reacted when first he proposed that she immigrate to America. "Perhaps not."

"So...better I didn't write."

"I'll be thinking she would have rather made the choice herself."

Neither spoke for a long moment. Then Danny grinned. "And what of your new babe—what did Moira have?"

Sean wrapped both hands around his glass, eyes fixed on the white froth on the rim. "Twins. Two lads." He looked at his friend. "Stillborn."

Danny closed his eyes and when he opened them again Sean could see his own pain mirrored there. "Oh Jaysus, I'm sorry. How is Moira doing?"

Sean downed the rest of his pint and watched as the barkeep filled the glass again. "She died too...a short while after."

"You can't know how sorry I am—"

"There's more Danny. You might as well know it all now. You've heard we're in famine again?"

"Aye."

"Kathleen left Ireland to help the family. She was coming to Newfoundland to work...and to find you."

"What?"

Sean swallowed hard. "But she's gone. She went overboard during a storm and never made it across."

"No—"

"It's my fault. I made her leave Ireland." His voice caught as the pain of losing Kathleen washed over him like it was fresh. "Said she had to go because Moira was with child and I'd just gotten back."

"Nay, she's not—"

"It's hard to believe, I know. I canna think of it overmuch or it breaks me down."

Danny grabbed Sean's arm with such force that he jostled Sean's glass and ale splashed out upon the bar. "Kathleen's not dead!"

"We got a letter—"

"Sean, stop! She's not dead. Look." Danny reached into his pocket and pulled out a folded piece of newspaper. "She's in Boston. I'll not be knowing how she got there if she fell off her ship, but she placed this notice—"

"When did ye see this?" Sean scanned the sheet.

"Last week."

He read the notice again, this time more slowly, then threw back his head and laughed out loud. "Mother of God, she's alive!"

"That's what I'm telling ye."

Sean pushed his beer away and dropped his head into this hands. Tears wet his palms. His sister lived; he hadn't sent her to her death. He felt Danny's hand on his shoulder, and lifted his head to look at his friend. "My sister's in Boston," he said in an awed voice as he wiped a rough hand across his eyes. "I wish me Ma and Da could know it right now."

Danny nodded and raised his glass. Sean thumped his against it in celebration and both drank heartily.

Sean slammed his mug down first. "Have you answered her yet?"

Danny shook his head.

"What if we went there?" Sean's voice dropped conspiratorially low. "The both of us. She thinks me to be in Ireland and you to be lost forever. Wouldn't ye love to see the look on her face when she opens the door to find the both of us on her doorstep?"

Danny chuckled and motioned the barkeep to fill their glasses again. "Aye, surprised she'd be," he said thoughtfully. "Near a year it's been."

Sean leaned toward him. "She's been waiting for ye all this time, Danny. A more bonnie lass you'll not find than me sister."

"I don't know if it's the ale thinking or me—"

"Ah, they're one and the same!"

"No doubt!" Danny took a long drink. "But have you money enough to get there yourself?"

Sean shook his head. "But if I could work at the fishery for a few days, even odd jobs and such…to be sure, I could earn enough. You're looking to be pretty important there now, Danny. Could you help get me a job?"

His friend frowned. "Ah well, there's the rub. We haven't any need for help, not until spring. And I'll be thinking anyway, it's a waste of time to stay in Newfoundland when your sister is in America. Sure and I'll lend you the funds to get to Boston, so ye can leave right away."

"But are you with me, Danny? You have to come too. Kathleen would never forgive me if I left you behind again. You owe it to her to show up. Jaysus, you owe it to me after what I went through with her when you didn't come back."

Danny chugged down half the glass of ale, then turned his gaze on Sean. "Aye," he said finally. "With ye I am. I'll be needing to talk with the boss come the morn." He nodded as if convincing himself. "Sure and I could say you've come to tell me of a sick relative in Boston… Me own Mam has come out of Ireland and is fevered, ready to die in Boston, and calling for her son. Aye, that might do," he said more to himself than to Sean. He looked up suddenly. "Ah well, I'll think of something."

"Why don't you just quit here? Once you're with Kathleen, the two of ye can settle in America."

"I've got a good job—"

"There's jobs everywhere in America, Danny. Haven't you heard—everyone gets rich." Sean waved his glass in the air for emphasis, then settled a serious look on his friend. "You haven't a lass here, now, have ye?"

Danny returned Sean's stare for a moment. "Of course not. I'll just be wanting to make sure I've a job in case Boston's not to me liking. Don't you be worrying now, Sean, I'll take care of it. I'll figure something out."

"So when do we go?"

Danny shrugged. "Morning after next? Have you a place to stay until then?"

Sean nodded. "A boardinghouse just down the road."

"I know the one. Be ready, for I'll be by early. We'll need to get over to the mainland to catch a train."

"Aye."

They downed the rest of their ale and Danny waved the barkeep over. "'Tis whiskey we'll be wanting now, bring a bottle of some fine Irish."

The barkeep poured several fingers of amber liquid into two glasses and, at Danny's insistence, left the bottle behind.

Danny raised his glass. "To America," he said and tossed it down.

"To America." Sean followed his lead, enjoying the burn of the liquor all the way to his stomach. Kathleen was alive. Danny had been found. It didn't get much grander than this.

CHAPTER TWENTY-SIX

S HE HAD NOT spoken of Danny in the days since their return from Lowell, had tried to banish him completely from her thoughts. Emma's only comment had been something about letting sleeping dogs lie. And Jack, bless him, hadn't said one word about the trip. Even when she found him watching her, surely remembering that day in Lowell, he didn't raise the subject.

Thank goodness there were other things to think of. The whole of Boston was caught up in the movement to send aid to Ireland. What had begun as a modest effort had blossomed into a huge program supported by virtually everyone in the city.

More than 4,000 people had attended a public meeting on February 18th at Fanfeuil Hall. When it was over, another relief group, the Boston Committee, had been formed.

Every day, the newspapers were filled with letters and reports of donations from churches, businesses and people of every walk of life. One letter writer this morning brought her nearly to tears with his words: *"Let us for a time lay aside party politics, president making, etc., and let us act upon the solemn conviction that from those to whom much is given, much shall be required."*

Hardly a day went by when there wasn't word of yet some

other fundraiser. Theater companies were donating their evening's proceeds, choirs and musical groups were putting on special performances. And tonight, the Howard Anthenaeum was holding a grand subscription ball for Ireland. All of Boston's finest citizens would be there, and she, Kathleen Deacey from Cobh, would be among them—if only as volunteer help.

She picked up the blue striped dress Father Williams had let her have from among the clothing that had been donated to the church for those less fortunate. Slipping it over her head, she turned to the mirror and dropped a curtsy. How elegant she looked. It was fortunate that Jack and his grandfather had already gone out for the evening, for surely the old man would voice his displeasure if he saw her dressed so fine—and on her way to a ball to help the Irish.

She ran a hand down the skirt of the dress, the color so like the spring sky over Ireland, when the air was cool and a gentle mist slipped in from the sea. On such a soft morning Danny had first told her he was going to Newfoundland, to work in the fisheries for the summer and make some money so they could be properly wed.

She turned away from the mirror, from the memories fostered by the blue fabric. Surely Boston was lovely in the spring as well. Pushing aside all thoughts except those of the evening ahead, she hurried downstairs to grab her cloak and slip out into the night. By the time she entered the Howard Anthenaeum a short while later, she jittered with excitement.

After getting a quick description of her duties from the woman overseeing the volunteers, Kathleen went to work collecting the wraps of people arriving for the ball. Before an hour had passed, it felt like she was wearing a path in the floor between the entrance and the cloakroom. Though there were two other young women besides herself collecting wraps, more help might have helped speed the process, at least until the rush passed. Still, she felt no cause to complain, even to herself, for her purpose this evening was to help the Irish. And if she went home exhausted, it would mean that she had done what she could for her homeland.

Several hundred people had already arrived and the arrivals did not appear to be slowing at all. To be sure, they would raise a goodly sum for the cause this evening.

The orchestra struck up a lively tune and the notes mingled with the sounds of laughter and of friends greeting one another. Amid this mood of gaiety, she set about collecting another armful of the wraps. As she headed for the cloakroom, a familiar laugh broke through the happy voices. *Jack?* A shiver settled itself upon her shoulders, waiting.

She clutched the cloaks to her chest and looked around for the source of the laughter. Jack had said he was meeting friends this evening. Surely he would have told her if he was coming to the ball, wouldn't he?

A hint of lavender rose up from the fur-trimmed mantle she carried and for a wistful moment she longed to be attending the ball instead of serving at it. She peeked inside the open ballroom doors. All of Boston's elite were here, the room awash in beautiful fabrics on every woman in attendance, jewel colored gowns shimmering beneath the chandeliers' glow. Though she'd heard of such events in Ireland, most were held by the English landlords for other English...and an Irish cottier's family was classes away from ever being invited to such an affair.

The parties she'd attended took place in homes, friends and neighbors spilling outside to dance to the fiddler's tunes, the dirt road their dance floor, the moon their chandelier.

She lingered a moment longer, as if her presence could make her belong with these people who lived in grand houses, and for whom the price of attending this ball was a mere pittance.

Then she heard it again, the laugh she would probably recognize even ten years from now, and a man called out, "Montgomery!" And the shiver that waited on her shoulders tripped down her spine.

He was here. She let her gaze slip over the crowd, spotting him near another entrance to the ballroom, formally dressed in a black jacket, waistcoat and trousers, crisp white shirt beneath. She watched, breath suspended, as he shook hands with several other men. She had never imagined Jack could be like this, so at ease among the gentry.

Leaning on his cane, he limped to the side of a striking blonde woman in a golden gown, cut low in the front and trimmed with lace flounces. He whispered something to her and she laughed gaily up at him.

Kathleen's stomach turned. Jack Montgomery was far more than just a whaling captain. He was a gentleman. An elegant gentleman. And what on heaven and earth might a gentleman want with her, a cottier's daughter, *a peasant*. She hurried toward the cloakroom, eager to escape before he saw her.

She was here to work, while he was here to…play. Indeed, there was no reason he would have to speak to her. Faith, why would he want to? She in her plain blue dress, ugly and striped, not a flounce nor a speck of lace, the neck so high as to label her a spinster—or a domestic.

She deposited the wraps in the cloakroom and returned to the entrance hall, certain that should their paths cross tonight he would not acknowledge her presence—unless of course, there was something he would be needing. She was the help this evening. And he was a guest.

Who was to care whether he was here anyway? What difference did it make? Surely, none to her. Jack was free to go wherever he liked, to be with whomever he chose. And tonight, she had other things to do as well.

Still, she couldn't help but look into the ballroom again, and now, damn his English soul, but there were many eyes cast in his direction—and they all belonged to beautiful young women, rich young women, elegant young women—and not a one of them in a striped blue gown.

Though she fought it, from that moment forward she could think of little besides who Jack might be with and what they might be doing. She had been assigned to help out in the ladies' retiring room once all the wraps were put away. And though she vowed to stay there the rest of the evening, part of her kept wanting to steal away, just once, to scan the ballroom and find him…to make sure he was still there and not off in some darkened corner with a beautiful woman.

She glanced at the retiring room doorway. 'Twas none of her business what Jack was doing out there. But he'd kissed her. *More than once.* And what had been his words? *"So you'll give up on us instead?"* he'd said, as though there was something special between them.

Ah, and no doubt he had kissed a great many women, had said those words to others before her. Her breath caught. Had he? She had never really thought on it before. She had known, she supposed, that he had kissed women, but in her mind they were regular women—not beautiful ladies from well-to-do families. *Everything she wasn't.*

A small group of women entered the room and she welcomed their presence as a respite from her thoughts. She plumped the pillows on nearby chairs and filled the washing pitchers with warm water from the fire. Only after the women were seated did she notice the gold dress and the woman wearing it—Jack's friend. Her blond hair shone in the lamplight, her blue eyes sparkled as she perched primly on the edge of her seat, the very vision of upper class.

"Tell us everything, all over again," one of the women said, leaning in.

"Has he spoken to your father yet?" another asked, also bending forward.

It was all Kathleen could do to keep from leaning in with them.

Gold dress laughed. "I'm sure he'll be paying a call on father soon."

"Really?" An excited tremor ran through the small group.

She nodded. "If I may say, he's been smitten with me for some time."

The women nodded knowingly and fanned themselves.

"He was sorely disappointed we couldn't dance—on account of his ankle," gold dress said with a sigh. "Of course, this nonsense about whaling will have to end if we're to be engaged."

Kathleen froze. His ankle? Was she talking about Jack? She busied herself wiping off the tops of the end tables in the room.

"I won't be the wife of a whaling captain...but a ship owner like my father, in the merchant trades, well, that is another thing entirely. Perhaps Jack will expand our holdings into the China trade..." Gold dress bestowed a royal smile on the ladies around her and they nodded agreement. Then she gave a little pout. "He's already making preparations to go to sea again unless father can convince him otherwise… Says he must make at least one more voyage. Oh, I cannot wait another year to become his wife." She brought a hand dramatically to her throat. "Emily Cuthbert Montgomery…sounds so lovely, don't you think?"

The women gave a collective nod. "If anyone can convince him, your father can," one said.

The women tittered as though sharing some private joke.

Kathleen turned away. Had Jack's grandfather been speaking the truth those weeks ago when he'd said Jack was nearly engaged? One more look at the small circle of women and she knew the answer without even acknowledging it.

So what had he been wanting from her?

Anger shot through her until even her fingertips seemed to be tingling from it. Sure, but there could only be one thing he was wanting from a poor Irish lass…aye, and it didn't involve a marriage certificate. By all that was holy, if she could see Jack this very minute, she would tell him exactly—

Her churning thoughts drew to a screeching halt as she caught sight of her face in the nearby mirror, eyes squinting, nose and mouth crunched into a look of deep concentration, lips nearly curled in a feral snarl like she was having a fit of sorts.

She forced composure onto her countenance, noticing only then that behind her own reflection were the faces of the ladies, gold dress included, their expressions ranging from amused disbelief to outright concern.

"Are you all right?" one asked.

Her face burned. Suddenly she could no longer stomach the scent of their mingled perfumes, the odor so sweetly overwhelming it choked the air from the room. The flames leapt high and golden

in the hearth, crackling wickedly as they devoured the logs. Waves
of heat rolled over her.

"I feel quite ill," she stammered and rushed out the door. Their
laughter followed her into the hall.

She rounded a corner into a deserted corridor and stopped to
regain control. Drawing several deep breaths, she thought again of
what had passed between her and Jack, and righteously embraced
her anger. Had she meant nothing to him at all?

The answer delivered an onslaught of disappointment, and
she almost gasped at the clarity with which she suddenly saw the
past few months. She brought a fist to her chest. First she'd lost
Danny...and now Jack.

She gave her head a firm shake. But this was ridiculous. What
right had she to be upset? He'd but kissed her; no promises had
he offered. And all along she'd made it quite clear that she was
betrothed, that Danny held her heart.

This thing with Jack was nothing but the merest dalliance. Still,
the day could not come soon enough that she might find Danny
and put these troubled thoughts to rest.

Strains of music from the orchestra slipped into the distant
corridor where she stood, reminding her that the Irish in Ireland
had problems far greater than hers. She would do well to remember
that.

She retraced her steps, passing by the ladies' retiring room on
her way to the main entrance, intent on getting some air before
returning to her station. Striding across the foyer, she burst through
the exterior doors and inhaled the frigid night air.

Out in the street the carriages waited, their drivers playing dice
with one another, laughing and talking away the winter night. It
didn't matter to them that Jack Montgomery was getting engaged.

It shouldn't matter to her. A whole world existed beyond this ballroom if she would but step out and find it. She watched the drivers until the cold made her shiver, then went back inside to return to work.

Surely by now, Gold Dress and her friends had returned to the party and other women would be using the retiring room. As she passed the ballroom, she glanced inside and let her gaze roam the crowded room. Aye, there she was, Emily Cuthbert, sparkling beneath the glow of the chandeliers, stretching up to whisper some secret to the gentleman bending low toward her. As if sensing Kathleen's perusal, the man raised his head to look toward the open doorway. Their eyes met. A slow smile spread across Jack's face.

Mortified, Kathleen quickened her steps toward the ladies' retiring room. By the saints, but she would not look in on the ball again. She'd not have Jack thinking her stalking him.

Hours later, true to her word, she had not been back to the ballroom, though she'd been far more successful restricting her actions than she had been at containing her thoughts. 'Twas now nearly one o'clock. She stifled a yawn. Supper had been served and the guests were enjoying the last dances of the evening. Her work obligation fulfilled, Kathleen retrieved her cloak and settled it over her shoulders before plodding toward the entrance hall. Her legs ached from standing and her mind was just as weary; her fatigue came as much from emotional turmoil as it did from hard work. She turned her thoughts to home, just a scant walk away. At this moment she could think of no place she would rather be than in her own bed. *Where she could dream of something other than Jack Montgomery.*

Thank goodness this night was done. By the morn she would

be fine, and she could go about her duties fully accepting that Jack was soon to be betrothed.

She passed the ballroom door and automatically turned to look inside, the room now much emptier than it had been just a few hours ago. Fatigue teased her imagination and filled her mind with visions of Jack Montgomery and Emily Cuthbert. Half the night had passed since she'd last looked in…sure and what could be the harm in a closer peek?

She stepped through the open doorway and slid into the shadows along the wall to watch the remaining dancers whirl about the floor. She tried to marvel at the elegance of this great hall and yet found herself no longer awed. Exhaustion made her eyes burn and she blinked hard to moisten them.

Jack was nowhere to be seen; no doubt he'd gone home already. Perhaps he'd departed once his soon-to-be-wife left the ball. Perhaps he'd walked her out to her carriage and asked to call on her in the morning. Perhaps he'd even asked to call on *her father* in the morning.

Why did she even care? Weariness rolled over her and her eyelids grew heavy. Eyes fixed on the exit door, her steps sluggish, she thought only of the relief that sleep would bring. A huge yawn overtook her and she made the sign of the cross over her open mouth.

"Why do you do that?" a low voice murmured in her ear.

Exhaustion fled with the race of her pulse and she cast a glance over her shoulder then turned slowly, an unbidden smile on her face. "Ye nearly stopped me heart, Captain."

He gave her a quick lopsided grin—no doubt the effect of much wine this evening. "Why do you make the sign of the cross over your mouth?" he asked again.

"You came to ask me that? Now?"

"Yes."

"You'd do well to cross your mouth each time ye yawn, else evil spirits will sweep in take abode."

He raised his eyebrows and a smile played at the corners of his mouth. "I'm probably full of evil spirits already."

"That I can believe. Perhaps you should drink some holy water just to be safe."

"I could do that," he replied in complete seriousness. His dark eyes shimmered in the dim light, reminding her of that afternoon in his bedroom. She glanced quickly away.

"I'll be done with my duties now. A good-night to you, sir." She stepped past him toward the door but he moved quickly to block her passage.

"Dance with me," he murmured.

CHAPTER TWENTY-SEVEN

HER HEAD SNAPPED up in surprise, the words so unexpected she thought perhaps she'd imagined them.

"Dance with me," he repeated.

Nay, her mind warned even as the idea sent a thrill through her. "I'm far too weary. Me legs might collapse," she said with an apologetic smile. "And I'm bound for home anyhow." She lifted her arms from her sides to demonstrate that she already wore her cloak.

"I'll hold you up."

"Oh aye." She gestured at his cane. "Your ankle is none too sturdy either. But tell me, Captain, how do ye come to be here? I thought you were meeting friends out this evening."

He shrugged. "I met them here."

"I'd noticed as much. A lady among them I gather." The words slipped out before she could stop herself.

He raised an eyebrow. "I have several friends who are ladies…"

"One in particular," Kathleen said. "Blond hair, gold dress. Perhaps *she'd* like to dance."

"Kathleen…are you jealous?"

"Hardly," she retorted. "But since you are about to be betrothed, Jack, ye should perhaps be dallying with her." Her eyes met his in challenge, an unspoken demand for explanation. The sounds of the orchestra floated over and around them and the beauty of the music swept into her soul. She dropped her gaze to the floor and tried to convince herself she didn't care what his answer was, for she had her own betrothed to be worrying about.

"I'm not getting engaged."

She looked up into his darkened eyes. "She said—"

"She wishes, like a child on a star. But you more than anyone should know only those dreams that are fated so, come true. I don't love her."

She swallowed down the knot in her throat, desperately wanting to believe him.

"Dance with me." He set aside his cane and stepped closer to her.

She hesitated, afraid that the nearness of him would be her undoing. He lowered his head until his lips nearly brushed her ear.

"Dance with me." The words were hardly more than a murmur.

"Aye," she whispered.

He unfastened the clasp at her throat and let her cloak slide slowly over her shoulders to the floor, then took one hand in his and drew her near enough that his other could rest at her waist. And though no other part of them touched, she could feel the heat of him as sure as if he were pressed against her. It took all her strength not to lean into him.

"Not afraid of the Good People any longer?" He took a step and she followed.

"Nay." 'Twas herself she feared—not the faeries.

Slow and halting, Jack favoring his sore ankle, they danced unnoticed in the shadows. He drew her close and Kathleen knew she should pull back—but didn't.

By the song's end she was trembling inside, acutely aware that though the music no longer played, Jack had not loosed his hold of her. And God help her, but she didn't want him to, her need to be near him so great she thought she might be rent in half if he moved away from her.

She looked up into his face and his expression made her feel as though she were about to leap off some great cliff with no knowledge of what lay below. She couldn't think, could scarce breathe. It was as if all the party had stopped and they were alone here in the darkness, a web of magic woven around them, rendering them invisible. What mischief were the faeries up to now?

"I must be going," she said, the shaking of her voice betraying her emotion. Pulling away from him, she picked up her cloak and fastened the front, intent on leaving without facing him again. What could he be wanting with her when he could have Emily Cuthbert?

He took hold of her arm. "I'll get my coat."

"You need not leave on my account."

"Wait for me." His tone said there would be no discussion on the matter.

"If you do not mind, sir, I'll wait outside where 'tis cooler." She hurried across the great foyer, as eager to escape her own emotions as she was to escape Jack Montgomery if only for a few minutes. She pushed through the outside door, gasping as the night embraced her with its icy fingers. Behind her the great doors swung shut like the immense jaws of a whale, swallowing the music and gaiety and abandoning her to the stillness of the wee morning. Outside, several carriages still waited under the bright full moon, the drivers huddled together, talking quietly while they waited in the cold for their passengers to finally quit the party.

Seconds later the door swung open again and Jack stepped outside to join her. The brisk air had cleared her mind and suddenly she saw his actions in the ballroom in a fresh light. She eyed him warily; no doubt the man thought to seduce her in his carriage.

"You didn't, perchance, rent a coach this eve, did ye?" She nodded toward the waiting conveyances.

"With home ten minutes away?"

"But your ankle—"

"Needs strengthening. Walking helps it."

Her shoulders felt infinitely lighter. "Oh, aye," she said with a smile.

Matching her grin, Jack stuck out his elbow, and after a moment's hesitation she slipped her hand into the crook of his arm. Though he walked slowly because of his cane, there was no weakness to the man and she was glad for his company at this late hour.

A gust of icy wind swirled around them and she shivered. "Too cold to be outside when a warm hearth and heavy blankets await at home," she murmured.

Jack drew his arm closer to his body as if to bring her into the circle of his warmth. She hunched her shoulders against the chill and leaned into him, too cold to worry about his intentions—or her response, for that matter.

"I was surprised to see you at the ball tonight, it being a benefit for the Irish and all. Does your grandfather know?" she asked.

He shook his head. "I'm sure he'll raise holy hell when he finds out."

"I wonder will the going be worth the fuss he'll be making for a few days over it."

He nodded, and they walked for several minutes without

speaking, past darkened storefronts, so different in the dead of the night, almost forlorn in their emptiness as though waiting for the magical spark of daybreak to bring them to life again. Jack halted in front of a milliner's shop.

"See something you like?" she teased.

His lips curved up and a prickle of anticipation swept through her.

He took a step backward. "Do you know what doorways are for?"

She shook her head in confusion. Taking her hand in his, he pulled her with him into the covered entry of the small shop.

"Kissing," he said with a mischievous grin. His lips brushed against her ear and Kathleen knew she was lost. He was going to kiss her. And she knew without a second's doubt that she could—would—do nothing but kiss him back.

His mouth trailed along the side of her jaw and he kissed her throat. She gasped and turned her face to meet him. His mouth closed over hers and she was once again swept into the place the Good People had created, where all the world had stopped and only she and Jack were left to linger.

The cold dissolved, replaced by a feeling inside her that Danny had never ignited. She softened into Jack and for the first time let herself truly care, let herself truly want this Englishman. When the kiss ended, he held her in the darkness, tight against him, one hand in her hair, and her head to his chest where she could hear the powerful beat of his heart.

"The going will be well worth any fuss my grandfather makes," he said.

She drew back and searched his face in the darkness, wanting to assure herself that his words were true. As if knowing her fear, he cupped her cheeks with his hands and put his lips to hers in a kiss so tender she sighed out his name when they parted.

"Are you still cold?" he asked.

She shook her head. He took her hand and tucked it into the crook of his arm once more and they started for home, walking even more slowly than before, as though neither was anxious to arrive. Kathleen looked up at the stars, their edges sharp as blades in a sky clear with cold, each one sparkling white in brilliant contrast to the opal universe. The odor of a thousand burning fireplaces mingled with the crisp, fresh air into a scent from her childhood, one that forever reminded her of racing across the fields for home and safety and warmth.

For the first time since leaving Ireland she felt the contentment of knowing she was somewhere she belonged. She sensed then the presence of powers greater than herself, of meaning behind all that had happened to her since the day Danny hadn't come back. She shivered and Jack pulled her closer.

"*Meileann muilte Dé go mall ach meileann siad go mín.* The mills of God grind slowly but they grind finely," she whispered. "Me ma said it often. Ah, to know what God's plan is, wouldn't you wish?"

"Perhaps. But I wonder how many of us would embrace our future willingly if we knew in advance what it would be?"

"You'll be sounding like me own mother now."

He grinned. "Somehow I'm flattered."

By the time they crossed the threshold into the foyer of Jack's home, Kathleen wished the night would never have to end.

She paused at the foot of the stair and turned to face him. He reached a finger out to trace the line of her jaw, then brushed his thumb across her bottom lip. The seconds passed unused. "Good night, Kathleen," he finally murmured before turning away and stepping into the parlor.

She heard the door to the sideboard open and the sound of a decanter set on the table. "Sleep well," she whispered. With a sigh, she mounted the stairs to her attic room, lonely beyond belief, and more confused than ever.

She threw her cloak over a chair, slipped out of her dress and into her nightclothes. Homesickness swept over her and she stepped to the window in the darkness to stare out at the quiet street. She longed for her family, for the comfort that came from being near those whose actions were predictable, whose words one could trust.

A tapping broke into her reverie, so quietly she first thought it her imagination. She went to the door but did not unlock it. "Is someone there?"

"Kathleen," Jack whispered.

She pulled on her wrapper and tied it tightly before cracking open the door. "What are ye wanting?"

His jacket was off, his shirttails out. He pushed the door open a bit more and took a step toward her, shoving the door quietly closed behind him with his foot. "Just this." He put a hand beneath her chin to tip her head up, then kissed her so long and hard she needed to lean into him for support.

His hands slid down her sides to loosen the tie of her wrapper, to slip beneath and caress the soft curves of her body through the thin fabric of her shift. The sigh that slipped from between her lips was enough to waken sanity in her fevered brain. She wrenched herself back and clutched the front of her wrapper closed.

"Ye must leave. We can't be doing this."

"It's not wrong—not between us. Surely you can feel it, too."

Aye, she could. She closed her eyes in silent desperation. He ran a hand up her arm and over her shoulder. She shivered and shook her head, knowing that if she let him touch her like he had minutes ago, her resistance would crumble. "Good night," she whispered just as he had done downstairs.

"Sweet dreams," he said after a long moment and exited the room.

Dazed, she shut the door and climbed into bed, weak with wanting. And though she could not forget that just days ago she was searching for Danny, she had only the slightest twinge of guilt that tonight she hoped her every dream was of Jack.

She slept restlessly and woke with a start before the sun, her mind caught up with thoughts of Jack and memories of the evening past and the clear knowledge that she no longer wanted to find Danny. She wanted Jack. Wanted him more than she'd ever wanted Danny. Though she didn't know what the future held, she could no longer deny to herself that Jack Montgomery was the man holding her heart.

CHAPTER TWENTY-EIGHT

JACK FINISHED HIS breakfast and settled back into his chair, all the while watching Kathleen as she bent over the table to clear away the dishes. She cast a shy smile his way and he grinned at her, their eyes meeting and holding before she carried the dishes to the kitchen.

"For bedding—not wedding," his grandfather said once she was gone. "Make sure you know the difference."

Anger rose up in his chest. "Pardon me?"

"I know you're taken with her, Jack. But she's Irish...and poor as they come."

"It seems to me this family was once poor, too."

"But we're not any longer. She'll drag you down again. Everything I've worked for, you've worked for, even what your father worked for—"

"My father didn't have the guts to stick around long enough to ever be poor. I'll tell you something—"

"I don't want to know."

"Even in our worst circumstance, we were never as bad off as she has been—and I've never once heard her talk of killing herself."

The old man shrugged. "The Irish aren't like you and me—they don't mind being poor. It's just part of their makeup."

Jack threw his hands up in disgust and bit back an uncouth reply. A tense silence settled over the room until Kathleen returned to clear away the remainder of the dishes.

"Kathleen," his grandfather said, "tell my grandson here why the Irish eat so many potatoes."

Hands full, she straightened her shoulders and faced the old man, looked him square in the face for a moment before answering. Suddenly Jack was very proud of her.

"We eat potatoes because all the wheat we grow is sent to England, payment for rent owed the English landlords," she said matter-of-factly. "Most families have but a small patch of land for themselves. Potatoes are the only plant that yields enough to feed a family for the year. So ye ask, sir, why we eat so many potatoes? It's because we have no choice."

She started to walk away, then turned back. "Even now, with Ireland in famine, the wheat—*our wheat*—is going to England, and the people of Ireland are left to starve." Her voice quivered and Jack knew she had overheard his grandfather's earlier words. "How dare you say we do not mind being poor! How dare you? Someday, perhaps not in this life, there will be a price to pay for this evil against me people—it will not go unpunished—for a sin against one man is a sin against all."

She strode back into the kitchen, leaving Jack and his grandfather to stare after her. A minute passed before the old man cleared his throat.

Jack slashed the air with one hand. "Don't even let the words cross your lips. I will not dismiss her—and neither will you."

The old man gave him an almost imperceptible nod. "Just make sure you don't confuse pity or lust with feelings of affection."

"I think I know the difference. Can we speak of something else now?"

His grandfather took a swallow of tea. "Will Cuthbert is stopping by later this afternoon," he said. "I saw him at the club last night...I think you'll be interested in what he has to say."

"Is it me he's coming to see? Or you?" Will was the prosperous owner of several merchant ships and an old friend of Jack's father.

"You, mostly."

"About his daughter?"

"I don't know. Just remember, she's a fine girl, Jack. And she's smitten with you."

"I don't—"

"For God's sake. Not so long ago you thought you couldn't do better than Emily Cuthbert." The old man pointed a finger at Jack. "You said her father's wealth would be a nice complement to your marriage."

"You said it. I only agreed."

"We owe a lot to Will. Don't forget that."

"I never would." Five years ago, when Jack and his grandfather had come over from England, Will had welcomed them, opening doors that otherwise would have stayed closed, enabling Jack to fit in with the upper classes long before he had the money to actually belong.

When he was between voyages, he and Emily Cuthbert had been thrown together because their families knew each other so well. There had been a time Jack had expected to marry her one day. But that was all before the last voyage. Before he'd plucked Kathleen Deacey from the ocean.

Kathleen slipped into the room and Jack watched as she set a pitcher of warm water and a clean basin on the small table in the corner. Her hair was pulled into a knot, and all he could think of was kissing her nape.

As though his thoughts reached her, she slid a hand across the back of her neck and glanced in his direction. A blush rose up her cheeks and he grinned at her.

"Jack!" his grandfather snapped.

He turned his attention reluctantly back to the old man. From the corner of his eye, he could see Kathleen slip from the room. "What?"

"Don't burn this bridge."

"Cuthbert? I won't."

His grandfather snorted. "The hell you won't. Keep your eyes off the help while Will is here." He sighed in resignation. "And then if you must, take the girl to your bed and get her out of your system."

*

Will Cuthbert took the offered glass of wine and absently turned it in his hand.

Jack settled into a chair on the opposite side of the hearth and hoped Cuthbert was here about business—and not matrimony. After the conversation he'd had with his grandfather this morning, he had thin patience for the subject. He would not be pushed into marriage, no matter how advantageous it might be to have Emily Cuthbert in the family.

"I don't think there's any easy way to lead into this," Cuthbert finally said. "So I shall just plow forward and hope you don't take offense."

Offense? Good, this couldn't be about Emily then. Jack relaxed and took another sip of wine. "I'm intrigued. Lead on."

"I've always admired your ambition, Jack. If I had a son, I would have wished him to be like you in that respect."

He shrugged, uncomfortable with the compliment.

"Ah, well," Cuthbert said with a sheepish grin. "I thought by now, you'd be coming to me on this matter."

"Excuse me?"

Cuthbert took a large swallow of wine. "I know you always said you wouldn't marry until you were financially secure. If I recall correctly, you wanted controlling interest in a whaling ship and investments in other voyages."

Jack nodded.

"I respect that. But while you pursue security, I must live with a daughter who grows increasingly anxious to wed. She's quite taken with you, you know."

Jack's jaw tightened. "I think highly of her myself."

"Dammit Jack, don't take this wrong, but your grandfather and I were talking last night at the club…"

So his grandfather did know what this was about. He opened his mouth to speak, but Cuthbert waved him silent.

"Hear me out. I know you're at least a year away from the financial security you want. Problem is, a year or two seems like forever to a young woman." He leaned forward.

"Would it help at all to know that, as a wedding present, I intend to sign over to you my interest in your current ship? My share added to yours will give you controlling interest. You'll be exactly where you want to be more than a year ahead of schedule. And free to… marry."

Jack's jaw dropped. This was far and away the last thing he expected from Cuthbert. The man had just guaranteed the financial security he'd been striving for all these years. With the controlling interest in a whaling ship, more than half of the profits from each voyage would be his. It would give him more than enough money to invest in several ships at once. He would soon be wealthy in his own right. All he had to do was agree.

But the price, was it worth the price? A lifetime with Emily Cuthbert? *A life without Kathleen?* He tossed down the remainder of his wine and fixed a look on Cuthbert. "I don't know what to say."

"I should add that at any point should you be interested, I would be happy to bring you into my company as a partner."

Jack reached across to the side table to refill his wine glass. He noticed that Cuthbert's glass was still nearly full.

"I know this is a bit of a surprise," Cuthbert said. "Take some time to think about it."

Jack held his glass up and watched the flames in the hearth through the burgundy liquid. Everything he'd ever wanted was being laid out for his taking and all he could think was that he didn't love Emily Cuthbert. He was amazed that such a thought bothered him. Not so long ago it wouldn't have even crossed his mind.

"I didn't expect to be thinking along these lines for at least a couple of years. But, your offer—well, are you sure Emily wants this match?"

Cuthbert laughed. "Would I be here otherwise? It's all she seems to speak of lately." He considered Jack for a moment. "But is it what *you* want?"

"Of course he does." Jack's grandfather shuffled through the doorway, a broad grin on his face.

Jack froze. He tried to warn off the old man with his eyes, but his grandfather merely grinned at him and reached out to shake hands with Cuthbert. One comment led to another, and before Jack could interject a word, the two were exchanging congratulations and welcoming one another into the family.

Jack bit back the words he wanted to say, fully aware that if he now voiced any concerns about the match, he would thoroughly insult Cuthbert. His grandfather would have hell to pay for this manipulation.

He tilted his head back and downed his wine and thought of Kathleen Deacey, of life without her. He thought of marriage to Emily Cuthbert. Then he stared into the empty hollow of his wineglass—and wished for whiskey.

His grandfather called for Kathleen to bring out another bottle of claret. She entered the room and he took the bottle from her, holding it up with great aplomb as she headed for the door.

"To the forthcoming engagement of my grandson and your daughter!" he boomed.

Jack stood, seething. "Excuse me, gentlemen, but this toast is a bit premature." He struggled to keep his tone light so as not to offend Will. "While Emily is charming and lovely and...every man's ideal...this is more than sudden. I need some time to look at my books and make certain this is the best decision at this time."

His grandfather chuckled and winked at Cuthbert. "He probably wants to ask your daughter first—on bended knee, no doubt."

Jack refused to dignify his grandfather's remark with so much as a look, let alone a response. Cuthbert got to his feet.

"Forgive me, Jack. I didn't mean to push. I'm only trying to help you and Emily move forward. Rest assured I'll not speak a word of this conversation to her until after you've proposed."

The two men walked to the foyer and Cuthbert extended a hand. "My offer stands," he said. "I'd be proud to have you in the family— and in my business. I'll see you this evening."

Jack pushed the heavy door closed after Cuthbert left. This evening? Did the man really expect him to propose tonight? He exhaled irritably. This day was taking on all the attributes of a nightmare.

His grandfather called from the other room and Jack welcomed the battle to come. He strode into the parlor, took the chair opposite his grandfather, and eyed the old man in silence. The fire snapped.

"What the hell do you think you're doing?" he finally asked.

His grandfather held up a hand. "It's a good match."

"For who?"

"For both of you, dammit. A woman of Emily Cuthbert's standing, with her father's wealth... It's what you've wanted all along. Half a year ago you would have jumped at this opportunity. Now look at you. Sulking because you have to marry a rich, beautiful woman."

"This is my decision to make, not yours."

"For the past several weeks you haven't been making wise decisions at all. About time someone took charge of the situation."

Jack sat up straight. "Situation? What situation? You mean *my life?*"

"No, I mean your wife."

"Ha! It seems they're the one and the same in your eyes."

"Emily Cuthbert isn't going to wait another year or two for you to make up your mind. I'm just trying to make sure you don't do something you'll live to regret."

"*Live to regret.* Well if I do, it'll be my life that's full of regret, now won't it? You had no right to imply to Will Cuthbert that I'm about to propose to his daughter." Jack's voice dropped a notch. "You've put me in a mess here and I'm not quite sure how to get out. I only hope he's true to his word—that he'll say nothing to Emily."

"So? Marry the girl."

Jack shook his head in disgust.

"That Irish girl is nothing more than a passing fancy," his grandfather snapped. "You saved her life. That's it. Somehow you've gotten everything mixed up with that. Your place is levels above hers."

"Leave me alone, Grandfather." Jack pushed at the air with one hand. "I've no patience for your prejudice."

The old man stood. "Fine. Don't forget we've dinner at the Thomson's tonight. All the Cuthberts will be there."

Of course, that's what Will had meant at the door. He wasn't expecting Jack to propose tonight. *Or was he?*

"I'm not going. Make some excuse for me. My ankle is swollen— whatever. I need time to think."

"That would be a terrible slight."

"It won't be a slight if you make my excuse good enough," Jack said in a low voice.

His grandfather said nothing for several moments. Then he turned and left the room.

*

Kathleen had been able to think of little else since the grandfather announced Jack's engagement several hours ago. Thank goodness it happened before she had a chance to tell Jack she'd decided to stop searching for Danny, before she'd had a chance to let him know of her feelings for him.

She stopped inside the parlor door. "I know you said you were wanting no dinner, but me day is coming to an end now and I'll be checking with you this last time before I go upstairs."

The lamplight flickered over Jack's face and, for an instant, he looked truly the devil she once thought him to be. And then, he was simply the darkly handsome man to whom she had almost professed her love.

He shook his head. "I'll find myself something to eat."

"Very good…sir." She made no move to leave.

"I'm not engaged."

A harsh laugh escaped her. "Best you be telling that to Mr. Cuthbert and your grandfather. It did surprise me though, after ye professed you didn't love her."

"Love's got nothing to do with it. It's no requirement for marriage. But a rich father and a family well-placed in society, well who could argue against the strength of those marital foundations?" Though he smiled, his eyes held no mirth.

She bit her lip to keep words of protest from rushing out of her mouth. 'Twas his choice to wed whomever he wanted, for whatever reasons he wished. She couldn't care. Marriages were arranged all the time, more often than not with no love between the bride and groom. Money, land, connections, those were what mattered. *And what of love?* her mind whispered.

"Is that all that matters to you?" The words burst out before she knew she was going to say them.

He shrugged. "Money and status are perhaps the only two things you can count on in this world."

"And love, a person can count on love—"

"Can they?" he shot back. "And where the hell is your Danny? My own lessons have come hard and each time, their essence has been the same." His words were clipped, his tone, biting. "My first teacher was my father, my second was my mother…" He shook his head. "Go to bed, Kathleen Deacey."

Aye, that's what she should do. Leave Jack alone with his problems for she had enough of her own. Still she did not leave. "And what will you do?"

His eyes bored into hers and she was suddenly afraid. "What would you have me do, Kathleen?"

She could scarce breathe. Faith, 'twas not her decision to make. She had to know that it did not matter to him that she was poor, that she was Irish, that she was a cottier's daughter. An ache pressed against the inside of her chest. He wanted things she could never give him—wealth and status. And she needed a man who believed in love.

And even if Jack became that man, even if he suddenly professed that her love was all that he wanted, would it be enough? For what would her family say of her loving this Englishman? Would they see Jack Montgomery, the man—or would they see only her betrayal of the Irish?

She didn't even have to ask the question to know the answer. What a fool she was. There was no future for them; there could be none with Moira dead and all of Ireland gasping beneath the foot of the English landlord. Her future lay with an Irishman, with Danny if she could find him.

And Jack—she could barely form the thought—would take Emily Cuthbert to his bed as his wife. Her self-control started to crumble.

"Kathleen?"

She blinked. "Wed whom ye must, Captain. I, myself, am already engaged, as ye know."

His expression hardened. "Then perhaps I shall have to make a point of calling on Miss Cuthbert." He glanced at his pocket watch. "Too late tonight, I suppose. Tomorrow will have to do."

The blood rushed from Kathleen's head. The room buzzed. "My congratulations to you, sir," she said. "I think ye've found your perfect match." She started for the door.

"What? No words of Irish wisdom to offer on my impending engagement?"

Kathleen kept walking. Thank God she was to marry an Irish man, a man who saw the world through eyes like hers.

"What would your mother have to say?" Jack shouted. "What proverb would she offer me now? Surely she would say something."

Kathleen whirled, cheeks flushed. "Aye, she'd have words for you, Captain. She would say…she would say…" Her mind raced for something, anything to shout back. "*Is uaigneach an níochán nach mbíonn léine ann.* I give you that from me mother on this eve of your engagement," she spat.

"And what does it mean?" he asked quietly.

She turned away.

"What does it mean," he repeated more loudly.

She strode from the room. She'd not tell him, ever, the meaning of the words. 'Twas not the proverb she meant to say anyway. She didn't know why this one had forced its way out of her mouth instead of some other. It was if her own brain had betrayed her just when she needed strength against the temptation Jack Montgomery offered. Her insides shook from the exchange; her head felt ready to burst. Why on earth had she shouted that proverb at him instead of some other?

She asked herself the question again and again, knowing full well the answer, knowing full well that she would spend a lifetime loving a man she couldn't have. She stepped into her room, then closed and locked the door behind her. *Is uaigneach an níochán nach mbíonn léine ann. It is a lonely washing that has no man's shirt in it.*

And such a lonely life it would be without his love.

CHAPTER TWENTY-NINE

JACK POURED HIMSELF a whiskey and slumped back into his chair. Hell, for a man who'd just been handed everything he ever wanted, he was surely in a foul mood. Perhaps his grandfather was right—he should just bed Kathleen and get her out of his system.

He grimaced. Problem was, bedding her wouldn't get her out of his system because, damnation, he didn't want her out of his system.

He stared at the fire, at the shadows dancing on the walls like specters from the past portending the future. Six months ago his future had seemed so clear. He closed his eyes and rubbed the bridge of his nose. Now he could hardly see beyond the next day.

All he had to do was say he didn't want to marry Emily Cuthbert. Simple as that. Yet, it wasn't really that simple and he knew it. No matter how he felt about Emily, the prospect of her wealth enticed him with the promise that he would never again know the pain of losing someone he loved because of lack of money.

But he would lose Kathleen.

He slammed a flat hand onto the armrest of his chair. If he'd never met Kathleen, he'd likely be proposing to Emily at this very moment. He'd not be concerned about whether he loved her, only pleased that the wealth of her family would soon be his. He shook his head. But he *had* met Kathleen and he couldn't change that. Dammit to hell, but what did he want?

An hour passed and then another and he refilled his glass several times as he forced himself to take stock of his life and his goals. Kathleen deserved someone who believed in love as much as she did. She'd been raised by a family who supported one another, who would always be there for one another, who knew that money wasn't as important as the bond between them.

He rested his head on the back of the sofa and stared up at the ceiling, seeing his own life more clearly than he had in years. Understanding washed through him. There were worse things than life as he had known it up to now. It was not money that made one man superior to another. It was not marriage into a proper Boston family that delivered respect. It was not wealth that made one worthy of loyalty.

His shoulders relaxed and a smile played at the corners of his mouth. It wasn't money and power that would give him what he sought; it was the love of a family, a family that stood beside him and behind him and loved him no matter what the circumstances. He wanted—had always wanted, he now realized—to love and be loved by a woman who would stay at his side no matter what fate threw their way, who cared not whether he was rich or poor. With Kathleen Deacey he could have that. She was the future he had been searching for all these years. He wanted her to love him, wanted to love her for the rest of his life. After so many years of women, none of whom ever even touched his heart, he had found love.

He made a move to stand, to go to Kathleen now and tell her

what it had taken him years to figure out. And then he stopped. It was far too late and she was surely asleep by now. Tomorrow would be soon enough.

*

He waited half the next day for both his grandfather and Emma to leave the house so he could talk to Kathleen without interruption or curious ears. As soon as both were gone, he went in search of Kathleen and found her polishing the wood steps on either side of the staircase runner. She worked at a furious pace, all the while humming a repetitive melody under her breath. From the bottom of the stairs he watched her. Now that he'd made a decision, she suddenly looked different, as though not quite real, like she could slip out of his life at any moment and he would only know she had been there by the chunk she'd torn from his heart upon her departure.

He waited a moment for her to notice him standing there but when she didn't, he mounted the stairs to touch her on the shoulder. She leapt to her feet, arms flailing as she uttered a startled cry. One hand shot out to grasp the banister for support and she twisted round to glare at him.

He grinned sheepishly and went down a couple of stairs. "Sorry—"

"You just took ten years off me life!"

"I didn't want to scare you by saying your name."

"Oh well, I'll be thanking ye for that." She drew in a breath to calm herself. "Is there something you'll be wanting?" Her voice held a chill that he knew he well deserved after last evening.

"Just a moment of your time."

"Aye." She looked at him expectantly.

Her eyes, God how blue were her eyes, like the ocean at its deepest point.

"I'm—sorry about last night," he said, struggling suddenly to find the right words. "Do you remember when I told you that my father died when I was eight?" He felt like a nervous schoolboy asking a girl to dance.

A perplexed expression crossed those incredible blue eyes and Jack had to fight the impulse to pull her into his arms and kiss her.

"Killed himself," he said, knowing he was repeating a story he didn't have to tell. He raked a hand through his hair. "Why don't we sit?" he said. He dropped down onto the stair and motioned for her to join him.

Kathleen settled beside him, brows pulled together in confusion. Her arm brushed his shoulder. The contact jolted him and he began again, eager to get through the explanations and into the important topics. "His company had failed, he lost everything. And my mother left—"

"Excuse me for asking, but why are ye telling me this again?"

"My father had no tolerance for weakness or failure, in himself—or anyone else. I've spent my life up to now trying to live up to his expectations." Jack looked straight ahead, avoided her gaze entirely and hoped his words would be enough to put things right between them again.

"Somehow, when I was younger I decided if I embraced the things that my parents valued— If I were rich enough or successful enough or socially respected enough then I would be worthy of their love—anyone's love…and I would never again lose someone I cared about. In some odd way it all made sense. Until I met you."

From the corner of his eye he could see her tilt her head to look at him.

"Last night I realized that if I married Emily Cuthbert, I would get everything I thought I needed—money, success, respect. But I would lose...you." He turned to face her.

Her eyes widened. "What are you saying?"

"I'm not going to marry Emily Cuthbert."

"What do you mean by *not*?"

"Not soon, not in two years, not ever."

"But all your plans... What of them? Can you give them up so easily?"

For her he could. He nodded. "I don't want to lose you."

He reached out a hand to cup her cheek, then bent forward to press a soft kiss to her mouth. Her lips parted and he deepened the kiss, took her by the shoulders and pulled her close.

Kathleen pushed back, her face alarmed. "But will you still be going back to sea?"

"I have to. It's my living."

"I saw me Danny go off on the ocean and he never came back. I couldn't stand it to happen again."

He ran a hand down her shoulder. "I can't guarantee nothing would ever go wrong, but—"

"How soon?"

"Two weeks." He took her hand and kissed her fingertips, happy that his next words would soothe all her worries. She didn't yet know that he'd not go back to sea without her at his side. She didn't know that it was common for married whaling captains to take their wives on their voyages. She didn't know that he intended to make her his wife before the week was out.

He took both her hands in his. "Kathleen, I want you to come with me."

"A woman on the ship?" She looked incredulous.

"Many whaling captains bring their wives—"

Pounding sounded upon the front door.

"Who in blazes?" he muttered.

She grinned at him. "I'll send them on their way." As she hurried down the stairs, she threw another smile over her shoulder and he had a sudden premonition that this joy would not last.

Kathleen grasped the handle and pulled open the door. Jack stood, suddenly needing to be at her side. He heard her long drawn gasp and, without even seeing who was there, knew his worst fear had come true.

*

"Danny?" she said in a hushed voice. She could swear her heart had just stopped beating. He stepped toward her, arms outstretched, the loose smile on his face like a beacon calling her home. She threw herself into his embrace and he gathered her in tight. She sobbed and laughed against his chest and prayed she wasn't dreaming. It had been nearly a year since last they'd been together.

He held her fiercely close and kissed her hair, her cheek, and murmured, "A fine sight you are for me eyes."

She threw her head back to look up at him. "Am I dreaming now? After all this time?"

From behind him stepped another man. "Sean!" She wrenched out of Danny's arms to fling herself at her brother. "What are ye doing here? How come ye to find me? How can you two be together?"

"Slow down." Sean laughed. "All in good time." He held her tight and when finally they separated she could see his blue eyes were moist.

"Ah, Seanie, you can't be knowing how good it is to see you

again. And Ma and Da? Is everyone...well?" She searched his eyes for the truth.

His smile faded. "Aye, they're all surviving. But—" He hesitated and she knew he was thinking of Moira and how to tell her. "We thought you dead, Kathleen. Drowned on the crossing. We got a letter telling us you were gone."

"From Lucy McKenna? I so feared she would write," she said. "Did Ma and Da—"

"They blamed themselves. As I blamed myself for insisting ye go." He grasped her shoulders and shook her slightly, as if he couldn't quite believe she was really alive.

"I wrote home nearly two months ago. They should know by now that I am in Boston—they should know."

"But tell me how come you to be here when your ship was headed for Canada?"

"Ye won't be believing the half of it."

"Kathleen." Danny gestured behind her.

Jack Montgomery stood in the doorway, his face a mask of non-expression. A pang of regret cut through her and she looked into his somber face and tried to smile. God in heaven, how could this be happening? Jack Montgomery had just professed his feelings for her...and Danny was back.

She took a step toward Jack. "Captain Montgomery, I'd like you to meet my brother, Sean." The two men shook hands as she continued, "And this is..." She swallowed. "...my betrothed, Daniel O'Sheehan. I've mentioned him before, do you remember?"

Jack nodded stiffly. "Once or twice, yes." He looked at Danny's outstretched hand for a long moment before reaching out to clasp it with his own.

Kathleen exhaled, until then unaware she had even been holding her breath.

"Are you planning to stay long in Boston?" Jack asked, a stiffness in his tone.

Danny put an arm around Kathleen's shoulders and pulled her close. "As long as she'll have me," he said. His eyes didn't waver from Jack's.

Kathleen glanced at him, surprised by his display of possessiveness. He had thrown down the gauntlet with his voice and she could see Jack bristle at the challenge. The animosity in the air was so strong, she almost feared the two men might start brawling at any moment.

Sliding out from under Danny's arm, she clasped her hands together and smiled broadly. "We needn't be taking any more of your time, Captain. Would it be all right if Sean and Danny come in through the kitchen for a wee bit? A few minutes so we can catch up?"

"Just don't forget you're still on duty."

Faith, but that was sounding too close to something his grandfather might say. Here were her brother and the man she was to wed, come to find her after all this time and the man's only thought was of work? She gave him a curt nod and set off toward the rear door with Danny and Sean following.

She glanced back before they rounded the corner of the house and saw Jack still on the stoop, watching them. Her happiness blurred. She gave him a tremulous smile, then turned away, fighting tears on what should have been her happiest day ever.

*

Jack limped back into the house and tossed the door shut behind him. Son of a bitch, the wandering bridegroom had appeared.

Where the devil had he been all this time? What right did he have to come in and pick up where he'd left off almost a year ago? He cursed under his breath. And what was to stop the man from hurting Kathleen once again?

He lowered himself into a chair in the sitting room and slumped back to stare at the ceiling, noting for the first time the intricate carving on the crown molding...and remembering the joy with which Kathleen threw herself into Danny's arms.

What did he expect after all? Danny was her betrothed. She had been searching for him for months. Of course, she would want him back. It would not matter what had kept him in Canada. It would not matter that Jack had almost asked her to marry him. All that mattered was that Danny had returned. This was Kathleen's betrothed. It would be only a matter of time before they set a date to wed.

But that didn't mean he would give her up without a fight.

CHAPTER THIRTY

OUT OF SIGHT of the captain, Danny swept Kathleen into his arms and kissed her. Once she would have been overcome with joy, but now her joy was tempered with confusion. This was her Danny, she'd known him all her life. He was her first love... Nay, he was *her only love*. She belonged with him. Now that he was here, everything would be right. Arms around one another, enveloped by the warmth of the winter sun, Kathleen felt as if she were back in Ireland and nothing had ever changed.

And still, the tears she held back threatened.

Sean cleared his throat and Danny pulled back, grinning.

"Sorry. But ye canna fault me for being happy to see your sister." He bent to look her closely in the face, reaching a finger to wipe the moisture from beneath her lashes. "Dry your eyes, lass, for I'll not leave you again. You've got me for good now."

The tears spilled over and Kathleen let them come. Her mind churned, a jumble of thoughts and emotions, not one of which seemed to stay around long enough for her to recognize it. She had found Danny, but had lost Jack. America would never be Ireland, the potatoes had rotted, Moira was dead, and hope as she might, nothing would ever be the same as it once had been.

Danny was back. *And Jack Montgomery would never be hers.*

But you have Danny, she fiercely reminded herself. Her prayers had been answered. 'Twas clearly meant to be, just as they had planned so long ago. She would bear his children, little boys with black hair and blue eyes— Jack's visage appeared in her mind and she had to turn away from Danny a moment to force the picture away.

"What's wrong, Kathleen?"

"Where were you Danny? What happened to you?"

"I've been searching for you," he said with a jaunty grin.

She refused to be drawn into his flirtation. "Nay, you have not. Now tell me Daniel O'Sheehan, why did ye didna come home last autumn."

His gaze slid away and seconds passed before he fixed his eyes on her face again. She felt a shiver of foreboding.

"It's too cold to be standing out here," Danny said. "Let's go inside."

"Nay. Tell me now. Why didn't ye come back?"

"I was offered work in Newfoundland. Steady work, a good wage. It was for you I stayed behind. So when finally I did come home to Ireland I would have money enough. We could build a real house—not a sod cottage. No more dirt floors."

She stared at him in disbelief. "Why didn't ye tell Sean before the boat left? Danny, do you know how I've worried over you?"

"They only offered me the job the night before the ship was to sail. I was having a pint with the boys when one of the fishery owners put it before me. I couldn't be turning such an offer down, now could I?"

"Ye might have written."

"But I did."

She glanced at Sean and he shrugged.

"I feared you died," she said.

He took her hand and kissed the palm. "I'll not leave you again, Kathleen. We'll be wed just as soon as we can arrange with a priest. In a few days, it will as though the past year never happened."

"You'll have to be waiting more than a few days," Sean said. "It's Lent. No priest will marry ye 'till after Easter. Church law, you know."

Kathleen nodded, relieved that the wedding must be postponed—and surprised at her reaction. To be sure, she wanted to marry Danny, but perhaps it would be best if she had some time to know him again after nearly a year apart.

Sean took her by the arm. "Enough of weddings for the time. Tell us how you come to be alive and in Boston."

"By rights I should be dead." A shiver ripped through her. "Let's go inside," she said, and pushed through the door into the kitchen. "I fell overboard during a storm and Captain Montgomery plucked me from the ocean. Saved me life."

In a quiet voice she told them of her rescue, of her voyage to America, and of looking for work in Boston. By the time she finished, her face was flushed. She'd said not a word of how Jack saved her life by warming her naked body with his, how he'd kissed her more than once without her doing anything to stop him, in fact to the contrary, she had kissed him back. Suddenly she found herself reliving each undisclosed moment and her stomach fluttered.

"Are ye hungry?" she asked in a rush, her words more a declaration than a question. She turned away so they couldn't see her face, as though it would somehow expose everything she was hiding. The two men sat at the table and she set the food before them. "Eat quickly, for the captain may not look so kindly on me feeding the two of you."

A black lock curled over Danny's left eye and she almost reached out to push it away. Once she would have thought nothing of brushing the hair from his eyes—now that simple gesture felt awkward.

"Kathleen I have something to tell you," Sean said quietly.

"I know." She knelt beside his chair and put an arm around his waist. "I know…about Moira and the babies."

"How?"

"Ye remember the Boyles? They used to live up the road? They're in Boston now and Mrs. Boyle had a letter from her brother's wife. I'm so sorry, Sean."

Anguish flicked across his eyes and he wrapped his arms around her. "I couldn't stay in Ireland any longer. I had to leave, if for nothing else than to forget."

Kathleen nodded and silence opened between them like a gaping wound.

Danny cleared his throat. "Ye should have seen him the day he came to the fishery, Kathleen. Surprised enough he was to find me there. But when I showed him the notice you'd placed in the newspaper, him thinking you had passed to the other side and it being proof you were alive…"

"Sure, the Lord was looking out for all of us," she said. "And bringing both of ye to me."

"You've a good situation." Danny pushed back his chair and strolled around the room. "Plenty to eat, a nice place to live." He picked up a spoon from the counter and twirled it between his fingers. "And silver, too, for the help. Your captain has a bit of money."

"Nay, we don't use that silver. 'Tis just in here being washed."

"Still, the fact is, he has it."

"Tell me of your job, Danny," she said. "Will they have you back when you return?"

"Perhaps we'll start fresh in America."

"It's not so easy for the Irish to find work in Boston—"

"Ah, but you have a fine job. Sure and ye make enough for the two of us to survive a while anyway—"

"I'm to be sending money home to help me family. Are you not doing the same? Have you not heard from your own about how they are faring?"

He shook his head.

"You've heard nothing?" Kathleen crossed her arms. "Your letters have gone unanswered?"

"I haven't written them."

"Danny. Your mam was beside herself worrying when ye didn't come back—and that was months ago. What can you be thinking to leave them like this? At least you owe them their peace of mind—"

"Aye, you're right. I was working so much and somehow the months just kept passing."

At a sound in the hallway, Kathleen turned. "Though it pains me to say it, you'll need to be on your way. I can't have the captain or his grandfather finding you eating their food, and me not working when I should."

"Especially since you're the only one of us with a job." Sean pushed back his chair and stood. "Come on, Danny, we'll be needing to find a place to stay."

Danny held up the silver spoon. "This should cover at least a few night's lodging, don't you think?"

"I'll be thinking you jest with us now, Daniel O'Sheehan," Kathleen said evenly.

"'Tis an English household, Kathleen. They've been stealing from *us* for centuries."

"This is my employer's silver," she said through clenched teeth. "I'll not lose me job—"

"Put it back Danny," Sean snapped. He buttoned his coat as he started for the door. "I'll be letting you know where we're staying Kathleen. Come on Danny. It's work we'll be needing—not stolen silver."

Danny tossed the spoon on the table and raised both hands in a gesture of surrender. "Just a little fun," he said. He put an arm around her shoulders and kissed her lightly on the mouth. "Don't be forgetting you're Irish, Kathleen, just because you're in America," he murmured. He flashed her a smile before following Sean outside, leaving the door ajar.

She stared at the thin opening between the jamb and the door, at the daylight sneaking in on the back of a frigid draft. Danny was back. Her betrothed, the man she'd been searching for all these months.

She stepped forward and gave the door a two-handed shove. It thudded into place, blocking out the offending breeze and crushing the sliver of light. She had to get back to work, back to her life, back to what she knew and could depend on. Aye, and just what was that? Once she'd thought it was Danny.

She rubbed a hand across her eyes and headed into the corridor to finish polishing the stairs. Surely all would be right once she spent some time with Danny again. She had loved him for so many years already. Perhaps that was all she needed—just a wee bit of time to get used to him again, time to find the love she hoped still waited in her heart.

And what of Jack? Was it just an hour ago that he had asked her to come on his voyage? Was it just last night that she'd lain awake dreaming of him?

Her nerves were stretched so taut she thought she might shatter like a dropped porcelain doll if one more thing went wrong.

Wrong? Nothing had gone wrong—today everything had gone right. She'd gotten everything she wanted, had prayed for. She'd found Danny. So why wasn't she happier? Why was she still thinking of Jack?

Don't be forgetting you're Irish, Kathleen, just because you're in America. Danny's words felt shouted in her head.

Jesus, Mary, and holy Joseph, but how had all this come to pass in her life? Nothing was turning out the way it should be. She should be home in Ireland, surrounded by her family, wed to Danny. And instead, here she was in America, trying not to love an Englishman.

*

"Kathleen," Jack called from his study as she passed the open doorway.

She stopped and looked into the room, a stricken expression on her face. He stood and held out a hand and she hesitated just a moment before stepping across the room into his arms.

She cried against his shoulder and he kissed her hair. "Smile," he whispered. "It can't be all that bad, now, can it?"

"It can. Finally I've found Danny and I don't know if I even love him. He's different—or perhaps I am."

He laughed in relief and took her face between his hands and kissed one corner of her mouth, and then the other, ready to ask her to become his wife.

"I've been such a fool—" she said.

"No." He handed her a handkerchief and she wiped her eyes and nose.

"Thinking I could have you…an Englishman…without me family ever knowing of it. Thinking that with them across the ocean in Ireland, they would never find out."

He felt time still.

"But while Danny being here is bad enough, I mean good, certainly…Sean being here changes everything." She looked up at him with darkened eyes. "With Moira dead because of the famine, he'll be thinking me a traitor… And me Da and Ma, faith, but I would be losing them, too. For all my life I would know they thought I had betrayed Ireland. Break their hearts, I would. But what makes me weep the most, is that I don't even want to care that it would happen."

Sadness draped itself around his shoulders like the arm of an old friend. After all that the Irish had endured over centuries beneath the English hand, he held out no hope that her family could overcome their hatred and accept him. He need only look at his own grandfather's view of the Irish to see how prejudice colored perception, reinforcing itself over and over again.

Too many years of Irish-English history had sealed her future— she could have him or her family, but not both. Though she had said as much before, until this moment he hadn't recognized what it truly meant for her. And now that he knew, he could think of nothing to say that would change the truth of it. A chill slipped under his skin and into his bones and he tightened his arms around her as though, somehow, his love would be enough to protect her. He did not push her away then, though he knew he was going to.

He had no right to try to take from her the very thing that made her who she was. He would not tear down her life so that he might finally have what she had always known—the love of a family.

She belonged with an Irishman, a man her family approved of. She had to stay with Danny, had to marry him— And he, Jack Montgomery, had to return to the sea. He took hold of her arms and gently pushed her away as he stepped back.

"You've searched and prayed for him, Kathleen. *You've found what you wanted.* This is good."

She shook her head. "But now that he's here, I'll not be knowing if I still want him. Jack, what of us?"

"Us?" He affected an air of indifference. "You've found your betrothed. And I'm going back to sea—the crew's been hired, the ship readied. I'm leaving before two weeks is out."

"But I thought ye wanted me to come along."

"I don't think Danny would take kindly to me bedding his betrothed." He cringed inside at the cruelness of his words.

Her eyes widened, and all he wanted to do was apologize, to pull her back into his arms and tell her he didn't mean it.

"Wouldn't I be your wife?"

He didn't answer.

"Jack?"

"What gave you the idea we would be married?"

Raw pain flashed across her eyes, and then they were shuttered and wary. "Nothing," she said in a weary voice. "Nothing at all." She turned and walked out the door.

Jack drew a rough breath and watched her go, amazed that he could both despise and respect himself at the same time.

*

Hours later, he opened the sideboard and poured a snifter of brandy. Thank God his ankle was nearly healed. Despite how much he disliked whaling, the thought of leaving on another voyage suddenly had immense appeal.

"You drink too much."

He looked up. His grandfather stood in the doorway.

"Got a lot on my mind."

"Obviously. Your ship is nearly ready to go and you still haven't talked with Emily Cuthbert."

Rankled, Jack took a swallow of brandy and mulled over his reply.

"I've as much as assured her father of your intentions, yet still you stall," the old man said.

"It might be wise not to make assumptions on my behalf."

His grandfather snorted. "No assumptions necessary. I know you. I know what you want—what you've wanted for twelve years. I know what motivates you."

"Really."

"Emily Cuthbert is a better match than you could ever have hoped for. A marriage to her will all but erase the stigma of your profession as a whaling captain."

"And elevate your status in the process?"

"If I gave a damn about my status, I wouldn't have taught you whaling." The old man gave a slight nod of the head. "It would help both of us."

Jack dipped his chin in acknowledgment of the truth.

"It's your life that stretches out ahead, Jack. You'll have to live with your choices." The old man's tone softened. "If not for the fact that Will Cuthbert was an old friend of your father's, I doubt he would ever have countenanced this match."

"I know, I know, I know."

His grandfather threw his hands up. "The woman wants to marry and I doubt she'll wait much longer for you to ask. Talk to her, Jack. You don't want to spend your life with regrets."

Regrets? Every action he thought of taking had the potential for bringing regret. What he needed was some time to wash Kathleen Deacey from his soul—a few months pounding the waves, tacking across a stiff breeze, face wet and cold with spray. The ocean would make him forget.

He rubbed a tired hand across his brow and searched for some way to postpone what seemed to be the inevitable. "It's too fast—"

"Cold feet is it?"

"If I take Will up on his offer, we'll need to hire a captain for this voyage. God knows how long that would take. The ship is nearly ready to sail *now*. Every extra day in port we lose money. We have seven other partners in this ship—my decision can't be based only on what I want."

The old man nodded. "Tell Will you can't skip this trip…but that it will be your last. Then tell his daughter she can spend the six months you're gone planning the wedding."

Jack blanched. It was all well and good to discuss this from a business point of view, quite another altogether to think of an actual wedding.

"Well?"

He didn't move.

"Jack! You've enough to do in the next week without having to worry about your future. It's time you asked for her hand."

There was no reason not to. This was what he had worked for all these years—wealth, status, security against pain. Many marriages begin without love, he rationalized. *And, Kathleen would be marrying Danny.*

"You'll forget about her," his grandfather said softly, as though reading Jack's mind. "We all have to forget someone."

He stared at his grandfather for a moment, hating the old man and loving him at the same time. Then he tossed down the remainder of his brandy, grabbed his coat, and set off for the Cuthbert's home.

CHAPTER THIRTY-ONE

JACK MONTGOMERY DIDN'T want her. Kathleen furiously cleaned the lamps on the second floor. Her thoughts and emotions collided with one another—Danny, Sean, Ma and Da, the grandfather, *Jack*, Ireland, America, Moira—all crowded into her head vying for influence until she could keep nothing straight anymore and all she wanted to do was throw a lamp across the room and scream.

Almost two weeks had passed since their conversation, two weeks during which she'd had more than enough time to embrace that Danny was back in her life. Two weeks during which she'd had enough time to accept the fact that Jack Montgomery was leaving this day to go back to sea. Without her.

If that wasn't enough to show her the right path, she didn't know what was. God had answered her prayers, had sent Danny back to her. Jack had made it clear that there was no place in his future for her. So dear Lord, why couldn't she sleep at night, why couldn't she eat anymore, why was her mind in constant turmoil?

She looked up as Emma puffed up the stairs toward her. "He's here again—at the back door. I told him to wait outside," Emma said in a voice laced with disapproval.

"Perhaps he's found work," Kathleen said.

"Hmmphh. Perhaps he's just hungry."

She slanted a glare at the cook. She didn't want to know Emma's concerns, she had enough of her own. She was tired of making excuses about Danny, tired of pretending that she was happy to see him when he showed up at the door wanting a bit of change or something to eat. "And just what are ye meaning by that?"

"I'm sixty-five years old. I've been cooking for nearly all of them. And I know the stink of rotten fish when I smell it."

"You've not even given him a chance. I'll be betting 'tis work he's found...and ashamed you'll be of how you're acting."

Not waiting for a reply, she hurried down the stairs and into the kitchen, praying all the way that her words were true. She tugged open the back door and motioned Danny inside. A blast of cold air entered with him and Kathleen shivered as he swept her into his arms and spun her around.

"You've found work, have ye?" she asked in delight.

He kissed her full on the mouth. "Soon. I've just been missing you."

Her enthusiasm dimmed. Every cent she gave him was that much less she could send home. "And Sean? Where is Sean this early morn?"

Danny tried to slip an arm around her waist and she twisted away. "He's looking for work, isn't he?" she asked.

The expression on Danny's face told her she was right. Anger surged within her. "Ye should be doing the same, Danny. I cannot support all of us and the family in Ireland, too."

"Don't be nagging at me, Kathleen. Ye may not have noticed, but they're not exactly jumping to hire the Irish in Boston. The English have planted their prejudice here and it's taken root."

"Aye, but others have found work. And need I remind you,

once you cared so much to work you stayed in Newfoundland, leaving me across the ocean." Her voice shook. "I cannot be supporting you when you are fully able to work, when me family is starving."

"But for the wedding ceremony, I, too, would be your family. Will you have me starve here in America?"

She drew a breath and exhaled slowly to contain her temper. "I'll be needing to get back to work now, Danny, for there are many counting on me," she said in a low voice.

Cook entered the kitchen and began to dust the cutting board with flour.

"Is it a pie you're making?" Danny asked.

"If I am, will you be coming back to have some?"

He grinned.

"Then no, I'm not making a pie." Cook turned her full attention to rolling out the dough.

Kathleen's stomach tightened. "Off with you now, Danny. I'll not have the captain's grandfather find you here and start thinking I'm shirking me duties."

"I'll be needing just a wee bit of money."

She could only stare.

"Don't be forgetting, 'twas my money that paid for your brother to travel from Newfoundland to find you, Kathleen. If I had what I gave to him, I'd not have to be asking now."

Guilt dissolved her anger. "Aye," she said softly. "Wait here a minute."

After retrieving money from her room, she raced down the stairs, afraid that every extra moment Danny was in the kitchen brought them one moment closer to Jack or his grandfather discovering him there. And if recent history was anything to count on, Danny would be eating when they found him. She chastised herself for thinking of him so.

Back in the kitchen, she shoved the coins into his hand. "Now you must be going. Please."

She heard the creak of the door behind her. "Go," she hissed.

Cook's rolling pin clattered to the floor. And Danny, damn him anyway, grinned and said, "A good day to ye, Captain Montgomery."

She turned, mouth frozen in a grimace. This was it, she would lose her job now. Her family would starve to death in Ireland. And all because Danny couldn't—wouldn't—do what he was supposed to.

"I called you as you passed my study, but you must not have heard," Jack said.

"No." Her face burned.

"I have a few things to go over with you before I leave."

"Would you like to do that now?"

Jack turned his attention back to Danny. "I told Kathleen I prefer you see one another during her time off. She is paid to work here and you'd do well to abide by the rules. My grandfather is unlikely to be as tolerant as I am."

Jack looked at her and in his eyes she saw, not anger, but something else. Sympathy?

"I'm sorry, Captain, it won't happen again," she said.

"Jaysus, but you're an English bastard, aren't ye?" Danny shot out.

Kathleen gaped at him. Indeed he'd gone mad these past months.

"All stiff, and stuck on rules that favor none but you and your own," he spat. "Thinking ye've hired an Irish girl and do her a favor now, eh? Pay her to work for a pittance—"

"Danny!" she exclaimed. He was itching for a fight, that she well knew.

"It's time you left," Jack said.

"I wouldn't put it past you to have tried to bed her, either. After all, the Irish may not be good enough to eat at your table, but we all know they're fine for warming your bed."

Kathleen turned slowly to face the captain. Save for the tenseness of his jaw, she could see no outward signs of anger.

"Get the hell out of my house." The words were spoken in such a low tone she could barely hear them.

"Ah, too close to the truth, am I? She wouldn't have you, would she?" Danny glanced between Jack and Kathleen, his lips curled upward in a tight smile. "Let me be telling you something, Captain Montgomery. Kathleen would never have ye. She hates the English with all her soul. Tell him Kathleen."

She hesitated.

"Kathleen?" Danny asked.

"It's true, I did hate the English—"

"Did?"

She looked from man to man, no longer clear about what she actually believed, only wishing that she was anywhere but here. "Danny, you must be going. We need not be talking of this now," she said finally.

"Oh, aye, we do. Where are your loyalties, Kathleen? The man looks at you like he owns you now. This is America—you need never be beholden to the English again. *He owns ye not.* So speak now your truth so I shall know you have not turned traitor to your own people. Tell him your place is among the Irish."

A wave of nausea rolled through her stomach as she met Danny's eyes with her own. He had given voice to the fears that had haunted her thoughts ever since she had first begun to care for Jack. He had laid her soul out for everyone to see.

"Don't be failing your people now," Danny said.

'Twas as if he knew what was in her heart, as if he could somehow tell that she had once—still—cared for this Englishman.

"Get out," Jack growled. He took a step toward Danny but the other held his ground.

Jesus, Mary, and Joseph, but Danny was about to get the fight he'd been wanting. And she'd never known him to lose a brawl. She scooped the rolling pin off the floor and rushed between the two men, brandishing it like a sword, turning from one side to the other forcing each of them to step back. Turning toward Danny, she gave him a shove in the chest with one end of the rolling pin.

"The captain doesn't own me, but neither do you, Danny O'Sheehan. Now he has asked ye to move on and I'll be asking the same. If you've things to discuss with me, then we'll be talking of them later. But not now. You've got what ye come for, now there is no reason for you to stay any longer." She strung one sentence onto the next without pause, afraid to leave room for him to slip in so much as a word, certain that she could convince him to leave if she didn't stop talking.

Finally he drew a breath and she knew she had won. He turned toward the door. "You haven't changed, Kathleen. Not much anyway," he said as he pulled open the door. "But whom do you love, lass? I'll have you say it now."

She knew by the determined look on his face that he wouldn't leave without an answer. Kathleen swallowed hard, knowing that she needed to say the words aloud as much for herself as for him.

"You, Danny," she whispered. "Me place is with you. Never should you doubt that." The hollow of her stomach ached.

"Nor should you then, Kathleen." He stepped outside and left the door hanging open behind him.

Kathleen gently pushed it shut. Her place was with an Irishman and she had just ensured it would be so. She turned slowly toward Jack. His cheeks were ruddy, chapped from the cold so that he looked to be sunburned. She thought of summer and suddenly wished it was him she had loved in Ireland, that it was him she had waited for that day so long ago. If only he were Irish... If only Danny hadn't come back.

She called herself a traitor to the Irish and locked her hands together to keep from reaching out to touch him. "I'll be asking your forgiveness for Danny's behavior, sir. I don't know what is the matter with him."

He waved her apology aside. "I need to get down to the dock. Let's get this finished."

She followed him to the study and tried to pay attention as he detailed additional instructions for the next half year. Her mind kept wandering ahead to that time when she would be married to Danny, and Jack would have wed Emily Cuthbert. The thought made her stomach churn.

"Are you listening, Kathleen?"

She started. "Aye. I've heard you, Captain."

He closed the roll top on his desk and stood, a small sheaf of papers in one hand. His trunk had been delivered to the ship the previous day, as had everything else he was taking on the voyage. They faced one another for several awkward seconds, then he touched her cheek.

"Since I'll not be here when you wed, Kathleen, I'll say my congratulations now." His hand dropped to his side. "I don't imagine you'll be staying on?"

She tried to quell the uneasiness that slipped over her at the stark reality of his words. "I must, at least for a bit," she said. "But Danny had a good job in St. John's, so I'll be thinking it best we return there…once the wedding is past."

"The date has been set?"

She wished he hadn't asked. "May the first."

"Well, know that you'll have a job here as long as you want one."

She nodded gratefully, all words snared in her throat.

He lifted his coat from the back of a nearby chair and glanced at it, shifting it from one hand to the other. He rubbed a finger over a dirt smudge on the collar and looked at her again, a faint smile lightening his face. "I'm glad that you're happy," he said. "I hope your life goes well. Goodbye Kathleen."

He slipped on his coat and walked out of the room. She heard his footsteps on the wood floor in the hall, heard him stop in the parlor and exchange farewells with his grandfather. She could tell the moment he stepped onto the rug in the foyer, waited for what seemed an eternity for the sound of the front door to open. Her heart sped up in anticipation and she pivoted, taking a step toward the hallway, pausing again at the sound of the bolt being pulled and the slight creak of the hinges as the door opened and thudded shut. *He was gone.*

Never again would Jack talk with her, never again would he touch her. *Never again would he kiss her.* Her throat knotted so tight that pain radiated into her breastbone.

Lifting her skirt, she raced into the hall and took the stairs two at a time. She rushed into the front bedroom and threw open the sash, leaning out the window to look down the street. She had to see him just once more. Spotting his dark coat, she exhaled a shaky breath. He wasn't gone, not yet. She watched until she could see him no longer, until he disappeared into the mass of people on the street, and still she did not move, just waited in the open window, drawing in the crisp March air until the cold forced her back inside.

"Good-bye Jack," she whispered.

CHAPTER THIRTY-TWO

HANDS CLASPED BEHIND his back, Jack strolled across the deck of his ship and gazed out over Boston Harbor toward the ocean. The wind was fresh and the sun bright enough to take the edge off the brisk temperature. The sea was calling. It was a perfect day to set sail.

He drew in a deep breath of salt air. When he was younger, he would have been filled with excitement at the prospect of going to sea again. But the adventure had gone out of the voyage for him. He knew there were captains for whom four weeks on land was three weeks too many. But not him, not anymore.

He'd looked forward to this for many years, his last voyage, expecting that once it was over he would settle down to a comfortable life as a ship owner and investor. He'd come to accept that he and the only daughter of Will Cuthbert would marry and raise a family. It had been a good plan...once. Emily had already opened doors for him, doors that had slammed shut the day his father took his own life.

He had hoped that asking her to marry him yesterday would return his mind to that same level of acceptance. But it hadn't happened—not yet anyway. Nothing was the same anymore, hadn't been the same since the ocean had delivered a woman to him—a woman he had come to love, a woman he had given up for love.

And though he once had no qualms about marrying Emily Cuthbert even though he didn't return her love, he was struggling with the idea of spending the rest of his life looking into the face of one woman and envisioning another.

Once he would have laughed at such a predicament. How many times, after all, had he said that marriage was little more than a business arrangement in which the product happened to be children?

He had never expected to feel anything more than fondness toward the woman he married. How ironic that now that he wanted to love the woman he wed, he couldn't wed the woman he loved.

What Kathleen had with her family, he would have given the world to share with her. But by building a family with him, she would lose the one she already had. He'd rather live without her than cause her that pain.

As soon as the last provisions were stowed, they would set sail. Though he was looking forward to the time away, a six-month voyage no longer seemed long enough. What he needed was two or three years whaling on the South Seas, the sun hot, and the island women so willing they would help him push Kathleen Deacey from his mind forever.

Ah, but the die had been cast, and he could only hope that six months and marriage to Emily Cuthbert would be enough to do the same.

Too restless to wait on board any longer, Jack headed down the gangplank, sidestepping to get out of the way of several crewmen loading more provisions. He wandered down the wharf, thoughts lost even to himself. Several minutes later he stopped before the great warship, the Jamestown, brought to Boston from Charleston for the Irish relief effort. From the ship's main mast flew a white flag emblazoned with a shamrock wreath around a thistle. Dozens of Irish men, all members of the Laborers' Aid Society, were loading the warship with provisions—thousands of barrels of food and clothing donated for Ireland. They had been working for days now.

"A fine sight, isn't it, Captain Montgomery?"

He turned and smiled. "Captain Forbes." He extended a hand to the captain of the Jamestown. "A fine sight indeed. Both the ship and the charity."

"Had I known the outpouring would be so great, I would have lined up more vessels. We've far more provisions than can fit on the Jamestown."

"Can't complain about too many blessings I guess."

"Absolutely not. We'll get it there somehow." He drew a hand across his brow. "And you, Jack, where are you headed?"

He shook his head and looked up at the clear sky. If only his thoughts were as cloudless. "Chasing baleen whale—up near Greenland. Just a short one, six months—"

"You're heading north?"

Jack nodded.

"With an empty ship?"

"Won't be empty for long I hope."

"But she'll be empty past the coast of Ireland," Forbes mused.

"I guess she would be."

"You're taking an empty ship up past Ireland? Let's just look at this—"

"Oh, no. Let's not."

Forbes held out his hands, palms up. "What would be the harm in filling it with provisions to drop in Ireland? I'd wager it would add but a few days to your voyage."

"In theory. But you know as well as I, nothing is ever as simple as it sounds," Jack said. "And I've got investors..."

"They could be convinced. And easily I think. After all, the Congress is pushing this effort. The couple of days you would lose are just a couple of days to you. But they could mean the difference between life and death for many Irish."

Jack nodded but didn't respond.

"Give it some thought," Forbes said as he set off again.

"Safe voyage," Jack murmured. He watched the workers haul barrels up the gangplank, each one a symbol of life, of the determination of the human spirit and the will to survive against adversity. Indeed, it had been a barrel that had kept Kathleen Deacey alive and brought her into his life.

Something stirred within him and, though English he was, he knew Ireland would someday stand again, to raise its fist to England and proclaim its independence. As surprised as he was to think it, he realized he wanted them to succeed.

They needed food. They needed ships to carry the food.

He looked toward his own ship, now nearly ready to depart. The hold was empty, awaiting the whale oil. It really would be nothing to fill it with barrels of food, nothing to stop in Ireland for a few days to unload. The breeze freshened, rippling through his hair and beckoning him to set sail without delay.

Jack frowned. He couldn't make decisions about the ship's destination without clearing it with all the owners. And God only knew how much their departure might be pushed back if he opened a discussion about detouring into Ireland. It just wasn't possible.

Unless... If his actions to help the Irish also brought benefit to the investors, he wouldn't need permission. He nodded to himself.

It could work. He spun on his heel and set off after Forbes with only the vaguest notion of what he was about to propose. It wasn't until he spotted the man and called his name, until Forbes looked round and smiled like he'd known all along that Jack would come after him, that Jack knew exactly what kind of a deal he wanted: a small portion of the food would remain with the whaling ship after they left Ireland as payment for transporting the provisions. Because this decision would save the investors money, no discussion nor permission would be required.

*

Four days after the Cyrena set sail, Jack's grandfather waved the newspaper angrily at Kathleen. "What did you know about this?" he demanded. "And how did you convince him to do it?"

"Sir?"

He swatted the paper on the dining table. "Jack's gone to Ireland and I know damn well you're behind it."

Some days she could swear the old man was slipping quickly into senility. "Sir," she said in the kind of voice one would use with an irrational child. "It's true, I am from Ireland. But Captain Montgomery has gone whaling...remember?"

"No reason to pretend, Kathleen, everything is in here." He opened the paper and read aloud, "*The Cyrena, with Captain Jack Montgomery at the helm, followed the Jamestown to Ireland, its hold filled with barrels of food and clothing from the relief effort.*"

He jabbed a stiff finger in her direction. "You had to know. The only reason he would do such a thing is because of you."

She opened her mouth but was so shocked it took a moment for her to speak. "The paper must be wrong! It's absurd! The captain would not have done such a thing."

"Once I would have agreed with you. But he did—and he made damn sure no one found out until he was gone."

"But it makes no sense, truly. Perhaps the newspaper listed the wrong ship."

"I verified it this afternoon. It's true."

The room seemed to spin and Kathleen bent forward to rest her hands on the table. "Forgive me, sir, but I'm feeling a wee bit faint."

"Sit down before you fall over," he snapped. His eyes narrowed. "Do you expect me to believe you knew nothing of this?"

Kathleen slid onto one of the dining chairs. "That he took food to Ireland? Never a word did he speak to me of such a thing." She couldn't contain her amazement.

"He did it for you." The old man ran a hand across his jaw and watched her for a long moment. Then he shook his head. "You're to be married soon," he finally said. "To that Irish boy."

Kathleen straightened. "In a few weeks now."

He stared at her so hard, she dropped her gaze to the floor.

"Do you love him?" he asked.

Her mouth dropped open at his forwardness. "I think so."

The old man scrubbed both hands tiredly over his face. "Think so? Don't you know?"

"Aye, I—I do love him."

"Well then, that's good, that's good. Don't you think?" He stared off, lost in his thoughts, not even noticing that she didn't answer.

After a moment, Kathleen stood and started across the room.

"I didn't marry the girl I loved," the old man said when she reached the door. "And I've never stopped wondering what happened to her."

She turned back to face him.

"Old people are always getting mixed up in the love affairs of the young," he muttered. "They didn't help me...and I haven't helped Jack. Doesn't mean I think he belongs with an Irish woman. Because I don't. Just means it's not my choice to make."

He waved her away without looking at her and she escaped to the kitchen, flabbergasted at his words and disconcerted over their meaning.

*

Jack shook his arms to dislodge the wet snow and headed down the companionway to his quarters. They had been at sea for nearly five weeks and he had to admit the predictions from some of the older captains had all come true. They'd warned him that March was the worst month to cross the Atlantic. And though March was now long past and they'd turned the page on April as well, the weather had not improved. Still, they were nearly there—another day of good winds and, barring unforeseen disaster, they'd soon be anchoring in Cork Harbor.

They had put up with some nasty weather on this voyage. From rain and hail to sloppy sleet and full snow. The wind could change in the span of five minutes from a fresh breeze to a gale. The rigging was stiff and hard to work, and the men were near frozen through—as was he.

Still he had no regrets except one: he should have told Kathleen he was going to Ireland. Should have found out whether she wanted him to check on her family or deliver a letter or bring them some money. She'd told him once that they lived outside Cobh. In the two extra days they'd stayed behind in Boston to load the ship, he should have risked his grandfather's wrath and gone home to tell her he was sailing to Ireland.

Shoving open the door to his quarters, he tossed his gloves on the floor and shrugged out of his jacket. The wood stove was warm and he sat in front of it, rubbing his hands together and blowing on his fingers to get the blood flowing. More than a month had passed since they set sail, since he'd seen Kathleen. He looked at the logbook on his chart table, glanced at the date. Tomorrow was the first of May. Tomorrow was when she would marry Danny, would move into the room—and bed—she would share with her new husband.

He thrust the thought away and peeled off the rest of his wet clothes, then toweled himself off before slipping on a dry layer and climbing into bed. A hard shiver coursed through him as the warmth penetrated his bones. He was good and tired of being cold—and no doubt, so were the men. There were several cases of frostbite among the crew and he had shortened the length of each watch to limit the men's exposure to the weather. Even then, it didn't take long on deck before the chill worked its way under your skin and grabbed hold of your ribs with fingers of frozen steel. His muscles relaxed in the warmth and he shivered again. His eyes drifted shut and he slid into the nebulous world before sleep, his last conscious thought of Kathleen, of kissing and kissing and kissing her.

*

A coolness skimmed along her jaw and down her throat. Kathleen woke slightly at the touch, pulled the blankets to her neck and let herself slip back into her dream. She didn't want to wake—not yet. Jack rolled her onto her back and kissed the curve of her jaw. His lips brushed the soft skin beneath her ear, and he turned her head toward his and kissed her on the mouth, softly at first, then with increasing urgency. He kissed her chin and ran his tongue along the line of her throat. Goosebumps rose on her skin and she reached up for him, ran her hands along the muscles of his shoulders and arms, over the flat plane of his stomach.

His hand slid up the side of the light gown she wore. The fabric slipped beneath his fingers and he played it against her breasts, his calloused fingers soft through the thin cotton as he toyed with it, drawing her nipples tight, each motion pulling the gown higher until her hips and stomach were exposed.

He kissed her harder and she pressed up toward him. And then her gown was gone and he cupped her breasts, the gentleness of his roughened fingers sending tremors rippling through her. She moaned out his name.

He pushed her legs apart with his knee, one hand cupping her bottom as he settled himself between her thighs. His mouth was on hers now, trapping her, and he held her tight by the hips and slid lower, pressing hard against her until he was nearly inside her. She shifted her hips, wanting him, needing him to take her now. "Jack," she whispered.

"You've married Danny."

"But my heart will always be yours." She waited, eyes closed for him to kiss her again, arching upward to meet him, her body yearning for his touch. She shifted restlessly, but he didn't respond. "Jack," she whispered again and opened her eyes, blinking with difficulty, as if coming out of a drugged sleep. "Jack?"

She blinked hard and pushed up on her elbows, struggling to focus her eyes, to find him in the darkness. Slowly her mind cleared and disappointment flooded through her. It was a dream. Jack had left weeks ago, back to sea. And she was to marry Danny this very day.

She dropped back onto the pillow and closed her eyes. The

dream lingered like a hazy photograph at the edges of her memory, and she reached for it, dragging it forward until it moved fully into her consciousness. She savored the memory until she could stand it no longer and then she opened her eyes and stared into the darkness.

What did she want? She had not long to decide. Yellow rays from the rising sun intruded from behind her closed draperies. Danny would be arriving soon and together they would go before the priest to take their vows. She had been so certain that happiness would be hers once they were together again. She remembered the depth of feeling she once had for him and tried to recapture that emotion, concentrating on memories in the hope that her heart would warm at the pictures in her mind.

The grandfather's question sneaked into her thoughts: *Do you love him?* She tossed off her blankets and sat up, swinging her legs over the side of the bed. A chill swept over her and she hurried to the hearth to stoke the fire.

Did she love him?

How could she not? He was her betrothed. She stabbed at the logs. "'Tis a fine kettle of fish you've got here for yourself now, Kathleen," she muttered. "Professing your love for one man and dreaming of another."

The fire flared gold and orange and she stepped back to watch it. "Tell me now, Ma, what would ye say to this quandary of mine?" she asked, though well she knew the answer. Ma would tell her to wed Danny—fine Irish lad that he was. Indeed, were her parents to learn that Kathleen had feelings for an Englishman they would never forgive her.

She must wed Danny. Of that she had no question. She must stand beside him for the rest of her life. Or lose her family.

Jack kissed her in her mind, just a touch of his mouth on hers— *But she had loved Danny since she was a child.* Jack ran his fingers down her throat and across her breasts. *Danny was Irish.* Jack touched a finger to her lips and whispered, "I could love you, Kathleen Deacey."

Her skin raised up in goosebumps. When had he said that? When? Then it came to her. That day he had taken her to find Danny, when the man they had found had not been Danny at all. She had slept on his shoulder and he had spoken of love. And just as surely as she knew he meant it then, she knew there was only one answer to her question.

She dropped to her knees on the carpet and prayed that she was wrong. For Danny was soon to arrive to take her to the church, and God help her, she'd lost her heart to an Englishman.

CHAPTER THIRTY-THREE

THE CYRENA SAILED into Cork Harbor late on a misty May morning to a greeting that astounded everyone on board. The hills were lined with people cheering the ship as it was towed to the depot to unload her stores. On the quay, crowds had gathered, grown men and women weeping with joy.

As soon as the ship dropped anchor, several dignitaries came aboard to welcome the crew to Ireland. "I'll be thinking all the bells in the city are ringing now in Cork," one of the men told Jack. "For they rang a full day once the news reached there that the Jamestown had arrived, near to three weeks ago now."

"They crossed the Atlantic in two weeks?" Jack shook his head in awe.

"Fifteen days, three hours. I heard that Captain Forbes said if the ship had been properly manned and rigged, they could have made it in thirteen and a half or fourteen days. They left on the return voyage more than a week ago already."

Jack planned to unload his own ship and head back to sea as quickly as possible, within a couple of days at most. There was, after all, another purpose to this trip—to hunt whales. Every day in port cost him money. Still, he graciously accepted the offer of lodging on shore and attended a welcoming dinner that first evening. After some persuasion, he even agreed to a walking tour of Cork with a local priest, Father Flynn, in the morning.

The priest was at his door early and Jack fleetingly wondered whether the man wanted to make sure Jack wouldn't be able to set sail and avoid the tour altogether. As they began their walk, the day fresh and the sun bright, he was heartened to see that conditions overall did not seem as bad as he'd expected. But once they turned off the main street onto a narrow lane, he had the sense that they had crossed into some inhuman place. The light seemed grayer, the people emaciated and faded as though their spirits were nearer to death than to life. No matter which direction he looked, he saw people in dire need.

He pulled out the few coins he had with him and began to pass them out, realizing immediately that his meager effort would have no effect on these lives except to prolong the suffering for another day.

Within minutes, a crowd had gathered around them, pressing forward, bony arms reaching out, weak voices coming from skeletal faces, begging for help. Suddenly, the horror that was Ireland was all he could see. He reached into his pockets again and came up empty.

"I'm sorry, I haven't any left."

Despite his words, the desperate crowd pushed forward, pleading for help. Father Flynn touched him on the arm and ducked into a nearby shop. Jack followed him into the safety behind its closed doors. He drew a sharp breath, shaken by what he had seen—human beings, no more than skeletons in rags.

"Are you all right?" the priest asked. "It's hard to face, I know, but I thought you would be wanting to see the people you're helping."

"I don't think I've done enough."

"Ah, but at least you've done something. Have ye any idea what it means to them to know that America, a country with no responsibility for the Irish, has given food and clothing, has brought provisions to Ireland at their own expense? It matters. For any of us, but particularly the Irish right now, it is good for them to know that someone in this world cares whether they live or die."

Guilt nagged at him for the terms he had worked out with Captain Forbes; his had not been a wholly charitable voyage. "Is all of Ireland like this?"

Father Flynn winced. "What you've seen, Captain, is not so bad. Those who are out are usually the healthiest. Open the door to any cottage or hovel along any lane and ye'll find people too weak to move, starving to death where last they lay down. They say there is no more painful death than starvation."

Jack's stomach turned.

The small crowd had dispersed and the priest motioned for Jack to follow him outside. "Out in the countryside is far worse," he said. "Almost the whole of Skibberdean is dead already."

The words settled over Jack like a chill and he felt as though he were trapped in a room with walls closing in on him. "And the English? What of their aid?"

The priest shook his head. "The government still refuses to help. A few landlords are spending their own money for the people on their land, but it's a very few. Most see the famine as a blessing, a means of clearing away the Irish so they can have more land to graze cattle for export. The British love beef."

Jack held up a hand to stop the man from saying any more. Kathleen had a right to hate the English, if for nothing else, but this. He looked up into the hills above the city. And what of her family? Mrs. Boyle had told him Kathleen's mother was giving her portion of food to her children. What if she now was dying? What if the whole family was?

He could not leave Ireland until he knew they were all right, until he made sure they had enough food, until he was satisfied that the money Kathleen sent each week was enough to feed and clothe the family. Though Kathleen would never know it, this would be his gift to her, a wedding present, so to speak.

"There's a family I need to find," he said, urgency speeding his words. "Parents of a friend. Deacey is their name. I believe they live somewhere just outside of Cobh."

"Have you a first name?"

"No. But there is a daughter named Kathleen and a son, Sean. Both are now in Boston. I know it isn't much to go on..."

Father Flynn rubbed his jaw. "One of the other priests may know of them. I can ask." He gave Jack a thoughtful look. "But you must be prepared for the worst. They may be dead already— or gone. Thousands have been thrown out of their homes by the landlords and if that is the case, ye'll never find them."

*

Danny stood at the back entry, all spit and polish, looking as fine as he ever had. It hurt Kathleen just to look at him. She had pulled on her cloak before he arrived and he knew not that underneath she was dressed in her usual work clothes.

"Are you ready now?" he asked. A big smile lit his face and his eyes sparkled.

She thought she might weep.

"Let's walk a bit, Danny." Without awaiting an answer, she stepped out the door.

"What's wrong? Have you bad news from home?" He followed her outside.

She shook her head. The air was warming, the cold winter temperatures long gone now that the calendar had turned to May. She drew a long inhale, as if the air's freshness deep in her lungs would somehow keep her from swaying from her decision.

"Tell me then, before I go crazy thinking," Danny said.

She stopped and looked straight at him. "I'll not be knowing any other way to tell you." Her heart wrenched at his stricken expression. "Ah, Danny, where were ye when I waited in Ireland? Why didn't you come back?"

"I told you, I got a job—"

"Ah, but I know there's more." She shook her head. "I waited for you, always afraid you might be dead and certain you weren't. I was so sure we would be together again. But now I can't marry you—"

"What?"

"I can't marry you." Her voice quivered.

He took hold of her arms. "What Kathleen, what is this? It's all right, common even, to be afraid right before the vows are taken."

"Fear is not what is driving me." Her eyes pricked with tears. How could she hurt him like this? How could she tell him she loved someone else? "I—" The words would not come.

His gaze dropped to the ground and he shoved his hands deep into his pockets. "I never meant to hurt you, Kathleen. Never meant for you to know. Sean never knew. My family either. That's why I stopped writing them."

She struggled to make sense of his words.

He raised his eyes to hers. "I never loved her, Kathleen."

She jerked back as though she had been slapped.

"I only stayed because her family had money. But when I saw your notice, knew you had come across, I couldn't go through with the wedding," he said, hands out in supplication.

Shock shattered her thoughts. "Wedding? You were to marry?"

He nodded slowly. "But you knew already. You knew…" Realization dawned on his face. "Did ye not?"

Kathleen shook her head. "How would I know such a thing?"

"Oh Jaysus."

"Who was it?" she asked in a hushed voice.

"It doesn't matter."

"It matters."

He glanced away. "Her father was one of the fishery owners."

Kathleen drew a shaky breath and an odd sound, half-sob, half-gasp tore from her throat. "You left me waiting in Ireland while ye courted another woman? Planned to marry her?"

"I never loved her."

Kathleen thought she might be sick. "And ye must never have loved me either or ye wouldn't have done it at all."

"I was tired of being poor, Kathleen, of having nothing—"

"We're all tired of it! The whole Irish race. Yet the rest of us are not betraying those we love over it."

"Please Kathleen—"

"So what did she say when you told her you were coming to find me?"

He met her gaze but said nothing, and in that moment she knew the rest.

"You didn't tell her."

"When I saw your notice in the paper, I had to come. I couldn't not. I've always loved you—"

"Have ye now? So you left her without a word."

"I never forgot you, Kathleen. I just thought you'd never leave Ireland—"

"You never asked me if I would come with you."

"It was a mistake not to. And I'll be thanking God for the rest of my life that I realized it before I said the vows with her."

"Do ye have any idea the prayers I said for you, the tears I shed for your safety—and all the while you were making a future for yourself with some other woman?"

"I just got lost for a bit. And you've a right to be angry, Kathleen. But we can start over, you and me." He took her hands. "We've always belonged together."

A hysterical laugh forced its way from her throat and she jerked her hands from his. "Once perhaps. But you didn't love me enough to come home, didn't love me enough to include me in your plans to leave Ireland." She raised her chin and wiped the back of her hand over her wet eyes. "I've news for you, Daniel O'Sheehan. I don't love you. I knew I didn't even when I saw you again that first day."

Danny threw back his head and laughed. "You'll have to do better than that." He pulled her into his arms and nuzzled her hair. "Come on now, lass, forgive me and let's be wed."

She twisted out of his grasp. "Nay! On this matter I would not be lying." She stood back from him, fists clenched, breath coming fast.

He reached his hands out in supplication. "Ah, Kathleen, you're not saying this, not really...are you?"

She nodded.

"You don't love me?" He glanced away for just a moment, then turned back suddenly. "Who?"

"It matters not."

His expression hardened and he let loose a chopped laugh. "The Englishman."

She knew her face gave her away.

"Irish you are," he said in a low voice. "And him of filthy English blood. You would betray Ireland for him?"

Danny's words pierced her spirit as surely as if he had taken a knife to her heart. She could not reply.

"Answer me true, Kathleen. You would turn away from your own country for this man?"

"I've not turned away from Ireland."

"Ha! And where is he now? Out to sea, a different woman in every port I wager. And an Irish mistress waiting in Boston."

"I'm not his mistress."

"You'll be it soon enough, for an English will never marry an Irish. He'll bed you, aye, but ye'll never be his wife."

Her vision clouded with the blackness of anger and it took all her self-control to keep from striking him.

"I am the man your parents approved of—not some English captain in America—"

"Enough!" The word was almost a growl. "If you'd truly cared about me, Danny, you would never have taken up with another woman, you would have come home to Ireland where I waited. And we'd have wed months ago. It's your own doing and you'll not change me mind with guilt—"

He took a step toward her. "I'll ask you just once. Will you come with me to the church and become my wife?"

"Nay."

He stared at her for nearly a minute. "Then I'll be saying good day to you—and good-bye. For I'll need to be catching a train for Canada. I'm engaged to a fine woman there, did you know?"

He spun on his heel and sauntered away, shoulders back, head up as though he didn't give a damn. She watched him through eyes blurred with tears, her mind in turmoil and her heart filled with relief, watched him until he rounded the street corner out of her life, never once glancing back.

CHAPTER THIRTY-FOUR

FATHER FLYNN WAS pounding on Jack's door before the sun had fully risen the next morning. Dragging himself from bed, Jack quickly pulled on some clothes. "What an ungodly hour for a man of God," he muttered as he unlatched the door.

The priest burst into the room, clearly no worse for the wear from his early morning excursions. "I've found them," he said with understated joy. "Your friends, the Deaceys. Father Bailey says he saw the family not a fortnight ago."

Jack was almost afraid to ask. "All well and alive?"

The other sobered. "At least alive," he answered. "I've arranged transport for ye later this morning to see them. You might take along a couple of your men as precaution, for along the road you'll pass many who are desperate. Were I a married man, I dare not even guess at what I might do to help me own children live."

Four hours later, Jack, Donnelly, and Matson set out in the carriage Father Flynn had procured, several bushels of food on the seats around them. Their mood was grim with apprehension and they spoke little, unnecessary conversation seeming almost disrespectful in the midst of such suffering. The further they got outside of Cobh, the more desolate the countryside became, eerily silent as though they were nearing the gates to the land of the dead. Clouds, heavy with rain, sank lower to earth and gray drizzle began to fall. The carriage lurched and bumped over the rutted road, kicking up dust that sifted down upon emaciated beings who watched their passing through sunken eyes. One woman reached toward them, pleading with her hand. Jack twisted in his seat to look back as they passed and watched as her outstretched arm dropped heavily against her side and she fell to her knees next to the body of a man lying beside the road.

Shaken, he sat back in his seat and struggled to ignore the images that kept appearing in his mind, pictures of what he might find at the Deacey home. He stared straight ahead, refusing to look out the window again until the carriage halted outside a small stone house squatting on the edge of the road like an unkempt child, traces of whitewash on its walls, an unruly mop of thatch for a roof. Though it was early afternoon, there did not appear to be anyone about. Fear skidded through him that he was too late.

He told Matson and Donnelly to wait, then stepped down into the road. As he started toward the cottage, the door opened and a gaunt, gray-faced older man shuffled out to stare at him.

"Good afternoon," Jack said. "I'm looking for Mr. Deacey. The father of Kathleen Deacey who went to America."

The man looked him over. "I'll be her father," he finally said. "Is she all right?"

Jack smiled. He took several steps forward and reached out with one hand. "She's well. I'm a friend of hers, Jack Montgomery."

The man smiled just a bit and stepped forward to clasp Jack's hand in welcome. His nails were broken and yellowed. "Micheal Deacey, I am. I know your name. I'll be thanking ye for saving me daughter's life and for taking her into your home. She's written us, you know, about what you've done to help her." He pulled open the door. "Will you come in?"

Without awaiting an answer, Micheal called into the cottage, "Anna, we've a guest—from America."

Jack took a breath to steel himself against whatever came next and stepped over the threshold. He paused just inside the door to let his eyes adjust to the dim light. With one glance he took in the entire house—a single room with a dirt floor, two windows, shutters closed. Three children lay curled upon a thin bed of straw in the corner, two boys and a girl, each wrapped in a threadbare blanket to ward off the damp chill. Though their expressions were blank, their eyes were open and all three watched him. A haggard woman with a black shawl tight around her shoulders sat in the room's only chair, close to the barely flickering peat fire. It was all Jack could do to keep from shuddering at the hollow planes of her face.

"Anna, this is Mr. Montgomery who has been helping our Kathleen in Boston," Micheal said.

The corners of her mouth turned up a bit.

"It's good to meet you, Mrs. Deacey." Jack struggled to keep the emotion from his voice.

She pushed herself up to stand beside the chair, bending forward to rest a hand on its back for support. "What a welcome surprise indeed to have you here. Will you sit down?"

"If you don't mind, I've been sitting for some time now and I'd just as soon stand."

She nodded and eased herself down, one hand on the back of the chair supporting her weight and shaking from the effort. She gestured toward the children. "These are Kathleen's brothers and sister—Thomas, Rory, and Nora."

His throat tightened and he hurt for Kathleen and for Sean

who he barely knew. God, he even hurt for Danny O'Sheehan whose family was surely trying to survive this horror too.

"Have you news from Kathleen?" Micheal prompted.

"Yes, yes. She sends you this." Jack pulled out 20 pounds and cursed himself for not bringing more.

Anna covered her eyes with one hand and began to weep.

Kathleen's father took the money, one hand curling around the other as though in prayer, wrapping it safely within his large palms. "We had nothing left. Thank you."

Jack turned for the door. "I've brought some food, too," he said. With Donnelly and Matson's help, he brought the bushels into the cottage and lined them along the hearth.

The children struggled to their feet, wasted bodies barely covered by tattered, too small clothing. Jack's stomach turned. It was hard to tell how old they were because of their physical condition, but he would guess the two boys were into their teens. How could he not have thought to bring some clothing from the ship? And more food?

Anna shuffled over to Jack and took his hand. Her eyes glistened with tears. "As long as the night is, the day still comes," she murmured. "I'll be thanking you for looking in on us. Ye'll be in my prayers every day of me life."

She sunk to her knees and reached into a basket. The children crowded close, hollow eyes wide with wanting. Anna broke off chunks of bread and passed them out. "Slowly now," she admonished. "Eat slowly or you'll have pains...and it will all come up again."

She pushed herself to standing and handed a piece to her husband, then hesitantly offered some to Jack and the other crewmen. All three shook their heads, and Donnelly and Matson excused themselves to wait out in the carriage.

"Micheal, if ye put a pot on, we'll have potatoes," Anna said.

"More bread, Ma?" one of the boys asked.

She encircled him with her arms and drew a weary breath. "I would give anything to let you have all you want. But, we've a long while to make this food last—and you've cousins down the road with nothing to eat. Will you have them starve now just so ye might fill your bellies to bursting this once?"

Jack clamped his teeth together and turned away, the tightness behind his ribs feeling like it might rend open his chest. Children—they were just children on the verge of adulthood. He wanted to urge them to eat, to fill their bellies to bursting. And they should be able to, shouldn't have to worry about where their next mouthful was coming from.

Did England care not at all what was happening to the children of Ireland? Where were the English as the Irish starved? And then, softly, he heard Kathleen as if she were standing beside him: *"They'll see the Irish die and be glad for it."*

So clearly did he hear the words that he twisted round expecting her to be beside him. "Kath—"

But only her family was there. He met her mother's eyes and she nodded as if she knew his thoughts.

"I thought I heard something," he said sheepishly.

"You did. You heard your heart."

She moved to check the water in the pot. "Have you any other news from Kathleen, Captain? We've not had a letter from her in a bit."

Surely they must know that Danny had been found. "Did you know that Sean found Kathleen in Boston?"

Anna clasped her hands together and dropped her head to her chest.

Micheal shook his head. "He went to Boston? We've had but one letter from him, saying he was safely in Canada. He thought Kathleen dead—as we all did. How did he find—"

"Ah, but it must have been a fine reunion. Were you there, Captain?" Kathleen's mother asked.

The question called up a vivid picture in Jack's mind, of Kathleen and Danny embracing when they first saw one another, of Kathleen's tears of joy, of his own sense of loss. "Yes. I was there," he said.

If they didn't know about Sean, they wouldn't know about Danny. Or the marriage. He steeled himself against the emotions he knew would surface when he said the rest of it out loud. "Kathleen placed a notice in the St. John's newspaper, looking for Danny in Newfoundland," he began.

"And Sean saw that notice?" Micheal asked.

"No. Danny did. Sean first found Danny..."

Anna and her daughter gasped. "Our Kathleen? Does she know Danny has been found?" Anna asked.

He nodded. "Danny came with Sean to Boston."

Anna took hold of her husband's arm for support. "And was she glad to have found him?"

In her eyes, Jack could see respect and gratitude and understanding. And in that moment he knew why Kathleen Deacey loved her mother so much, why she turned to her mother for advice when they were a million miles apart.

"Yes," he said. "She was very glad." He smiled then, mouth only, for he could bring no joy to his eyes. "They were married just a couple of days ago." He paused. "She was very glad."

In the ensuing silence, the only sound was that of the water bubbling on the hearth. Jack shifted uncomfortably. "Well, I should probably be going. I have a ship to ready for a whaling voyage."

"Give our love to Kathleen when next you see her," Anna said.

Jack nodded and clasped Micheal's hand in farewell. "I'll send someone tomorrow with more food." He stepped outside and quietly drew the door shut. The dampness crept through his coat and into his bones and he thought of the three children in rags in the cottage behind him and how their mother had not taken a piece of bread for herself.

He thought of how his own father had abandoned his family, killed himself, unwilling to stay and fight for their survival once his money was gone. How his mother left him behind as she chased wealth. Would that his parents had been like Kathleen's, how much different his life might have been.

The cloud cover had begun to lift and he looked up at the white blue sky hinting of spring and knew that the change of seasons would bring no help to the family slowly dying inside the stone walls of this cottage. He shoved his hands into his pockets and did not turn round, though he knew he was going to. He thought of the whales he needed to catch, of the funds invested in this voyage by the other owners and of the profit they expected to make. And he knew without a doubt that none of that really mattered.

He turned and stepped into the cottage without knocking. The family looked at him in surprise.

"I've—" He blew out his breath. "Damn, I don't know how to do this." He shoved a nervous hand through his hair. "Look, I want you to come with me. To America. To Boston."

*

Kathleen drew a tired hand across her eyes and wished she knew what was right anymore. At this moment, with Danny walking out of her life and Jack already gone, with her family so far across the ocean, she thanked God that Sean was here, for without him she would have felt completely adrift.

Church bells began to chime the hour, and though this path today had been her choice, still she could not hold back her grief. This was the moment when she was to have stood at the altar and pledged her love to Danny, when she would have vowed to cherish him for the rest of her life.

She lifted the front of her skirt with one hand and hurried for Holy Cross Cathedral. Though there was to be no wedding, Sean and the Boyles waited at the church, and she knew without a doubt that Danny wouldn't be going there to tell them it was off.

By the time she reached the steps of the cathedral, she was winded. A small group had gathered on the steps, Irish all, dressed in their best clothes. Another wedding. The thought weighed heavy on her heart. With a nod at them, she dashed up the steps and tugged open the heavy door.

Sean was at the altar in consultation with the priest. The Boyles waited together in a pew. Kathleen drew a breath of the inside air, heavy with the scent of incense and burning candles, and welcomed the peacefulness inside the silent stone church. She started down the aisle.

All four turned as she neared.

"Kathleen!" Mrs. Boyle hastened toward her with Sean not far behind. "We were getting to be worried." She looked toward the entrance doors. "Where's Danny now? Father says he has another wedding to perform at half past the hour."

The prickle in Kathleen's throat became a lump.

"What's the matter? Sure, Danny came to get you, didn't he?" Mrs. Boyle put a hand on Kathleen's arm.

"Aye, he came," she said. "But we'll not wed today…nor will we ever, Danny and me." She glanced at the priest waiting at the altar. "Please give Father my apologies, tell him I'm sorry we troubled him."

"What happened?" Sean's brow was creased, his eyes dark. "Where is Danny now?"

"Come outside and I'll tell ye the whole of it."

Five minutes later amid the clatter of passing wagons, Kathleen related the story, making it sound as though Danny had called off the wedding because he wished to return to the other woman in Newfoundland. There was no reason anyone ever had to know of her feelings for Captain Montgomery, for nothing would ever come of it.

"Jaysus, Kathleen," Sean said. "It makes no sense. If he didn't plan to go through with it, why did he push you to wed so quickly? And why would he tell you this on your wedding day? If he wanted to go back to Newfoundland, why not tell you last week—or the week before?"

Mrs. Boyle clucked her tongue. "Why did he come to Boston at all?"

"Perhaps when we were nearly facing the vows, that was when he realized the woman he wanted wasn't me." It may not be the pure truth but it was true enough, no matter what Danny might say if anyone ever asked him.

Sean put an arm around her shoulders and gave her a squeeze. "It'll be all right, you know. How often has Ma said, *it's a long road that has no turning?*"

A small laugh escaped her, followed by a wave of longing. Her words caught. "More than I can remember."

They said good-bye to the Boyles and Sean walked her home, hugging her tightly before she went into the house. She quietly closed the kitchen door and headed for the stair, relieved to discover Cook was nowhere to be seen and she wouldn't have to tell the story again, not yet.

As she passed the parlor, an incredulous voiced barked out, "You're back already?"

The grandfather. She was tempted to ignore him, for she did have the entire day off, it being her wedding day. Still, he was her employer and 'twould be unforgivable not to acknowledge the man.

She pasted a smile on her face and stepped into the room. The old man sat in a wingback chair by the hearth, a thick book in his hands. "Is there something you'll be needing, sir?"

"Is *he* with you?"

Kathleen bristled. "He?"

"Your Irish husband."

She pressed her lips together. Obviously she'd not be avoiding this conversation as she had hoped. "We didn't get married," she said in a voice loud enough to carry across the room and, with any luck, brusque enough to discourage further questions.

The grandfather dropped his book and it landed with a dull thud on his foot, followed by a clearly audible curse. "So he called it off," he said with smug satisfaction. He bent to pick his book off the floor.

"Nay."

"Good Lord, don't tell me he's been killed!"

Hysterical laughter welled up inside her.

The old man lay a steady gaze on her and she knew he was waiting for her to provide the details. It gave her a perverse pleasure not to accommodate him. She knew he'd ask.

"Well then?" he finally said. "Why aren't you married?"

"I decided not to."

He gave a snort of derisive laughter. "You?"

"If there's nothing else, sir, I'll be going to me room." She was nearly out the door when he spoke again.

"He was no good for you anyway."

She turned. "Excuse me?"

The old man tilted his head slightly and gave her a small nod. "I may have underestimated you, Kathleen. I saw what he was when he first starting coming around—but I thought you'd never see it. You both being Irish, I didn't think it would matter to you."

"If you'll pardon me for saying so, sir, it isn't like you not to have said so back then."

"What would I say? That one Irish shouldn't wed another? That you shouldn't marry the man you've waited to find for nearly a year? Why would I say that? It would only have encouraged... Jack. Anyway, you needed to learn that yourself."

"Me Ma used to say, *'tis impossible to love and be wise.*"

"Ah, so now that you do not love, you have found wisdom."

She gave a small shrug. "Perhaps only as relates to Danny."

He gave her a thoughtful nod and a defeated smile. "The best laid schemes of mice and men often go awry. Robert Burns."

"Sir?"

He shook his head. "Ask me in six months."

He opened his book, dismissing her without a word.

CHAPTER THIRTY-FIVE

"COME TO AMERICA?" Kathleen's younger sister asked, her eyes wide and so much like Kathleen's it almost hurt to look at her. "I thought you were going whale hunting."

"I considered that, but the more I've thought on it, you see, I'm engaged. To be married. She's waiting in Boston. It would be good that I go back," he said, knowing as he spoke that his words made little sense. He turned to Kathleen's parents. "Will you come?"

"But Ireland is our home," Anna whispered.

Micheal dropped his gaze and shook his head. "We have no money for passage."

"I'll not charge you for passage—I own the ship." *One-eighth of it anyway.* "Kathleen and Sean are there already. Will you watch your youngest children perish on Irish soil? Or will you let them live—in America?"

No one answered and he gestured with one hand. "If things improve in Ireland, you can always return."

"I didn't want Kathleen to go, nor Sean...and now you say I should leave this place that is me home," Micheal said in a thick voice. "You've never seen it when all is green, Captain Montgomery. You've never felt the joy of a soft day. She holds us here. We are as much a part of Ireland as she is of us. This island is woven into our hearts and through our souls. And yet, ye say we must leave." He shook his head. "My heart aches at even the thought."

"I'll not pressure you now," Jack said quietly. "Think on it tonight. I'll return tomorrow for your answer. But know this— Kathleen left Ireland to save you. She said to me once, the only way the Irish will save the Irish is from America. Let me help Kathleen help you to live. Let me do this for her." He put a hand on the door handle and stepped back to the waiting carriage, fully determined that the Deacey family would come with him to Boston.

He slept little that night, his dreams a tortured jumble of images he had seen the past two days. In the dark loneliness of early morning, he gave up on rest and stared at the ceiling, working out rebuttals to the arguments he expected the Deaceys to make. Though he knew not how long the convincing would take, there was one thing of which he was certain—he would not leave Ireland without them.

By the time the sun broke the horizon, he was up and dressed. He'd told the crew yesterday about the change in plans, had promised them full wages upon docking in Boston—a decision that would financially set him back but good, but he didn't care. Then he'd put Matson in charge of building berths in the hold for the family to use during the voyage. In a span of ten minutes he'd said what needed to be said and escaped off his ship so he wouldn't have to look at the crew's incredulous expressions any longer.

*

Jack looked out the carriage window as the driver brought the vehicle to a halt in front of the Deacey's cottage. Like yesterday, the house looked to be uninhabited, but he knew Kathleen's family was inside. The cottages of Ireland were filled with its people, each family facing a banshee of its own.

Jack's shoulders tensed in anticipation of the discussion ahead. He hoped the family wasn't too determined to stay, that the conversation wouldn't turn into battle. He stepped to the ground and lifted out the basket of clothing he'd brought along. The sun had risen through clear skies today and he welcomed its warmth.

He rapped on the door. It swung open with a creak and Micheal Deacey stood before him, unmoving, unwelcoming. Then, with a defeated sigh, he stepped aside and bid Jack to enter.

The family stood in a row facing him, the children close together, shivering beneath the too-small blankets across their shoulders. Jack set the basket on the floor.

"I've brought some clothing. I think it should fit." He held up a shirt to gauge the size, then handed it to the youngest boy who murmured a grinning thank-you and pulled it on. "Mrs. Deacey, a hand if you will," Jack said.

Minutes later amid laughter and tears, the clothing had been passed out and pulled on, shoes tied over wool socks, coats tried on and then laid aside for later.

"You look fine," Jack said around the knot in his throat. Five gaunt faces looked back at him, eyes shining from hollow sockets. "You look grand." He turned to Kathleen's father. "Have you talked it over?" he asked. "I don't want to argue, but if I must—"

"We'll go."

Jack grinned. He clapped the other on the back and nodded, unable to speak for a moment. "I know how hard this must be, but I promise you won't regret it." He hesitated. "Can you come now? Do you have to say goodbye to anyone?"

Micheal shook his head. "We did that yesterday, once we'd decided. But there's one thing, Captain Montgomery, just one thing—" A knock rattled the door and he exchanged a look with his wife before going to answer.

Jack could hear nothing of the conversation there, just the low murmur of voices. Finally, Micheal opened the door and a man, woman, and two children came into the room. Their feet were wrapped in rags, their clothing thin and torn, their faces pinched. But their eyes shone.

Anna Deacey stepped forward. "This is my sister, Brigid, and her husband, Colm. We buried their baby girl a fortnight ago."

Colm clutched the front of his coat with both hands and drew a rough breath. "Micheal told us how ye were taking them to Boston. And we were wondering—"

He dug in his pocket, pulled out a few coins and held them out to Jack. "'Tisn't even passage for one, I know, but I promise on me word, that I will pay you back for all our passages, once I get work… if you might take us with you. To America." His face held an odd mixture of hope and fear.

Four more people. He'd had been so concerned about convincing the Deaceys to leave Ireland, it hadn't occurred to him they might want to bring other relatives along. Four more to feed on the month-long journey. Still, how could he leave them behind? They'd already lost one child.

"A few more, a few less, is there a difference really?" Anna offered.

Jack cocked his head to look at her. What difference would four more make really? He himself might die tomorrow and then what good would his money do him anyway?

"All right. We'll all squeeze into the carriage somehow," he said with a grin. "Have you anything you need to get to bring along?"

Another knock sounded at the door. Micheal glanced at Jack, frowning slightly as he went to answer. Without more than a sentence exchanged between him and the caller, he opened the door just enough to let a lanky, skinny man enter. "Our neighbor, James Duffy," he said gruffly.

The man took several slow steps into the room. Under one arm he had tucked a fiddle, the wood mellowed to a rich patina. He drew it forward and lovingly held it across his chest. "I've come to ask you for passage, Captain Montgomery. All I have is me fiddle. 'Twas me father's. And his father's before that. It plays a pretty note."

The man set the instrument on his shoulder and ran the bow across the strings, the notes weaving into a melody Jack had often heard Kathleen humming while she worked. He touched the strings with his hand to silence them and shook his head. He wanted no reminders of Kathleen right now.

Duffy looked stricken. "Please Captain. You could sell it once we reach America—"

"You misunderstand me. I don't want your fiddle. But I expect you'll entertain us on the voyage with your music."

A grin broke across the man's face. "Oh, aye, that I will, sir. And me family? I have a family."

Jack suppressed a frown. "How many?"

"Just a wife…and five wee ones."

Six more? How was he going to feed all these people? As he hesitated, he saw Duffy freeze with the fear that his family would be turned away. Jack exhaled softly, then smiled. "Well, you couldn't leave them behind now, could you?" Oh, his grandfather would have a great time with this when Jack was home again.

A light tap at the door drew the attention of everyone in the room. Jack lay an accusing look on Micheal.

The other shrugged innocently. "Word seems to have spread," he said.

"Let me get it this time." Jack strode to the door and pulled it open, intent on discouraging the next caller from asking for passage. A lone woman stood closest to the door, but behind her a line of people stretched out into the road, starving people with faces drawn like death, hair thin and tangled, and none in clothing that would keep them warm even on this fine May morning. Children lay on the ground at their parents' feet, too weak to stand. They had come he knew already, for a chance at life.

But was it his place to make sure they got it? Wasn't he doing enough already? *Was he?* He took a quick count as he stepped outside. More than thirty. "Are you all looking for passage to America?" he asked in a raised voice.

A chorus of quiet "ayes" was the reply. He nodded, more to himself than to them. It would cost him a fortune to feed this many people for a month on the passage. He glanced back at the cottage where Anna Deacey stood in the doorway, watching, one hand holding her sweater close to her throat. *Kathleen's mother.*

He gave her an almost imperceptible nod. "Ah well, a few more, a few less, what's the difference really?" he said.

The slightest smile touched Anna's lips.

He turned back to the crowd. "I have a whaling ship. It's not made for transporting people. My crew will have to build berths enough for all of you to sleep in." He quickly calculated how much time they needed. "Even so, I'd like to set sail in five days."

A tall, emaciated man stepped forward. "I can help build the berths. I'm a carpenter by trade."

He hardly appeared strong enough to swing a hammer.

"All right. Good."

"I, too, can help." Another man stepped forward. Several others followed, and though none looked healthy enough to work, Jack had not the heart to turn them away.

He considered the task ahead. The ship should be able to carry this many people. They could build smaller berths for the children—that would save room. And clothing. Not a soul here was properly dressed for the weather—all would need garments for the voyage. Spring could be as cold as winter on the ocean. Oh, hell, and blankets, too. Then there was food—just how much they would need for all these people was anybody's guess.

"Micheal, I'll need a list of names and ages of all passengers," he said. He'd also have to get Matson involved in the planning. If they were able to weigh anchor in five days it would be a miracle.

*

Jack woke that night in the moonlit darkness of his borrowed room and began to question his own sanity. What could he have been thinking, telling all those people he'd take them to America? Between the wages he'd promised the crew and the cost of feeding everyone, this would cost him an ungodly sum.

Then he'd have to deal with the investors' anger once he got back. Not to mention the argument he could already foresee having with his grandfather. And, oh, hell, then there was Emily Cuthbert. No doubt she'd think they should wed as soon as he arrived. *No doubt her father and his grandfather would agree with her.*

He sat up and swung his legs over the side of the bed. Second guessing always came so easy in the middle of the night. He'd done the right thing—the *only* thing. He'd made a decision and he'd not look back with regrets.

He padded barefoot across the room to rummage around in the bag of things he'd brought ashore. He'd stashed a half-finished bottle of whiskey in here somewhere, now where—ahhh. His fingers closed around the smooth glass neck and he allowed himself a smile. Sleeping potion.

He climbed back into bed, sat back against the headboard and put the bottle to his lips. There was no need for a glass, not when one was drinking alone. Not when one's sole purpose was to find sleep. He savored the liquid's burn all the way down to the core of his stomach and thought of Kathleen and the time she'd chastised him for being stingy with the whiskey. And then he thought of how she was married to Danny now, how she was laughing with him and kissing him and sleeping with him.

And he drank some more.

An hour passed and still he lay awake, not the least bit drowsy, but now well into his cups. He wrapped a blanket around his shoulders and slipped across the room to stare out the window. The empty street below was desolate in the darkness, the harbor a black hole stretching out to eternity. Never had the night felt as lonely as it did at this moment, never had the sea seemed so foreign, never had he had felt so unsettled.

He'd thought that once Kathleen was married to Danny, it would be easy to go back to being the man he'd once been. That he'd again see the benefits of marriage to Emily Cuthbert. But now he knew he could never go back. All the money in the world wouldn't make him forget Kathleen, wouldn't make his marriage to Emily right.

He held the bottle up in the dim light and eyed the remaining whiskey. Still, of what worth were such thoughts when Kathleen was married to someone else? He took another swallow of whiskey and mentally hashed over all the reasons he should go ahead with marriage to Emily. It was a worthy list, he had to admit. But was it enough?

He tossed the blanket onto the bed, drew a sheet of paper from the desk in the corner and began to write a letter to Emily. The packet ships were so fast, if he posted it with the ship that now lay in the harbor, Emily would receive it weeks before his own ship docked— plenty of time for her to get used to the idea of *not* marrying him before he arrived home.

Half an hour later, he sat back and exhaled. It was finished. The desk around him was littered with crumpled sheets of paper, each holding little more than a sentence or two, each discarded in turn for being too blunt, too cruel, too inane, too something. He reread the final version, then sat back and crumpled the paper into a ball.

What in God's name was he thinking? He shoved back the chair and crossed the room to stir the fire. The red flames twisted like arms, beckoning him as though they knew his intent already. With a sigh, he dropped the letter into their midst and watched as the edges curled and the letter burst into flame, gone forever—like the man he once had been.

He remained standing long after the letter was ash. There had been a time he would have sent that letter to Emily Cuthbert and thought nothing more of it. Just as there was a time he would have married her though he didn't love her.

He cleared the rest of the crumpled papers off the desk and threw them into the fire, then climbed back into bed, the burden of his future once again heavy on his shoulders. He would not take the easy road, not when he would be home in little more than a month, not when he knew that Emily deserved more than a letter telling her of his change of heart. He owed her the dignity of ending their engagement properly.

*

Kathleen hooked her arm through her brother's and grinned at him as they walked the narrow Boston lane, their shoes making a quiet scuff on the cobblestones. Though it had only been two days since she'd called off the wedding, it already seemed like weeks had passed, like that part of her life was in the distant past. The sky was clear, the sun bright, the scent of lilacs filled the air.

"I saw Danny at the pub last night," Sean said, a hint of accusation in his voice.

Her stomach took a turn and she looked directly at him.

"He said you called the wedding off—not him. That you ended it before ye even knew of the other lass."

"I was going to tell you…"

"When?"

"Someday." She stopped walking and stepped back from him. "Seanie, things with Danny were…nothing was the same. Perhaps we'd been apart too long. Couldn't you see it?"

His brows drew together. "Sometimes, but I just thought the two of you would overcome it. He says you're in love with the English captain."

"He's not English to me," she said softly and raised a hand, begging understanding. "Surely, now that ye know what Danny did in Newfoundland, ye cannot think I should have wed him still."

"I said nothing of marrying Danny." Sean looked away and immediately turned back. "I hardly know anymore, Kathleen. You should be with an Irishman, I think—"

"Ye need not worry about the captain. Did I not tell you, he's to marry?"

Sean raised his brows.

"Aye, to a woman of means. He'll join her father's shipping business. So you see, it's not me he's wanting." Saying the words aloud made them all the more real, all the more painful.

"Stupid fool."

She laughed.

"So is Danny right? Do you love him?"

Her smile faded and she looked up at the sapphire sky that wrapped around the horizon, slipping around the earth to connect her to Ireland. "Aye. Like I never loved Danny."

"Da would be furious if he know."

"So he must never know." She took hold of Sean's arm. "Promise me now, on your honor. Da and Ma must never know."

"Don't you be worrying. Not a word of this will they ever hear from me." Sean began to walk again and Kathleen fell into step beside him.

"I heard how your captain took a shipload of supplies to Ireland," he said.

"He's not *my* captain."

"Have ye heard anything from him?"

She drew back in surprise and narrowed her eyes. "Ye needn't worry, Sean. He's not writing me—nor do I expect him to."

"Aye, well…" He gave a sigh of resignation. "I suppose ye could do worse."

"Like Danny," she muttered.

"Aye."

"Have you lost your mind now? A minute ago you were wanting me to forget all about the captain."

He let out a wry laugh. "I just wish you had someone to take care of you, that's all. It was me who forced ye to come across after all."

"I'm doing fine. You cannot know how it helps to have ye nearby. I'll be happier still when you are able to find work."

"Smile then, for I have."

She let out a screech and threw her arms around him. "You found work? What will ye be doing?"

"Building the railroad across Ohio. I've known for a few days, but I thought you'd be wedded to Danny... That it would be all right if I left, for you'd have someone to look out for ye."

"You're leaving?" She pressed a hand to her chest above her heart. "But you only just arrived."

"There's no work here. No one wants the Irish. And the few who will hire us, they're paying next to nothing. But the railroad—they promise a good wage and steady work."

"Now that you're here, I can hardly stomach you'll be leaving." How could she live in this home with Jack married to Emily Cuthbert...and not even Sean nearby for support?

"I know. But I can't go on like this, every day trying to find even a bit of work and most often finding nothing. Depending on you for money when we both should be sending whatever we can home..."

Kathleen felt the same despair as the day she left Ireland, saw again her country just a tiny speck on the ocean's horizon as the ship carried her away from everything she knew. "Ye'll write?" she asked.

"All the time."

She threw her arms around him and burst into tears at her family torn apart, brought together and separated once again. *"Is fada an bóthar nach mbíonn casadh ann,"* she whispered. "I just didn't expect the road to turn again so soon."

CHAPTER THIRTY-SIX

JACK STROLLED ACROSS the deck of the ship and stopped to watch a small group of children listening to one of the crew members explain the repair he was making in a sail. Before long, each of the children had touched the point of the needle and a few had tried to shove it through the heavy canvas. Their laughter tumbled across the deck and he was amazed at how much healthier they looked after just three weeks of plentiful food.

The return voyage had been uneventful, though they had some sixty passengers instead of the forty or so he'd expected. Most of the extra people had arrived the morning they were to leave—cousins, brothers, sisters, friends, parents of those already on the list. What could he have said? They came to him with hope in their eyes and fear in their voices and asked whether he might take one more, or two, or three. What could he have said? *No, you'll have to stay behind and die?*

He thought of Emily Cuthbert and wished there was some way he could talk with her now, tell her he couldn't marry her, put an end to the anticipation that must be building within her as each day drew her closer to marriage.

"'Tis official now," Anna Deacey said.

He turned and smiled as she drew near. "What is?"

"The McFarlen's baby. They've named it Jack."

"Didn't they have some relative they'd rather name him after?"

"To save a life, Captain, is no small matter. She'd likely have lost the child had she stayed in Ireland…that is, if she herself lived long enough to miscarry." She gestured toward the nearby children. "These are all lives that might have ended if not for you."

He glanced back at the children, the whole group now repeating the words to a sea shanty that one of the crew was teaching them, any questionable language replaced with other words. He leaned his elbows onto the bulwark and contemplated the vast ocean. "What's it all for? Birth, life, death… How is it that some live and others die, some rise to fame and wealth and others never rise above the hovel in which they were born?"

The ship leapt in the freshening breeze, the stays creaking as the masts responded to the pressure. Anna took hold of the rail for balance.

"To be sure, I've wondered that meself at times, struggling as we have to feed our family all these years," Anna said. "But now, as we travel to America, a new land with such hope, I think I know why God put me on this earth."

Jack watched her and waited.

"Me purpose on earth was to bear a daughter who would meet a man…" She smiled. "A man who would love her. And because of this love, so strong it could have been ordained by God himself, this man would save the lives of sixty Irish he had never met before. Me daughter is the reason I was put here."

"How did you know?"

"That you love Kathleen?" She shook her head. "Och, but it is for a mother to know. I could see it in your eyes the first day ye came to our home." She reached out and touched his hand. "She'd have done well to love you, too."

"I'm English, you see."

"Ahhh. And what did she say about you coming to Ireland with food, then?"

"I never told her."

Anna put a hand to her heart. "You are more fine a man than I even had thought."

"No. It wasn't from the goodness of my heart that I did it. I was coming north anyway, whaling. I worked out a pay arrangement—a percentage of the food."

"And look what happened. Why, you're not whaling at all. And you're feeding sixty extra passengers on the voyage home—a voyage you didn't intend to take. Nay, Captain, how you began the journey is not so important as the path you chose once the road forked."

*

Nearly five weeks after leaving Ireland, on a warm June afternoon, Jack brought the ship into Boston Harbor. The water sparkled in the brilliant sunshine and the beauty of the day made even the seediest areas of the city look appealing.

The passengers chattered as they crowded the rail, small children hoisted high, anticipation running through the group like a shiver, all eyes aglow at this first sight of their new country. Gradually the talking died down into silent awe.

For the first time since he had immigrated to the United States, Jack's stomach flopped with excitement at the prospect of stepping onto American soil, though his reasons were entirely different than those of his passengers. Today he would see Emily Cuthbert and end their engagement.

Once the gangplank had been hoisted into position, Jack sent two crewmen ashore—one to hire a coach for him, and another to bring an immigration agent aboard so the passengers could be processed. Because everyone on board was healthy, they were quickly cleared to enter the country. Joy and excitement hovered over the deck as the passengers gathered their few belongings and shook Jack's hand or threw their arms about him in gratitude before stepping down the gangplank and disappearing onto Boston's busy streets. Finally, only Kathleen's family members remained.

Jack stared out at the city, marveling at how it could still look the same when he was so different than he had been just a few months ago. He thought of Kathleen, of Danny, of Emily, and rubbed a hand across the back of his neck. The time had come to take care of unfinished business, to put things to rights again. He'd initially planned to call on Emily later in the day, once he'd found Kathleen's family a place to stay. But now all he could think of was putting an end to the engagement as soon as he could.

A coach drew to a halt on the nearby wharf and Jack waved to the driver before turning to Kathleen's father. "That carriage is for you," he said. "I expect Kathleen and Danny went to Newfoundland after the wedding, but I'm hoping my cook will know how to find Sean."

Five minutes later the two families had filled the carriage. "Looks like we ride outside," Micheal said as he climbed up to sit beside the driver.

Jack shook his head. "I'll meet you there. I've something to take care of first." He gave his address to the driver, and instructed the man to take the family on a short tour of Boston before delivering them to his home. Then he handed an envelope up to Micheal. "If you arrive before I do…" He grimaced. "Just give my grandfather this note."

A dubious look crossed Micheal's face and Jack laughed. "Don't let the old man bully you." He strode off in the opposite direction, turned at the next corner and nearly broke into a run, tamping down his guilt at sending the Deaceys, an Irish family, to meet his grandfather without him. Hopefully the tour through Boston would delay them enough that he would be able to talk with Emily and get home before they arrived.

Impatience drove him forward at a brisk clip and before long he stood outside the ornate wrought iron fence that surrounded the Cuthbert's stately home. For the first time since making this decision, his stomach knotted. He clenched his jaw tight and mounted the stairs to the door.

*

From the far bedroom on the second floor, Kathleen could hear the knocker pounding on the front door. She froze on hands and knees, scrub brush in hand and listened to see if the grandfather would answer the door himself. There was silence for several moments and then the vague sounds of conversation floated up the stairs. She sat back on her heels and surveyed the section of floor she still had to wash.

Downstairs, the voices grew louder, as though the caller had come into the foyer. A word drifted like a whisper up to her: *Kathleen.*

She cocked her head and strained to hear, to make sense of the few syllables and sounds rising and falling to her ears. *Harbor. Captain Montgomery. Kathleen.*

Goosebumps rose on her arms. Had something happened to Jack? She set the scrub brush on the floor and slowly stood, drying her hands on her apron as she walked to the door. Only silence rose from the foyer now, not a word spoken by any of those she knew must still be there.

Suddenly the old man shouted— "Kath—leen!"

The urgency in his voice propelled her to motion and she raced to the top of the stairs. Below her in the foyer, the grandfather was reading a sheet of paper while a stranger holding two worn satchels stood nearby, waiting, his back to the stair.

"Did you need something, sir?" she asked, afraid something was terribly wrong.

He raised the white sheet of paper in the air as though she would find meaning in the sight of it. God help them both, it couldn't be bad news of Jack. She was halfway down the staircase before she bothered a second glance at the other man. He had turned to watch her, a half smile on his face. She stopped. Her heart stilled.

"Da?" she whispered. *"Da?"*

"Aye lass. 'Tis your own Da." He set down the satchels.

She took the remaining stairs nearly blinded by tears and he met her with arms open and wrapped her in his embrace. She had never thought to see him again. She sobbed on his shoulder and roughly wiped a hand across her eyes. "What are you doing here?"

"Ah, well, your Ma thought we should take a visit," he said in a voice thick with emotion. "And you know how determined she gets when she has something in her head."

One arm still around her father, Kathleen twisted toward the open doorway. Her mother stepped in from the stoop, a dark shape silhouetted against the shining afternoon sun.

"Ma?" She hurled herself into her mother's arms, talking and crying all at once. And then her siblings came through the door, and her aunt and uncle and their children, and there was more noise in the foyer than she'd ever heard before in the whole of the house. And every time she wiped her eyes, a fresh batch of tears rolled over her cheeks like the sky had opened on fine Irish morn.

"It's as if I am dreaming," she said. "And if I am, I never want to wake. How do ye all come to be here?"

Her mother smiled, and the grandfather held out the sheet of paper he had waved at her. She read what Jack had written, how he had brought her family out of Ireland, how he was at this moment ending his engagement to Emily Cuthbert. The words blurred on the page and her throat constricted. When finally she looked up, it was into the smiling faces of her parents.

Jack's grandfather shook his head in resignation and a wry smile almost touched his lips. "Like I said, the best laid plans..."

The front door creaked open and Jack Montgomery stepped over the threshold. Kathleen drank him in, memorizing every detail of his face, his frame, locking him into her mind and heart so that no matter what ever happened, she would never forget what he looked like at this moment.

His gaze riveted on her. "Kathleen," he said with restrained surprise. "Hello."

She nodded, unable to trust her voice.

"I thought you'd be gone to Newfoundland. I told your parents as much—"

"Danny went back alone—"

"Without his wife?"

"Nay. You see, we didna wed, Danny and me."

Their gazes locked and held across the now silent room.

"You didn't?"

"I didn't love him." *Not like I love you.* "I've read your note," she said quietly. "And you? Why did you end it?"

He looked at the floor a moment, then raised his eyes to meet hers again. "I couldn't imagine spending my life with one woman…when I was in love with another."

Like a whisper of a breeze, hardly heard, Kathleen's mother murmured, *"An áit a bhfuil do chroí is ann a thabharfas do chosa thú."*

Kathleen's throat tightened.

"What does it mean?" he asked.

It meant that her parents knew of her feelings for Jack, that they were giving her their approval of this Englishman. It meant that she was free to love him without fear of losing them.

"Your feet will bring you to where your heart is," she said quietly. She brought a fisted hand up to press against her breastbone, to still the ache where her heart pounded within her chest. She smiled at her parents, then raised her eyes to Jack's and spoke the words he had once whispered to her. "I could love you, Jack Montgomery."

In two steps he had her in his arms and the cheer that went up in the room was just an echo of the joy in her heart.

The End

If you enjoyed this book, please consider
reviewing it online.

AUTHOR'S NOTE

MANY OF THE historical events in this novel are true, some are products of my imagination. Irish animosity toward England is based on 700 years of history. Britain first invaded Ireland in the 12th century. After the Irish rebellion of 1641 put most of Ireland under the control of the Irish Catholics, Oliver Cromwell invaded the country and brutally re-conquered Ireland for England. At that time, more than 90% of the Irish people were Catholics. Tens of thousands of Irish were slaughtered after surrendering and tens of thousands others were sent into indentured servitude in the British colonies. Hundreds of thousands of Irish Catholics in Northern Ireland were forced off their lands, which were then given to English and Scottish Protestants.

In 1601, 90% of Irish land was owned by Catholics; in 1660, it was 20%; by 1776, just 5%. The Irish had become tenants in their own country.

Penal laws were passed by the ruling Protestant minority outlawing Catholicism and Gaelic (the Irish language), restricting Catholics' right to education, and prohibiting them from voting, holding public office, serving in the army, owning firearms, entering the legal profession, buying land, engaging in trade or commerce, and more.

The typical Irish family paid rent to an absentee English landlord for land to farm—typically about a half-acre. Potatoes were the only crop that came close to yielding enough to feed a family. Even so, there were often weeks at the end of summer where the Irish went hungry waiting for the next crop to mature.

After a partial failure of the Irish potato crop in 1845, a blight in late summer 1846 destroyed three-fourths of Ireland's crop. Because of the country's dependence on potatoes, famine struck instantly. It was followed by one of the most severe winters in Irish history.

In Britain, many viewed the famine through religious, moralist eyes. Charles Trevelyan, who oversaw the relief effort for the British government, firmly believed that God had sent the famine, and described it as an "effective mechanism for reducing surplus population," and a means of breaking "the cancer of dependency." Lord John Russell, Britain's prime minister during most of the famine years, wrote in 1847, "It must be thoroughly understood that we cannot feed the people..."

Even though a solution existed within Ireland—the country was producing more than enough wheat, oats, and barley to feed its people—the British continued to export those grains out of the country under armed guard, while the Irish starved.

Blight struck again in 1848, completely wiping out the potato crop again. Between 1846 and 1852, one in eight Irish, more than a million people, died in Ireland during the Great Famine. Another 1.25 million Irish fled the country in ill-equipped, under-provisioned, and overcrowded ships that came to be known as coffin ships.

Upon crossing the ocean in search of a better life, the Irish discovered they were pariahs in America, and "No Irish Need

Apply," was the norm. The influx of Irish Catholics produced an outpouring of anti-Irish, anti-Catholic sentiment—particularly by Protestants.

When word reached the United States of the suffering in Ireland, the Catholic Bishop in Boston, John Fitzpatrick, spoke to the congregation of Holy Cross Cathedral and called for a relief effort to be formed. The sermon Kathleen hears him give in the story is his actual sermon.

The U.S. government made two warships available to ferry supplies, one of which, the U.S.S. Jamestown, was captained to Ireland by Robert Bennett Forbes. In all, the New England Relief Committee sent more than 100 ships with supplies to Ireland in 1847.

Kathleen Deacey and her family, and Jack Montgomery and his are all figments of my imagination. Kathleen's mother, Anna Deacey, is named after my great-grandmother who emigrated from Ireland; her sister's name was Brigid. Many of the other names in this book—Clark, Goggins, Hurley, O'Connell, McDermott, and Sullivan—were also borrowed from my Irish roots.

I am very grateful to the following authors and experts whose books, websites, and knowledge have helped me research this period in history. Any mistakes are my own.

The Cobh Heritage Center, Cobh, Ireland. www.cobhheritage.com

Ireland's Great Hunger Museum, Múseam An Ghorta Mhóir, Quinnipiac University, Hamden, CT. www.ighm.nfshost.com

The New Bedford Whaling Museum, New Bedford, MA. www.whalingmuseum.org

Ashley, Clifford. *The Yankee Whaler.* Dover, 1991.

Boid, Edward. *A Description of the Azores or Western Islands from Personal Observation.* Ulan, 1834.

Briggs, Katherine. *An Encyclopedia of Fairies.* Pantheon Books, 1978.

Browne, J. Ross. *Etchings of a Whaling Cruise.* Belknap, 1968.

Creighton, Margaret S. *Rites and Passages: The Experience of American Whaling, 1830-1870.* Cambridge University Press, 1995.

Curran, Bob. *A Field Guide to Irish Fairies.* Appletree Press, 2008.

Druett, Joan. *Petticoat Whalers: Whaling Wives at Sea, 1820-1920.* UPNE, 2001.

Forbes, H.A. Crosby and Lee, Henry. *Massachusetts Help to Ireland During the Great Famine.* T.O. Metcalf, 1967.

Froud, Brian and Lee, Allen. *Faeries.* Bantam, 1979.

Gallagher, Thomas. *Paddy's Lament, Ireland 1846-1847, Prelude to Hatred. Harcourt,* Brace & Company, 1982.

Gray, Peter. *The Irish Famine.* Harry N. Abrams, 1995.

Kee, Robert. *Ireland: A History.* Book Sales, 1984.

Laxton, Edward. *The Famine Ships, the Irish Exodus to America.* Henry Holt, 1996.

Laing, Alexander. *The American Heritage History of Seafaring America.* McGraw-Hill, 1974.

Logan, Patrick. *Irish Country Cures.* Sterling, 1981.

Mac Con Iomaire, Liam. *Ireland of the Proverb.* Roberts Rinehart, 1995.

Miller, Kerby and Wagner, Paul. *Out of Ireland.* Elliott & Clark, 1994.

O'Connor, Thomas H. *The Boston Irish, a Political History.* Back Bay Books, 1995.

O'Connor, Thomas H. *Fitzpatrick's Boston 1846-1866: John Bernard Fitzpatrick, Third Bishop of Boston.* Northeastern, 1984.

O'Farrell, Padraic. *Irish Toasts, Curses & Blessings.* Sterling, 1995.

Olmsted, Francis. *Incidents of a Whaling Voyage.* C.E. Tuttle, 1969 (1841).

Sanderson, Ivan T. *Follow the Whale.* Little Brown, 1956.

Wilde, Lady. *Ancient Legends of Ireland.* Sterling, 1991.

Wilde, Lady. *Irish Cures, Mystic Charms & Superstitions.* Sterling, 1990.

Yeats, William Butler. *Fairy and Folk Tales of Ireland.* Scribner, 1998 (1888).

ABOUT THE AUTHOR

PAMELA FORD IS the award-winning author of contemporary and historical romance. She grew up watching old movies, blissfully sighing over the romance; and reading sci-fi and adventure novels, vicariously living the action. The combination probably explains why the books she writes are romantic, happily-ever-afters with plenty of fast-paced plot.

After graduating from college with a degree in Advertising, Pam merrily set off to earn a living, searching for that perfect career as she became a graphic designer, print buyer, waitress, pantyhose sales rep, public relations specialist, copywriter, freelance writer—and finally, author. Pam has won numerous awards including the Booksellers Best, a Gold Medal in the IPPY Awards, and is a two-time Golden Heart Finalist. She lives in Wisconsin with her husband and children.

Contact Pam at pam@pamelaford.net.

For news and sneak peaks of upcoming novels visit:

pamelaford.net
facebook.com/pamelafordauthor
twitter.com/pamfordauthor

CPSIA information can be obtained at www.ICGtesting.com
Printed in the USA
LVOW10s1627150715

446355LV00009B/1086/P